The Oyster House Siege

JAY RAYNER is an award-winning journalist and broadcaster who is also the *Observer's* restaurant critic. In 2006 he was awarded 'Critic of the Year' at the British Press Awards. He is married and lives in London. This is his fifth novel.

'A tightly crafted, socially observant, stand-off thriller... Genuine tension [...] with some fine set pieces... Thriller, social commentary [and] black comedy, well handled and in the right quantities, make good ingredients in a recipe for success.' Peter Millar, *The Times*

'[Rayner] might be expected to know a thing of two about dining out, but as this solidly written crime caper suggests, he knows something about crime, too... The supporting cast are strong and credible characters, each with their own cross to bear... Cleverly constructed with conflict and tension and drama.' Toby Clements, *Daily Telegraph*

'Engaging [and] impeccably plotted.' Tom Cox, *Daily Mail*

'Behind all of the siege shenanigans the message is clear: whatever your political beliefs, civilisation thrives in times of prosperity, and an individual's psychology and character is best understood by what they choose to put in their stomach.' Matt Thorne, *Sunday Telegraph*

'[Rayner] mixes comedy with drama to intriguing effect... A most entertaining read. I hope there will be a sequel.' Peter Guttridge, *Observer*

'Deliciously gripping... An engaging, witty tale.' Melissa Thompson, *Big Issue*

The Oyster House Siege

Jay Rayner

Atlantic Books
London

First published in Great Britain in hardback in 2007 by Atlantic Books, an imprint of Grove Atlantic Ltd.

This paperback edition published in Great Britain in 2007 by Atlantic Books.

9 8 7 6 5 4 3 2 1

A CIP catalogue record for this book is available from the British Library.

978 1 84354 566 8

Typeset in Sabon by Avon DataSet Ltd, Bidford on Avon, Warwickshire, B50 4JH

Printed in the UK by CPI Bookmarque, Croydon, CR0 4TD

Atlantic Books
An imprint of Grove Atlantic Ltd
Ormond House
26–27 Boswell Street
London WC1N 3JZ

For Andreas Loizou

Yesterday

The Oyster House Siege ended on its fourth day shortly before 10 a.m. At a noisy press conference afterwards the authorities emphasized that, during the operation to end it, only four shots were fired inside the Oyster House kitchen by officers of the Special Air Services. They also said that neither police marksmen nor the army had been responsible for wounding or killing a single hostage during the previous four days. They said this was an achievement, for which they deserved to be given credit.

When the smoke from the stun grenades had cleared, two of the four bullets were found to have penetrated the stomach and chest of a man who had fallen to the floor close to the doors. He was wearing chef's whites, and was lying on his back. His eyes were open, and his lips parted to present an oval of surprise. Once an SAS officer had pressed two fingers against his carotid artery, just below his jaw, and satisfied himself that the man was dead, another figure in whites came and knelt by the body, as if in supplication. The chef drew a finger through the crimson puddle spreading across the victim's chest, checking the liquid for consistency, then leaned down and whispered into the dead man's face, 'You weren't supposed to die.'

I

Four days ago

In the early hours of the 8th of September 1915 a bomb, dropped from a Zeppelin airship, struck 87 Jermyn Street in central London. It detonated in the basement kitchen, killing the three bakers who were working there and filling the street outside with a cloud of dust so thick it was likened to an autumnal fog by those caught in it. The subsequent renovation of the Jermyn Street Oyster House tidied away the back staircase that had been used by Edward VII and his mistress Lillie Langtry for secret trysts, and the dining room with its long mahogany bar, red upholstered banquettes and brass rails was restored and expanded. However the Oyster House never returned to baking its own bread. The force of the explosion had been so great that there was nothing of the victims' bodies to recover and the Guild of Master Bakers declared the site sacred ground. None of its members would work there. Despite this, the restaurant's reopening in the spring of 1919 was seen by the politicians and businessmen who booked its tables as a symbol of continuity, in a city traumatized by the long agony of the Great War.

By the time the last bakers who could recall the deaths at the Oyster House had retired only London's grandest hotels could afford to bake their own bread. Instead, the work was contracted out and on the morning of the 9th of June 1983, it was the driver of a baker's van who made the first delivery to the restaurant. The box was placed in the doorway shortly after 7 a.m. and retrieved half an hour later by a cook called Tony Simpson who, as on most mornings, was the first to arrive. Inside the box there was coarse, open-textured wholemeal to go with the plates of smoked salmon. There were great, domed bricks of white bread with a crust the colour of burnt butter for the Welsh rarebit and baguettes for those who did not want oatcakes with their cheese. Downstairs in the kitchen, the cook unpacked the bread into the dry stores cupboard and sniffed the base of the loaves for the sweet, comforting smell of yeast. It was the smell of the morning bread which made him question his capabilities as a cook; for all his skills in the kitchen he had never once been able to bake anything other than an amateur's misshapen loaf. Tony had been a chef for four years but saw himself still as a refugee from his home town of Sheffield, who, in another age, would have been getting his hands dirty in the city's steel mills and foundries like his father and uncles had done before him.

It depressed Tony that it hadn't turned out that way. The steel industry had gone and by the time he left school there were no jobs. He realized that he had to learn a trade and that eventually he would have to leave the city. When he arrived at the Oyster House, two years after becoming a chef, he was immediately nicknamed Sheffield Tony. Sheffield for short. After that the other cooks would pick up knives that had been left lying around and, with their thumb obscuring the 'Made in' stamp, ask if they belonged to him, because his name was on the blade. They thought this was very funny but for a long time Sheffield felt the reference to his home on all the knives as a rebuke.

The bread was away, and Sheffield was cutting up vegetables for the stock pot, when the head chef arrived. At first Bobby Heller stood leaning back against the pass, eyes closed, sipping black coffee from a chipped mug and saying nothing. In other kitchens where Sheffield had worked, the head chefs came in shouting orders. They tore up menus or abused the front-of-house staff. Bobby preferred a different approach and Sheffield, who had four brothers and no sisters, assumed this was because she was a woman. She insisted that every order be followed with a shout of 'Yes, chef', rather than something in the clumsy, mispronounced French London's old-fashioned kitchens favoured, and if she needed to berate a member of her brigade it was always done beside the walk-ins out of earshot of the others. The cooks liked the atmosphere in her kitchen and told her that was why they stayed.

The chefs in London's other restaurants had a different explanation. It wasn't about the sweetness of the kitchen regime, they said. It was about Bobby Heller's blue eyes and the golden peroxided hair, tied up with a colourful gash of silk scarf. The cooks wanted to take her to bed, they said, and to hear her whisper in her rich mid-Western burr. They also said she was unstable, and carried a boning knife with her at all times which she would be happy to use. Sheffield knew the truth behind that story. Occasionally, in the all-night Chinese cafés of Soho, where London's cooks gathered after hours for bowls of rice and sticky roast duck, a drunken cook from one of the other kitchens would try to make a pass at her. One night, confronted by such an approach, Bobby withdrew a crescent of horn-handled blade from somewhere unseen by her waist and placed it gently, tip upwards, leaning against the edge of the bowl, as if ready for use. Without looking up she said, 'What was that you were after?' The cook stared at the knife, and then walked away. Sheffield thought it was a measured and subtle response; he did not regard it as the behaviour of an unstable woman.

After finishing her coffee, Bobby fetched her leather knife roll from a drawer and chose a mid-sized blade, which she sharpened on her knife steel. Then she went to work removing the tendons from a long, purple beef fillet. While she worked she stowed the steel in the waist band of her apron for easy access, where it hung like a pirate's cutlass.

Stevie McGrath was the last of the cooks who would be working that day and he did not arrive until shortly after 10 a.m. 'Sorry, chef. It was a bit full-on last night.'

Bobby looked over at Sheffield, who was preparing vegetables. 'Glad somebody here's got a social life.'

'Don't know where he gets the energy, chef.'

Stevie, who was tying an ankle-length apron low around his narrow waist, allowed himself a shy grin.

Bobby returned to the sole she was filleting. 'You might as well tell us his name.'

Stevie took a breath, as if more air would refresh his memory. 'Patrick. I think.'

'You think?'

'It was noisy,' he said with an apologetic shrug, and Sheffield and Bobby laughed.

The kitchen staff was completed by Kingston, the broad-shouldered Jamaican-born kitchen porter, who had been at the Oyster House for only two weeks. As agreed, he arrived at noon, because Bobby knew there would be a large enough pile of oven trays and pans by then, and the coming promise of the lunch service.

Not that there was much of a lunch service today. Just four tables were booked and one of those was by the owner, Marcus Caster-Johns, who ate there every day and, as today, always alone. He liked soups and grilled chops and oysters, though only the natives, which he could eat by the dozen, splashed with sherry vinegar. The Caster-Johns family had owned the restaurant for much of the twentieth century and Marcus spent so much time there as a child that, from his usual table opposite the bar, he could identify the places around the room to which his most important memories were attached. At the bar was the high stool where he sat while his father prepared for him his first oyster, cupping the open shell in the well of his palm as he separated the bivalve from its sticking place with a stubby knife. Marcus was six years old and he kept his eyes closed as his father poured it over his bottom lip with the instruction to 'taste the sea'. And he did taste the sea, a wash of sweet and salt which made him think of the Northumbrian shore where the family kept the big house.

'Look at my little oyster-catcher,' his father said proudly, and Marcus asked for another one, because he wanted to please him.

In one corner of the dining room was the table where he had once joined his father, Princess Margaret and the actor Peter Sellers for dinner, and been introduced by them to what they all agreed was 'a pretty good Bordeaux' to accompany the grouse that Marcus and his father had shot on the family's land. He had just turned thirteen. 'In some countries you could get married now, Marcus,' his father said, 'and if you're old enough to marry you're old enough for a little claret.'

Then there was the store room behind the bar, separated from the dining room by a red velvet curtain, behind which a young waitress, with quick soft hands and shining eyes, had eased him from his trousers one lunchtime in the last summer before university, while on the other side ladies ate poached salmon with mayonnaise.

He knew what people said about the Oyster House because, for a few years while he was a student, he had said it too. He told his father one day that it was a restaurant with 'too much history and not enough future' and for six months after that they did not speak. But when his mother died he realized that he had not a single food memory of her. She was too busy going out each evening, jewelled and smelling of lilac, to cook for her children, and every taste he could recall came from the Oyster House. His father died in 1981, when Marcus was twenty-six. The executors of his will asked Marcus if he wished to sell the restaurant to developers but he refused. The restaurant had opened for business in 1825 and he didn't want to be the one who brought that history to a close. 'It would be like selling England,' he said.

So the restaurant stayed as it was, and Marcus Caster-Johns came every day for his lunch of soup and chops. Today, as he drained his coffee, he called over the head waiter and asked him why the room was so empty.

Mr Andrews leaned in towards him and let his eyebrows knot at the centre of his moon face. 'I believe there is a general election today, sir, for which I am most awfully sorry.'

Downstairs Bobby claimed she had expected election day to be quiet, because people would be voting during their lunch breaks, but she was also relieved because there were so few cooks in the kitchen. When she saw that the restaurant was booked out for the evening, she tried calling in more help but none was available. At 6.30 p.m. a waiter appeared in the pool of light cast by the pass. He delivered a ticket, written up with an order and announced that the first table had arrived. The cooks called on Bobby to play them some sounds, as they did every night, and she thumbed through the kitchen's music collection, looking for something which she thought might raise their energy levels.

Bobby found an unlabelled black cassette, which she waved above her head, saying, 'I hold in my hands your redemption,' and she pushed it into the mouth of the ancient, paint-splattered tape machine up on a high shelf. She pursed her lips as she turned the volume up to nine, and glanced up to the ceiling with a look of delight on her face.

2

Upstairs in the dining room the head waiter placed a finger lightly against the rim of a wine glass. He could feel the vibrations of the music being played downstairs through the table to the glass. He disliked the way such an ugly sound could make itself felt through such a beautiful object, and he allowed the contrast to encourage his anger. Mr Andrews had given up complaining about the noise to the head chef, but he still felt the need to make his disapproval known. He nodded politely at the lone couple sitting at a back table, tugged at the hem of his waistcoat in an attempt to stop it rising up over the curve of his huge belly, then turned and walked to the front of the restaurant from where he took the stairs to the basement kitchen.

He did not recognize the music of the Ramones as he came through the swing doors, just as he did not recognize recordings by the New York Dolls or the Dead Kennedys when they were being played on other nights. But he did hear in the mix of voice, drums and electrified guitars a sound that he considered inappropriate. After thirty-two years at the Jermyn Street Oyster House, Mr Andrews believed he was one of the few people qualified to decide what was appropriate to the restaurant and what was not.

He looked at the cooks briefly enough to confirm that there were just three of them working that evening; this gave him pleasure. Mr Andrews knew that the kitchen would be under the kind of pressure which would make it an unattractive and inhospitable place, and he liked to think of the cooks sweating. He did not, however, acknowledge them. He turned instead to a work surface just inside the door, above which were shelves stacked with crockery and glasses. He took down a tray of champagne flutes and two large Tupperware boxes. Working quickly he half filled both boxes with hot water and added to one of them a champagne glass full of white wine vinegar from a bottle kept on the shelves for the purpose. He laid a second tray with a clean tea towel. He then dipped a glass in the water and vinegar mixture, before rinsing it in the second box. Finally he stood the glass on the new tray where it could dry to a clean, drip-free shine, and started on the next one. After two and a half minutes the Ramones track came to an end. There was a pause punctuated only by the satisfied laughter of the cooks behind him, and a new track began playing. Mr Andrews held his position, dipping glasses. The head waiter felt that engaging in an activity like this, which was necessary to the smooth running of the restaurant, was a fine rebuke to the kitchen's lack of professionalism. He felt the gesture was appropriate.

In the break between songs Sheffield took a drink of water from one of the cleaned, glass milk bottles that all the cooks used for the purpose. As he drank he gestured rudely at the head waiter's back with his free hand, which made the other cooks laugh. He put the bottle back on a shelf behind him and, as Joey Ramone counted in the next song – 'One, two, three four' – prepared to mime lead guitar, one hand clawed over his belly to play the strings, the other outstretched at the neck, thumb cocked. Stevie bashed at the side of the solid top stove with two knife steels, and Bobby took on the bass, nimble fingers flicking at the empty air.

As the second Ramones track came to an end Mr Andrews picked up his tray and shouldered his way out through the doors. Bobby walked over to the tape machine and turned down the volume. She picked up the first ticket.

'One grapefruit, one avocado. Two steak medium.'

'Yes, chef.'

The Ramones gave way to the Talking Heads, by way of the B52s. Starters gave way to main courses. Flames leapt from the stove and steam hissed from pots. The solid top fizzed, the temperature rose and the cooks took long drinks from their water bottles. At his sinks, a pile of oven trays and dirty crockery built up next to Kingston, and hot water splashed against the front of his blue, nylon housecoat.

The last of the diners was seated by 9.30 p.m. and Mr Andrews was finally able to survey the dining room, which he did with satisfaction. Up the three stairs in the L-shaped back room he could see MPs and industrialists. There was a brace of Thatcher-supporting tabloid newspaper editors and a famous political columnist who looked nothing like his youthful picture by-line. There were PR men who had turned their gifts to the black arts of politics and bankers on to their second bottle of Pomerol. On table one, in the restaurant's prized front section, there was Lord Connaston, whom he recognized from behind because of his great mane of silver hair. He was accompanied by his wife Carla and a friend, who rocked in his seat when he laughed in a manner which suggested to Mr Andrews that he had drunk most of the bottle of Burgundy standing empty in front of him. The small table at the top of the stairs leading down to the kitchen was occupied by the art dealer Carl Walker and his friend Grey Thomas. The head waiter disliked them both, as much for the flamboyance of their dress as the pitch of their voices, but thought it wise to keep on good terms with men like this who had enough money to order wines from the bottom of the list.

In the bay window there was a trio of advertising men whom Mr Andrews knew slightly and, on the table next to them, an elderly couple he had not seen before, treating a younger couple to dinner. It was the evening of the 1983 General Election. The Conservative Party was on course for a landslide victory, and it was clear to Mr Andrews that everybody dining at the Jermyn Street Oyster House was pleased, both with the predicted result and their part in it. As they ate their profiteroles and their sherry trifles, the election was what they discussed, to the exclusion of any other subject.

So nobody paid any attention to the loud boom from somewhere nearby, assuming it to be nothing more sinister than a car backfiring. Nobody noticed when a man's shout echoed down the street outside or when the shutter on the archway directly across the road, the entrance to a narrow arcade of expensive shops and boutiques, lifted a couple of feet. They didn't spot the man dressed in black who rolled out on to the pavement, followed by another, who stayed wedged under the shutter on his knees for a moment, looking back into the arcade. Soused with wine and giddy with the coming victory, none of them bothered to look up when the first of those men shoved his way into the restaurant and stood in the open doorway, panting, despite the bashed leather jacket on his back, the black balaclava on his head, and the oily pistol in his tattooed right hand.

3

Mr Andrews reacted on instinct. He approached the man standing in the open doorway and, bowing a few degrees from the waist, said, 'Good evening, sir. May I help you?'

If it had not been for the balaclava, the waiter would have seen a blink of surprise.

Mr Andrews smiled thinly and moved closer in the hope that the width of his barrel-chest and his shoulders, correctly positioned, would bar entry to the man. When there was no response he moved closer still, and repeated the question. 'I said, sir, may I help you?'

Before the man could answer, there was a crack of gunfire from outside.

The man swung about frantically at the noise, only to be pushed backwards into the restaurant by another figure in a black jacket and balaclava. Together, the three of them crashed into the dining room. Mr Andrews just managed to say 'Really!' as they hit Thomas and Walker's table at the top of the kitchen stairs, knocking the two men off their chairs. There was the sound of splintering wood as the table's front legs gave way and it fell to the floor, table-top facing the front door. It was followed instantaneously by the crack and shatter of crockery and glassware, banging against each other on the way down and the ripe-fruit splatter of osso bucco and boeuf bourguignon landing amid the wreckage.

The two masked men lay sprawled against the table-top at their backs, stunned. There was silence in the dining room. Slowly the first of the men turned to look at the gallery of faces staring back at him. A number of people had half risen from their seats, and were fixed there, knees bent, watching. Red wine dribbled off tables where glasses had been knocked over by diners, startled by the commotion. Waiters stood between them, staring down at the masked men, knuckles white from the tightness of the grip on the plates in their hands. The regulars at the Oyster House regarded the restaurant as a place that could be relied upon to keep the world at bay. It was their place, and in these first seconds they saw the intrusion by the masked men as something they should be outraged by rather than afraid of. This, after all, was exactly what they had been voting against all day. How dare these men just barge in? Some talked later of a moment of calm and described how the two men stayed fixed with their backs to the upturned table, staring out at the street, arguing with each other.

'You shouldn't have fired.'

'They were coming for us.'

'They were just girls.'

'I didn't hit them.'

But there was still the winded Mr Andrews, who had been thrown by the impact on to his back a few feet from the gunman and who lay there now, surrounded by the chaos of sauce and crockery, listening to the hoarse exchange of words, regaining his breath and planning his next move. As the two men talked, their sentences becoming ever more staccato, he turned himself slowly on his side and looked at the weapon, still clutched in the second gunman's hand, which lay in his lap. Sensing an opportunity he took a deep breath and lunged, one soft hand reaching out for the gun, hoping the momentum offered by his weight and the unexpectedness of his actions would knock the intruders off balance.

Unused to physical activity of any kind, he miscalculated badly and threw himself beyond the hand with the gun. As he landed across the men's legs, the impact forcing the breath from his lungs once more, he felt somebody grab him and then he was rolling across the floor, over jagged shards of broken plate and clanking pieces of cutlery, one of the men behind him, the hand with the gun about his neck. He reached up to take it, his fat fingers scrabbling against the cold metal. Now they had stopped rolling and he felt the other man underneath him and pressed down, sensing for once that his excessive weight might give him an advantage. The two of them scrambled with their feet to gain purchase on the sauce-slicked carpet.

It was as he finally got his hand around the barrel of the gun, held hard against his cheek, that Mr Andrews felt a sharp stabbing pain in his throat which was so intense it radiated out across his shoulders and into his chest. For a moment the head waiter flailed his arms as though he were trying to stop himself from falling, and then finally he became still as the effects of the injury overwhelmed him.

The gunman tightened his neck-hold on the head waiter and pulled him upwards into a seating position sprawled next to him, Mr Andrews' soft back held against the hardness of his bony chest. The two men were leaning against the side wall of the restaurant, by the front door, facing into the dining room. The gunman twisted the silver fork that he had just stabbed into Mr Andrews' throat so that it moved deeper through the layer of fat covering his gullet. The wound released a thick stream of blood. It soaked into the front of his white shirt and down across the lapels of his black suit. Mr Andrews gasped and his eyes bulged and the gunman tightened his grip further, until he was satisfied by the speed of the haemorrhage.

'Did you want something, fat man?' he said, whispering hoarsely into the waiter's ear.

The gunman heard screams and looking up he saw that, at the sight of Mr Andrews' blood, the diners in the front section of the restaurant were finally rising fully to their feet. Chairs fell backwards. More glasses tumbled to the carpet in a spray of expensive claret. He let go of the fork for a moment, tossed the Browning pistol into his free hand and pointed it around the room. He shouted, 'Downstairs.'

The customers and staff of the Oyster House did as they were ordered, slipping through the narrow gap between the upturned table and the top of the stairs, screaming and hollering at each other to move more quickly so that some stumbled on the way down and called out in pain as they banged against the walls or the doors at the bottom. When the last of them had gone through the gap the two gunmen scrambled behind the upturned table, taking the waiter with them. The first gunman looked down the stairs behind him, at the diners pushing their way through. He turned to his companion and hissed, 'Trevor!'

'Insurance,' Trevor said.

The head waiter tried to right himself. Trevor dropped the gun again and reached over to the fork. He twisted it so that his victim gave a tight, wet groan, and his tongue flopped out of his mouth. Mr Andrews stopped moving. His breathing was coming in shallow pants now, and there was a blue tinge to his lips. Blood was pooling on the carpet and was smeared across Trevor's hands. Nathan James looked at the punctured skin and the fork protruding from it which his accomplice was still holding, a lever for the administration of pain, and felt a rush of nausea which only subsided when he took a deep breath and turned away from the bloody mess. He told himself Trevor had done the only thing possible, that this was exactly why he had brought him on the job in the first place. He was in no position to worry about such things now.

From their position behind the upturned table, the two men heard the sound of sirens followed by the rapid, nightclub strobe of blue lights, which flashed against the buildings outside, cutting into the Georgian façades. Trevor picked up his gun and fired another shot that took out the glass frontage of the restaurant. It shattered, turning cobweb-white from the impact and holding for a split second before collapsing to the floor like a satin sheet released to gravity's will.

Nathan pressed his hands against his ears to ease the ringing caused by the noise of gunfire. 'Stop,' he shouted, and for a moment he sounded desperate.

The head waiter's eyes were glazed and rolling back in his head. 'And ease up on him.'

Trevor released his neck-hold, so that the waiter slumped to the floor and gasped.

The two men peered over the edge of the upturned table, at the shuddering blue flashes outside and the shadows moving among them. The light show was punctuated by the wail and crack of the police klaxons.

Trevor said, 'You sure about the door?'

Nathan nodded and, eyeing the waiter, said, 'Leave him here.'

'He comes with us.'

'He'll slow us down.'

'I told you. Insurance. Warning to others.'

There was no time to argue. They could decide what to do with him later. They would have to decide a lot of things later. The two men slipped a hand under an armpit each and dragged the limp body of the head waiter towards the restaurant kitchen, his head banging on each stair as they went.

As they worked their way down, Nathan James looked at the damage his accomplice had done to the man's throat and at the trail of blood it had left behind on the carpet. He felt a familiar rush of anger that made his cheeks burn beneath the harsh mesh of the balaclava. He had spent his life trying to be a man who made things happen. Instead he was a man things happened to.

4

When Nathan James was seven years old, his parents were killed in a car crash. That day it was his grandmother who was waiting for him at the school gates. She held her arms stiff at her sides and looked past Nathan into the distance and he wondered if she was watching out for someone else. Then he called, 'Nan,' and she turned to him with an empty stare. She told him that his mother could not collect him today because of a 'problem' and waited until she had walked him silently to his house to give him the news. Even then she was unable to find the right words. She said: 'Mummy and Daddy were in an accident.' She told him 'it was the kind of accident that makes people go to sleep for ever', and she hated the way it made his parents sound lazy. She finished by announcing that he would now be coming to live with her and his grandfather in Streatham. Mrs James assumed she had supplied enough pieces of information for Nathan to work out what she meant without distressing him with needless detail, and told him briskly to pack a case with his favourite toys to go with the one of his clothes that she had already prepared. That September afternoon in 1966 Nathan James began his journey back from London's middle-class suburbs to the fringes of the inner city, a journey that his father had completed in the other direction some years previously.

Nathan's grandparents, Terry and Frieda, decided early on that it would be best for the boy if they did as little as possible to remind him of his previous life. Every night at bedtime Frieda asked Nathan if he was all right, but she would never suggest any reason why he might not be. The first night she leaned over to kiss him goodnight on the cheek, and he forced his face down into the soft part of her shoulder, his slender arms looped about her neck, and wept noiselessly. Nathan did this every night and Frieda held him tightly while saying nothing before gently releasing him to his pillow. After a few weeks of this, she said it was time for the crying to stop. Nathan accepted the instruction.

Terry James ran a removals business, and at first the furniture in Nathan's new room was made of old wooden tea chests: a high bed of upended chests pushed together with a mattress on top and tea chests on their sides for open cupboards from which he got splinters. Nathan thought that they smelt of other people's lives. Over the next few weeks each piece was replaced by objects Terry had scavenged from households that no longer required them. Every one, Terry said, was 'a lovely find', though Nathan regarded them suspiciously as cast-offs like himself. Nathan went to a new primary school in Brixton, further north into the city. At school he had a hook for his coat, just as at his old school. There was hard shiny paper printed with the words 'Now wash your hands' in the toilets, and wall bars in the school hall for PE lessons. There were many of the things he had known before, but they were all in the wrong place.

In the school holidays Nathan joined Terry on his removal jobs. Each day began the same way, the empty van parked up on a residential street in Streatham or Tooting, while Nathan and his grandfather waited for the rest of the removal team – impressive, solid men called Ken, Tom and Jack – who would help ease another family towards a life elsewhere. Every day Terry read his copy of the *Morning Star*. He had three copies of the newspaper delivered, two of which were meant to be read by the others, but they never were and these tightly rolled copies formed an unlit pyre in the space behind the dark green vinyl seats in the van's cab. As he read his paper Terry maintained a commentary, mostly about a war in Vietnam, or about America's 'imperialist ambitions', which Nathan understood was something his grandfather disliked. Occasionally he tapped an announcement of an event – a summer camp run by the Communist Youth League or a fun day from the Young Socialist Alliance – and said, 'We should get you on to that,' but he never sounded convinced and nothing came of it. Sometimes he taught his grandson slogans from the Communist Manifesto because he thought it was funny to hear a small boy shouting, 'The proletarians have nothing to lose but their chains.'

At night, over dinner, he talked to Frieda about the newspaper stories he had read. Workers were organizing in Sunderland, he told her one evening. The bosses had gone too far this time in Birmingham. Then he looked over at Nathan. 'Listen to me trying to put you to sleep with all this talk,' he said, and he winked. 'Kick a ball about after tea?' Terry said, businesslike, as he scooped peas on to his fork.

Nathan said 'Yeah' even though his grandfather was bad at football and lost interest quickly. Most evenings, after an initial burst of activity, Terry stood staring at the house, while Nathan ran around him, the ball at his feet, and he knew that his grandfather would rather be at his desk, tearing articles out of newspapers and scribbling notes in the margins. Still, he was glad of the offer, and happy that the talk of workers and bosses was done with for now, even though he knew it could start again at any moment. Terry had fought Mosley's Fascists at Cable Street in 1936 and liked to impress his grandson with stories about the crowds who gathered that day, unafraid of violence. Terry James was a man with a great memory. His sense of betrayal at the news of Soviet tanks moving into Hungary in 1956 was as intense as if it had happened yesterday, and when in the summer of 1968 they rolled again, this time into Czechoslovakia to put down the Prague Spring, he fell into a depression. He turned the small plaster bust of Lenin that he kept on the mantelpiece in the front room to face the wall, and took his party membership card from his wallet and placed it on the table in the hall by the telephone. 'I'll get rid of that tomorrow,' he said, though he didn't, nor the day after that. One morning, watching unseen from the shadowed half landing, Nathan saw Terry slip it back into a slot in his brown leather wallet.

Before the car crash, Terry had been a distant figure in Nathan's life. He never seemed pleased to see his son's family when they visited, and even on a Sunday he retreated to his desk to deal with paperwork, wearing the brown warehouseman's coat that he kept for weekdays. Terry's son – Nathan's father – had joked about his father's membership of the Communist Party, as if it were an embarrassing hobby, and made good his rebellion by becoming an accountant. Now that the son was gone, the grandson became Terry's project. He bought him a large dictionary and told him that everything he would need in life was on its pages. Sometimes he tested him on the spellings of difficult words and gave him a coin or two as a reward, which Nathan put in the toy safe he had hidden under his bed, illicit bounty stolen during a moving job. In his early teens, Terry gave Nathan books to read – *Down and Out in Paris and London* by George Orwell, *The Ragged Trousered Philanthropists* by Robert Tressell – though he didn't get far with them. Reading single words in a dictionary was one thing, Nathan decided. Reading whole chapters took him further inside his head than he ever wanted to go.

Frieda James died when Nathan was twelve and, wanting to make Terry feel less sad, Nathan went with him a few times to his political meetings. They were held in small halls around Brixton that smelt of bleach and overheated dust and seemed to Nathan to be attended mostly by angry men in duffel coats. The meetings were terribly dull. Still, his grandfather's revolutionary narrative appealed to Nathan's sense of himself as an outsider and once, attending a lecture on anarchism, he felt that he had found an ideology that would suit him. Wasn't the death of his parents so early the 'abolition of government' that the definition of anarchism described? He decided he had been living in a state of personal anarchism for years, and liked to imagine that the circumstances of his upbringing released him from any responsibility to the laws which bound others.

After Terry died, and Nathan's life changed again, he threw away all his books. He didn't attend any more political meetings and soon stopped describing himself as an anarchist, because he didn't like any of the other anarchists that he met. He had hung out for a while at the squats on Villa Road in central Brixton and, though he was intrigued by the sense of family they had created, too many of them were middle-class college kids mouthing slogans they only half understood, and he doubted their commitment.

Nathan was twenty years old in 1979, and eligible to vote for the first time at a General Election, though he didn't bother. So many of the brick walls in Brixton had been daubed with the smudged black swastikas of the National Front by then, and all he ever heard in response were the empty platitudes of the Villa Road crowd. Stinking piles of black-bagged rubbish piled up during the winter of early 1979. Every office building was guarded by a cadre of strikers, shouting at passers by and adding to their freight of morning gloom, and Nathan couldn't see how voting for the Labour Party was going to change any of that. He reserved equal contempt for Margaret Thatcher's easy rhetoric and wished that Terry was still alive so he could hear him rage with authentic anger. Terry would have called her an 'embezzler', as he did anyone who took the side of business.

On polling day Nathan met Ken, one of Terry's former removal men, who told him that the new owner of his grandfather's business had erected a poster of the Conservative leader by the depot's gates. After dark Nathan went alone to the depot and found the poster. She had her teeth set in a grin and her hair fixed in a crashing golden wave that could only be maintained with a heavy dose of lacquer. The poster was attached to a wooden stake, which in turn was nailed loosely to the gatepost. Nathan took a swing at the poster in the darkness, hoping to knock Margaret Thatcher to the pavement. He regarded it as an act of revenge on his grandfather's behalf, but he did not see the long rusting nail protruding from her mouth, where the poster had been nailed to the stake, until his fist was impaled upon it. The blood rushed out over his hand, down his forearm and dribbled off his elbow to the ground, and he had to pull hard to free himself. He went to hospital after that, and saw out the rest of election night watching the blood soak into the muslin strips the nurses had given him when he arrived. By the time they had stitched him up and given him a tetanus shot it was dawn and Margaret Thatcher was the new Prime Minister.

5

They laid the unconscious waiter carelessly down on the floor to one side of the swing doors. A pinkness was returning to his cheeks and lips now that Trevor had released his grip, but the blood around the tines of the fork, where it was stuck in his throat, was beginning to darken and coagulate. Behind them the diners, who had been herded into the kitchen, crackled with terror and pushed towards the back of the room. Most had turned away from the kitchen doors towards a point in the back wall that Nathan could not see. A few were dressed in white jackets and aprons. Others wore their night-time costumes, jewellery shining beneath the kitchen's white lights.

Nathan said, as if to himself, 'Quiet.' He turned to Trevor, who was standing by the partially open door and watching the police lights flash against the walls of the stairwell. 'There are too many people down here,' he said. There was a tightness in the way he spoke that made him sound impatient. 'We can't control this many people.' Trevor stared at him, his eyes unblinking through the holes in his mask, and then looked past him to examine the kitchen for possibilities. Close by, next to the stove, was a stainless steel deep-fat fryer. The vat of amber oil was on a gentle roll. A few feet away, his back turned to the gunman, the art dealer was trying to push himself to the back of the room with every-one else. Trevor walked over and took him in a neck-hold from behind. With his free hand, the gunman grabbed one of Walker's arms and forced it up his back. It took two steps to manoeuvre him so he could be pushed forward over the boiling fat.

Walker screamed, and a silence fell on the kitchen. The cooks and the diners turned to look, and seeing the involvement of the man who had so eagerly bloodied the head waiter just minutes before, they stiffened. From his position at one side of the kitchen Lord Connaston watched the gunman and saw in him an uncommon and disturbing physical self-confidence. He recognized an animal of instincts who knew how to control others. The art dealer was trying to lift his body away from the oil that was only a few inches below his face, but Trevor's hold was tight. Walker twisted and bucked his body. Sweat rolled down his face to the end of his nose, and dropped into the hot oil forcing it to splash back into his face. He screamed again and opened his mouth wide so that a dribble of saliva spooled into the oil, causing it to fizz and spit once more. Trevor didn't flinch.

Nathan watched, and swallowed hard. 'Trevor,' he said quietly.

'Tell them,' the other gunman said, nodding towards the crowd behind him. His voice sounded hoarse from the exertion of keeping the man in place, and his teeth were gritted.

Nathan looked at the crowd. 'Clear away from the back of the room,' he said. Slowly they began to walk towards him.

'Faster. Do exactly what we say. Do it now.'

Soon a narrow channel had opened up through the crowd of diners so he could walk towards the back wall of the kitchen. He turned to Trevor. 'Leave him.'

The gunman kept his hold.

'I said, leave him.'

Reluctantly, Trevor released his grip on Walker's neck and arm, and took a step backwards. The art dealer pushed himself upwards, gasping. He turned and slid down the side of a cabinet, his head in his hands. Through the art dealer's fingers, Nathan could see a crust of white blisters beginning to form on his cheek where the boiling oil had made contact, and once more felt the contents of his stomach rise towards his throat and then settle again. Grey Thomas slipped down on to the floor next to Walker, and wrapped one arm around his slumped shoulders.

Nathan looked about the room. It was full of smells – of hot alcohol and meat cooking over naked flames. When he was a child in his grandparents' house, kitchens smelt only of frying onions or crisping bacon. This was a different experience entirely. It distracted him from the heat which was causing sweat to build up behind his coarse woollen mask. Nathan pulled the gun from his own waistband and felt the unfamiliar weight of the weapon. He waved it around the room and said to himself, 'I'm taking control.'

Now he shouted, in a voice that surprised him: 'Everybody back off. Give us space.' Pleasingly, they recoiled from him. He might not have Trevor's intent or violent commitment, he thought, but with the gun in his hand he could be effective.

He sniffed the air again and told himself to focus. He had to treat this as part of the job, not the job gone wrong. He looked towards the doors behind him and, through the small safety-glass windows, saw the strobe of police lights. That way was not an option. The solution therefore lay in the other direction.

'Stay here,' he said, redundantly. And, 'guard the door.' He walked through the crowd, taking in the changing smells as he passed copper saucepans of thick brown liquor. 'Out the way,' he said, and 'coming through' like it was a busy Saturday night at the pub and he was trying to carry a pint. He felt sweat building on his temples and slipping down the back of his neck, and he gave thanks that nobody could see his face. He didn't have to worry about looking anxious, confused or concerned. He was what he was: the man in a mask with the gun.

At the back of the kitchen he could see the open door, and around it a tight huddle of diners. As he approached, people drifted away until he was facing the doorway. He stared at what was behind the door, his weapon slack at his side.

'Not what you were hoping to find?'

He turned at the sound of a American woman's voice. He took in the chef's whites and the silk scarf tied around her head.

'When did they do this?' Nathan waved towards the doorway with his pistol. The rest of the room was watching.

'Two weeks ago. Trying to keep the vermin from getting in,' Bobby said. 'They didn't think about any vermin that might be trying to get out.'

'It's a fire hazard.'

'You think so? Like, illegal?'

'Well…'

'Nice, coming from the guy with the rusty gun.'

Involuntarily he ran a hand over his head, as if through his hair. He felt the rough weave of the balaclava beneath his palm. Sweat sucked the material in against his scalp.

'Who are you?'

'Bobby Heller,' she said. 'I'm the chef here, and this is my kitchen.'

He kicked the back door open further with his foot so they could all look at the bricked-up doorway.

'Not any more it isn't,' he said. And he shoved the barrel of the gun up and under her chin so she was forced to look down her nose at him.

6

Up above they heard the diners who had rushed to the back of the dining room when the gunmen arrived leaving the restaurant. Each footfall made a heavy thud that forced those in the kitchen to look upwards and wish they were doing the same. Nathan had a tight grip on Bobby's wrist, and he was walking her back to the kitchen doors. Sheffield stepped forward as they passed, as if to drag him off, but Bobby shook her head. She mouthed 'No' and he sunk back towards the cabinets that lined the kitchen.

When they reached the swing doors Bobby stood quietly next to the gunman, waiting, watching the second man who was still staring out through the partially open door, his narrow back turned to her. Slowly, Trevor turned to look at her. She saw him blink behind his mask. The very tip of his tongue emerged from the mouth hole in the mask to rest against the rough material, a flash of pink against the blackness. Even with the mask she could feel his sudden interest in her. He was staring at her. As Nathan had moved through the kitchen the silence had been replaced by quiet voices of diners trying to reassure each other that they would all be fine, as long as they did nothing stupid. Once more the voices stopped. Everybody turned to watch Trevor.

'You look nice,' he said softly, and he took a few steps forward so he was standing in front of her. Bobby could smell cigarette smoke and involuntarily she leaned backwards to maintain the distance between them.

Nathan laid his hand flat against the other man's chest. 'Trevor—' But Trevor ignored the gesture. It was as if Nathan was not there.

'I bet you smell nice too.' He leaned in towards Bobby and she turned her head away, to expose inadvertently a long stretch of pale neck. She heard him breathe in, and then sigh, so that a warm rush of air brushed against her skin.

'You're hot.'

'Leave her be, Trevor.'

'You've been sweating.' He sounded exhilarated by the discovery. 'I can smell that you've been sweating. I like that.'

He reached out to touch her, his fingers splayed, and she saw the hard bony structure of his hand and the pale grey flesh pulled taut over the knuckles. She took shallow breaths and swallowed, watching the hand, waiting for whatever it was that he was going to do, feeling exposed and vulnerable with her wrist held tight by the other man.

'Pretty skin.'

Quietly, in a voice only just above a whisper, she said, 'Don't touch me.'

And he didn't. 'I want to taste you,' he said. His hand hovered over her neck and, without getting any closer, traced a path from her ear to the hollow of her collarbone just inside the open neck of her chef's jacket. 'I want to find out what you taste like when the sweat runs down into there.'

'We don't have time for this, Trevor,' Nathan said anxiously, turning to watch the door. His voice was forceful but quiet, as if he was dealing with a child he did not wish to startle. For a few seconds more Trevor kept his gaze on Bobby, then slowly turned to the second man. 'That's a pity,' he said, and he laughed so that his stained teeth appeared from behind red, chapped lips. Casually, and without taking his eyes off Bobby, he returned to his position by the swing doors.

Bobby could feel Nathan's tight, solid frame next to hers. She was thinking fast now. She was weighing up possibilities. He was six inches taller than she was and she thought he could be as much as sixty pounds heavier, though she believed that would be to her advantage. He wouldn't be expecting anything from such a slight woman. With her free hand, she felt in the waistband of her trousers for the hard curve of horn-handle that she knew was there.

He turned to her. 'Are there any other doors in or out?'

She shook her head. 'No. Just this one.'

'Where does that lead?'

He was pointing to an open doorway in the same wall as the swing doors. He assumed it led back under the dining room towards the front of the restaurant. Bobby peered around him.

'Wine cellar at the back under the pavement. Staff changing area to the right, plus dry stores and walk-ins.'

'Walk-ins?'

'Fridges. It's where we keep the food, which is the stuff we cook in a kitchen.' She was regaining her equilibrium. She knew what she was going to do.

He ignored the challenge. 'No way out through there?'

'I told you. Just these doors here. And the dumb waiter.' She nodded towards the east wall of the room to their immediate left, where a pair of closed cupboard doors were flush into the white tiling. Next to them were two heavy buttons and two dead lights.

'What's one of them?'

'Hand-operated lift. We use it to bring the dirty dishes down.'

He looked at the cupboard doors. 'How big is it?'

'Not big enough for you.'

From the floor they heard a loud groan and everybody turned to look. Mr Andrews was coming round and, in turning his head, had moved the fork enough to reignite the pain. Bobby decided the distraction was the only opportunity she was likely to get and swung herself around so swiftly that she was suddenly behind the gunman. She pulled out the boning knife and, in one clean movement, pressed it to his throat just below his Adam's apple. He let go of her wrist in surprise and she reached up to wrap her other arm tight about his forehead. This is what boning out ten legs of lamb a week gets you, she thought to herself. This was what peeling a hundred pounds of potatoes and shucking a gross of oysters every day had done to her arms. It had given her the strength to take a big man down.

Nathan stood rigid and still. Trevor stared from his position by the door. Mr Andrews lay beside him, blinking.

'Now you're going to let us all go,' Bobby said quietly.

From between gritted teeth, Nathan said, 'Trevor?'

'Right.' He turned, lifted his weapon and shoved the barrel into the mouth of the head waiter. Mr Andrews stared back down the gun.

Trevor turned to look at her. Nathan remained still, his head back as if waiting for a dental consultation.

'Be my guest,' she said. 'Blow his brains out. You'll be doing us all a favour.' Her blade stayed in place.

Trevor said, 'Fair enough.' He withdrew the gun from the man's mouth and patted him on the cheek. Mr Andrews gulped. Trevor stood up and took a step towards the crowd. He walked along the line, staring closely at them – a young man in collar, tie and brass-buttoned blazer, the twenty-something woman next to him with her arm looped tightly through his, an elderly man with narrow nose and high cheekbones. He stopped before the small bird-like woman stand-ing next to him who had grey piled hair and a floral dress, and who smelt lightly of lavender. 'Fine,' he said and he put the gun against her right temple.

'What about her?' He turned to her. 'Name?'

'Susan Guthrie,' she said in a whisper.

'What about Suzy?' He pushed the gun harder against her head, and the woman let out a small squeal. She said, 'Please—'

Bobby blinked and swallowed. Trevor stared back at her and jerked the weapon once more against the elderly woman's head. 'Shall I?'

Reluctantly, Bobby released her grip. She let the knife slip away from the man's throat. Her arms fell to her sides as Nathan shook himself out.

'Thank you, Trevor,' Nathan said, as if his friend had offered him a cup of tea. He took the boning knife from Bobby's hand. He nodded towards the old woman. 'You can stop now.'

Trevor pulled the gun away from her head, as though he was always open to suggestions, and she turned to be comforted by the older man next to her. He closed his eyes and let out a puff of air, his papery cheeks deflating.

Nathan walked across to where the head waiter was lying on the floor and squatted down next to him. There was now a thick, black clot around the fork and running down over his neck to cake his skin. Blood had run into the folds of fat and dried there. Nathan knew what he needed to do, though the thought of it brought a familiar and uneasy lightness to his stomach. He looked into Mr Andrews' eyes and then away from him as he slipped two fingers either side of the fork's tines. With his other hand he pulled on the handle. At first it wouldn't move and the head waiter gave a piglet-like squeal and began to pant. Nathan decided the task had to be done quickly. He pushed down with one hand and at the same time, pulled so that with a crisp sucking noise the fork withdrew. A small amount of fresh blood welled up in the puncture holes and slipped out and over the clot.

Before he stood up Nathan wiped his hands casually on Andrews's clothes then he turned to face the room. He held the bloodied fork upwards, tines to the ceiling. Only a small amount of the metal was clean enough to catch the lights. The rest was smeared with black or brown matter.

Nathan said, 'Look at this.' He presented it slowly to the room, turning in a semi-circle so that everybody could see it. 'And the next time any of you think of trying something like that, remember it. Do I need to say any more?'

Nobody spoke.

He said it again, only louder. 'Do I?' There was a dull murmur of 'No' from around the kitchen.

Nathan dropped the fork on to a work surface. He wiped his hand on his leg and turned again to study the shape of the kitchen. He needed a distraction, something with which to keep the attention of his hostages. On a shelf he saw what he was looking for.

Nathan looked at Bobby. 'Does that work?' he said, nodding towards a small, portable television. Bobby looked over at the set. 'Yeah. It works.'

'Good.' He looked at his watch. 'This is what we're going to do. We're going to watch a little telly. You—' He pointed to Stevie, who was nearest. 'Do the honours.' The cook flicked the switch and the black and white picture fizzed into life.

7

Sergeant Willy Cosgrave dreamed about food much as other men dream about women. Good dishes, fully imagined, made him feel whole. By rehearsing the stages of a classic daube – barding the beef with pork fat, enriching the wine with brandy for the marinade – he could keep the world at bay. And when, in his imaginings, he reached the moment when he raised the casserole's lid to release the first breath of steam, a feeling of calm would overcome him. Only then could he open his eyes and face whatever irritation the commander had foisted upon him.

'My husband,' Marion Cosgrave would say to her friends, with a hand pressed to her well-fed heart, 'he's only himself by the stove.' And the rest of the time he is trying to find his way back there, Willy might have added.

He understood himself most clearly as a father in the kitchen, because that was where he had the cleanest purchase on his role in life. That was where he offered Alex the first taste of Marie Rose sauce (before the introduction of Tabasco) to be licked away by a baby's trusting tongue from his fingertip; of crisped lardons handed down to Paula's open mouth; of whipped, sugared cream from a spoon to both of them. Then the tutorials, as the children grew: the garlicky liquor about a true dauphinoise; a teaspoonful of lobster bisque as the flavours surfaced, and then again after the addition of cream.

'See what it does, Alex? See how the fishiness softens, Paula?'

And the willing child's blink of recognition, better still, followed by a plea for more. His one regret as a parent, he always said, was that his shift patterns meant he could not be there to cook his children's every meal. 'This is what I do as a father,' he said one day. 'I feed.'

At first he recognized this as the sacrifice a family man made to be a good staff sergeant. It was meant to be a job for up-and-comers, for those with ambitions who liked having the ear of the superior they were employed to serve. But nobody now regarded Sergeant Willy Cosgrave as an ambitious man. They did not believe he sought rank or command and he did not look like he sought them either, for, in the service of both his fantasies and his children's appetites, he had become a man of heft who wore his trousers high about his belly in a way that was unfashionable in the Metropolitan Police Service. They wanted their senior officers to look lean and hungry as the commander did and, as Willy Cosgrave said, he had not been hungry since October 1963. He liked to make these jokes about himself before anybody else thought of doing so.

It had been different once. When he left the Wiltshire force to take the job with the Met, it was with whispers in his ears from the older officers who had never made it out of the countryside. He was going to do all the things they had never managed to do. Willy was hungry for everything then, and he thought Commander Roy Peterson was eager to feed him. 'I'm here to put some city dirt under your fingernails,' he said on Willy's first day. 'You can waste valuable police time trying to stay too clean.'

A few weeks into the job Peterson had a visitor, a big man in a three-piece suit, with a flash of gold-watch chain under the jacket and the shine of silver cufflinks at his wrists. They sat facing each other in high-backed armchairs, holding tumblers of whisky and sucking on cigars, and Willy was instructed to find someone to watch over the visitor's car, which was parked illegally outside. When nobody from uniform was available Willy did it himself, and stood on the pavement for forty-five minutes calculating how long he would have to work to afford the grey Bentley in front of him. He reminded himself that, officially, this was not one of his duties. As the man climbed back into the car, lifting his stomach a little with one hand to help fit it behind the steering wheel, he tucked a roll of notes into Willy's top jacket pocket and patted it with the flat of his palm. Later, embarrassed, Willy told the commander, who said tersely, 'He was showing his gratitude. It's rude to decline.' Willy sensed he had failed a test.

Other visitors came to the Commander's office. They were businessmen who owned clubs in Mayfair and Soho or who ran magazine publishing companies from industrial estates in South London. There were always clouds of cigar smoke and tumblers of whisky and jokes half heard through a closed door, which Willy thought were at his expense. Sometimes, at day's end, there was an excuse for Peterson to put on the black tie and dinner jacket that he kept hanging in the cupboard next to his dress uniform. He was off to see a boxing match in the East End with a contact. There was an invitation to dinner at the Café Royal. Once he was given a box at the Royal Albert Hall to watch Sinatra sing. 'He's an old boy now,' Peterson said the next morning. 'But he still has it.' He hummed 'My Way' to himself all morning. Later Peterson graduated to the last night of the Proms, and the big West End musicals. He thought *Cats* was a masterpiece and after that could be heard humming 'Memory' under his breath instead.

Peterson was less impressed by the detail of police work. Sometimes he did call up a case file, telling the detective in charge that he would 'take it from here'. Shortly afterwards, Willy would be given the file and told to 'put it away for now. Some of those boys downstairs couldn't tell a crime from their elbow.' Most of the time Peterson chaired committees and was talked of in the canteen as a future candidate for commissioner, so skilled was he at the politics of the job. But promotions were never offered and, as the rejections piled up, he took it out on his staff sergeant. Willy was sent to fetch dry-cleaning and collect unnecessary pieces of shopping. He was required to get the commander's private car into the garage for servicing. When he wasn't being forced to run around town, Peterson would lecture him. 'Up here, sergeant, you're still thinking like a country copper. There is no space for that in the Met.' And it was true that Willy didn't get on, because promotions didn't come his way either. Around the Yard it was assumed that Willy Cosgrave would not be moved elsewhere unless Commander Peterson moved too and as the years passed that seemed increasingly unlikely. 'We're growing old together,' the commander would say, irritably. On days off Willy prepared ever more complex dishes, from recipes in his copy of *Larousse Gastronomique*, and enjoyed the rare feeling of control that their completion gave him. He attempted Sole Veronique and Tornedos Rossini. He boned out a whole chicken and stuffed it with a light mousse of chopped pork, green herbs and morels. He discovered the secret to a good Béarnaise sauce and told his wife: 'white wine vinegar, egg yolks, a little butter, and the confidence not to let it know you are afraid', and she laughed with him. He liked having expertise for which he could be respected, if only at home.

Tonight, however, there was not enough of the evening left for an adventure at the stove, and when the Oyster House Siege began he was in the living room, dozing in an armchair, dreaming about an authentic cassoulet into its second day of preparation. On the television, men were talking excitably about exit polls and landslides. Someone in a beige suit was predicting that either Guildford or Torbay would be the first to report a result, as if those results, when they came, would have an impact on the Conservative landslide victory. Willy was not listening to any of this. He was working the breadcrumb crust back into the cassoulet, shifting the lumps of goose confit and Toulouse sausage from their sticking places and reaching into the deepest recesses of his head for the appropriate smell-memory of pig, goose and bean that he knew should be there.

The telephone rang. 'Will.' And more insistently, 'Willy!'

He opened his eyes. He knew from her face, the look maintained by a wife too accustomed to getting into bed alone, that it was New Scotland Yard. He took the call and looked at his watch as he accepted the inevitable. Peterson was on duty that night, while his colleagues policed the election, and now there was an incident from which even the commander could not escape.

'They need me,' he said to his wife afterwards, and she straightened his tie.

'At the Yard,' she said. It was a statement.

'No. Jermyn Street. Something going down.'

'On election night?'

'Criminals don't stay at home just because it's election night.'

She nodded. And then, as the thought occurred to her, she said, 'What about the steaks?'

Willy frowned. 'I'm not packing my bags. I'll be back in a few hours, I'm sure.'

'But if you're not?'

'I'll be here for dinner tomorrow night.'

'You promised you wouldn't miss our anniversary this time.'

'I'll make it home.'

'You always say that.'

'Am I boring you, love?'

She kissed him lightly on the forehead. 'Just make sure you come back in time to eat it, Willy Cosgrave.'

'It's a robbery gone wrong. That's all. I'll see you in the morning. Kiss the kids for me.'

8

Within five minutes of Nathan James and his accomplice storming the Oyster House a cordon had been thrown around the area. Strands of striped police tape, guarded by a car and four officers, had been strung across both the eastern end of Jermyn Street where it met Regent Street and the western end at St James's Street. Police cars were lined up along the south side of Piccadilly, blue lights flashing, closing off Duke Street and the gate through to the courtyard and gardens of Christopher Wren's church of St James's. The entrance to the church led into a series of small foyers and entrance halls which also had an identical doorway on the other side out to Jermyn Street itself, seventy-five yards east of the restaurant. Closing off the southern approaches, an exclusive clutter of art galleries and expensive Georgian townhouses, was a more complex proposition. For the moment, police cars and tape stretched out across the entire distance from west to east, cutting off everything north of St James's Square.

'So the square isn't inside the cordon?'

'No, sir.'

Commander Roy Peterson nodded at the torch-lit map spread out across the bonnet of a police car which was parked on Jermyn Street alongside the eastern end of the church. Above him, in the glow of a street light, insects danced against the city's sodium-diluted night sky. 'Give thanks for small mercies,' Peterson said. 'It's mostly residential and they are not the sort of residents to take kindly to being turfed out of their homes.' He looked down Jermyn Street towards the two police vehicles blocking the road, past the shirt-makers and the milliners, the boot-makers and barbers and the cheese shop with its ancient crooked frontage; the businesses that have kept the British aristocracy clothed, shod and fed for decades. In the electric blur of the police lights, black-clad figures could be seen squatting down beside their vehicles for cover.

In a basement just behind where the cars were parked, was Tramp, the expensive members-only club, with its entrance on Jermyn Street. Peterson knew Tramp well enough and was aware that tonight, as every night, it would be full. There would be blondes with hair like spun sugar and men who were too old for them. There would be financiers and ageing aristocrats who could measure their status in the weight of the cotton shirts on their backs and the thickness of the gold rings on their fingers. The commander had spent evenings down there, sharing a bottle of champagne with a contact, and he could visualize the situation. He tapped the spot on the map.

'Has Tramp been emptied?'

'One of the clearing banks is holding an election night party down there.'

'Get them out. There aren't any other entrances apart from the one on to this street, are there?'

'The fire exit has a route out into the arcade. We can then lead them up to Piccadilly from there.'

'Do it. What about the other club?'

'Xenon?'

'That's the one.' Peterson only knew Xenon by reputation, as a disco for rich kids who liked to spend their parents' money on expensive cocktails. When it opened, a few years before, the press had made much of rumours that a star attraction would be a caged black panther wearing a diamond necklace which would be placed by the neon-lit entrance on Piccadilly. Peterson had dispatched an officer to investigate who had returned to report that he had enjoyed his night out, and that the panther was not by the door but was an occasional – and fully licensed – attraction on the stage. He said that, when the wild animals came on, a wire mesh was lowered to save the clubbers from a mauling. This still did not make the appeal of Xenon obvious to Peterson, who could not see why anybody would wish to visit a nightclub to see a giant cat.

He said, 'Can we leave that lot in peace?'

The officer shook his head. 'Don't think so, sir. Their fire exits also lead out into the arcade. Actually we think it's how the gang first accessed the jewellery shop. If there's a sudden emergency in the club then we could have 400 kids trying to—'

He didn't have to finish the sentence. Peterson could see the problem: an armed hostage situation, interrupted by a crowd of young, spoilt drunks tripping over their own heels on their way to safety. 'Clear that too.'

Peterson studied the map one last time. 'What about residential on Jermyn Street itself? How many people are there living over the restaurant or across from it?'

'Not sure, sir.'

'Well, find out. While you're at it get an ETA on the command unit. I can't run this thing from the bonnet of a squad car. And where's Cosgrave? Did anybody call Willy Cosgrave?'

'Here, sir.'

Peterson looked his staff sergeant up and down, as if inspecting his uniform. 'You're late.' He turned back to his map.

'Sorry, sir. Just got the call.'

The commander took off his peaked cap and ran one hand over his greying, closely cropped hair. He said, 'No flabby thinking tonight, Sergeant,' and Willy blushed. 'Do what I tell you, when I tell you.'

'Yes, sir.'

'I need you to get hold of the top man. The commissioner's people need to know that we have a situation down here. You know the drill.'

'Of course, sir.'

'Keep it pleasant and businesslike.'

'What do I tell him?'

'Bloody good question.' He turned and shouted to a cluster of officers standing by a car parked behind his own, staring at another pile of maps. 'Harris, we need a full briefing. Where's the first on scene?'

An officer pointed back down the road towards the cars. 'DCI Marshall is down behind the furthest squad car, sir, weapon drawn.'

'Well, pull him out of there. Get one of the SO19 boys in to replace him and get him round here.'

'Yes, sir.' The officer muttered into the radio clipped to his lapel.

Peterson stood up straight and looked down the street, and then, as though he had only just noticed its presence, at the old church behind him. Its high, arched windows shimmered in the burst and fall of police lights. He pointed up at the building. 'Willy, we need to set up an HQ in the church. Go find the vicar, priest, whatever, and see if you can—'

From down the street, they heard a deep, guttural roar: the muffled sound of a dozen voices crying out as one. Every police officer turned towards the noise, which was coming from the Oyster House, as if expecting to see it manifested on the road.

'Jesus! Harris, what the—'

'Checking, sir.' The officer turned his chin urgently to his lapel again. 'Marshall, DCI Marshall...' There was a pause, and then a burst of compressed noise and static from the officer's radio. Harris looked up. 'DCI Marshall says an incident is occurring, sir, in the Oyster House, sir. He's asking for permission to go in.'

Commander Roy Peterson turned and stared down the street towards the restaurant. He pressed one open-palmed hand against the centre of his chest, let free the slightest of burps and said only, 'Why tonight?'

9

The cheering pressed itself in against the low, ducted ceiling of the Oyster House kitchen and filled the ears of the crowd who had given it voice. Their heads were tilted forwards now, the better to catch every word and, for a moment, they were oblivious to the heat. Nathan watched too as the first important Conservative Party win of the night was announced. He had known this was coming, and yet he felt a hollowness in his stomach, even though he was still a stranger to the ballot box and had done nothing that might affect the situation. Whatever changes were happening to Britain, he was certain nothing was going to alter in his neighbourhood. A short lick of music played in his head, the sad opening refrain from 'Ghost Town' by the Specials. When the single had been released a couple of years earlier it had been dismissed by Nathan and his friends for being too commercial and its success was taken as proof of betrayal. One Jamaican friend called it 'black music for people who don't know black people', and Nathan agreed. Then the riots broke out in Toxteth and Moss Side. 'Ghost Town' became an unofficial soundtrack to the scenes of petrol bombs and the barricades, an anthem for the mob, and Nathan quietly allowed the music hall melody to seduce him. He hummed the song to himself now as pictures of a victorious Conservative Party appeared on the screen. Soon the tune faded from his thoughts and he was drawn back to the reality of the room.

As the cheering gave way to applause, Nathan James found himself thinking about floor space. If he was going to get himself and Trevor out of there safely he would have to keep control of the situation and it would be difficult to do so with this many hostages. He needed the room to empty out.

'Oi!' A few of the captives turned to him. The rest kept their eyes on the screen, immersed in the moment. They were trying to convince themselves that it was still what this night was about. Nathan banged the steel of his gun barrel against the side of a stove. Suddenly the only noise was the tinny chatter of the pundits on the television. Now he had everybody's attention. Nathan nodded towards the screen. 'Kill the sound.' Stevie reached up and turned the volume down to zero. It was reduced to a mime.

He pointed his gun at Susan Guthrie. She shrunk into the older man's embrace. 'You,' Nathan said. He indicated the doors with his gun. 'Out.'

'You're letting us go?' Her voice was small but precise.

'No. I'm letting *you* go. Get out of here.'

'What about my husband?'

'He stays. You go.'

She opened her mouth to speak but the old man silenced her with a single finger pressed to her lips.

She looked to the younger man in the blazer, whom Nathan took to be her son, and back to her husband. 'If you're both staying I'm staying,' but she didn't sound convinced.

Nathan pressed the gun hard against the old woman's sunken cheek. 'If I tell you to go, you go.' Back behind the mask he blinked.

Slowly, wordlessly, Susan Guthrie made towards the door. 'And you.' He waved the son and his girlfriend after her. Now he worked his way around the room, clearing it of people. He released businessmen and wives, executives and waiters. He stopped two men at the door and told them to carry Mr Andrews out with them.

Trevor protested. 'He should stay.' He didn't want anyone who had challenged him to get away that easily. And anyway he liked looking at the man's wound.

Quickly Nathan said, 'He needs a doctor. We need to let him out before he gets any sicker. And what you did to him will prove we mean business.'

Trevor seemed satisfied that his efforts would be recognized and helped to get the head waiter to his feet so he could be dragged away. He did not object when Nathan released Walker, who was still sitting on the floor with one hand pressed to the burns on his face, moaning quietly.

Nathan looked at Bobby. 'And you too.'

She didn't want to stay in there any longer than necessary, but she wasn't leaving until all the hostages had been freed. 'Don't talk crazy. This is my kitchen.'

'I told you, not any more.'

'I'm the head chef here. I know how this place works. You need me. I'm staying.'

Nathan considered her. She was probably right. She could be useful.

'Can you deal with the heat in here?' He ran a single finger around the inside of the mask where it clung to his neck.

She turned to her cooks. 'Boys?' Stevie and Sheffield moved towards the stoves.

'Stop! You move when I say you move.'

'They're turning off the stoves.'

Nathan nodded, as if it was his idea. 'Fine, you stay. And them. They stay too.' He turned to Grey Thomas. 'But you're done. Get out.'

The little man with the silk cravat, the hounds tooth jacket and the tiny feet clad in brogues of ox-blood coloured leather, pressed his hands together and said, 'Thank you.' He turned towards the door.

'No.' Bobby had a hand on his shoulder.

Thomas recoiled. 'I beg your pardon?'

'If I'm staying this little shit's staying too.'

Thomas's eyelids fluttered. It made him look vulnerable. Nathan thought it made him look female. Thomas said, 'He just tried to set you free.'

'But I'm not going, so you're not going either.'

Nathan intervened. 'Why doesn't she want you to go?'

'You'll have to ask her.'

'So?'

She stared at the other hostage, like he was a tray of cheap fish gone bad. 'I've got my reasons.'

'Whatever you say. He stays.'

Nathan turned back to the kitchen. He had reduced the head count from over twenty to just nine of them, including Trevor, himself and the staff of the kitchen. He had also kept the restaurant critic, a middle-aged man with a sweep of shoulder-length silver hair, who looked expensive enough to be worth holding on to, plus the older man whose wife Trevor had threatened. The man held himself straight and the unemotional way in which he surveyed the room suggested he was used to an audience, Nathan decided. This meant he might have seniority and therefore be valuable. Plus an older man was unlikely to challenge them.

Finally Nathan could take in the shape of the kitchen. It was a simple rectangle. The swing doors through which they had come were situated at the eastern end of the long side and directly across from him was the bricked-up back door. Down the centre of the room, taking up much of the space, was a large solid top stove. The floor was squared out in tiles the colour of clotted blood. The stainless-steel work surfaces were strewn with the debris of a kitchen caught mid-service, and diagonally across from him, in the south-western corner, tucked back into its own alcove, was the sink area. Standing over it with his back to the kitchen, was a large black man wearing a blue polyester house coat. Nathan hadn't noticed him up to now. He'd been aware of a looming presence, towards the back of the room. But the presence had stayed there in the margins, and in the chaos of their entry to the kitchen anything that was not an immediate threat had not been granted room in his thoughts.

But now he couldn't avoid looking at the man. The steep curve of the wide shoulders; the way the back of the housecoat's collar bowed away from the back of the thick, black neck; the way the material creased and pulled under the armpits, as if it was two sizes too small for the body it was meant to contain, because his clothes always were. He couldn't avoid looking at it because it was all so familiar.

Nathan lifted his gun once more. 'You!'

The man didn't move.

'You! At the sink. Turn around.'

His shoulders rose up and then down again as if he had taken a deep, sad breath.

'Now!'

Slowly, clumsily, the kitchen porter stood up straight at the sink and turned about to face the masked gunman. Nathan stared and, once more, let the weapon drop to his side.

'Kingston?'

Trevor turned to look too. Nathan took a step towards him. 'What are you doing in here?'

Kingston opened his mouth to say something, thought better of it and closed both his mouth and eyes at the same time, as if his face were trying to shut down altogether to avoid expressing any emotion.

Now it was Bobby's turn. 'Kingston? Do you know these guys?'

The kitchen porter opened his eyes and looked at her for a second, before letting his gaze drop to his feet. 'Yeah, Chef,' he said, as if his world had ended. 'Afraid I do.'

10

Kingston was a year above Nathan at the Cardinal Wolsey Secondary Modern school and big for his age, made taller still by a black nimbus of Afro hair. Every day he arrived at school carrying a square plastic carrier bag containing a record, which he would not put down even when he had abandoned the rest of his possessions. There were other boys at the Cardinal Wolsey, black and white, who brought records to school, mostly recordings by Jamaican ska acts. In breaks, or at lunch-time when they stood outside the chip shop, they would compare their records and swap them. Nathan watched the boys over his bag of chips, admired the bold album covers as they changed hands and decided that he wanted to be a part of their society.

One Saturday he went to Ragged Records on Brixton High Street and bought a second-hand copy of an album by Millie Small. The title track was 'My Boy Lollipop', the only Ska track that Nathan knew because he had heard it played on the radio. He carried it to school in its Ragged Records carrier bag for three days, but nobody took any notice. On the fourth day Kingston stopped Nathan on the way out of school and asked to be shown what was in the bag. He nodded slowly at the Millie Small album and asked Nathan what he thought of it. Nathan said he thought it was good, which was true. He liked the happy sound of 'My Boy Lollipop' and assumed the rest *was* good but had no way of knowing because he did not own a record-player. He did not admit this. Kingston was carrying his own bag which he handed to Nathan. 'Have a listen to this,' he said. 'You might like it too.' It was an album by someone called Prince Buster. Nathan asked when he should return it. Kingston turned his gaze to the distance and said, 'Later. When you're done with it.' Nathan was impressed. It would never have occurred to him to lend out something like this.

At home he asked his grandfather if he might borrow some money to buy a record-player. Terry said he would think about it, and two days later returned from a move with a simple grey deck and two small speakers, which had been left out for collection as rubbish. He said, 'Just don't make the ceiling shake,' but gave the impression that he wouldn't mind if he did. The record-player's sound was thin and the needle jumped if Nathan moved too vigorously about his bedroom, but he didn't mind. He stood next to the record-player bouncing gently on his heels to the pulsing, offbeat shuffle of 'Al Capone' by Prince Buster, and the call and response of the saxophones. He loved the sound of Buster's rhythmic voice on 'Judge Dread' and mouthed along to 'I am the rude boy today', with its rising intonation, even though he had no idea what it meant. 'My Boy Lollipop' still made him happy for three minutes.

At school he returned the Prince Buster record to Kingston and said it was one of the best things he had ever heard. Kingston grinned and said, 'There's better,' and invited Nathan to go with him to Ragged Records after school to search out rare recordings. It became a regular fixture and on weekends they went by tube to Camden in North London to hang out in the crowded Jamaican record shop down from the canal, and flick through the racks of discs. When he was thirteen he learnt to smoke cannabis with Kingston and his three older brothers – Red Lebanese mostly, or Moroccan Gold, crumbled over tobacco – and he liked the gentle high which made him laugh, even on days when he had few reasons to do so. He was an uneven student at school, and though he understood everything, he preferred the approval of his classmates. His accuracy with an elastic band and a ball of paper earned him punishments and he spent a lot of time waiting by himself in empty classrooms after school.

By then his grandmother had died, and his grandfather's sadness lay heavily on the house in Streatham. He felt sorry for Terry, and for himself, and for a while the only thing he wanted to do was be near him in the evenings, for fear that his grandfather would go away when he wasn't there, as all the others had. They watched television together in silence. Soon, though, Terry chose to work longer hours to fill the space in his life and Nathan did not want to go home to the tall empty house. A few weekday evenings, and every weekend, Nathan went instead to yeasty ska and reggae pubs in Highbury or Notting Hill with Kingston, where they smoked and listened to music. The men at these pubs, cured by smoke, preserved in alcohol, knew they were underage, but liked their confidence and did not trouble them. Nathan became a keen reader of the *New Musical Express* and *Sounds*. He admired the look of the black Ska artists and the white Mods in their narrow-cut suits who followed them. He found a suit of his own in a second-hand shop, a light, grey wool and polyester two piece with narrow lapels, and a white shirt with a button-down collar to go with it, and wore it to the gigs they went to on Saturday nights. He cut his hair short and though he was not a suedehead, with a scalp of strokeable fur, he believed his taste in music was recognizable from his appearance. In a neighbourhood as black as Brixton he believed this was a useful quality in a white boy.

Often after school, Kingston took Nathan home to his house on Dalberg Road, where he sat around the table with Kingston's three older brothers. Pinned up on the wall over the fireplace were curling postcards of too-yellow beaches infested with palm trees beneath a too-blue sky, sent over by family in Jamaica. Mrs McDonald handed out large bowls full of oxtail stew and rice and peas or snapper with ackee, and the boys shouted jokes across the table, trampling on each other's punchlines. Nathan liked the noise because his own house was too quiet, though he also became aware of the flat, rounded vowels in his own voice; what Kingston's brothers called his 'posh boy' sound. He worked hard to lose it, shortening the vowels and dropping hard letters when it felt right. He didn't want to stand out anymore.

One evening Nathan and Kingston went to see Prince Buster play at the National Ballroom in Kilburn, and Nathan took with him a tape-recorder, which he wore under his shirt on a strap around his neck. He was pleased with the recording, which hissed and crackled, but still let the driving sound of the Prince come through. He played it to friends at school. They liked it so much they asked him if they could have copies and he made a few. These he sold at a profit and soon he realized he had a way of paying for his music habit. He decided he was also rebelling against the big business interests that exploited both the musicians and the fans. Each weekend he went to concerts by Desmond Dekker or the Melodians, Jimmy Cliff or the Paragons, and the following Monday he sold the few tapes that he had made. When one boy asked Nathan if he could also supply a little dope to go with the tape, Nathan quickly said he could. Now he would be allowing those who could not get to concerts themselves to enjoy the full experience at second hand.

One of Kingston's brothers helped them to pay for half an ounce of crumbly, sweet-smelling Red Leb, and together the two boys cut it up into thumbnail-sized pieces which they wrapped tightly in clingfilm. Most people were now buying a stick of dope with their tape. Nathan and Kingston began to make enough money to buy their dope themselves.

When he was fourteen years old Nathan suggested to Kingston that they get tattoos, as proof of their friendship.

'What kind of tattoo?' Kingston said. 'My ma will kill me.'

Nathan said, 'Love?'

Kingston looked appalled, but Nathan was determined.

'Like the Borstal boys,' Nathan said. 'They've got love on the knuckles of one hand and hate on the other.' He made two pale pink fists and held them forward.

'We don't want to be like them,' Kingston said. 'People will think we're like that Trevor.'

Nathan agreed this would not be to their advantage, but he still wanted to pursue the idea. On the floor of the bedroom that Kingston shared with his older brother Raymond was a large collection of reggae imported direct from Jamaica. The LPs were stacked up by the fireplace, at the boys' feet, and the album covers were dressed with pictures of men with dreadlocks. There were roaring lions on them too or burning spears and sometimes all three, in livid saturated shades of red, green and gold. 'A lion's head,' Kingston said quickly, and Nathan said he thought it was the perfect idea.

But they couldn't find a parlour that would do a tattoo for them in Brixton let alone a lion's head, not even in those places under the soot-blackened railway arches along Atlantic Road where anything could be bought at a price. 'Come back when you got some pubes,' the Jamaican men with the metal front teeth shouted at them or, 'What you want on there, bwoy? Andy Pandy?' And they would still be laughing when they slammed the door.

They went up to Brockwell Park instead. They took some sewing needles and some ink and two joints. They hunkered down in one of the old gardener's sheds by the ponds. It was where they always went when there was business that needed attending to. But neither of them was skilled enough to draw a lion's head, because it demanded too much detail. They settled instead on the moon for Kingston. 'Because you're black,' said Nathan, with authority, and the sun for him.

'And when we put our hands together we'll have night and day,' said Kingston, and they touched fists, knuckle to knuckle. They smoked their joints and laughed and decided that it hadn't hurt very much.

Their hands quickly swelled up like balloons after that. They wrapped them in strips torn from an old T-shirt and told Mrs McDonald they had hurt them climbing over the park's iron fence when they got caught there by early winter closing. She sent them to the Bengali doctor in the big house on Brixton Water Lane. He shook his head at the damage, but said nothing as he gave them both a shot and a bottle of pills. One day after school at the kitchen table, after they had healed, Mrs McDonald spotted the outline of a crescent on the back of Kingston's hand, above the second and third knuckle. She cuffed him around the head and said, 'Who told you to mark the skin God gave you? Who, child?' She was so cross she sent him away before his plate was empty. She saw the disc in the same place on the back of Nathan's hand, with its skinny trails to indicate the sun's rays, but said nothing about it. She crossed her arms across her bosom and said to Nathan, 'Don't let that boy lead you astray. He always leadin' and not to a good place.'

11

A decade later, the two men stood facing each other in the restaurant kitchen.

'You shouldn't be down here, Kingston.'

'It was your idea. That time, when we were upstairs.'

Bobby Heller took a sharp, outraged breath. 'You bastards have eaten in my restaurant?'

Nathan silenced her with one raised finger and turned back to Kingston. 'I remember being here.'

'And you said we were invisible.'

Nathan finished the sentence, with a dying fall. 'So you got a job.'

'I told you about Natalie and about Josh. I told you I wanted out. And then you said we were invisible sitting in the restaurant and I thought well, this is the place.' He looked apologetically about the room. 'I didn't think—' He scanned the faces of the hostages looking back at him. 'There was no way I could have known.'

Bobby breathed in again, and jutted her head towards her kitchen porter. 'But you thought it could happen? You thought it might? You knew about this?' The tone of her voice was rising and the words were coming out so fast it sounded like she might never stop talking. 'You know these guys and what they were going to do tonight and that they were going to come in here and—'

Nathan pressed his gun under her chin. 'Please stay quiet.' He pushed his masked face into hers and said, very carefully, 'He didn't know anything about what was going to happen because *we* didn't know what was going to happen.'

Trevor clapped a hand on Kingston's shoulder. 'Good you're here, though.' At the appearance of Trevor on this side of the room, Bobby stepped backwards and away from the men. She didn't want to do anything that might encourage his attention.

Kingston stared at Trevor. 'Good how? How can this be good?'

Trevor said, 'You can help.' He reached into the waistband of his black jeans and pulled out a second pistol, which he held by the barrel. He proffered it to Kingston.

'What you want me to do with that?'

'Lend a hand.'

Kingston turned to his friend. 'Nathan, I can't. That's not what I do. I'm about Natalie and Josh now. Not...' He stared at the weapon. '... this.'

A dilemma, Nathan thought to himself. Trevor was right. Another person on their side would be useful, particularly someone like Kingston whom he knew so well. Then again his friend had been trying to walk away and he respected that. He was just in a bad place at a bad time.

Before Nathan could say anything Trevor pushed the butt of the pistol into Kingston's chest and, impassively, said, 'We'll grass you.' Kingston understood immediately, and the potential outcomes came to him, not as words, but as a set of flash images: Trevor, having escaped from the Oyster House, now in a South London phone box, the receiver tucked under his chin as anonymously he calls in Kingston's name to the police, and lists his offences; Trevor, having failed to escape, now being interviewed by the police and leaning forward eagerly over the table towards the officers to make sure they spell Kingston's name correctly; Trevor and Nathan lying dead on the floor of the kitchen, bullet holes in their chests. Kingston realized that if he rejected Trevor's proposition it would have to be because he expected them both to die, but in this scenario he saw himself lying on the floor of the kitchen too, victim of a stray bullet, bleeding from a hole in his stomach.

Nathan said, 'It will be fine, Kingston. I'll look after you. Just take it.'

Kingston looked from one to the other. He said, 'You've got masks, though. No one knows what you look like. Everybody can see. They know who I am.'

Nathan nodded. 'Good point.' He reached up with one hand, slipped his fingertips under the rim of his mask where it met his neck and pulled it off in a single swift movement. Bobby looked at the face of her captor. Now she could see him as a real person. She could see him as a man with angular features and a sharp buzz cut, flattened on to his head by the mask, with hard distant blue eyes. The sudden revelation of her captor's humanity lightened her mood. He was just a man. The removal of the mask diluted his threat.

Her surge of confidence lasted only the few seconds before Trevor pulled off his mask. Now the room could take in the spider's web tattoo that ran up one side of his neck to disappear behind his ear, and the tangle of greasy brown hair, and the restless scar on his cheek that meandered from beneath one eye down towards the lip. Too much human history on one face.

Nathan screwed his eyes up tight and ran a hand across his pale, sweaty skin, blotched and creased from its incarceration. He said, 'I was looking for a reason to get that off.' He threw it on to the work surface, where it lay like a deflated balloon. 'If getting this sorted is down to the masks we're in trouble too.'

Trevor lit up a cigarette from a packet in his back trouser pocket, and exhaled a long plume of smoke. 'We're all going to get out of here,' he said, and he grinned at Kingston. He dug into a front trouser pocket and pulled out a small piece of folded paper from a glossy magazine and holding it by one corner, waved it in the air. 'Want some whiz, Kingston, while we're waiting.'

The kitchen porter shook his head. Trevor shrugged. 'Suit yourself.' He unfolded the paper and with a quick snort hoovered up the grey-white crush of amphetamine sulphate. He tipped his head back, sniffed and then blinked.

'Go easy,' Nathan said. 'You don't want to crack through too much of that.'

Trevor leaned his face into Nathan's. 'I know what's good for me. Question is, do you?' He ran his tongue around his teeth then walked back to his place by the door.

Kingston and Nathan watched him go. Kingston said, 'Can you manage him?'

'He'll do what I say. As long as we throw him the odd bone or two.' He turned back to Kingston. 'Which is why…' He nodded at the gun in his friend's hand.

Kingston managed a defeated half-smile and, accepting all his options were gone, retreated back to his position by the sink.

Nathan watched his friend walk across the room and felt a feeling of calm flow over him. He tried to tell himself that it was because he was pleased to have his friend close by, but he knew that it was less straightforward than that. Nathan felt like a victim of events rather than the director of them and, by forcing Kingston to join him, his friend had become a victim of events too. Their predicament – their inability to avoid situations – was shared.

'Kingston!' The kitchen porter turned to face him. 'Make us a cup of tea.' Kingston said he would. 'That's your job now,' Nathan said, trying to lighten the mood. 'Tea monitor.'

He turned to Bobby and, pointing to her cooks, said, 'How many of those white jackets have you got?'

'Laundry came in earlier. A couple of dozen.'

He turned to the hostages who weren't part of the kitchen staff. 'Right, you three. The cooks here are going to get you nice white jackets like they've got. I want you all to change into them.'

'Expecting us to cook your breakfast, are you?'

Nathan took a couple of strides towards where the man with the thick silver hair was standing, his back to the stove, chin up. 'Who are you?'

'Harry Connaston.'

'Well, Harry, old chap,' he said, mimicking well his accent with its flattened vowels and clipped consonants, 'if it's an offer, I jolly well might take you up on it.' Connaston stared back.

Behind him Stevie and Sheffield were handing out the jackets and searching for one big enough to fit Kingston. The judge and Grey Thomas were taking off their clothes and throwing them into a pile in one corner of the room. Nathan called for a jacket which was flung across the room. He caught it and presented it to him.

'Think of it as camouflage. We don't want the police to do anything stupid, do we.'

Within a few minutes the kitchen appeared to be staffed by the largest brigade of chefs it had ever known. Nathan surveyed them with satisfaction, impressed by the way a uniform made people look like each other. Except for Kingston who could only ever look like himself, in a jacket two sizes too small that was straining at the buttons.

Nathan pulled on his own jacket and looked at his watch. It was just coming up to midnight. 'Everybody get comfortable. Find a place to sit. Get some sleep. It's going to be a long night. But do what I say and it will all be over soon enough. Trevor, you take the doors. And you, mate,' he nodded towards Stevie, 'you turn the volume back up on the telly. Let's see how Maggie Thatcher is doing with that election of hers.' As one, the gunmen and hostages of the Jermyn Street Oyster House Siege turned towards the screen. Nathan James was about to find out how much trouble he was in.

12

From her position by the grill Bobby listened to her cooks sniping at each other and allowed herself the lightest of smiles.

'You clean down like a girl, Stevie.'

'No, I don't.'

'Look. You've got the pinkie up.'

The two cooks were bent over the solid-top, scraping away at scraps of food that had become burnt on during service.

'If you did it like that where I come from, they'd make you a necklace out of your guts.'

'If the good men of Yorkshire were to find my little finger so arousing they'd have their way with me, what can I do about it?'

'You wouldn't know what hit you.'

'You make it sound like lots of fun.'

Her crew was bantering again and that had to be a good thing, however whispered and hissed the abuse. They were taking control of their space, which was the point of the clean down. It took back ownership. A good kitchen service, full of flame and singed fingers, was meant to be about disorder. As long as the *mise-en-place* had been prepared correctly, Bobby always said, the kitchen could be allowed its air of chaos during service. They could change a dish, go off menu, set fire to each other's hair, brand the new cook in the corner with the red-hot tongs. (All of these things had happened in the Oyster House kitchen.) None of it mattered. The food would still get out on to the tables. 'Be good to the Meez,' Bobby would say, 'and the Meez will be good to you.' And then, once all the tickets had been sent, they got out the brushes and the mops and they cleaned down and took back control and applied the ice and bandages to the damaged skin. And that's when they opened the beer.

Once, in a bar in Paris, Bobby was set upon by three Algerian men who smelt of old sweat and cheap whisky. They crowded around her as she leaned over a cigarette machine down a dimly lit back corridor and pressed themselves against her. Two of them held her arms up to the cold, gloss-painted wall so that the third could force his face on to hers and his tongue in so hard between her teeth that she was too busy gagging to bite down. All of them reached in with a hand then, to find a corner of flesh. They dug away inexpertly at the hardness of her pelvic bone until she was bruised. Then the men stopped and pulled away. They walked off laughing.

She didn't bother to tell the police because she knew they would only shrug and look at her like the incident had been an opportunity missed. Later, in her studio, she stood beneath the rush of cold water that passed for a shower in the darkest hours of the Parisian night. But she wasn't trying to wash away their smell because it did not linger, nor even remove the sensation of their touch because that too had gone. She was putting herself back in charge of her own body. That was how she felt about her kitchen after the men with the guns arrived. She needed to clean it to restate her ownership.

'This shithole needs to be cleaned down,' she said to Nathan after he had turned to the television again.

'Are you asking me?' The gunman did not look away from the screen.

'No, I'm telling you. Me and the boys are going to clean down now.'

Nathan kept his eyes forward, watching closely as each new Conservative seat flashed on the bottom of the screen. He held on to his mug of tea with both hands.

'Give the blades to Kingston.'

She looked around at the heavy-handled knives that she knew were still lying on the work surfaces where they had been dropped when the gunmen had arrived. She had hoped he hadn't noticed them.

'We'll clean those too.'

'Give the metal work to Kingston. Kingston? Do the honours. Put them out of harms way, yeah?'

'I'll clean 'em first.'

'Do what you like. Just pack the blades away.'

So she handed over the knives, and started work on the carbonized grill. And the more she worked the more the kitchen felt like hers again and the less it felt like his.

She had just started scrubbing down the sauce station when the picture on the screen changed to a long-distance shot of a deserted Piccadilly. There was the fluttering tape stretched out across the road and a herd of police cars parked up kerbside, their lights flashing. At the bottom of the screen it said 'Live from central London'.

Nathan leaned towards the screen. 'Turn it up.' Stevie flicked the dial.

'You're famous,' Bobby said.

'Quiet. I'm listening.' There was not much detail: a siege situation; gunmen ambushed the restaurant shortly after 10 p.m.; unknown number of hostages; no word of demands; police marksmen on the scene; sources saying it was a robbery on a nearby jeweller's shop gone wrong; speculation from 'other quarters' that this may be an IRA 'spectacular'.

Nathan frowned. 'I R A?'

'It's an armed terrorist organization. They blow people up and stuff like that.'

Nathan pointed one finger at Bobby. 'I told you to stay quiet.'

'Police don't like the IRA. They won't be happy if they think you're Irish terrorists.'

'We're not I R –' But before he could finish his sentence the picture changed again. Two photographs: one of a judge, complete with shoulder-length judicial wig; the other a solid-jawed middle-aged man with his own leonine sweep of silver hair. '... both High Court Judge Sir Philip Guthrie, and the Conservative Party Treasurer Lord Connaston are believed to be among the hostages. The Prime Minister, who is in her Finchley constituency for the count, is being kept informed of developments. She has already spoken by telephone to Lord Connaston's wife, Carla, who herself was reported to have been held by the gunmen for a short while. Police say...'

Nathan looked away from the screen at the two men on the other side of the kitchen who were now staring back at him.

Bobby pushed cheerfully at her scrubbing brush. 'You are in such heavy shit.'

Nathan didn't look at her.

'Lords and judges. Oh my! A very bad call, my friend.'

Nathan chewed hard on his bottom lip. He had wanted something to bargain with but this was too much. He said, 'This is you?' The judge nodded. Connaston winked, as if he had just got one up on his captor.

From his position by the door Trevor jerked his head round towards the judge. 'What's your name?'

'Sir Philip Guthrie.'

'Guthrie?'

'Yes.'

And again, 'Guthrie?' Like he was trying to separate out the syllables into different words. Trevor turned away and stared blankly out of the window in the kitchen door, as if waiting for someone to arrive.

Lord Connaston said, 'You could end this now, you know.'

Nathan stared back at him. 'This ends when I say so.'

'When's that?'

'When I get what I need.'

'What do you need?'

'We're going to make a deal.'

'It doesn't look good for you.'

'Looks like my bargaining power just went up.'

Connaston said, 'I wouldn't see it like that.'

'You think I care how you see it?'

'Sir Philip is a highly respected member of the judiciary.'

'So they'll want him out.'

'Of course. But they'll also want to make sure nobody else tries to take a judge hostage.'

The judge nodded slowly and his bottom lip came forward as if he were considering the issue in real time. 'Indeed. There must, I imagine, always be an element of deterrence to any police action in a situation such as this.'

Nathan felt a flush of anger. He said, 'We didn't plan this.'

Connaston nodded. 'That much is obvious.'

'It just happened.'

'We all understand.'

'No one's going to get hurt.'

'That's good to hear. So why don't you just let us all go.'

Without turning around from his position by the door, Trevor barked, 'I'm not going to let them take me.'

'They won't take you. Trust me. I'll get it sorted.'

Quietly, in a voice just shy of a whisper, Connaston said, 'Are you entirely sure of that?'

13

From across the kitchen Bobby looked at the judge, who was seated on the floor now, his back against one of the steel-fronted cupboards that lined the back wall. She liked Guthrie's appearance because he reminded her of her grandfather, and not simply because of his age. Conrad Heller had been a great observer. He always sat at one end of the kitchen table in her parents' farmhouse outside Marion, Ohio, watching the family wrestle each other's jealousies, with the edge of a smile on his lips. Bobby liked to catch sight of this smile during rows with her brother because it suggested the old man thought she was in the right, though looking back she knew she was fooling herself, because she could never remember him taking sides. In old age he had retreated to a sagacious neutrality which put him in conflict with nobody. The judge had that same look about him. It was a distance from events which suggested insight. He looked to Bobby like he understood what was going on in this kitchen better than anyone else who was there, and she found the notion comforting.

After her parents divorced and her brother left, an unnatural peace fell on the Heller house near Marion. Bobby took to cooking then, eager to return to it a necessary smell of domesticity. 'A home that does not smell of supper,' she said, sounding many times her fifteen years, 'is just a house,' and she thumbed through the stained cookbooks that her mother kept on the shelf above the Frigidaire. What she wanted was her parents back together; instead she created the dishes she had eaten with them. Conrad still came most days. He still took his place at the top of the table, and Bobby cooked for him. She made Boston brown bread with thick molasses, and a beef and oyster stew, and her grandfather always cleaned his bowl. She made her own Tollhouse cookies with chunks of Hershey bar that she froze and broke up with a hammer. She roasted pork and even made sauerkraut with caraway seeds because, in his plaid shirt and jeans, Conrad liked to think of himself as having roots in the old country, even though it had been his own grandparents who had settled from Germany. Conrad had passed his working life not as a farmsteader or frontiersman but in life insurance, studying actuarial tables.

What mattered to Bobby, though, was the process of cooking and feeding, which suspended all other activity, and it mattered to her now. From a high shelf in the Oyster House kitchen she took down a Tupperware box of shortbread biscuits and another of dense Madeira cake. She carried these over to the judge and, sliding down next to him, asked if his dinner had been interrupted before he had reached pudding. She knew the question was absurd. No one was likely to recall the dinner they had been eating that evening, only the events that had brought it to an end. Dutifully he managed a smile. 'My doctor has told me to tame my sweet tooth,' he said, with a solicitous dip of the head. She pulled open the lid to the biscuits and he looked inside. He asked if she had made them herself and she hoped the question was not about the restaurant's standards. She wanted the judge to think about the kitchen as a place where food was prepared rather than one where hostages were held. She lifted the other box, so he could see the faint, hazed outline of the dark matter inside. 'And the Madeira cake,' she said.

'In that case,' he said as he took a biscuit, 'I think my doctor will forgive me just this once.' It broke up on his lips and left a crust of crumbs and sugar which he licked away economically. Suddenly he had a coughing fit, pursing his lips, as if trying to keep the air in, his chest bucking beneath his chef's jacket. She laid a concerned hand on his shoulder, and asked him if he wanted her to thump him on the back to dislodge a piece of biscuit, but he waved her away.

'Touch of asthma,' he said, taking a noisy breath when the coughing had subsided. 'Reward for getting to my age. Nothing to worry about.' He nodded towards the box. 'They're good.'

She thanked him and looked sadly at her biscuits. It seemed such a pathetic offering in the circumstances.

She said to the judge, 'What should I be doing now?' The question had sounded reasonable enough inside her head, but spoken out loud it felt foolish.

Guthrie leaned in towards her so that she could smell the shortbread biscuit on his breath. 'There is nothing you should be doing now.'

'It's my kitchen.'

'That doesn't make you responsible for everybody in it.'

'I feel responsible.' Her voice was becoming thinner and tighter.

'The only people who are responsible are those who are holding us here against our will.' His voice was a hoarse whisper.

She blinked, and turned away. She recalled the moment when her knife had been pressed to the gunman's throat, and she had felt the bulge of his Adam's apple above her blade. She had felt powerful, until the stakes had been raised, and then she had felt compromised.

'What's happening here was not caused by you,' the judge said. 'Nothing you did created any likelihood that it might happen, and the outcome is not your responsibility either.' He tipped his head to one side, as he thought about the shape of his last sentence. He wanted something that sounded less like he might have delivered it in his courtroom, and said, 'It's just a bugger it happened at all.' He opened his eyes wide and smiled at his own sudden coarseness.

Bobby nodded. 'Is there anything else I can get you?'

He looked at the box of biscuits. 'You can leave those with me,' he said. He tapped the side of the box with one hard-nailed finger. 'I've been thinking of changing my doctor for a while now.'

Bobby placed the open box in his lap and eased herself up from the floor. She said, 'Don't eat them all at once,' and admired the cheerful presumption in her voice.

Guthrie acknowledged the command. 'Well now, that may prove a challenge. We shall have to see if I am equal to it.'

Bobby whispered, 'Thank you,' because she felt she had been complimented, and walked back to the other side of the kitchen.

14

A short distance away at the church of St James's, God had moved out and the Metropolitan Police had moved in. Beneath Christopher Wren's gilded ceiling, the space had already been divided. On the north side, beneath the gallery, was a makeshift mess, dispensing weak coffee and limp cheese sandwiches to the dozens of officers who were now on site. SO19, the firearms unit, had taken over a back corner, as much because of their tribal instincts as the need for an operations centre. (All the firepower was, in any case, locked away outside in a van parked up on Haymarket.) The wooden pews were strewn with police helmets and items of discarded uniform. Huddles of officers, some in black combat trousers and multi-pocketed vests, others in standard issue, stood about sipping from polystyrene cups or studying two large maps of the area pinned up on notice boards, which had been erected down by the carved wooden pulpit at the front right of the church. A man in overly clean jeans and a bright white shirt pulled tight beneath an empty brown leather gun-holster strapped across his chest was pointing out key locations on the map, with the furious movements of someone trying to understand his story by retelling it as quickly as possible.

Commander Peterson, now in shirtsleeves, had his own paper-smothered trestle table on the north side of the church, beneath a window. He studied maps and gathered information from officers at the scene.

'Not a good night for it, Sergeant.'

'No, sir.'

'Not that there is such a thing as a good night for an armed siege. Still at least we know these hostages won't go hungry. They'll just have to get by on oysters, won't they'.

Willy stared across the church at its southwest corner, as though he could see through the walls to the restaurant beyond. 'Actually, there aren't any oysters, sir. The Jermyn Street Oyster House doesn't serve oysters in June.'

Peterson looked up at his staff sergeant. 'If you've got anything useful to tell me, do so, Sergeant. Otherwise keep quiet.'

'Yes, sir.'

Willy's radio crackled into life. He stepped a few metres away to the privacy of a corner behind the pulpit. When he returned he said, 'The Prime Minister's convoy has been rerouted down by the Embankment.'

Peterson glanced at his watch. It was approaching 2 a.m. 'When are they expected?'

'Round about now. They did ask for last-minute clearance to use Piccadilly to get to Downing Street but I told them we were denying all requests.'

'Exactly. Don't need that lot cruising past the middle of this.'

'They said she wasn't very pleased about it.'

'Who said that?'

'Her Special Branch boys. Said she felt like she was being dictated to by criminals.'

'She's being dictated to by the police, which is a different matter entirely. Any more trouble put them over to me.'

'Yes, sir.'

Peterson admired the authority in his own voice, though even he recognized it as mere bravado. Normally, with a siege situation of this seriousness, the Home Secretary would convene a Cabinet-level committee to make key decisions, as they had during the Iranian Embassy siege three years before. Not tonight. The Cabinet was scattered about the country waiting to hear whether they were going to remain in politics. The Home Secretary still held the title, until the electorate decided otherwise, but while the votes were being counted he was in no position to convene anything. Peterson knew the politicians were being kept informed but, for the moment, operational control would remain with the police. The Commissioner of the Metropolitan Police Service had made that much clear. Peterson was to refer only the most serious of decisions upwards to New Scotland Yard, the Commissioner had said when they spoke by telephone earlier in the evening, but for now, it remained his case.

The Commander checked his watch and decided it was time to begin. Willy clapped his hands, called the church to order and the audience drifted towards the notice boards. Some sprawled in the pews. Others rested their arms on the back of the pew in front.

Peterson nodded towards the man with the empty holster. 'DCI Marshall?'

'Yes, sir.' He flipped open the black-covered notebook he was holding and stared at the pages.

'At 22.02 hours last night, we received reports of gunfire, from within Princes Arcade, which runs...' he looked up at one of the maps, a large-scale close-up of the area immediately surrounding the Oyster House, '... here, from Piccadilly, south to Jermyn Street. Initial reports were of an attempted burglary on the premises of a jewellers within the arcade which had been disturbed.'

'By security guards?'

'No, sir. Our understanding is that two young women attending the Xenon night club last night had followed the suspects through a fire exit door that leads from the basement club and up into the arcade, whereupon they came under fire.'

'Who called in SO19?'

'I did, sir, when first reports were received.'

'Go on.'

'During their escape from the arcade, via the Jermyn Street entrance, here,' Marshall pointed at the map again, 'we believe two shots were fired. They proceeded into the restaurant opposite said entrance, known as the Oyster House at number 87 Jermyn Street. I and my colleagues arrived on the scene at 22.05, followed by the armed response unit three minutes later, when a third shot was fired at police from within the premises.'

He closed his notebook. Despite the cold, measured language of the description nothing could disguise the gravity of the situation. London was in the midst of its most serious hostage crisis since the Iranian Embassy siege, and everyone in the room remembered how that one had finished: stun grenades, fires, the SAS swinging through windows, corpses, and all of it live on television. Nobody wanted a repeat of that.

Peterson took up position by the map. 'Right, gentlemen. We play this by the book. We have... how many hostages is it?'

He lifted his chin to receive the response. 'We understand from a debrief of the released hostages that it's seven, sir,' came a voice from the pews. 'There are four members of the kitchen staff, including the head chef. A journalist, Sir Philip Guthrie who is...'

Peterson finished the sentence. '... who is a high-court judge, plus Lord Connaston – who many of you will know is a leading figure in the Conservative Party, which is otherwise having rather a good night.' He looked at the map behind him. 'Currently we have six police marksmen surrounding the front of the building, both at street level and in elevated positions,' – as he spoke he pointed out locations on the smaller-scale map – 'and a further four plus back-up surrounding the back of the premises down by Mason's Yard.'

There was a shout from the back of the church. 'Don't waste your time on the back door. There isn't one.'

Peterson looked up. 'Who the—?'

'Marcus Caster-Johns. I own the joint.' He was striding down the central aisle towards the crowd of officers, a long canvas bag slung over one shoulder, the material of his dun-coloured, waxed cotton trousers and dark green hunting jacket rustling as he moved. There was a policeman at his side who was pleading with him to hold back.

'Let him come.'

Caster-Johns stood panting slightly at the front of the church, his cheeks pinking with excitement, strands of hair slicked to his forehead by a light gloss of sweat. 'Thank you.'

'You are the owner?'

'Yes, indeed. The Oyster House has been in my family for seventy-three years.'

'Has it been without a back door for seventy-three years?'

'Of course not. Only got rid of the bollocking thing about a fortnight ago. Had it bricked up.'

'I'm sorry?'

'Rodent problem. Few rats. Couldn't stop the bastards. Health and Safety didn't like that at all.'

'So you bricked up the back door?'

'Exactly. Did the trick. Bit dicey on fire regs, but we'll sort it.'

Peterson rubbed his face with one open palm. 'Mr Caster-Johns, if you could just wait at the back of the hall until we're finished here I'm sure your knowledge will be very helpful to us. One of my officers will be along presently to talk to you.'

'Actually, I was thinking I could be rather more useful than that. I'm a terrific shot.'

'Mr Caster-Johns—'

'You don't even need to give me a gun.' He lifted the canvas bag off his shoulder and began opening the top strap. 'Brought my own. A lovely Enfield 303. Use it for deer hunting.' Peterson didn't need to issue an order. Before Caster-Johns could pull the weapon from its bag or finish the sentence four officers were out of the pews and dragging the man down the church, one at each corner.

'Take your hands off me. Put me down. I'm trying to help. Let go of my armpit.' He was still shouting as he was pulled out into the vestibule.

Peterson watched them go. 'Sergeant, get them to put him in my car. I'll talk to him in a few minutes. And check he's got a licence for that thing.' As Willy Cosgrave set off down the aisle, the Commander looked up at the ancient clock set into the wood panelling below the organ at the back of the church. 'Right, gentlemen. It's 02.15 or thereabouts. The negotiators are on their way and should be here by 04.00 hours. Let's make sure there's still a situation here for them to negotiate. Maintain the cordon as set. Nothing done unless on my say-so. For the moment silence is a very good thing.'

Briskly, the officers of the Metropolitan Police Service returned to their positions to see out what was left of the short summer's night.

15

Three days ago

The voice at the end of the phone said, 'Who am I talking to?'

Nathan looked up at a stack of books on a high shelf, with foreign-sounding names on the spines. There was one by someone called Roger Verge and another by an Anton Mosimann. There were books by Frédy Girardet and Paul Bocuse and someone else called Larousse, which he didn't know how to pronounce.

He said, 'Call me Freddie.'

'My name's Denis.'

'OK, Denis.'

'Right, Freddie. Well, it seems we have a bit of a situation here.'

'Yes. We have a situation.'

'And we need to help you to conclude the situation. Is everybody OK in there, Freddie?'

'They're all fine. We're not monsters.'

'I'm sure.'

'And we're not the IRA.'

'Why do you mention the IRA, Freddie?'

'I'm just saying, we're not them.'

'Who are you then?'

'We're just... I'm Freddie. That's all you need to know.'

'Freddie, we're going to have to work together.'

'We're going to want a car.'

'And what are you going to do with the car?'

'It will have to have blacked-out windows.'

'Where will it be going, this car?'

'You know who we've got in here?'

'We know who's in there. All the police marksmen know who you've got in there.'

'That sounds like a threat.'

'Not at all, Freddie. You don't seem the sort of man to scare easily.'

'I'm not.'

'You seem very clear-headed, actually.'

'I am.'

'We'll take this nice and slow, Freddie.'

'You use my name a lot.'

'Do I?'

'Is that what they train you to do? Use my name?'

'I'm just trying to put you at ease.'

'It's not my real name.'

'We're going to have to learn to trust each other, Fre—'

'There you go again.'

'I'll try to watch it.'

'I'm the one who needs to know I can trust you. I need to know you're not going to screw us over.'

'I'm not going to do that.'

'Good to hear.'

'Have you got everything down there? Food? Water? Medicines? Is there anybody down there on medication?'

He looked around the kitchen. It was a little after 6 a.m. and most of them seemed to be asleep, on makeshift beds of plump, green canvas bags full of dirty linen that the cooks had dragged into the main kitchen from down beside the walk-ins. A few had been startled awake when the phone rang but now they had their eyes closed. Trevor was wide awake, though. Trevor hadn't moved all night. He had his finger tight around the trigger and his eyes set on the doors. Bobby was watching too, from her place on the floor on the other side of the kitchen as far away from Trevor as possible, back against one of the storage units. She blinked but her features stayed still.

'Everyone's fine.'

'You must need something, though.'

Nathan squeezed the phone in tighter against his neck.

'Freddie?'

'I'm still here.'

'What do you need?'

Nathan looked around the kitchen, at the piles of copper pans and stainless steel trays, the hanging implements and plastic pots of powders and herbs. He recognized that he had been presented with an opportunity. He could get the police to respond to his demands. For the moment it wouldn't matter what he asked for, just as long as they complied with his requests. His eyes fell upon a set of lists taped to the tiled walls.

'Right. Here's what I want.'

'Go on.'

'Ten pounds of veal, from the cushion.'

'What does that mean?'

Nathan didn't know. He said, 'Write it down. From the cushion. Veal.'

'OK, Freddie.'

'Four dozen eggs.'

'Yes.'

'Two pounds fresh breadcrumbs. One pound butter.'

'One pound, did you say?'

'Yes. A pound. Butter.'

'Right.' -

'A pound of capers.'

'Is that it?'

'Yes. That's it. We want them by...' he looked at his watch, '10 a.m. Put them in the...' He hesitated as he tried to recall the words.

From her place on the floor Bobby hissed, 'Dumb waiter.'

He looked down at her as he spoke. 'Dumb waiter. Send them

down in the dumb waiter. Telephone first. Then one man comes in, puts it all in the dumb waiter and leaves.'

'Right, Freddie. And if you want to talk to me this line will be open. All you have to do is pick up the phone and I'll be here.'

'Just get us what I asked for.'

'Bye bye, Freddie.'

Nathan put the receiver back on its wall-mounted hanging place and looked down at Bobby, who was staring back at him, one thin eyebrow raised.

'What's up with you?'

'So, it's Wiener Holstein for lunch then, is it?'

16

The policemen took off their headsets and dropped them on to the fake wood grain of the Formica-topped desks. They were sitting in the first of the mobile police control units, which had been delivered on to Jermyn Street in the early hours of the morning and parked up in front of the church. From the roof a tangle of wires reached up to the nearest telegraph pole to cut into the phone line to the Oyster House kitchen. Inside, there was the beginning of an office: papers, pin-boards papered with plans of the kitchen, phones, swivel chairs and the smell of weak coffee.

Peterson said, 'What do we think?'

The negotiator stared down at the phone. 'He's calm. He's collected. I'd say he's smart.'

'Not Provo?'

Denis Thompson frowned.

'I'm just removing it as a possibility,' Peterson said, defensively. 'The question will be asked and I want to be able to say a conclusive no.'

'Definitely not IRA.'

'You're not just going on accent?'

'Well, partly, of course. That's a London accent. South London, I'd say, with something else mixed in. In any case, the IRA don't attempt robberies and they don't deny they're IRA when they are.'

Peterson needed the negotiator to make an unambiguous assessment. If the siege was regarded in any way as a terrorist-led event, he would be required to refer all decisions to New Scotland Yard and through them to some hastily assembled collection of politicians overly eager to exercise their newly acquired mandate. If it was downgraded to the actions of ordinary criminals it would remain his case and present him with the chance to prove himself in operational conditions. That was something he felt his CV lacked. To Commander Roy Peterson the Oyster House Siege had just begun to look like an opportunity for serious career advancement.

Peterson leaned forward. 'What about the demand?'

Thompson picked up the sheet of paper and stared at it. 'I think he was reading off a list or something.'

'Fine. Whatever they want for now, we do.'

'It looks like a list of ingredients.'

Peterson turned to his sergeant, who was head-down over papers at a desk in the corner of the cabin.

'Willy. One for you.' He handed over the sheet and turned back to the negotiator. 'What do we do next?'

Thompson leaned back in his chair. He stretched out his legs and crossed them at the ankle, heel to the cheap office carpet. 'We fill the order.'

'Excuse me, sir.'

'Hang on, sergeant. Then what? We fill the order and call up again?'

'Exactly. Take it step by step. Do as Freddie asks. We shouldn't be in a hurry.'

'We're not in a hurry.'

'Good. That's when these things go wrong. When people hurry.'

'Sir, they've forgotten…'

'Give us a minute, sergeant.' And to the negotiator: 'But we'll still be drawing up plans.'

'… it's the anchovies.'

The men in the room turned to look at him. Peterson barked, 'Do you have something useful to say?'

Willy looked down at the sheet, sheepishly as if he regretted opening his mouth. 'I was just thinking, sir, this here is a recipe for Wiener Holstein.'

The men looked back at him blankly. 'Er, breaded veal escalope. It's fried, with a fried egg on top. Without the egg it's a Viennoise. With the egg it's—'

'What about the anchovies?'

'Well, this is a classic recipe list for Wiener Holstein, but it should come garnished with capers and anchovies. They've only got the capers.'

The negotiator pulled a face. 'Sounds rank, if you ask me.'

'Oh, it's not. The veal's very rich so you need something salty to cut through that and the anchovies.'

'I don't believe anybody here is interested, Sergeant.'

'No, sir.'

'Get it all together. Put it in a box. Get it back here by 9.30 a.m.'

'Of course, sir.'

For once Willy Cosgrave had an assignment he could enjoy. It drew on his own particular area of expertise, it didn't involve paperwork, and it was of no strategic importance to the operation whatsoever. Over the years, as the relationship with his superior officer had deteriorated, Willy Cosgrave had concluded that his best hope of an easy life now lay in never being of strategic importance. This, more than anything else, was his specialism. He didn't intend to change that now.

17

Terry James died suddenly one morning while trying to lift a box of expensive crockery that dropped to the pavement as his knees gave way. The contents spilled out and lay in jagged, gilt-edged shards around him as his men pulled open his coat and shirt and attempted to thump the life back into his body. Ken, who had worked for Terry the longest, was waiting for Nathan on the doorstep when he returned to Streatham in the early evening. Nathan was fifteen years old and there were so few weeks remaining until he left school that he and Kingston, both of whom had always been irregular students, had stopped attending Cardinal Wolsey altogether. They preferred instead to roam the record shops and pubs of London, impressing the older rastas and rude boys with their knowledge of ska and their competence in the rolling of refined and complex joints. Nathan's eyes were bloodshot from a day's smoking in Notting Hill.

Ken gave Nathan the news, and punctuated it by the lighting of a cigarette, so that the final declaration of Terry's death was followed by a great plume of grey mist from his nostrils. Though he had never seen the boy smoke, Ken offered Nathan one, as a sign that he had been accepted into an early adulthood. Nathan took the cigarette, which Ken lit for him. Nathan took a drag and said, 'I'll be fine.' Ken offered to take him to his house 'just for a few days, until the arrangements are made', but Nathan heard the reluctance in his voice and declined. He asked instead that he be driven to Kingston's house in Brixton where he asked Mrs McDonald if he might stay for a while.

'Child, with four mouths already what's a fifth?' She ladled out some thick black bean soup and sat at the head of the table watching him eat, a hand rested softly on his shoulder. Kingston came downstairs. He stood leaning in the kitchen doorway, his arms crossed, and watched too. 'Nathan will be in with you and Ray,' his mother said quietly, over Nathan's head.

'Now we'll never get rid of you.'

'Child!'

The boys smirked at each other. Kingston was over six feet tall. He filled the doorway and did not fit well his mother's description of him. 'It's all right, Mrs McDonald.'

One evening, a few days later, two social workers arrived at Mrs McDonald's house. They had been tipped off by Terry's employees and sat now in her kitchen, a bearded man in corduroy with shoulder-length hair and a silent woman in thick tortoise-shell-framed glasses, and drank her tea. The man sounded satisfied with the situation, though he did not bother to meet anybody's eye. 'And what arrangements have been made for the maintenance of the boy?' he said, without looking up from his notebook at Nathan who was just across the table. Kingston and his brothers were crowded into the kitchen, watching the proceedings, and shifted their weight irritably from foot to foot at the man's rudeness.

'We'll look after him,' Mrs McDonald said briskly.

'I'll get a job,' Nathan said. 'And my granddad was worth a bit.' Mrs McDonald looked at him. The thought had not occurred to her.

'Acceptable,' the social worker said and closed his notebook.

But Terry James was not worth anything. He had paid his employees too much. He had charged too little for his firm's services and it had fallen into such debt that he had been forced to mortgage the house against the business. Everything was taken.

'I'll get a job,' Nathan said again when he heard the news.

'A first for this house,' Mrs McDonald said.

But Nathan was adamant. 'I'll bring in some money.'

'You stay under my roof,' she said. 'But you clean what I tell you to clean and you tidy what I tell you to tidy.'

'Yes, Mrs McDonald.'

'And that's how you join this family.'

'Right, Mrs McDonald.'

She patted him on the cheek. 'We make a good Jamaican boy of you yet.' After that she left him in peace.

Still, he knew that she was watching him. Sometimes Mrs McDonald watched Kingston and Nathan, whispering with their heads down over the corner of the kitchen table, and he heard her mutter 'Thick as thieves'. It was as if she knew more than any woman should know about the things the young adults in her house were doing when she couldn't see them. Mrs McDonald was clever, Nathan decided.

But he did need a way to make money which was compatible with his talents, and Mrs McDonald couldn't help him solve that problem. It fell to Kingston to propose a plan. They were in Brockwell Park and Kingston was watching Nathan carefully stick together a patchwork of small Rizla cigarette papers to make a sheet big enough for the joint he had in mind. White boys rarely had the skill for rolling joints, Kingston said, admiringly. Somebody could make a fortune if they started selling joints ready rolled. Nathan was dragging the tip of his tongue across the gummy strip of the Rizla, and smiled at his friend. 'That's a thought,' he said.

They went home and set up a factory in their bedroom: a Desmond Dekker album on Kingston's lap, something by Jimmy Cliff for Nathan. Papers to the left, cigarettes to the right, sticky lumps of hash in the middle. They rolled one each and, as encouragement to the long night's work ahead, lifted the bottom sash window, knelt down on the floor and smoked it over the London rooftops. They nodded at their handiwork and blew lightly on the burning tip so that it sent sparks into the darkness. They laughed at each other's jokes, lay on their beds, told stories and fell asleep.

The next morning Nathan yawned and said, 'We've got to find a different system.'

Kingston agreed, and suggested using the men who patronized the Hamilton Arms. The pub was at the southern end of Railton Road, opposite a line of unmodernized Victorian terraced houses, and a distance from the dope-dealing pubs of central Brixton. During the day, before the sound system at the back began to vibrate with the music of the Skatalites and the Pioneers, the Hamilton was the pub where the older Jamaican men went to drink their beer. It was dark in there, and the men stayed all day to share racing tips and smoke their cigarettes, which most of them could roll one-handed because they had nothing else to do with their time but learn tricks. It was agreed that Kingston would talk to the men, and Nathan returned to the house to wait.

Kingston came back a few hours later with a brown paper bag of tightly rolled joints, twisted to a tip at one end, tamped down with a cardboard roach at the other. He emptied them out on to their bedroom carpet. 'Nice work,' Nathan said.

He selected one at random, pulled open the window and lit it. He took a long drag, held the smoke then let it go. For a moment he stared out over the surrounding houses. Then he looked at the joint held tightly between thumb and index finger. He took another drag.

'Here.' He passed it over. Kingston sucked deep, so the tip burnt red, then he looked at the joint too. He passed it back to Nathan and chose another from the bag on the floor. Nathan watched while he lit it. He said, 'Well?'

Kingston shook his head. 'Nothing.'

'You sure?'

'I'm sure.'

Nathan picked up a third, lit it and instead of inhaling sniffed the curl of smoke as it came off the tip. 'There's nothing in this either.'

'Really?'

'I'm telling you.'

'I don't understand it.'

'You gave them the gear and you watched them do it?'

'Well I –'

'You stayed and watched them?'

Kingston let out a deep sigh which made his huge shoulders rise and fall.

'Kingston?'

'I was going to, Nathan, but I was hungry. They knew what they were doing. I thought it wouldn't be right just staring them down so I went to the caff up the road.' The words died on his lips.

Nathan stubbed out the two dopeless joints he was holding against the outside of the windowsill and sat down on the edge of the bed. He picked up a few more of the joints and tore open the paper wrappings, so he could look through the tobacco with his thumbs. A sprinkle of torn papers and strands of tobacco dropped on to the carpet at his feet.

'So you left a bunch of Jamaican stoners with two ounces of our gear and told them to get on with it?' When he was angry, the pinched South London accent Nathan had worked so hard to acquire began to fade away to leave sweet, flat vowels which Kingston found all the more intimidating. It was the voice of authority over him.

Kingston pressed his lips together. He had supplied a pub full of men with enough free quality cannabis resin to keep them happy for a long afternoon, and there was nothing he could say that would make it better.

18

'Kingston!'

The kitchen porter looked up from his place by the sink. 'What?'

'You gave her a blade.'

Bobby Heller was leaning over a chopping board. She held half an onion flat against the wood with one hand. In the other was the knife, with which she was slicing in a controlled rhythmic motion. The blade never lifted more than half an inch above the pearly dome of the onion.

'It's all right. She knows what she's doing. She's a chef.'

'Kingston, you Joey. You don't give weapons to hostages.' Over by the door Trevor stood up to watch. Nathan turned to him, quickly. Trevor's eyes were red-rimmed and the hollows beneath them a sickly blue-grey. 'I'll handle this.'

'The bitch has got a blade.' He sounded excited by the notion, as though this surprising turn of events opened up many possibilities.

'Trevor, leave it to me.' The two men stood facing each other across the corner of the stove. 'She's my concern,' Nathan said. Trevor looked past him to where Bobby was standing. 'She'll slice you,' he said. 'Then I'll slice her back, won't I.' And he smiled thinly. Just the shape of the words gave him pleasure.

'Sit, Trevor.' Slowly, the man sunk back down to his place on the floor, the smile still on his lips.

Bobby didn't look up. She went on slicing, happier to concentrate on the task than the confrontation just a few feet away. She didn't have a reason for cutting up onions. It just felt good, as if she was being herself in her own kitchen. She was doing her job and that was what mattered. She turned the onion around, cut in the other direction, lifted her left hand away and swept the result to one side with the knife, so it collapsed into uniform fragments. She picked up the other half of the onion and began again, inserting the tip of the blade just shy of the root so it stayed in one piece. This, to Bobby Heller, was the essence of the cook's work in the kitchen. Any cook might claim a great palate. They might think they knew how to pair flavours, mount sauces or garnish with fans of strawberries and kiwis, as they were taught at catering college. But if they couldn't take the raw ingredients and machine-cut them to their will, it was dinner party cooking. It didn't count.

'What's the matter?' she said. 'Never seen a knife used properly?' Nathan was standing by her now, close enough so that she could smell him. 'Must be a shock for you, this. Discovering you can do things with blades that don't involve stabbing people.'

'I don't stab people.'

'No?' She swept the onion to the side of the board. She dried both sides of her blade against her apron and picked up the next one from the pile by the board. 'Bet you've waved the odd knife around though.'

Nathan said nothing.

'Bet you just love yourself with a bit of steel in your hand. Bet it makes you feel quite the guy.' As she spoke, the speed and attack of her knife work increased. Slice, slice, slice. Chop, chop, chop. 'Men like you, it's all about the toys, isn't it? Knife. Gun. Cock. Same difference. Wave them about for long enough, and the world is yours.' In one motion she swept the fragments off the board, picked up the next, sliced it in half and then looked up at him. 'No idea how to use them, though. Look at this.' She held out one index finger. The hands which had been in constant motion were now still. She balanced the knife on her finger tip, at the point where handle met blade. 'Look at that. Real craftsmanship. And all some guy like you can think about is how much damage you can do to somebody's skin with one of these; how much fear you can generate.' She threw the knife tip down into the board, so it vibrated like an arrow that had found its mark. 'And that's where it ends, isn't it?' Now she looked up at him. 'Maybe we should see what the tough guy can do with the blade? Or have you only got the moves for slashing skin?' She stepped back from the board. The kitchen was silent now. They could hear the electrical hum of the walk-ins. There was the buzz of the strip lights.

Nathan stared at the knife, unsure what to do. He knew he could pass the blade to Kingston and walk away, but he understood that he would be seen to have ducked the challenge and would therefore forfeit his authority. But if he accepted the challenge and got it wrong, she would still have the upper hand. They were two equally undesirable alternatives, he thought to himself. And yet there was a third possibility, which was the successful completion of the task.

He stepped up to the board and pressed the onion down with his left hand. Slowly he gripped the handle of the knife with his right hand and pulled it from the board. For half a second he rested the tip just above the root of the onion, at the spot he had seen Bobby cut in. Now he applied the necessary pressure to slice down. With a blade this sharp, he quickly realized, the weight of his hand would provide most of the down-thrust he would need, so he kept his grip loose. Up, across and down. Show the bitch, he thought to himself. The action of his right hand was accelerating all the time now. It felt natural, like the blade and his hand were one and the same, working their way across the taut outer layers of the onion.

Nathan lifted his blade again, and spun the onion around 90 degrees. He began to cut once more, feeling the sharpness of the steel taking it apart to his design. He swept it off the board with the blade, watched expressionless as it fell apart into uniform pieces, grabbed another and worked it over too. He was lost in the moment. The fatigue, the nervous exhaustion, the situation, all retreated until there was just the hand and the blade, the board and the onion. Now it was about the process. That was the only thing which mattered to him. He didn't want to stop.

But he knew he had done enough. He had won, at least for now. Nathan swept the debris of the last onion to the side and threw the knife, so it landed tip down in the board again. He looked back at Bobby, who said, wide-eyed, 'Have you done that before?'

There was no time to answer. The telephone was ringing.

19

Up above them they heard the footsteps of the policeman retreating from the dining room. The green light next to the dumb waiter was on. Stevie opened the cupboard doors, reached inside and pulled on the down rope, hand over hand, until the unit holding the cardboard box had dropped into view. He was about to drag it out into the kitchen when Nathan told him to step aside.

He stood in front of the dumb waiter, and tapped the barrel of his gun gently against the side of the box.

Trevor looked up from his position by the door. He rolled his head from side to side so that his neck cracked and took a drag on his cigarette. He said, 'You thinking it's a trap?'

'Don't know,' Nathan said. 'I'm just thinking.' He placed his hand flat against the side of the box, as if by touch alone he might be able to work out what was inside.

Bobby was leaning back against the stove with her arms tightly crossed. 'You know it's probably just a big hunk-a-veal.'

Nathan ignored her. He walked over to where the list of ingredients was taped to the wall and ripped it off. 'You two.' He pointed at Sheffield and Stevie. 'Pick up the box and follow me.'

He walked out of the kitchen to the walk-in fridges. The two cooks followed, carrying the box. They found him standing behind an open fridge door, as if he was using it as a shield. 'Inside,' he said, pointing the way with the gun. 'And here. Take this.' He gave the piece of paper to Sheffield as he passed. The two cooks stared out from the brightly lit interior of the cold room. 'What do you want us to do?' Stevie said.

From behind the door, Nathan said. 'Check what's in the box. I'll wait out here.' He pushed the door so that it closed with a heavy clunk. With the door out of the way he was now facing Bobby, who was standing in the entrance-way from the kitchen, a hand pressed against each door post as if she were trying to steady herself.

'Let me do it.'

'Men's work.'

'They're practically boys.'

'What are you then? Mother hen?'

'Just let me…'

He raised one finger to silence her and shouted, 'Well?'

Sheffield's voice was muffled by the thick fridge door. 'We're just opening it.'

Nathan and Bobby stared at each other.

'Bloody hell!'

Bobby ran to the fridge and pressed her forehead against the door. 'Sheffield! Stevie!' She slapped the door with one flat-palmed hand. 'Talk to me. What is it? What's going on in there?'

Another muffled cry. 'Jesus.'

'*What?*'

'It's this veal, chef.'

She frowned and pressed her head harder against the door, as if she could push her way through it. 'What about the veal? Is it wired?'

'It's bloody lovely, chef. That's what it is. Far better than the stuff we normally get.'

Nathan jutted his head towards here. 'What they talking about?'

'The veal. They're talking about the veal.'

'Chef?'

'Yes, Sheffield?'

'Looks like it's come from the Roux brothers' new butchery place. It's got their name on the paper and everything.'

Now it was Stevie's voice. 'I'd say it was French. Delicious deep rosy colour.'

Bobby pushed herself away from the door. 'Serious gear.'

Nathan sniffed with irritation. 'So?'

'Best meat you can get in London,' Bobby said, turning towards him. She rubbed one thumb against her index finger. 'Big money.'

Now Nathan shouted again. 'What about the rest of the box? Is there anything else in the box?'

'Hang on a sec. We're just...'

From outside they heard Sheffield say, 'That's weird.'

Stevie's voice this time: 'What's that in there?'

'I think it's...'

Nathan stepped back from the closed door as if stung. 'Everyone. Back into the kitchen.' The huddle watching from around the entrance-way swiftly retreated. Bobby stood her ground.

'Talk to me, boys. What you got in there?'

'It's... anchovies.'

Ignoring Nathan, Bobby pulled open the fridge door. 'So? Big deal. It's Wiener Holstein. It should have anchovies.'

'Not according to the ingredients sheet, chef.'

She grabbed the small rectangular tins from Sheffield's hands and studied their livery of white and yellow. 'Albo. That's cool. Must have come from Garcia's over on Portobello Road.'

'There aren't any anchovies on the ingredients list.'

'Well there should be. Wiener Holstein has a fried egg, capers and anchovies.'

'But there aren't.' Sheffield pressed the piece of paper into her other hand and she quickly scanned it. 'You must have left it off by accident,' he said.

Nathan was standing behind her now. 'Have they been screwing with my demands?' She raised a hand to silence him. 'Hush. I'm reading.'

She looked from the list to the small tin cans and back again.

'Chef?'

She didn't look up.

'Chef, can we...'

'Sorry, Stevie. I was miles away. What?'

'I'm freezing my gorgeous arse off in here, chef. Can we get out?'

'Course. Come on.'

They packed up the box and carried it back to the warm, damp fug of the kitchen where they opened out the contents on to a work surface. Nathan trailed behind. His pistol was back beneath his white apron, in the waistband of his trousers. He looked at the ingredients laid out across the stainless steel table: the large cut of pale pink meat, the cartons of eggs, the bags of pre-ground white breadcrumbs, those tins of anchovies.

'What are you telling me?'

Bobby looked up from the cushion of veal which she was caressing gently, her thumb flat against the grain of the meat. 'That we've got someone outside who knows his food.'

Stevie said, 'Maybe he's trying to send you a message.'

Sheffield laughed. 'What? Like, I'm hungry?'

'Or... can I come to dinner, please?'

Bobby looked at Nathan. 'I think Stevie's right. I think someone out there is trying to talk your language.'

Nathan picked up one of the tins. 'What? Anchovies?' He dropped it again, so that it clattered against the metal surface. 'I don't know anything about anchovies. I don't even like them.'

'Yeah, but they don't know that. You were the one who called in the ingredients. So now they think we're being held hostage by a bunch of, I don't know, gangster cooks.'

'So?'

'All I'm saying is it might be worth going along with. Perhaps this is their way of saying you've got nothing to fear. It's cool. We're here to negotiate. Maybe.'

His eyes narrowed. 'What should I do now then?'

Stevie said, 'Send out for another set of ingredients.'

'But with something else missing,' Sheffield added.

'And see if they spot it and put it in anyway.'

Sheffield said, 'Call in the ingredients for a steak and kidney pudding.'

Stevie groaned and rolled his eyes to the ceiling. 'In June? Don't be an arse.'

'I'm not being an arse. We do a list for steak and kidney without the kidney.'

'Then it's just a steak pudding. How would they know if anything was missing?'

'OK. You suggest something then.'

'All right then. Goulash. Without the paprika.'

'Don't be a jerk. That's like a daube without the beef.'

'What about a *pot-au-feu*?'

'What? Without the pot?'

'You can be very mean sometimes, Sheffield.'

From the other side of the kitchen came a deep rasping noise. Nathan and the cooks turned to look. The judge was standing on the other side of the solid top stove, clearing his throat in preparation for addressing the room. 'Coq au bloody vin,' he said, finally, when he had everybody's attention.

Nathan walked over to face him across the stove. 'What's that, old man?'

'I said, coq au vin.' And then, as if talking to the hard of hearing, 'chicken in wine. But leave out the button mushrooms.'

Bobby moved in closer to the judge.

'Nobody seems to know how to make a decent coq au vin these days.' He looked at Bobby. 'Present company excepted.'

Bobby raised both hands. 'Don't worry about me, judge. I think you've got a point.'

'There's always something missing isn't there? They've got the lardons but not the mushrooms. Or they've got the damn mushrooms and forgotten the onions. I remember during the last push for Paris at the end of the war we stopped at this tiny village bistro. Nothing to look at, really. Just an old stone house. Woman of the house cooked, one big pot it was. But they served this coq au vin which really was the essence of French paysanne cooking. Intense, rich, and made with a real old bird, not one of these baby chicks they use nowadays. Even had the cockscomb in there.'

Nathan looked at Bobby. 'You got a recipe?'

'I can do it from memory. Stevie, fetch me a pen and paper.' The cook brought over a large notepad from beside the cookery books and the chef set to work drawing up a partial list of ingredients.

20

The men seated in the back pews of the church of St James's, tapping their ring-bound notebooks against their knees or finishing off the crossword on a folded tile of newsprint, were happy to be there. For the previous three weeks they had been wandering the suburbs, watching politicians grasp for votes. Some had been in northern towns of the sort they would normally only visit when a husband had murdered his wife in an original manner. Others had been navigating country lanes in unsuitable shoes, trying to avoid livestock and ruddy-faced farmers. All of them had been on the campaign trail, attempting to find a diverting newspaper story in a foregone conclusion, and dreaming otherwise about beer in London pubs or the comfort of a bed laid with a duvet rather than the sheets and blankets which still held sway in the rest of Britain.

Now the vote was over. Margaret Thatcher and the Conservative Party had been re-elected with a landslide, and the job of reporting the last results fell to television. These newspaper men with their patina of disappointment, their cheap suits and rubber-soled shoes could safely ignore the politicians again. To them the reporting of a siege in the heart of London, so close to their offices on Fleet Street and the drinking halls that surrounded them, felt like a welcome from the city. Off the record, police sources were telling them that it could be over in just a few hours, which had the virtue of compactness. The plan was to talk the gunmen out, police sources said, and negotiations were proceeding. And then Commander Peterson was in front of them, looking tired in shirt-sleeves and open collar, but ready to give them the official line. Not an IRA gang, just a small jewellery heist gone wrong. Yes, some of the hostages were well-known public figures, but everybody who remained inside was unhurt. They had been assured of that. None of the other injuries were serious, even those to the head waiter which had already been much reported.

'Have they made any demands?'

'No, not yet. All I can say is that negotiations are underway.'

'They haven't asked for any food?'

'Yes. They have asked for food, though of course they are in a restaurant kitchen so there should be some at hand.'

Another journalist: 'What did they ask for?'

'Various items.' Peterson wasn't trying to be obstructive; he simply couldn't recall the detail of the list. A list of ingredients was of no interest to him. 'It was delivered to them this morning via the dumb waiter in the restaurant. And I would like to take this opportunity to commend the bravery of my officers who performed that duty.'

'Could we have some specifics?' said one.

Commander Peterson was irritated by the request. He was expecting a visit from the commissioner's deputy, to whom he was now reporting, and he didn't want to be caught in a press conference when his superior arrived on site. He turned and shouted across the church. 'Sergeant Cosgrave, can I borrow you for a moment.' When his Sergeant was standing in front of him he said, 'You still have the food list?'

'Yes, sir.' Willy withdrew the crumpled sheet from a top pocket and held it out to his superior.

Peterson waved the list away and looked around the church. 'You read it. Entertain the gentlemen while I return to the small matter of an armed siege.' He fixed him with a sharp, sarcastic smile, before striding back across the church.

Willy turned to the reporters sprawled in the pews.

'You want to know what they called in?

The journalists nodded.

'Everything?'

They agreed that they wanted everything.

'Right.' Willy unfolded the piece of paper and began to read: 'Ten pounds of veal cut from the cushion, four dozen eggs, two pounds fresh breadcrumbs, one pound butter...'

A reporter looked up from the page of the notebook he was scribbling in. 'Sounds like a recipe.'

'It is. Well, it can be.'

'For what?'

'Wiener Holstein. If you add some anchovies, which they didn't include.'

'Is that Wiener with a V?'

'And how do you spell Holstein?'

'No. It's Wiener with a Germanic 'w'. That's W-I-E-N-E-R Holstein, which is H-O-L-S-T-E-I-N. It's a veal escalope, breaded and then fried and garnished with a fried egg, capers and anchovies.'

As one, the reporters had the same idea. They knew their editors would approve of what would be a new take on the reporting of an armed siege.

'Could you give us the recipe?' said one of the journalists.

'What? Tell you how to make it?'

'Yes.'

'From the beginning?'

'Exactly. If that's what they're eating down there we ought to know about it. Only take it slowly. None of us are that handy in the kitchen.'

Willy scratched the back of his neck, and said, 'OK then. There's enough veal here for twenty steaks, if cut thinly enough, only across the grain, and then you would have to beat it out.' The reporters hunched down over their pens and began to take detailed shorthand notes.

21

The judge pushed the box of biscuits across the floor towards Harry Connaston who was sitting with his knees up, an arm rested limply on each one. He was staring at the doors of the oven in front of him. His shirt was undone to the third button and his sleeves were rolled up, to expose the brushed metal of an expensive sports watch at his left wrist.

'Have another?' Guthrie said. 'They really are rather good.'

The Conservative Party Treasurer looked at the judge. Outside the kitchen Connaston would have known precisely how to engage with a man of Guthrie's standing: the raised eyebrows of recognition on hearing his name, regardless of its familiarity; the firm handshake followed by a grip on the forearm with his free hand, so he could draw the man towards him; the Prime Minister's admiration for the judge, confided in a whisper: 'She can't discuss it in public, of course, but I know Margaret takes a keen interest in your work.' In Harry Connaston's experience all successful men had their vanities, and even those who claimed not to like the Prime Minister were titillated by the revelation. It didn't matter if it was true or not; Margaret Thatcher understood the necessary deceits of the political fundraiser's art.

The situation inside the Oyster House made these games irrelevant. Harry Connaston was stripped of the advantage that his position in politics gave him, and he felt naked. Instead he said only, 'Don't mind if I do,' and he chose a biscuit. He smacked his lips as he ate. 'The food is always good here,' he said. It was a knowing retreat into small talk.

Guthrie yawned. 'Wouldn't know. My first time. Treat for our son and his girlfriend.'

'Some treat.'

The judge said 'indeed' and told Connaston that the dinner had almost been postponed. First his son had been told he would be needed abroad for work, until the trip was cancelled. Then his wife had announced a headache, her usual response to a meeting with one of the boys' girlfriends. Her husband had been required to apply cool flannels and fetch aspirins. Then, when they got there, the gunmen arrived. He looked over at Connaston and nodded towards the television screen, where the election results were being discussed.

'Still, your lot did well last night.'

'Deserved, I think.'

'Perhaps. Better if I don't comment either way.'

Connaston looked up at the picture. 'Yes, of course. I understand.' He listened to the television pundits talking about the Conservative's landslide. 'I've missed some terrific parties, though.'

'I should imagine so.'

Connaston said, 'It would have been fun.' And then, casually, 'Do you think they understand the depth of their predicament?', and the judge knew immediately that he was referring to their captors, rather than the defeated Labour Party.

'Most of these people do not understand the situation they are in, until I am sentencing them.' With the slightest motion of his hand he pointed to Trevor by the door. 'That one is calculating his next action from one minute to the next, which makes him terribly dangerous. If I offered him a biscuit he'd interpret it as a threat.'

'Better not offer him a biscuit, then.'

'Good idea. More for us.'

Connaston looked around the room 'We ought to do something, though. We're smart men, aren't we, you and I. We should be able to out-think them.'

'In my experience the clever chaps are the ones who do nothing to put themselves or others in harm's way. It's the stupid ones who try the heroics.'

'There must be something down here we can turn to our advantage,' he said, as if he had not heard Guthrie at all, and he was suddenly impressed by how lethal an environment the kitchen was. On a work surface across the room he could see a food processor. Connaston had never used one, but he assumed that the blade turned at speed. If they could force a gunman's finger's inside the jug, they could quickly disable him. He recognized, however, that it would prove difficult to keep a man's hand in place while the blades did their work, and that the blood would make any hold slippery.

The deep-fat fryer had already shown its potential, though that had been switched off, and there was always the likelihood of being splashed with boiling oil. There was an eye-level grill, but that would only be of use if it were possible to get a man's head inside it, which was impractical, given its position above the stove. There were the knives, but he was certain their captors had more experience with those than he did. That left the simplest solution: holding the men's hands down on to the solid top of the stove, until they were sufficiently blistered. But if they were able to get them into that position they would also be able to overwhelm them and take from them their guns. The solid top – the food processor, the deep-fat fryer, all of it – would be irrelevant.

The judge interrupted his thoughts. 'I know this sounds peculiar, but there is, to me, something rather liberating about this situation.'

'You need a little more sugar,' Connaston said, and he rattled the biscuit box at him.

The judge shook his head. 'In my daily life I am expected to take a lead. I am required to have a certain responsibility. Down here there's absolutely nothing I can do about anything. I must simply wait and see. I am rarely invited to do that.' Next to him Thomas was asleep, his chin down on his chest. 'Perhaps we should do the same as him, and catch up on our sleep,' the judge said.

Connaston shook his head. 'I'm sorry,' he said. 'But I really don't think I could. I find this all very...' He paused as he searched for the right word. He could manage only, 'difficult'.

'Some people feel otherwise,' Guthrie said, and indicated Trevor. Beside the door, and extending a little distance into the room, he had built a wall of catering-sized cans of food, fetched from out by the staff lockers. The heavy cylinders were piled one on top of one another. He had assembled a collection of newly cleaned kitchen knives, taken from Kingston's station, and in the small space between the wall of cans and the first of the kitchen cabinets, he was now arranging them in order of size, and humming to himself cheerfully as he worked. He lifted a blade, and ran the pad of his thumb over the leading edge, before placing it with the others on the floor. Most of the time he had his back turned to Connaston and Guthrie.

Connaston turned to the judge, his mouth open in a wide grin of schoolboy enthusiasm. 'He's not watching us. We could...' But Guthrie silenced him before he could finish the sentence.

'Whatever you're thinking of doing,' he said. 'Don't. It's bound to be a bloody lousy idea.' He turned away from the treasurer so their eyes would not meet, to indicate that the subject was closed.

22

One February morning in 1979, while crossing Leicester Square, Bobby Heller saw a rat. She had not been in London long and though she had witnessed the occasional mouse dancing between the rails below underground station platforms, she had not expected to encounter anything so substantial. Its fur was grey. It had black eyes and had tucked itself in beside a pile of fat, plastic refuse sacks stacked up on a corner by the Empire cinema. It was at least eight inches long excluding the tail. She had first noticed the pile of rubbish a week before, and had wondered when someone might come to take it away, but it only got bigger. Then she heard radio reports of the strikes which were spreading across the country and understood that the rubbish would be there for a while. Each morning she observed the way the pile had grown overnight. There was a new summit to one side. A hollow was filled in to create a plateau. Other piles began appearing around the Square – on the south side by the Odeon cinema, on the street to the west that led to Piccadilly Circus – each with its own unique and shifting geography. Every day the smell grew more putrid, as if the volume was being turned up on only one of her senses, and she anticipated that vermin would soon come. Bobby grew up on a farm where rats and mice were always attracted to the easiest pickings, and these bags were the easiest of all. Many of them had split open and were spilling their rotting guts on to the pavements.

In the days after she saw her first rat she saw many more, moving in twos or threes around the rubbish sacks. Occasionally she saw a sleek rodent disappear into a crevice between bags, the tail slipping smoothly away like a piece of grey spaghetti sucked up between lips. She hated the rats and she hated London for allowing them to get so fat and docile.

They cleared the rubbish away eventually, and the smell soon died down, but that winter the city still felt like it was decaying. The trains didn't work. The newspapers were full of stories about the unburied dead. A few weeks later the owner of the restaurant where she cooked announced he was closing down the business. He was moving instead to New York to try his luck there. When he told her how much he was paying in taxes she understood why he was going and she decided that being in Britain was depressing her. Bobby went to Paris after that and though it made her no happier, she told herself that every chef should spend some time in France if they were serious about their profession. She was in Paris in the spring of 1979 when Margaret Thatcher was elected Prime Minister, and returned to London early the following year.

The city still had problems. The trains often didn't work, people were losing their jobs and the effects of the recession could be seen in the sales advertised desperately in the high street shop windows. But then the Falklands war came and, when it had been won, she sensed a new optimism. In the restaurants where she worked people didn't just buy generic Côte du Rhônes and clarets anymore. They bought Châteaux Haut-Brion and Beaucastel. It was the preparations of lobster, foie gras and truffles that sold the quickest. The British were no longer embarrassed about spending money. London stopped being depressing.

Three years later Margaret Thatcher had won a second election and now she was on the screen of the black and white portable television in the Oyster House kitchen. She was walking along Downing Street, receiving the congratulations of an organized crowd of well-wishers. Bobby took in the shape of the Prime Minister's narrow ankles and the carefully considered cut of her pale A-line skirt. It was disconcerting to see her out in the bright sunlight of an early summer's day like this with its sharp contrasts, when they had been locked away down here in the basement for more than twelve hours, with just the strip-lights to show the way. Down here time was halted. Out there, viewed only through the tight aperture of the television's screen, the world was moving on.

'Watch her like that,' Nathan said, 'and people will begin to think you like her.'

Bobby didn't look away from the picture. 'Like her? Nobody *likes* Margaret Thatcher.'

'Exactly what I'm saying.'

'But it doesn't stop me admiring her.'

Nathan pointed at the screen. 'You admire that vicious old harpy?' He was appalled and intrigued. Living in Brixton it was impossible to imagine why anybody might have something good to say about her. He had seen her once but only from a distance. He was walking up Brixton High Street when he noticed police outriders holding up the traffic that joined the High Street from Acre Lane by idling their motorbikes across the traffic lights on green, so that the route into London cleared. Then came a procession of limousines – black Jaguars in Nathan's memory – and everyone turned to look, expecting to see a member of the royal family in the back seat of one. It was the helmet of blonde hair he recognized first and then, in profile, the sharp nose, but only in profile because she was looking down at something on her lap. This was what Nathan recalled most clearly. He could not imagine that Margaret Thatcher had been to Brixton often, if at all. And yet, as she passed through the area, she did not once look up to see what was passing by her window. This, Nathan decided, was what made the people feel so weak and powerless: not so much her policies as her lack of interest in those adversely affected by them. He wanted to see her embarrassed and ashamed by the intensity with which people hated her and he still regretted he was in Amsterdam the night the Brixton riots broke out in 1981. He suspected he would have been good at throwing petrol bombs, and that he would have done so with commitment. He would have felt Terry at his back, urging him on towards the gestures he could no longer make himself.

Nathan said, 'How much of this country have you seen?' Bobby said she had seen enough to know that Margaret Thatcher was making things better than they had been.

'How much of London have you seen then?'

'I have seen enough of everything,' and she remembered the sleek, fat rats. They watched the Prime Minister move towards the door of number 10 Downing Street, and then turn to wave at the cameras with a broad smile that didn't appear to be directed at any of the cameras focused on her. 'Anyway, there's not much point us having this argument, is there? We know where you stand.'

'You know nothing about me.'

She turned to him. 'I know you tried to take down a jewellery store. I know there aren't many petty thieves who are welcomed as members of the Conservative Party.'

'They're all thieves.'

'You'll have to do better than that.' And then, 'You hate her because she wants people to do a proper day's work. You hate her because she believes in people standing on their own two feet.' Bobby was enjoying herself now. She felt fluent and focused and heard, in her own rhetoric, a pleasing authority. 'She doesn't like people who have their hands out. She doesn't like people who take what isn't theirs.' Her argument returned to her some of the power that the other gunman had taken away.

'You have no idea what I was doing last night.'

'You want to tell me about it?' He ignored her, and stared at the image on the screen. 'As you hate her so much I guess you voted against her yesterday.'

'I don't have a vote.'

'Not that committed to opposing Maggie then?'

'It's better in my line of work not to have your name down for things like that.'

Bobby pierced the wooden board in front of her with the tip of the knife she was holding. 'Line of work? You call what you do a line of work? You are trying to make thieving sound like a profession. Now this –' She pulled out the knife, and stabbed at the piece of veal on the board in front of her. '– this is work.'

In one controlled movement, Nathan turned from the screen, pushed Bobby out of the way and grabbed the knife.

23

Stevie and Sheffield were at the other end of the stove, beating eggs and preparing breadcrumbs. When Nathan took the knife, they moved towards him but Bobby told them to stay back. Nathan stood over the chopping board for a few seconds, looking at the bolder of muscle. He rested his left hand on the top and with the right began to cut a single slice an inch thick. Bobby watched the blade slip through the fibres. She watched the way it stayed exactly on line to produce an even steak. Most of her cooks attempted this for weeks and still got it wrong. The knife skewed off in one direction under too much pressure, or the weight of the left hand pushed the separate lobes of muscle out of alignment so that when the steak came off it was uneven. But Nathan's hands were steady and even. The cut was clean. The steak was perfect.

'You sure you haven't done this before?' she said.

He wrinkled his nose. 'It's not rocket science.' He lifted the blade out and cut a third and a fourth steak. He liked the way the metal moved through the meat. It was satisfying to take this misshapen cut of muscle and carve from it something uniform and regular.

Bobby moved to stand beside him. She took a clean tea-towel from a drawer and wrapped one of the steaks in it. Then, using a wooden mallet, she beat it out, until it formed a long flat oval. She repeated the process with each new steak that Nathan cut, until there was a pile of veal escalopes at her side. When he came to the end of the muscle Bobby said quietly, 'Discard it. We'll use it for stock,' and Nathan did as he was told, shifting the nodule of meat to the side of the chopping board with the flat of his knife. He felt disappointed. The job was finished and he wished it wasn't. He felt like he could stand there and slice veal steaks all day. He stayed where he was, staring at the empty board until Bobby said: 'We've got nine Wiener Holstein to cook. We could use an extra pair of hands.'

Nathan didn't look up. 'What do you need?'

'Someone to crumb the steaks.' She collected the other ingredients from her cooks and brought them back to where Nathan was standing. She seasoned the beaten eggs and the breadcrumbs with a little salt and pepper. 'Like this,' she said, dredging a piece of the meat through the ripe pool of butter yellow egg, and then tossing it into the breadcrumbs until it was covered. 'Think you can manage that?'

'I told you. It's not rocket science.'

'Right.' And then to her cooks, 'OK, ladies. Let's do what we do best. Sheffield, you're with me on the range, two to a pan. Stevie, you're on the eggs, the *beurre noisette* and the garnish.'

'Yes, chef.'

There was a hiss of gas and then a bright pop as the burners beneath the solid top of the stove ignited in quick succession. It would be a few minutes before the heat was sufficient. The cooks used the time to line up pans, and put ingredients in place: Tupperware pots of butter to one side, another of jellified veal *jus* quickly melting down in the emerging heat, the eggs in their blue-grey carton.

Without looking up Stevie said, 'Sounds, chef?'

Sheffield grinned. 'Yeah, chef. Sounds.'

'Leave it out, girls.'

'Aww, come on, chef. Give us some sounds.'

'Something to wake us up a bit.'

'No!' She said it so sharply she surprised herself. The cooks fell silent.

She crossed the kitchen to where the judge, Lord Connaston and

Thomas were sitting in a line on the floor. She told them she was preparing some food.

The judge indicated the box of biscuits which was close to empty. 'I might just be able to find a little more space,' and he smiled at her.

She looked at Thomas, who was sitting with his knees up and his tiny feet together. The sound of her voice had woken him. 'Do you have any objection?' she said briskly.

He narrowed his eyes. 'None at all. Why should I?'

'You could be polite. I'm offering you food.'

'If you had not obstructed my release you would not need to.' And he looked away from her.

Connaston interrupted. 'The other one,' he hissed. He indicated the kitchen door.

Bobby looked around. 'What about him?'

'He's not paying attention.' Trevor had his back turned again, as he hunkered down over his knife collection.

'We could take him,' he said.

Guthrie sighed deeply at the man's insistence, a long breath that turned into a spasm of coughing. She turned back to Connaston. 'Someone will get hurt even if it isn't you.'

'But he keeps presenting us with perfect opportunities. If we don't act now –' His lips were pursed and he was frowning so hard that his heavy brow placed his eyes in shadow.

'The other two are still watching us.' She indicated Kingston, standing over by the sink, and Guthrie nodded. 'Both of them are armed. Please give it time. The main guy's settling down. I think I can talk him round.' She felt she understood better than any of them what Trevor was capable of. She had seen it when he had leaned towards her to breathe in her scent. She was sure they could only take him down if Nathan and Kingston, the people he trusted, were also on side, but there was no prospect of that.

'Oi!'

She looked up. Nathan was standing over her, slapping the palm of one hand with the bowl of a large wooden spoon. 'Are we going to cook?'

'Yeah, we're going to cook. That's exactly what we're going to do.' She pulled herself up, and walked him back to her station by the stove. The moment the butter hit the pans she was drawn back to the rhythm of the kitchen. She saw her cooks slip easily into their allotted roles and watched Nathan dredging the veal escalopes with a clean flick of the wrist. That was what made him so effective, she decided. He had the economy of movement of all great cooks, and he wasn't even aware of it. He knew what was expected. Two turns in the egg, two more in the crumb, a quick shake and start again with the next.

The first four of his breaded escalopes went into the butter, which foamed around them in fine bubbles of copper and bronze. Then it went down the line. First it was drained. Next it was plated. On top came the egg, fresh out of the pan, the white solid, the yolk still runny. A sprinkle of capers, a criss-cross of two anchovies, a dribble of caramel-coloured veal *jus* enriched with the *beurre noisette* around the sides and down again to the first takers on the floor. It took seven minutes to cook all of them and soon Nathan was standing over his own plateful, taking his first food in nearly twenty-four hours. He liked the crunch of the coating he had made. After that came the soft yield of the meat beneath, better still with a dribble of the egg yolk and the salty hit of the dense anchovy fillet, all on one forkful. It tasted like nothing else he had ever eaten.

'Veener Hol-steen?'

'More like Hol-sh-teen,' Bobby said, shaping each syllable carefully.

'It's good.'

'It's OK, as far as it goes.'

'You sound like you don't like it.'

'I love it, but it's not the kind of food I want to be cooking. If I had my way we'd be doing something lighter, more up to date.'

He took another mouthful. 'Don't know anything about that. This tastes good enough to me.'

'That's what they say upstairs too. What they said.' She watched him eat. 'You should get some sleep, you know.'

He chased a piece of veal through the slick of egg yolk on his plate. 'Are you thinking of making a run for it?'

She nodded towards the door where his accomplice was sitting, scraping the anchovies to the side of his plate before eating what remained. 'With him in my kitchen?' she said. Nathan looked across at his companion. She was right. Nobody was going anywhere with Trevor in the room.

24

Bobby had just turned off the light in the toilet cubicle opposite the walk-ins, and was coming out when she spotted the burning tip of a cigarette, hovering in the darkness. The strip lights had been on out there when she went in, but now they were off. The end of the cigarette fizzed and sparked as Trevor took a deep drag, the extra smudge of light illuminating the hollows of his face. He was standing inside the doorway from the kitchen, out of sight of the others.

He said, 'Did you enjoy that?' His voice was soft.

Bobby looked around in the darkness, in the hope of finding something she might be able to use as a weapon if the need arose, but could see nothing other than the metallic glint of some catering-sized cans of vegetables used for staff meals which were out of reach on a shelf. 'What do you want?' she said, nervously. She took shallow, shuddering breaths.

Trevor pushed himself away from the wall and quickly backed her up against the side of the toilet cubicle. Her eyes were becoming used to the darkness now. He sniffed and pursed his lips. 'It smells in here, doesn't it?'

'Leave me alone.'

Trevor smiled and took another drag on his cigarette. He blew gently on the tip so that it burned angrily for a moment. 'I saw a programme on the telly last week. About lions.'

She blinked. 'I didn't see it.'

'It was on in the night-time.'

'I work here at nights.'

He nodded, as if to say, we each of us have the lives we must lead. 'Lions have amazing tongues.'

'As I say, I didn't see—'

'They can taste the air.' And he clicked his own tongue against the roof of his mouth.

'Where's your friend?' She looked around his shoulder, in the hope that somebody might be coming.

'Nathan's sleeping now,' he said. 'Most people are asleep. Not us, though. We're not asleep, are we?'

'Maybe you should sleep.'

He smiled and sniffed. 'That's why the whiz is so good. Don't need to sleep.'

He was so close to her that she could feel the heat from the tip of his cigarette against her cheek when he inhaled.

'Do you know the other thing about the lion's tongue?'

She shook her head. Maybe he just wanted to talk at her. Maybe he would get his satisfaction that way, by leering and talking.

'It's so rough it can lick the meat off of bones.' He ran his tongue around his bottom lip, then licked the tip of his finger and ran it down her cheek towards her open neck, and the dark, shadowed line of her cleavage. She turned her face away, trying to escape him. The slippery finger tip dried as it went, so that the further down it moved the more it dragged against her skin. She stopped breathing and, glancing down, saw the muzzle of the pistol pressed against her, the black gunmetal obvious against her whites. He pressed himself in against her too, as his finger slipped beneath the lapel of her jacket.

'I would like to have a tongue like that. Then I could lick the flesh from your bones, couldn't I?' Bobby felt a slick of cold sweat dribble down the middle of her back.

Kingston had decided to wait until Nathan was asleep before approaching Bobby, although he wasn't sure what to say to her. He didn't know if words could be used to make the situation better, and anyway words were not his strong point. Nathan was better at those.

He had watched her by the stove while she was cooking the veal, her head bowed, so that loose strands of golden hair hung down over her forehead. She had looked self-contained then and for a moment Kingston had given up on the idea of trying to explain himself at all. He had seen the way she looked at him when she was talking to the other hostages, glancing up to register his location, but away again swiftly so as not to make eye contact. She had been like this since the moment, the night before, when Nathan had spotted him. He had tried to catch her eye, to see if it was possible to re-establish any of the rapport they had developed over the previous two weeks, but she was intent on avoiding him. He didn't blame her. As far as she was concerned he was just another dangerous presence in her kitchen. He was one of 'them'. He knew that she suspected him of being involved with the events that had led to this siege from the moment he had started working for her, that she saw him as part of some complex conspiracy; and he needed her to know it wasn't like that at all. He wanted her to see beyond the facts as she understood them.

He watched her walk off towards the wine store and the walk-ins and decided to wait until she came back.

What frustrated him most was the familiarity of the situation; not the guns and the hostages – that was all new – but the way he was being misunderstood. It had always been like this, even when he was a kid. He put it down to his size. In his experience people always made assumptions about large men, because it was the easiest thing to do. There was the time when he was fifteen years old and, stoned on his brother's sensimilla, he fell asleep in the front hall of a friend's house during a party. A little while later gatecrashers turned up. Nathan told them to go away, but they refused, so he led them up the hall to where Kingston was lying, rolled in on himself, his massive domed back filling the space.

'See him,' Nathan said. 'He's asleep now, but when he wakes up he will be very angry.' The gatecrashers left.

Nathan was still laughing about it hours later when Kingston did awake. 'You're the perfect doorman, Kingston. You can do it in your sleep.' And Kingston laughed too, though he didn't like the fact that violence had been associated with him while he was sleeping. He wasn't even sure how violence worked. Once, up in Brockwell Park, Nathan told him to help punch down a soft, rotten door on an old shed so they could get out of the rain, but he stopped Kingston before his knuckles made contact.

'You'll break your hand if you do it like that,' Nathan said. Kingston studied the fist he had made, the thumb held tightly beneath the fingers rather than over them. 'I'm not good at hitting things,' he said. 'I haven't had much experience.'

Even so, Nathan made Kingston come along with him on the rare occasions when there were debts that needed recovering. 'You don't need to do anything. The whole point is that you don't do anything. You just stand there looking big. It's our advantage, your bigness.' Even though Nathan was right and he never did have to do anything – these people paid up the moment they saw him – the jobs made him worry about the way others viewed him. He knew the police always assumed he was up to something, just because of the way he looked. He had lost count of the number of times he had been arrested and spent the night in a police cell, only to be released the next morning without charge. He was hardened to being shown the door by white police officers muttering threats about unspecified crimes he might or might not have committed. It made him angry but he could cope with it, because all the black boys in Brixton went through the same thing from time to time. He also knew that it was only luck they hadn't yet picked him up for the offence of which he was actually guilty.

What troubled him more was what girls might think of him. Nathan always seemed to find someone to go home with at the end of a night's dancing at the Fridge or in the hall at the back of the Prince of Wales pub. He saw the way these girls liked to rest their hands on the back of Nathan's thighs as they took a last slow dance, and let their fingertips brush against the curve of his arse. But no one wanted to dance with Kingston like this and he assumed it was because he looked intimidating.

A girl said to him once: 'I thought you were terrifying the first time I saw you but that was before I got to know you.' By the time he had made the effort to get to know her they were friends and apparently that meant they could not have any other kind of relationship – and certainly not the kind he wanted, in which she might rest her hands against the back of his thighs occasionally. She said she really liked him as a friend but didn't feel 'like that' about him, and he decided to believe her. How could he escape that contradiction? To convince girls he wasn't frightening he had to get to know them. And if they became his friends they didn't want to kiss him. It had taken Natalie to show him there was another way, but she wasn't like all the others.

And now, here he was at the Oyster House and those things – his size, his assumed scariness – had been drawn into the mess that Nathan had made, and had been misinterpreted by Bobby. He didn't expect her to understand. He wasn't sure he would if the roles were reversed, but at least he had to try.

He glanced over at the doorway on the other side of the kitchen every now and then, while washing the pans used for the meal just gone, but there was no sign of her. He didn't just want to stand watching the doorway. That would be too obvious, too insistent. He wanted it all to look casual and unthreatening, so he kept his back turned, but it occurred to him now that she had been gone a while. He looked around the room: at the judge and Connaston and Grey Thomas, with their eyes closed on one side, at Nathan, clearly asleep on a laundry sack on the other, at Sheffield and Stevie, playing a quick game of cards. He looked at the swing doors.

Trevor wasn't there. He looked around the room again. He was not in the kitchen. He looked over at the doorway. Now he noticed that the light which had been on when Bobby went through had been turned off. It was a black rectangle.

Quickly, Kingston walked across the kitchen and stood in the doorway looking into the gloom. 'Chef?' He called out hesitantly, not wishing to bother her unnecessarily, if she was all right.

In the darkness he could smell fresh cigarette smoke. He heard a muffled voice, somewhere over to his right, as if someone had been trying to call out but then thought better of it. He called for Bobby again and, reaching instinctively for the switch, turned on the lights. Trevor jumped away from Bobby, as though the power to the lights had also given him a shock. There was a furtiveness about him, like a child caught in the act, which he tried to disguise behind the mechanics of lighting a cigarette. Bobby was pressed up against the toilet cubicle, the top of her chef's jacket open one button lower than usual. There was a sheen of sweat on her forehead and a dampness around her eyes which she reached up to smear away with the ball of her hand. With the other she held her jacket closed at the throat.

'You all right, chef?'

She said nothing but stared, wildly, at Trevor, who was cupping a match in his hands.

'All right, Kingston,' he said casually, as he took the first drag.

'What have you done?'

'Me and chef here have been talking nature programmes,' he said, jabbing in her direction with the cigarette. Bobby flinched and stared back at him. He was smiling to himself, as if it was all just one big game, which he was certain to win eventually.

'Leave her alone, Trevor.'

Trevor took another drag and exhaled a long lazy plume of smoke. He looked Kingston up and down, reviewing his shape. 'We'll finish that talk another time, won't we, love,' he said to Bobby, and fixed her with a rictus grin of pink lips and nicotine-stained teeth. He looked like a man who had more time than he knew what to do with. He turned and slowly walked back into the kitchen.

When he had gone, Kingston said, 'You OK?'

Bobby nodded and dried away another tear from the edge of one eye. For a moment they stood silently together, watching the doorway to the kitchen as if they expected Trevor to return.

Kingston took a deep breath. 'I just wanted to say—'

'There's nothing to say.'

'I just wanted to tell you that I understand why you think I'm mixed up in all this.'

She turned to him. His shoulders dropped. Just the way she stared at him now made him feel defeated before he had begun. He had chosen the wrong time to speak. He had said the wrong thing. He shouldn't have opened his mouth at all. She nodded at the butt of the pistol sticking out from the waistband of his trousers. 'That looks very comfortable in there.' He could hear the anger in her voice. It didn't matter that he had just intervened to fend off Trevor. The way she saw it, if Kingston hadn't been in her kitchen, Trevor wouldn't have been there either. He understood this.

His hands went to the gun and hovered over it, like it was some leaking wound he didn't want to touch. 'He made me take the gun.'

'You only had to take the gun because he had something on you.'

Quickly, as though worried she might interrupt, he said, 'I was trying to get away from all this. That was why I wanted the job. If I had known what was going to happen here I would never have come.'

'Keep away from me.' She was straightening her jacket and buttoning it high on the throat to hide any skin. 'Keep him away from me.'

'I won't do anything to hurt anyone.'

'Clean the pans and stay out of my way.'

'Yes, chef,' Kingston said, as she pushed past him and out into the kitchen, and in that moment he decided he would clean every plate and every cup and every knife too, and keep cleaning them. If he couldn't convince her of his innocence by his words, he would do so by his gestures. He would make looking after the kitchen his job, and in washing away the stains of cookery perhaps he could wash away the stain of criminality too. Maybe he could make her believe in him that way. He followed her back through the doorway to the kitchen.

25

Nathan was woken by a sharp jab to the ribs, and knew immediately where he was from the dense smell of food. Trevor was standing over him.

'The box is here.'

He sat up and rubbed one eye with the ball of his hand. 'How long have I been out?'

'Four hours.'

He took a deep breath and stretched his legs.

Trevor opened his mouth to say something and then thought better of it. Nathan encouraged him to speak. It was better to know everything that Trevor was thinking, however disturbing the thoughts might be.

'Don't trust the bitch.' Trevor spat out the words.

'What's she done?' He looked over to where Bobby was standing at the other end of the kitchen, looking at an opened cardboard box.

'She lies. That's all I'm saying.'

'We need to concentrate on getting out of here.'

'I won't let her get in the way.'

Nathan looked at the purple-tinged creases of ruined skin running down Trevor's cheek; those inscriptions left by a night of old-style drinking violence. Bobby had been right when she said that no one would try to escape a room guarded by Trevor, Nathan thought to himself. Trevor's knowledge of violence and the threat of it were invaluable in a situation like this. But he was also a liability. He might know everything there was to know about violence, but he could offer no insights into the suffering it caused.

Nathan said, 'I understand. I've thought things through,' and 'Leave her to me. She's my problem.'

He placed one hand on Trevor's shoulder and held it there in silence.

Slowly Trevor shook his head as if to say, you have no idea what is going on in this kitchen. He took another wrap of speed from his pocket, dropped to the floor, folded it out and buried his nose in its contents, hungrily.

Bobby and Stevie were at the other end of the kitchen. When Nathan approached she looked over his shoulder to where Trevor was sitting, and Nathan turned to look too.

'He's all right,' Nathan said quietly. 'I've got him under control.'

'He's dangerous.'

'He's my problem.' And then, from Bobby, the same look that Trevor had given him, the one that said, you don't have a clue.

Nathan looked to the work surface. He needed to reassert his authority. He wanted things back on his terms. 'The box?'

'It's all here,' Stevie said.

Nathan looked inside. The cook pulled up a white paper bag and opened it for him to inspect. The smell of earth and old grass rose to meet him from the damp paper.

'Some darling little button mushrooms,' Stevie said, keenly.

Bobby held up a greaseproof paper package. 'And some thick rashers of smoked bacon for the lardons. We left both off the list and both have been added to the box.' Then, shouting across the kitchen to where the judge was sitting. 'Did you hear that, your honour? Mushrooms and lardons.' She found reassurance in these ingredients. The smell of pig and earth brought her back on to home territory.

The judge pushed himself up from the floor and came to have a look. He picked up a single button mushroom between thumb and index finger. In his chef's whites and grey hair, he looked like a scientist inspecting the outcome of an experiment. 'Someone out there is as greedy as I am, by the looks of things,' he said.

'Plus this.' Stevie opened up another fold of paper and showed it to the group.

In the middle, curled in on itself, lay a scrap of something red and leathery. It reminded Nathan of the dead, featherless chicks that he would find on the pavements around his grandparents' house in the spring: the stillborn blackbirds with their oversized beaks and bulging, useless eyes, which he poked at with twigs. He peered at the scrap of flesh. 'What is it?'

'Cockscomb,' the judge said. He stuck his hand on the top of his head and wiggled his fingers. Bobby laughed. 'From the cockerel's head,' the judge continued. 'Shows a commitment to authenticity.' Nathan stared at him blankly. The judge leaned into him. 'That's a good thing.'

Bobby said, 'They've got the rest of the cockerel in there too. Whoever's doing this knows their stuff.'

Nathan considered the box.

Bobby started rewrapping the ingredients. 'You going to tell them you got the message?'

'What message is that, then?'

She patted the box. 'That they share your interest in food.'

'I haven't got an interest in food.'

She raised her eyebrows. 'No? The way you cut that veal—'

'You asked me to help out.'

'The way you breaded the escalopes—'

'I was lending a hand.'

'The way you ate it, then.'

'I was hungry.'

'Fine. Whatever you say.' She stared at him, her jaw clenched. 'You want to know something? I don't actually care.' She was shouting now, a sudden damburst of pent-up tension. 'All I care about is that you and your friends are in my kitchen and I want you bastards out. I want to make sure nobody gets hurt, at least none of my guys. Fine if you end up getting your balls sliced off and dunked in the deep-fat fryer over there. That to me would be a good day at the office, but frankly it would be less complicated if that didn't happen and what's in this box might make it easier to stop that happening, so if you just made the call...' She looked like she was on the edge of tears.

Nathan kept his face still. His ability to neutralize another's rage by showing no reaction was a talent he'd learned years ago, but it was only a mask. Underneath the smoothness of his cheeks and the flatness of his brow, calculations were being made. Nathan knew exactly how to build advantage from this box. 'I'll make the call when I'm ready.'

'And when's that?'

'Soon.'

'Well, when you do...' She pulled another ingredient sheet off the wall and shoved it into Nathan's hands. 'Get this in. If we're going to be stuck down here we might as well use the time efficiently.'

'Do you cook, Denis?'

'I know *you* cook, Freddie.'

'You already think you know so much about me.'

'That was a detailed list of ingredients. It didn't make much sense to me.'

'Exactly. You don't cook.'

'No, not really, Freddie. Cheese on toast is about my limit. Not bad at scrambled eggs.'

'And that's it?'

'I'm afraid so.'

'Who filled the boxes, Denis?' There was silence from the other end of the line. 'Who ordered up the ingredients? Who checked them all? Someone went and got them and put them in the box and it wasn't you, was it, Denis?'

'I think you need to keep your calm here, Freddie. It's only a few bits and pieces.'

'Important things were left off the lists, Denis. And each time those things were added to the boxes when I hadn't asked for them.'

Another moment's silence. 'I'm really sorry about that, Freddie. I don't think anybody here meant to interfere with your wishes.'

'I want to talk to them.'

'Tell me what you want to say and I'll pass on the message.'

'I don't want to send them a message. I want to negotiate with them.'

'You're negotiating with me.'

'I don't think I am, Denis. I don't think we have anything in common.'

'I thought we were doing pretty well.'

'I know that if I asked you to describe a Wiener Holstein you wouldn't have a clue and I'm sure you've never cooked one.'

'As I say, Freddie, cheese on toast is my limit.'

Nathan allowed himself the luxury of a smile. He was finished with this man. 'So we haven't got anything in common, because I have cooked Wiener Holstein. I want to talk to the man who did the boxes. I'm going to hang up the phone now and when it rings again I want them to be on the end of this line. Do you understand?'

'Yes, Freddie, I think I do.'

26

'Is that Freddie?'

Nathan glanced up at the bookshelves to remind himself. The spine of Frédy Girardet's book stared back at him.

'Yes, this is Freddie. Who's that?'

'This is Sergeant William Cosgrave.'

'Bit of a mouthful.'

'You can call me Willy if you like.'

'All right, then. So tell me, Willy, did you do the boxes?'

'Yes, I did. I mean, what I want to say is, I'm terribly sorry if I've upset you. I didn't intend to. I just thought that, if things were missing from the ingredients sheets it might be a help if I put them in.'

'It did help. Wiener Holstein's much better with the anchovies.'

Eagerly Willy said, 'It cuts through the richness, doesn't it, the salt?' Nathan said nothing. Willy filled the silence. 'And now you're going to make coq au vin?'

'Looks like it.'

'I like a good coq au vin.'

'Do you, Willy? Why's that?'

'It's one of those self-contained dishes.'

'I expect it is.'

'Do it properly at the beginning and everything is there. Use the right bacon and you don't even need to season it.'

Neither of them spoke. There was just the distant rush of white noise on the phone lines.

'You're my contact now, Willy.'

The policeman said only, 'I see.'

'We have shared interests so we're going to work together to fix this.'

'I hear you want a car. They'll be wanting you to release the hostages before they start talking about things like that.'

'Now, Willy, don't get all hard knuckles with me. We've got an understanding, and I don't want to see it go wrong at the start.'

'Of course not.'

'I don't expect something for nothing. But I'm going to need to know about the car and get a few assurances.'

'Right.'

'First though, I've got another list, except nothing's missing this time.'

'Good to know.'

'I need a bottle of Jamaican rum, two pounds of flour, four ounces of fresh yeast, half a pound of caster sugar...'

'Making rum babas are you?'

Nathan read the heading on the sheet. 'You're good, aren't you, Willy?'

'I try my best.'

'That's all I can ask. Two lemons...'

'It's all right. I know what you need. I'll give you a call when it's done.'

'It's like I said, Willy. You're my man.'

'Thank you, Freddie.'

27

Willy Cosgrave dropped the receiver on to the handset, leaned back in his chair and placed his soft, fleshy palms flat on his face so as to wipe away the sheen of sweat.

Commander Peterson pulled off his headset and sniffed. 'Well, at least you didn't make a hash of it.'

The negotiator smiled. 'I thought he did very well, actually. No commitments made. Dialogue maintained. Textbook, I'd say.'

'I was just trying to keep it civil, really,' Willy said.

'The important thing is the emotional connection. That's a very exciting development.' Willy stared at the negotiator. He did not like the man's enthusiasm. He wanted to feel he had completed his task but there was a lightness in the man's voice which suggested he was not finished with him. Denis Thompson licked his bottom lip. 'The classical theory in these negotiations is that you build up an emotional relationship which makes it harder and harder for the hostage-taker to displease you. He will want to be your friend. He will want to do what you ask him to do. But to get there you have first to find a point of contact.' Food, he said, had become this hostage-taker's point of contact. He described it as an 'emotional marker' and, as he did so, walked over and perched on the corner of the office desk so that he was staring down at Willy. It made the police sergeant feel small and foolish. 'Do you understand what I mean by emotional marker, sergeant?'

Willy shrugged. He didn't want to be having the conversation at all, let alone understand it. He was thinking about a large sirloin steak two inches thick and a span across. He had thought of nothing else since 3 p.m. that afternoon. In the corner of his mind reserved for matters of the stomach he had been working through the manufacture of the chips, the whisking of the Béarnaise, the plating of the whole. He tried to retreat back into that mental space, but the negotiator would not let him go there.

'Over the next few hours and possibly even days you are going to be having a series of conversations with Freddie,' Thompson said.

Both the sergeant and the commander grasped the point at the same time.

'The man's not trained as a negotiator,' Peterson said, quickly. 'He's a staff sergeant. Nothing more.' Willy wanted to agree with the argument but not with the man making it. He didn't want the responsibility of this negotiation. He certainly didn't want to phone Marion to let her know he wouldn't be coming home for dinner this evening. Equally, he didn't want to be dismissed by Peterson as an incompetent.

Thompson said, 'Willy has shown he's more than capable. In any case, the decision is not ours. Freddie has chosen him. During those conversations he will attempt to dictate to you an exit strategy. He will want to know about a car. He will want to know about safe passage for himself and his co-conspirators. He will be looking for reassurance that his position is secure.'

Willy, looking to gain Thompson's further approval, said he would do his best to provide that reassurance. Thompson shook his head. It was, he told him, exactly the wrong thing to do. Those subjects would make the gunman agitated and nervous. He would become suspicious and wary. In pursuing a place of security he would be exhibiting his clear insecurity. 'We don't want him like that because in such a state of mind a man with access to guns is unstable and therefore dangerous.' Peterson shook his head vigorously. It was obvious to him that his sergeant was proving his unsuitability for the task. He wasn't clever enough to understand the subtleties and nuances of the job. The commander opened his mouth to speak but Thompson silenced him.

'You will have to draw him back each time into his emotional comfort zone,' the negotiator said. 'You must actively seek to get him to talk about food. Discuss recipes, ingredients, the best place for a prawn cocktail and a Black Forest gateau in London. I don't care what you discuss. Just keep him talking food. While he's talking about that he will be relaxed and at ease.'

Sadly, Willy said, 'It's more than I'll be.'

Thompson ignored him. 'You can even start sending him in a few ingredients of your own choosing, if you like. We need to reward him for the efforts he makes to please us. Keep talking. Keep rewarding. And later, when he's as far away from the violent behaviour as we can get him, we'll move into the endgame.'

'Are you going to let me know what that is now?'

Denis opened his eyes wide and grinned. 'You can offer to cook him the best steak in London, can't you Willy? That should lure him out, like a mouse to a piece of cheese. I'm sure you don't just talk a good game.'

Willy said, 'I cook a little.'

'And if the steak offer doesn't work,' Denis said, cheerfully, 'we'll send in the bloody SAS.'

At the mention of the SAS Willy looked at his watch. He saw the minute hand careering towards the bottom of the hour. It was later than he wanted it to be. Time was slipping out of his grasp and with it so was his steak.

Commander Peterson stood up and leaned forward so he could look out through the window of the mobile unit and down the street towards the front of the restaurant. Without looking back at his sergeant he said, 'You can take one of the beds that are being set up in the gallery of the church.'

Willy turned to look at the telephone and said he would need to call his wife. The two men left him alone while he dialled the number.

When he had made the call he didn't want to make, been given the lecture by his wife that he didn't want to hear, and arranged for the sacrilege of the steaks' freezing, Willy Cosgrave hung up the phone and stared out into a deserted Jermyn Street. He had seen streets emptied of people before, and mostly they just looked naked, like swimming pools without water. But this one was different. It didn't just look naked. It looked defeated. Without cars browsing along the kerb and people dodging each other on the pavements, or pushing each other through the narrow, creaking doorways, Jermyn Street looked wrong. Willy Cosgrave was now the man charged with making it right again. Suddenly, and for the first time in many years, he felt very hungry indeed.

28

The old man reached into the pocket of his dun-coloured overalls and pulled out a large bunch of keys, strung on a wide chrome hoop. He felt along them, as if they were a rosary, until his fingers found the right combination of silver Yale and copper-coloured Chubb. He hesitated and looked east down Piccadilly towards the line of police cars and vans that stretched kerbside for the entire length of the church.

'Do hurry up. There's a good chap.' Marcus Caster-Johns shifted the weight of the two large canvas holdalls so that the leather handles were back up over his shoulders. He pulled his arms in tight across his chest so that the rest of his load didn't slip down either: the metal-framed camp bed, folded in on itself, the small cardboard box on a piece of twine, the bed roll, the supermarket bag of groceries.

'Really, Mr Caster-Johns, the policeman was very clear. Nobody, he said. Not a soul.'

'I know that, Eric, but I'm not nobody, am I?'

'Well—'

'You and my old man got on famously, didn't you?'

The caretaker let out a puff of air and stared away over the younger man's shoulder. 'He was a good bloke, your father. That's true.'

'Exactly. And he'd have wanted me to keep an eye on the place, wouldn't he?'

'I suppose so.'

'And I can't exactly do it from out here, now, can I?' Caster-Johns looked up and down the street, uneasily. He didn't want to stay on the pavement for too long with this much equipment on his back.

Eric squinted at the police cars again, and the line of tape that had cordoned off the pavement in front of the church. It was a bright early summer's day, and behind them a line of red buses moved down the street, oblivious, belching and hiccuping at each set of traffic lights.

'I told you I'd make it worth your while,' Caster-Johns said.

Gloomily, as if hoping someone would intervene to stop him, the old man turned to the grey, unmarked door, tucked in between Hatchard's to the left and Swayne, Adeney, Brigg to the right. He unlocked it slowly and ushered him inside. The door closed on to its draught excluders with a solemn thump. The corridor behind the door was laid with scuffed pink lino which ran up a flight of stairs fringed by a heavy wooden banister, painted magnolia. The hallway smelt of dust and disinfectant and there was the hollow silence of an empty building. The caretaker looked down at a heap of uncollected post scattered about the floor and was bending down to pick it up when Caster-Johns stopped him.

'On your way out,' he said.

'Yes,' Eric said. 'Of course. On the way out.'

The two men walked slowly through the building: up eight flights of stairs to the fourth floor, through a fire door to a corridor lined with locked and evacuated offices, and then took a sharp right to the Jermyn Street side of the building. At the end of a short corridor they came to another flight of stairs. They took this down one floor, and passed through an odd, misshapen and ill-hung interlinking door between the old Georgian houses on this side of the block. Finally, sweating from the effort, they reached a dead end and a last unmarked door.

'Anybody sees you coming out, it will be my neck on the block,' the caretaker said.

Caster-Johns nodded towards the freight on his back. 'Got everything I need here, haven't I? I won't even leave the room, let alone the building.' He put the bags down on the floor. 'Plus, you're going to put this on the outside of the door as you leave.' He dug around in the side pocket of one of the bags and found a rolled-up piece of paper, which he handed over.

Eric unrolled it. At the top was an obvious photocopy of the Metropolitan Police logo and under that, scrawled in marker-pen, the words 'Searched and evacuated'. Caster-Johns gave him a small plastic bag. 'There are some drawing pins in there and a roll of red and white tape. Put up the poster and then stretch the tape across the doorway. No one will give it another look once that lot's up.'

The caretaker stared at the things he had been given as if he thought them an unwise collection of objects.

'Oh, for God's sake, man,' Caster-Johns said sharply. He reached into a pocket of his waxed jacket and pulled out a roll of banknotes. 'Here. Take this.'

The caretaker palmed the money. He unlocked the door and walked away without pushing it open. Caster-Johns waited until the caretaker had turned the corner and his shuffling footsteps had faded, before shouldering his way into the room.

It was empty save for an office desk pushed up against one wall. A wooden chair was stacked on it, next to which stood an Anglepoise lamp whose cable hung off the edge of the table, plugless and frayed. On the other side of the room was a blocked-off fireplace, painted in the same shade of magnolia as the rest of the woodwork in the building. There was a hard, dark brown carpet, a bare lightbulb hanging from the ceiling and one long window looking out over the street which filled the space with light. For the moment Caster-Johns ignored the window.

He folded out the camp bed against one wall and laid it with the bed roll. He opened the cardboard box and took out a Primus stove which he placed in a back corner of the room, alongside a set of camping pans, a few tins of food – soup, cheap stews, fruit salad, condensed milk – a loaf of bread, a box of tea bags and three bottles of Johnnie Walker whisky, all of which came from the supermarket bag. From the holdalls he unloaded two replacement gas canisters for the stove, a small telescope, a pair of binoculars, a sheathed hunting knife and a battery-operated transistor radio.

Now he stood in the middle of the room and considered the tall sash window, which sat in a shallow alcove. He walked to the right-hand side of the window and pushed himself against the wall. From here he could see down to the deserted street below and the frontage of the Oyster House. He knew now that he was going to take it back, whether the police liked it or not.

Keeping his body as far back into the room as possible, to avoid being seen, he opened the window and moved the table so that it was in front and to the side of it. Now he reached into the bottom of one of the holdalls and took out a long object wrapped in a tartan rug that was half sticking out of it. Gently he unwrapped the hunting rifle, and ran the pad of his index finger along the barrel for signs of dust or dirt. He fitted a telescopic sight and placed the whole on a tripod and set it on the desk, angled down so that, perched side-saddle on the desk, he could look down the sight and get a clear shot at the doorway to his restaurant. He did this methodically and with an economy of movement as if it was a task he had performed many times before. If he swivelled the gun an inch to the right he found, with some satisfaction, that he could also get a clean shot at the now glassless front window of his restaurant. Caster-Johns sat up and looked down over the gun to the street below. He was exactly where he needed to be.

He slipped off the table, went to the mantelpiece over the dead fireplace, and unloaded on to it the handfuls of ammunition with which he had filled his pockets on the way out of his flat that morning. Carefully, he placed each round on its base, until he had just one left in his hand which he loaded into the rifle. He had just slipped the safety catch when he heard a rustle and coo from the window sill.

He looked up. A pigeon was staring back at him, its head cocked on one side as if surprised to find it had company up here.

Caster-Johns smiled. 'Hello, old chap,' he said gently. 'Invading your territory, am I?'

The pigeon took a few steps along the window sill on its gnarled, London-callused claws. It pecked at an unseen something.

'Looking for a little nibble to eat, are we?' The bird pecked again. 'Let's see if we can't help you.'

Caster-Johns went to his food store, opened the loaf of white bread and took out a single slice which he tore up into fragments. Gingerly, still at arm's length, he dropped a few pieces on to the sill. He retreated and watched as the bird picked one up and held it in its beak.

'Excellent,' Caster Johns said. 'Bloody good. We can be pals now, can't we, you and me? What do you say?'

The bird said nothing. 'Might be up here a little time,' he said. Caster-Johns stared past the bird to the street below and his clean sight of the restaurant doorway. 'But that's all right, isn't it, my friend? Because we've got everything we need up here, haven't we?' He ran his fingertips along the smooth, oiled metal of the rifle's barrel and smiled to himself. Everything, he decided, was exactly the way he wanted it. Now all he had to do was wait.

29

The mid-afternoon edition of the London *Evening Standard* on Friday, 10 June, dedicated much of its space to the results of the General Election, but gave over pages 4 and 5 to the siege. In a report at the bottom of page 5, under the headline 'Hungry work for Jermyn Street gunmen', the newspaper listed the ingredients that had been requested by the hostage-takers. There was a short description of Wiener Holstein and admiring quotes from London chefs, one of whom called it 'a timeless classic' and 'a bold riposte to the effete posturing of nouvelle cuisine'. The report concluded with a recipe for the dish.

Raymond Morris, an insurance underwriter at Lloyds of London, read the report and immediately wished he was eating the same food as the hostages. Fried eggs reminded him of childhood breakfasts cooked by his late mother and made him think fondly of cold winter mornings and the smell of rendering bacon fat rising from the kitchen downstairs. A fried egg was a cheerful item which, with its dam-burst of yolk, could shatter the formality of any restaurant dish. He imagined the hostages sitting about in the kitchen by candlelight, willing refugees from the demands of everyday life, enjoying an eggy dinner. He decided that, in these circumstances, he might enjoy being a hostage.

After reading his newspaper he telephoned Rules, a restaurant in Covent Garden specializing in game, and asked the head waiter whether the chef might be willing to prepare Wiener Holstein for himself and his wife that evening. The head waiter, who had also read that day's *Standard*, said the chef would be happy to do so. Other restaurants in London – the Savoy Grill and Green's, Shepherd's and the Guinea – received similar requests. London's restaurant-goers had been reminded of an old friend, one they had always liked but with whom they had lost touch. News of the interest in Wiener Holstein soon reached the media and the early evening television news bulletins, eager for relief from election coverage, concluded with live reports from various London's restaurants. In the BBC report, the journalist was outside Rules holding a plate of Wiener Holstein and looking pleased with himself, as if he had won a prize. He said this food was 'exactly what the hungry gunmen are eating right now'. He took a mouthful of the crumbed veal and fixed the lens with a prearranged grin.

Nathan leaned into the screen. Like most of those in the kitchen he was sipping from another mug of strong, milky tea. Kingston's cups of tea were less a drink now than something to do, more punctuation mark than refreshment.

'Theirs looks a bit small.'

Bobby looked up. She was amused by his sudden expertise. 'Probably cut from lower down the muscle where it tapers off,' she said, making a slicing motion just above her left knee with the side of her hand. She was dragging pieces of chicken through a plate of seasoned flour. In a large earthenware pot on the stove, mushrooms, onions and pieces of bacon were cooking. The pot rocked lightly on its uneven base as the bacon fizzed, and curls of steam lifted from its lidless mouth. When she had floured the last piece of chicken she reached into the pot with a slotted spoon and began removing the contents to a clean plate.

'So,' she said without looking up, 'is the hungry gunman getting peckish?' She smiled at her own cleverness.

Nathan said, 'I don't know where they got that from.'

'You should be pleased. You're famous. Only famous people have nicknames.'

He said, 'If I had wanted to be famous I would have taken acting lessons.'

One by one, she placed the pieces of chicken into the pot, where they hissed in the hot, flavoured fat. Each new piece increased the volume, as if they were instruments taking up their part in a band.

Nathan watched her work. He did not want to be famous. In his experience, fame – being known by more people than you know – carried no advantage. He had never forgotten the interest shown in him during his first weeks at his new primary school after his parents were killed, and the discomfort it caused him. He had concluded then that being too interesting to others could not be good, and he felt the same way now. Fame led to confusion and misunderstandings, like the reporter who said they were eating Wiener Holstein 'right now' when they weren't. As Nathan saw it, the better you became known for something, the harder it was to control what people thought of you. He could still recall the anxiety he felt when boys he had never talked to before at secondary school asked if he could supply them with a fingernail of dope. If the boys he wasn't friends with knew he was dealing, who else knew and what did they think about it? What had they said to others? How far had the fame spread? When he was dealing to his friends he was part of an informal club. Although the supply of the hashish was more of a crime than the smoking of it, there was a shared criminality which ensured Nathan's security. Most importantly he understood the geography of these boys' relationships. He knew who they regarded as their real friends – that Billy was tight with Neil, that Neil had gone to primary school with Gavin and Rob – and who they spoke to as a matter of convenience. He knew who hated whom. He could describe circles of animosity and affection and he understood instinctively his place within those circles and how bad blood could impact upon him.

Nothing had changed in his method as the enterprises got bigger and more complex. He knew other men around Brixton in the dope-dealing business who made their success public by the purchase of expensive cars and over-sized jewellery and who wore two-tone shoes.

He knew these men believed they were sending out signals to anyone who might wish to challenge them, by presenting a front of raw, financial power. Nathan, in contrast, kept to his narrow-lapelled grey suit and his white button-down shirts. He made a virtue of quietness and though, like many young people in Brixton, he had not been able to avoid the police entirely, the worst he had experienced was a conviction for a small amount of grass which even the magistrate had described as a minor offence. Meanwhile he watched, intrigued, as the other big dealers in their loud silk suits and their BMWs were picked up repeatedly by the police, while he was left alone.

He recognized now that by breaking with his usual methods to raise cash – by attempting to rob a central London jewellers – he had also compromised that quietness. In doing so he had forfeited control. It had started with the suggestion that he might be an IRA terrorist. People might not know him, but as a result of this hostage situation they had started forming opinions of him and there was nothing he could do about it. The idea that he might be a terrorist had now been abandoned but instead he was the 'hungry gunman', a cartoon character who had locked himself in a restaurant so he could raid the fridge. He needed to take back that control.

It seemed to Nathan that, despite being held hostage, control was something Bobby still retained. For all the powerlessness he and Trevor had forced upon her she remained in charge of what was going on at the stove. As each group of chicken pieces was browned in the pot, she removed them to the same plate as the vegetables to make way for the next. Once all the chicken had been sealed she returned everything to the casserole and added salt, pepper, a crushed clove of garlic and herbs. There was order here, a sequence of events to be followed which would turn raw, pink chicken and grey mushrooms into something other.

It was just gone seven in the evening and a torpor that had hung heavily over the kitchen during the late afternoon was giving way now to a mood of anticipation as the smells of cooking began to expand into the space. The judge was standing on one side of the stove watching, the top button of his chef's jacket undone. Grey Thomas was also on his feet, and while he was still keeping his distance it was clear he was engaged with the process. Kingston went around offering refills from a stainless steel teapot he had found in a cupboard but for now there were no takers. After the tensions early in the day, it appeared to him that a kind of calm had descended. Occasionally he saw Bobby look in the direction of Trevor, fixed to his place by the door, but with everyone now awake, she seemed relaxed.

Bobby dropped the cockscomb into the pot and gave the judge a wink. He nodded, approvingly. She put the lid in place and lifted the casserole down to the oven.

Guthrie said, 'How long will you give it?'

Bobby wiped her hands on her apron and squinted up at the clock over the swing doors. 'Half an hour, maybe forty-five minutes to get it really tender. Then the wine.'

'I was always told one should use the very best wine one could afford.'

Bobby turned and looked through the doorway behind them which led to the walk-ins and beyond it, to the wine store tucked in under the pavement. 'I think we've got a bottle of a 1961 Château Lafitte back there.'

The judge laughed. 'Perhaps that would be a little too good.'

'You're right. The situation is nowhere near desperate enough for that kind of gesture. Still, a glass of something wouldn't go amiss, would it?' She turned to Nathan. 'All right with you if we open a bottle?'

He jutted out his bottom lip to indicate he didn't care either way.

She turned to her cooks. 'Stevie, can you fetch us a couple of bottles of the Brouilly? Make it the '79.'

Soon, she was pulling the corks on the bottles and filling glasses. Stevie said, 'Just give me what's left in the bottle. It will save on the washing up.' Connaston took a large mouthful. He swallowed and, staring at Nathan, said, 'The taste of civilization.'

Guthrie slipped his nose over the rim of his glass and sniffed. 'I suppose we should let the air get to it.'

Bobby took a sip, and swilled it around from cheek to cheek. 'Special circumstances,' she said. She picked up the bottle and poured another glass. She pushed it across to Nathan. 'Live a little,' she said.

'I'm living too much at the moment.'

'Live some more.'

They sipped their wine and stared at each other, as if the opening of the bottle had marked a truce. She seemed comfortable with the wine glass in her hand, its bowl resting on, but not held by, her thumb and index finger. By contrast Nathan felt clumsy. He usually drank beer or spirits – vodka, mostly, with a splash of orange cordial to soften the blow – and he wasn't used to wine or its accessories. He took a long sip, trying to look delicate. There was a rush of fruit in his mouth and then, if he held the liquid on his tongue for long enough, an urgent astringency from the alcohol, which was a more detailed sensation than anything he ever got from vodka. He swallowed and felt it move to the back of his throat before drying away. The newness of the experience made him feel unworldly. He turned to look at Trevor who was dozing by the door again. Bobby turned to look too.

'Should we wake him?' Nathan said. 'He's missing the party.'

Bobby shook her head. 'Leave him there. It's safer when we know where he is.' She realized she liked admitting to Nathan that she found the other man frightening, however tentatively.

The phone began to ring. The conversation stopped and they turned to look at it. Nathan didn't move. Trevor shook himself awake and stared up at the phone, irritably. Bobby lifted her glass to toast the ringing phone and said, 'You should answer that. It's probably your fan club calling.' She drank more of her wine. Unhappily, Nathan put down his glass and walked across the kitchen to take the call.

30

Willy Cosgrave listened uneasily to the ringing tone. He rested his hand on the sheet of paper in front of him, where, under Thompson's instruction, he had written:

Keep on topic.
Promise nothing.
Be his friend.

He looked across at the negotiator for encouragement but Thompson was staring out of the window, one side of the headset held casually against his ear, while the other side dangled free. There was a click and then a gentle hiss of white noise. Willy turned back to face the piece of paper. There was silence at the other end.

Willy said, 'Freddie?'

A weary voice said, 'I'm here.' Thompson turned to Willy and nodded his approval. The hostage-taker sounded tired. Thompson clearly thought this was a good sign. Willy looked back at his piece of paper. It said: 'Be his friend.'

'I was just wondering how you were all doing down there.'

'We're cooking coq au vin.'

Willy hunched over the desk. 'What wine are you using? Elizabeth David says you should use an old Burgundy but I've always thought that was rather too good for a dish which is essentially farmhouse food. It needs to be something good but not too good.'

'Elizabeth who?'

'David. She's a cookery writer. A food writer really. She writes stories about food, which happen to have recipes in them. I would have thought someone like you would have read David.'

Nathan said, 'We need to talk about the car.'

Willy turned around to look at Thompson and opened his mouth; the sergeant wanted to look like he was shaping a response, though none came to him. The negotiator gestured at him to continue. Willy picked up the sheet of paper, hoping he might find certainties there. It said: 'Keep on topic.'

At first he said, 'I drive an Austin Allegro.' And then, 'But I've always hated the colour. It's orange.' Thompson frowned at him. Willy gave a desperate shrug, as if to say 'I couldn't think of anything else'. He looked out at the forced emptiness of Jermyn Street. Parked on the other side of the road, a little way short of the restaurant, was a highly polished E-type Jaguar which had been there when the siege began and had not been moved since. Willy noted the two exhausts peeking shyly from under its rear bumper, the impracticality of its two seats and the long, lazy slope of its bonnet.

He went on, eagerly, 'I used to do a lot of cooking in my car, actually.' Thompson managed a light smile which Willy took as encouragement. 'Under the bonnet, I mean, rather than on the back seat with a camping stove, which would be bloody messy, not to mention dangerous.'

A few years ago, he said, he had read an article in an American food magazine about in-car cooking, in which heat generated by the engine block was used to cook foil-wrapped cuts of fish and meat during long journeys. One Sunday morning he oiled some pieces of foil and double-wrapped four salmon fillets with a little salted butter and a sprinkling of dill. He made a creamy potato salad with his own homemade mayonnaise and packed it away in a Tupperware box, and then told the family to get in the car because they were going on a trip.

He felt like a pioneer, bringing a brave new world of on-road gastronomy to Britain. They drove fifty miles – the recommended cooking distance for fish in a medium-sized car – which took them out towards the Cotswolds, and had their picnic in the shelter of a horse chestnut tree because it was raining lightly that day. The children, who didn't much like salmon when it was cooked at home, liked it no better here on a damp Oxfordshire hillside, but Willy was enthused. He saw a bright future in front of them, full of happy family outings to the countryside, a roast lunch cooking under the bonnet of their modest family saloon. Once they could smell the roasting meat, the article said, they would know their food was ready and they could pull across to the side of the road. It seemed bizarre to Willy that everybody wasn't doing this all the time. It was a sensible use of otherwise-wasted energy, and a great way to improve the quality of food on such trips.

He said to his wife, 'We could even drive up to your sister's and take lunch with us. You know how bad her cooking is.' Willy liked to imagine that any tense family situation could be catered away. But Marion Cosgrave sided with her children. The sort of weather which invited a hot meal did not call for it to be eaten outside. And she was not going to embarrass her sister by turning up on the doorstep clutching a roast joint smelling of engine oil, she said.

'Not that anything I ever cooked on my engine block did smell of oil because I always keep it good and clean under there,' Willy said.

Nathan listened to Willy's story, and found it unsettling. He had neither eaten baked salmon nor been part of a family which would complain about it. The policeman was describing a club which he would never be a part of, and it suggested a social element to eating that had never before occurred to him. At the point when he picked up the phone, there was a clear picture in his head of what he wanted. He saw a car with blacked-out windows drawing up to the front of the restaurant. He saw himself, Trevor and Kingston getting into it, with Bobby alongside them as a hostage. He saw them driving at speed to one of the big south London housing estates, maybe the Angel or the East Peckham, somewhere they could lose themselves in the shadowed hive of underground parking spaces. They would dump the car and, using their superior knowledge of the walkways and corridors, escape easily. But now, unbidden, came another image: the car parked up in south London; Trevor flicking the hood open and, before they ran, Nathan grabbing the foil package from its hiding place on top of the engine.

And then there he was, with Bobby, in his living room above the shopping parade on Acre Lane, sipping wine and eating salmon from its foil plate, and laughing about the ease of their escape.

As Willy spoke, Nathan turned to look at Bobby. She had the pot back on the stove and the lid was off. He watched her fill a glass with brandy and upend it into the pot. She lit a match and, dropping her hand gently inside the pot, ignited the alcohol so there was a pop which encouraged the other hostages standing around the stove to gasp admiringly.

Nathan reacted automatically. 'Ooh.'

Willy stopped mid-sentence. '– what's up?'

'The chef just set fire to the pot.'

'Brandy?'

'Yeah.'

'Well, of course.'

A halo of blue flame flickered over the rim of the pot and Trevor got to his feet. He took three steps towards Bobby, his fist inside the waistband of his trousers, grasping for the pistol. Trevor had already used the paraphernalia of cookery as a weapon and therefore, in other people's hands, he saw it as a threat, but Nathan raised his hand palm-forward to tell him to stop. Trevor stared at him, his face tense and hard so that the scar under his eye seemed to deepen beneath the lights. Fixing Trevor with a stare, Bobby added another spoonful of brandy so that the blue flames popped and burst over the rim again. She enjoyed the provocation, with so many people here in the room to watch.

Nathan turned back to the phone and said, forcefully, so that Trevor could hear, 'We're going to need a car, with blacked-out windows. It must be driven up to the front door. We will take some of the hostages with us. We must not be followed or —' He let the last word hang. He wanted the policeman to understand that he was in charge of the situation. He wanted to feel the sense of authority that the gun in his hand had given him when he first entered the Oyster House. He wanted Trevor to be reassured.

Willy said, 'I could put something on the engine to cook for you, couldn't I?'

'I'm not thinking about food,' Nathan said, though he was. Bobby was emptying the bottles of wine into the pot, and the air in the kitchen smelt thick and alcoholic now. He wanted to know what this combination of chicken and bacon and onions and mushrooms and cognac and garlic and herbs and wine would taste like.

He said, 'Get us the car.'

Willy looked at his sheet of paper. It said: 'Promise nothing.'

'I'll have to talk to my superiors about that.' Thompson ran a single finger across his throat to indicate he should bring the phone call to an end. 'Goodbye, Freddie.'

Distractedly, Nathan said, 'Goodbye.' Slowly he dropped the phone away from his ear, and watched Bobby mash together a knob of butter and some flour in a small bowl. The conversation was over. It would soon be time to eat.

31

They ate the coq au vin standing around the stove, and mopped at the dense, dark sauce with pieces of the previous day's baguettes which had been moistened with milk and heated in the oven to reinvigorate them.

Bobby studied the men in their chef's whites, pulling at a chicken leg with their teeth or scraping together a forkful of lardon and mushroom. It was a curiously familiar sight. In many restaurants, kitchen meals were often taken like this before service, the cooks on their feet about the stove. The major difference was the quality of the food they were eating. Here, in the middle of a hostage situation, it was so much better. In a Michelin-starred Parisian restaurant where she had once worked, the brigade was often given the duck carcasses to gnaw at, after the legs had been taken off for confit and the breasts for pan frying and just before they were entombed in the stock pot. She had lost a lot of weight working there. In another, there was nothing but stews of offal – liver and kidney, or heart and lung, or tripe and spleen – because the meat supplier was willing to offload cheaply the deepest parts nobody else wanted. Some of these she liked but others carried about them the faint tang of urine, which reminded her too much of the smell in the city's streets. None of them had served a coq au vin, properly made.

Food aside, the feeling of lives on pause from the business at hand – in this case the business of being a hostage – was the same. Nathan even looked the part and she wondered again whether he had ever worked in a kitchen. She noticed how he stood, the heel of one foot rested on the toe of the other, a classic position for cooks who spend too much time on their feet. Though the blanks in his knowledge suggested he was telling the truth – that he just happened to be a natural – he did also fit the profile. Many of the cooks she had worked with were outsiders of one sort or another who took refuge in kitchen life because the chaos down there sated their appetite for causing chaos elsewhere. She knew from what he had said that Sheffield had passed some of his childhood in the local magistrates' court, having his riper adventures retold to him, and Stevie's entire life in gay London was acted out in the margins. For him the kitchen was family. It was somewhere he could trust when the rest of his life was so unreliable. Even Trevor didn't look out of place. She had known kitchen staff – mostly butchers in the big hotels, mostly ex-servicemen – who had even more scars and tattoos than he did.

It was Connaston who looked wrong. The wave of silver hair was now a matted tangle, loose strands of which he had taken to tucking behind his ears. There was a growth of grey stubble on the pleats of fat that made up his double chin and there were dark shadows beneath his eyes. And yet, for all this, he still maintained an imperious air as if he, among them all, was being most insulted by the situation in which they found themselves. He fidgeted with his food and eased out more space for himself at the stove with his elbows. When Kingston came around to collect the empties he dug him in the chest with the edge of his plate.

'There's no call for that,' Guthrie said, resting a hand on the bigger man's shoulder, but Connaston shook off the contact. Kingston stayed where he was, the plates held tightly between his big flat hands, considering his options. Connaston looked Kingston up and down. 'Trust a judge to side with a black criminal,' he said, spitting out the words.

Nathan pulled his gun and strode around from his corner of the stove, with the butt clasped in both hands. He lifted the weapon and dug it into the marshy flesh covering Connaston's jaw. Forks stopped midway between plate and mouth, and hovered in the space between.

'Apologize,' Nathan said. 'Now!'

Kingston put down the plates and moved towards his friend, to pull him back. He said, 'Leave it Nathan.'

But Nathan kept the gun in the man's skin. The only sounds were the rush of ignited gas under the stove and the hum of the fridges. Connaston swallowed and stared straight ahead. Nathan eased his finger on to the trigger and wondered, for a moment, what it might feel like to pull on the narrow curve of metal that would release the hammer that would fire the bullet. Behind him he could hear Kingston breathing. He was surprised by the amount of pleasure he was taking in the control he now had of the room. Suddenly he felt he understood what it might be like to be Trevor, to have no grasp of consequences. Or better still to understand consequences but not to fear them. Since this whole situation had begun he had been so controlled, so absorbed by outcomes, that every muscle in his body ached from the tension. Now, just standing here, his weapon drawn, a man's life in his hands, he felt a release.

When he looked to his left he could see Trevor grinning, his lips wet with anticipation. Trevor liked the idea of what could happen next. It thrilled him and, in that instant, Nathan knew he had made his point. He knew too that he could never be Trevor, never live that easily in the moment. Finally, in a sibilant hiss, Connaston whispered, 'Sorry.' Slowly, to make it clear the gesture was at his discretion, Nathan slipped the gun back into his waistband. He returned to his plate and the silence was filled again by the clink of cutlery against plate.

The newly solemn mood was broken when Sheffield suggested a game of cards. Stevie proposed poker and Connaston, who had the politician's instinct for survival, cheerfully said he would join in too. Then he manoeuvred to place himself at the heart of the venture by proposing they play Texas Hold 'em. The cooks agreed, and Guthrie said he was eager to learn a new card game if nobody minded 'a poker novice' joining them. He was invited to take a position standing around the high stainless steel prep table, while Sheffield went to the dry stores and fetched three bags of pulses. The white ṃ.ageolet beans were worth a pound, he said. Kidney beans were worth five pounds and the large butter beans were worth ten. They agreed to start off with £100 each and laughed when Stevie wondered out loud whether they would have to pay up when 'this whole thing' was over.

'Yeah,' said Sheffield, 'But there will be no three-bean stew for you, my friend, because you are going to be one big loser.'

Nathan took Trevor's place by the doors and Trevor walked across to watch the drop of cards and the beans scattering across the metal surface as the first hands played out. Sheffield muttered, 'Sounds, chef,' as he reviewed his cards. This time Bobby didn't argue. She went to the tape machine and found a recording of The Clash, which she played with the volume down low. The pulsing baseline of 'London Calling' sounded out in the kitchen like a heartbeat. She returned to examine the contents of the rum baba box which had arrived early that evening, and nodded her head to the music. At his station, Kingston cleaned the dishes and pots from dinner, one hip rested against the damp edge of the sink, the other turned half out to the kitchen so he could watch the game. Only Thomas kept himself apart. He slumped down again by the cabinets, knees up, an arm perched limply on each one, head bowed between them to the floor.

After four hands, Sheffield said to Trevor, 'Shall we deal you in?' He wanted to remove the man from his peripheral vision, but he also felt that the poker table was a place where usual conduct could be suspended. He had played poker with people he hated before, because the rules of the game established a cordon around their history. He thought that having Trevor in the game might prove a way to neutralize his threat, at least while the cards were being dealt. The gunman turned to Nathan for approval, which he gave with a curt nod. Trevor took his place by the table and was given a wallet full of pulses. For a while play moved on, broken only by mutterings of 'call', 'see' and 'raise', and the crack of hard, dry beans on smooth metal. The lead switched politely between Sheffield, Stevie and, for a short while, Trevor. After almost an hour a contested hand produced a large pot in the middle of the table with three of the five players still in. Trevor said he would see Sheffield, and the cook turned over a three and seven of hearts which made a flush with the two, ten and queen of hearts in the middle of the table. Stevie closed his cards and threw them down to signal he was out. With a proud lift of his chin, Trevor flicked over his cards and reached across to drag in the pot. 'Mine, I think.'

Sheffield put his hand on top of Trevor's and said, 'I don't think so.' The gunman had a jack of diamonds, king of spades and ace of clubs which gave him an ace-high straight, with the ten and queen in the middle.

'A flush beats a straight, any time,' Sheffield said.

'Your eyes not working? I got pictures.' Trevor tapped his cards.

'A flush beats a straight.'

'I won.'

'Not with that straight.'

Trevor leaned in towards him across the table so that the three other players backed away. Connaston closed his eyes as if, by shutting out the moment, it would cease to be. Guthrie let his features fall flat. Trevor moved one hand to the pistol in his waistband. The other hand pressed down on the pot in the middle of the table. He said firmly, 'These butter beans are mine.'

Sheffield held his stare for a couple of seconds, before pulling back from the table and laughing. He pushed all the beans across the table towards the other man. 'You're right. They're yours. Knock yourself out. We'll get you some smoked sausage tomorrow and you can make us lunch.' Trevor allowed himself a half smile, as he took possession of the pot. 'That's right. They're mine.'

They played on for a few more hands but the intensity had leaked out of the game. Guthrie had bet away his butter beans early on and when he lost the last of his purple kidney beans he pushed what was left of his flageolet over to Trevor and retired from the table. The rest of them played one more hand before declaring Trevor the winner.

In a police van parked in Mason's Yard behind the restaurant, a Special Branch officer who had installed listening devices around the bricked-up rear door on the first day, picked up the sound of The Clash and informed his superiors that the gunmen were listening to music. On the other side of the building in Jermyn Street, the SO19 dayshift gave way to the marksmen who would work the nightshift. Over by the lines of police tape at the junction with Regent's Street, television news reporters prepared to inform the nation that the hungry gunmen had feasted that evening on coq au vin and were now preparing to make rum babas.

Forty feet above the street, in the gallery of the Church of St James's, Sergeant Willy Cosgrave slept fitfully on his camp bed, while down below, seated in the pews, Commander Peterson and police negotiator Denis Thompson stared at the altar, drank a thumbs-depth of whisky from plastic cups and congratulated themselves on keeping the situation under control. The siege was developing its own rhythms and routines. What the police had referred to, at first, as a 'serious acute incident' was moving into what the analysts now described as 'the chronic stage'. It had reached the point where commanding officers drank whisky and reviewed events.

The music went off in the Oyster House kitchen just after 11.30 p.m. and Trevor, exhilarated by his win, said he would take the first watch by the door. Hearing this, and offering no explanation, Bobby pulled a green laundry sack over to the side of the kitchen where Stevie and Sheffield had staked out space and announced she would be sleeping between them. At midnight, certain Willy would not call him again that evening, Nathan dragged a couple of sacks out to the walk-ins where he lay down, his knees up to his chest, his hands under his head. Within minutes he was asleep, and a form of peace had settled on the Oyster House siege.

He was woken four hours later by the brittle sound of breaking glass.

32

Two days ago

Nathan propped himself up on one elbow and squinted into the darkness. His hand went to the butt of the pistol in his waistband, made warm by the tight cover of his belly while he had slept curled in on himself. He turned around and looked at the lit rectangle of the doorway through to the kitchen, expecting to see Trevor silhouetted against the light, but nobody was there. Across the narrow aisle from where he lay he could see the outlines of Connaston and Guthrie, asleep on their own litter of laundry bags. They didn't move.

Nathan eased himself from his place on the floor. When he was upright he stopped and listened to the breath in his nostrils and the pumping of blood in his ears. He pulled the pistol from his trousers and flicked the safety catch. In the night-silence of the basement the noise felt huge. He heard a rustling to his right and looked down at the Tory Party Treasurer as he turned over and settled once more. In front of Nathan there was the flicker of movement again, and that sound of broken glass. Slowly he stepped forwards, heel down carefully to enable control of the ball of the foot as it lowered. He held the butt of the gun in both hands and pointed it at the place where the sodium blush from the street lights up above came through the dirty glass bricks set into the pavement and illuminated the wine racks. The curves of oil-dark glass glinted in their wooden frames. He could feel his pulse in the tight grip he had about the gun. He lifted his weapon and squeezed his finger around the trigger. He felt his heart in his grip again, and took a deep breath to feed it.

From behind him he heard a click. He swung around as the ceiling strip lights illuminated in sequence over his head. He could tell from the curve of hip that it was Bobby standing in the backlit doorway from the kitchen, looking past him at something on the floor.

She said, 'Thomas, you little shit, what have you done?'

Guthrie and Connaston sat up. Nathan turned back to look. Grey Thomas was sitting on the floor, leaning against the wine racks, his legs out in front of him, feet slack at a 45-degree angle from each other. One hand was around the neck of an almost-empty wine bottle, which stood upright on the floor next to him. An empty bottle lay on its side, with a corkscrew next to it. His other hand lay bloodied on the floor, the lacerated palm surrounded by shards from a broken wine glass and a smashed wine bottle, which had been full when it hit the floor. The blood from the cut to his hand ran into a purple puddle of wine off to one side, where it was joined by a third stain which darkened the crotch of his trousers and ran down the inside of his trouser leg. The smell of red wine mingled with the higher-pitched aroma of urine. His eyelids drooped but his eyes were not yet completely closed. With great effort he managed to lift up his head as Bobby and Nathan approached.

'I just have a little drink,' he said, allowing each word to flow into the next. 'Now bugger off.' His head dropped again.

Bobby hunkered down next to him, and Nathan stooped to join her. She picked up the empty bottle first. She studied the label and shook her head. 'He's drunk the '61 Lafitte.'

Nathan said, 'Good was it?'

She didn't look up. 'Four hundred pounds' good.'

'Four hundred for one bottle?'

Bobby ignored him. She was looking at the bottle he was still holding. 'It had to be the Cheval didn't it, you little– I've got a mind to smack you over the head with this.'

'Another £400, I suppose.'

'Something like that. It's a '57 Cheval Blanc.'

'I should have been trying to rob this place instead of the jewellery shop.'

Kingston appeared behind him. 'Everything all right, boss?'

Nathan looked up at his friend. 'This one decided to have a party all by himself.'

'Looks like he did a good job of it too.'

Bobby sent Kingston to get the first aid box. She bathed Thomas's injured hand in antiseptic, examined it for any fragments of glass and when she was satisfied there were none, she applied a cotton wool swab and, to protect it, wrapped it in a bandage which she secured with a safety pin. By the time she was finished Thomas was unconscious. She suggested that, for his own safety, they place him in the recovery position so that he wouldn't choke if he vomited in his sleep. Nathan fetched one of the laundry sacks he had been sleeping on and, together, they lay him on his side, his head tilted down slightly. They stood over him and listened as his heavy breathing gave way to a loud snore.

'What a bloody mess,' she whispered, looking down at Thomas in the meagre light at the back of the basement. And then to Nathan, 'Proud of what you've done?'

Nathan said, 'I tried to release him. You were the one who insisted he stay.'

'But if you hadn't come in here in the first place—'

'I wanted to let him go. I had let him go.' Nathan thought for a moment. 'Why did you want him to stay?'

'I didn't think we'd be down here this long.'

Nathan shook his head. 'That's not an answer.'

Bobby looked at him, then slumped down on to the floor, her back to a pillar, her hands in her lap. She did not want to explain because she knew the reason was not good enough. By giving it voice she would be swapping some of her self-righteousness for some of Nathan's culpability. She felt they would become more alike and she did not want to be like Nathan in any way. Still, she knew she had to tell him. Thomas was a restaurant critic for one of the monthly glossy magazines, she said eventually, which was reason enough in itself. He made his living by eating in restaurants at other people's expense and then writing rude things about the experience.

Nathan was baffled; was it really possible that an income could be achieved simply by the lifting of a knife and a fork? Was this what went on in the world of abundance which people like Grey Thomas moved in? It had not occurred to him that there might be ways of earning a living which did not, in any way, correspond to his understanding of what work was; that there might be non-jobs, like that of restaurant critic, which could bring with it enough money to buy tightly stitched brogues in oxblood leather and hound's-tooth trousers.

Two years before, Bobby said, the head chef in the restaurant where she then worked had been killed in a drink-driving accident, which was not unexpected. He was always drunk, even on service. Sometimes he drove. An incident was likely. No one foresaw the problems his death would cause, however. The chef was a partner in the business and had not revealed the depths of the restaurant's financial problems. Suppliers were not being paid and waiters were owed salaries. Bobby, who was sous chef, took over the kitchen and attempted to keep the place running.

'That was when Thomas decided to review us,' Bobby said. 'He knew the trouble we were in. The car crash had been well reported in the papers. The suppliers we owed had been talking about it all over town.'

'He didn't say anything nice, then?'

She turned to look at him and, as if reciting a poem, said, 'It would be a service to British gastronomy if, in an act of solidarity with the late chef, every other member of the kitchen brigade dispatched a bottle of whisky and then climbed behind the wheel of a car and drove towards the nearest willing oak. Ingredients – and diners – need protecting from incompetents like these.' She turned back to look at the restaurant critic. 'I remember every word of that review. It was cruel.'

Nathan looked at Thomas too and nodded his head slowly in agreement. 'Quite funny, though.'

Bobby gasped and stared at him, mouth open. Nathan raised his hands in mock surrender. 'I take it back. I take it all back.' He nodded towards Thomas. 'Anyway, I think you've got your revenge.'

Kingston appeared in the doorway, filling the space. He asked if they wanted help clearing up the mess that Thomas had made, but Nathan said they could leave it until the morning. He asked where Trevor was and Kingston told him he was asleep.

'Typical.'

'I'll take over now, if you like.'

Nathan looked at his watch. It was just coming up to 5 a.m. and, through the glass bricks in the ceiling, he could see that dawn was advancing. He couldn't imagine getting any more sleep tonight. 'It's all right Kingston, go get some kip. We'll be getting out of here tomorrow. I want you good and alert for that.'

'Cup of tea?'

Nathan smiled. 'No, Kingston. Just get your head down.'

When he had gone, Bobby said, 'Do you really think this will be over tomorrow?'

Nathan shrugged. 'Don't know. Hope so. I'm not asking for much.'

Bobby looked past him to the now empty doorway where Kingston had been standing. 'You guys are close, aren't you? '

Nathan turned to the empty space where Kingston had been. 'We used to live together,' he said, simply, and he thought of the smell of oxtail stew in Mrs McDonald's kitchen. He pictured the curling postcards above the fireplace with their images of custard-yellow sand and blue sky, and it all felt a long time ago.

33

When Kingston was nineteen he told his mother that he wanted to move out. His brothers were furious, and shouted at him while he sat on the corner of his bed, the only personal territory he could claim in the crowded house. The last person to leave had been their father, who announced one day that he was tired of being cold and that he was going home. Kingston was only three at the time but the older boys still recalled their mother sitting at the kitchen table for days after that, in pink dressing gown and slippers, weeping over an empty tea mug. She gave up cooking and instead made rounds of jam sandwiches, which she buttered with such ferocity that the knife went through the white bread. The boys often had to hold their sandwiches tightly to make sure they didn't fall apart. When she wasn't at the kitchen table, they moved quietly about the house for fear of coming across her unexpectedly. Their mother's crying worried them more than the absence of their father, and they wanted to prepare themselves for it.

Then, one day, the house smelt of frying onions again, and they knew the emergency was over. Each morning, while her sons ate their breakfast, too many knees crammed under too small a table, she made stews which she left in the oven to cook during the day. The boys arrived home from school each afternoon before she had returned from work, and the scent of those slow-cooked dishes – of oxtail, or curry goat or braised cow's foot – had impressed itself upon every corner of the house. It was a surrogate for her physical presence. The older boys found the smell comforting but also regarded it as a symbol of the change in circumstances. Their mother could no longer be available to them all the time because of their father's decision to return to Jamaica. After that, there was an understanding that leaving home was never going to be an option. They believed it was a form of stress their mother could not tolerate.

Kingston's memories of the episode were slight, however. He saw his brothers' dramatic recollection of the events, and the pride they took in the privilege of that knowledge, as just another means by which older siblings discriminate against the youngest. When Nathan suggested they get a flat together he said he liked the idea very much. 'I'll have my own room.'

Nathan was pleased. He had been grateful to Mrs McDonald for giving him somewhere to live, but increasingly he felt that he was perpetrating a fraud upon himself by staying there. He had been denied the experience of family as a child, with its rituals and boisterousness, and staying in this noisy Caribbean household only emphasized the fact. He didn't want to be a fraud any more. He wanted independence; to live like the adult that he felt circumstance had forced him to become so early. He could be beholden to, and responsible for, no one. He found a flat above a café on Acre Lane. It smelt lightly of chip oil and damp, and there was a growth of mould around the edge of the bath. The carpets were rubbed raw to the underfelt in places and once, standing alone in the living room before moving in, he heard the scrape of claws, which he took to be mice. But he had heard mice in the McDonald house too and he wasn't going to let that put him off. The rent was affordable and, by paying it, he would be living somewhere he had chosen for himself, rather than because the selfish deaths of others demanded it. He was determined it would stay tidy.

When Kingston told his mother she said, 'I always thought it would be you first,' and his brothers shouted at her instead. But she said to them, 'Stop your noise. Maybe it's time I had the house to myself.' There was a shocked silence.

On the day the boys moved out, she stopped Nathan as he was picking up a box of records from the hall floor. 'You're the smart one,' she said. She nodded over his shoulder towards her youngest son, who was loading a chair into the back of the van outside. 'He's a sweet child, but he needs taking care of.' She tapped a finger against the side of her head. 'He don't think.'

Nathan promised that he would look after him, even though he was certain Kingston could look after himself. She patted his cheek with one hand and then let her hand rest there, so he could feel the warmth of her palm against his face. She smiled apologetically. She knew he found the contact embarrassing but she was not dissuaded. 'Such a good boy,' she said, and she drew him into an embrace. He stood stiffly, his palms hovering above the curve of her back, not knowing how best to react. Slowly he dropped his hands on to the slippery nylon of her dress and she tightened her grip. He allowed his head to rest momentarily upon her shoulder. 'Such a good boy,' she said again, and when she pulled back, her eyes were damp. 'Ignore an old woman,' she said. 'Go take your box.'

She was satisfied they could support themselves. Nathan and Kingston weren't dole boys like so many of the others, who managed to make a daily trip to the job centre on the high street look like an occupation. Instead they worked each day on a fruit stall in the Electric Avenue market, though she was not aware of the arrangement they had made with the stall holder. He was a small Jamaican man called Frankie who had a gold front tooth. He wore an old tweed waistcoat with lapels over a frayed white shirt, and he liked a smoke. The boys supplied him with dope for free. In return he let them store their stash under his fruit boxes and to supply their customers by dropping their wraps into the bottom of a brown paper bag of apples or grapes. No money was exchanged between Frankie, Nathan and Kingston. It was safer than working the street corners like others did up on Railton Road and Coldharbour Lane, and it gave them access to the rivers of gossip which flowed around the heart of Brixton. They knew the police were approaching long before they arrived, and could have their blocks of resin buried in the deepest parts of the cart where the hard, green bananas were stored to ripen.

At night they drank in the Prince Albert where the music was reliable: New Wave mostly, or reggae and, later, the best of Two-Tone. They liked Mary, the large Irish landlady who kept a wooden stick behind the bar which she would bang on the tables at last orders, and they approved of the room's shape. If they chose the right tables, to the right of the bar, it was always possible to see who was coming and going. They took pride in their understanding of things like this, and talked to each other with great seriousness about the mechanics of their jobs as dope dealers. Nathan kept a record in a notebook of the money they had spent on each bulk purchase, and next to it listed the amount it had been sold on for. In the back he recorded the details of major drugs busts in and around Brixton, in the hope that he might spot a pattern and be alerted to any risk to their enterprise. He read local newspapers closely. Together, Nathan and Kingston knew the tight knot of streets in central Brixton well, and regarded their ethnic mix as an advantage, because it meant they could sell comfortably to anybody.

During the day Kingston made the deals with the black boys who stopped by the stall. At night, in the pub, Nathan negotiated with the white middle-class kids, who stood self-consciously at the bar, scanning the room as they sipped their pints, trying to look like they had another purpose this evening; that the pub was just a staging post en route to somewhere else rather than the point of the journey itself. Nathan and Kingston became expert at spotting these potential clients, and at making eye contact in a way that would initiate business. Nathan believed he could find a way to talk to anybody, however far from home they happened to be, and argued that friendship or, more usually, the pretence of friendship, was the way to secure a hard core of reliable purchasers. He made a point of locking them in conversation before they were invited to follow Kingston into the men's toilets, where a wrap of resin would be exchanged under the toilet cubicle wall for a roll of banknotes. He believed this system reduced their exposure. Though he had never discussed the issue of recreational drugs with his grandfather, he liked to think that Terry would have understood the silent challenge they were laying down to the authorities, through their sale of dope, and that he would also have appreciated the rigour with which Nathan approached the business.

'We should always be able to move quickly,' Nathan said one evening. And, 'Nothing should ever surprise us.' He firmly believed that nothing would, until he met Lucy.

34

Lucinda Cranbourne had unruly auburn hair to her shoulders and wore ankle-length gypsy skirts in panels of red and gold. Later, Nathan told her that she had looked like a sunrise the first time he saw her, standing in the doorway of the Albert, searching the bar for her friends.

'You thought I was an idiot.'

He denied it. 'At that point you hadn't actually said anything.' She cuffed him playfully.

Nathan didn't notice her until the man he was sitting next to stiffened on his bar stool. He was a history student at the London School of Economics who had just bought half an ounce of Moroccan black.

'Lucy,' he whispered urgently to his friend, who was rolling a cigarette and had his head bowed to the floor. 'And she's alone.' Carl looked up.

Nathan looked too. At the same time, she spotted them. She raised her hand in salute, so that a collection of thin silver bangles clattered down her arm towards her elbow.

'Charlie! Darling!'

Nathan wasn't surprised by the ripeness of the voice. Most of the wealthy, suburban kids who bought dope from him in the Albert had the same kind of unmarked accents. But they attempted to hide it, by assuming an uneven mockney of dropped aitches and clumsy abbreviations they thought might sound cool. This woman didn't seem to care, though. He heard in those two words – 'Charlie! Darling!' – the kind of fat flattened vowels that he had also once used, before school, and an instinct for assimilation had encouraged him to mislay them.

The pub did not fall silent. The Albert was never silent, but drinkers did turn to look.

'Friend of yours?' Nathan said to Charlie. Neither he nor Carl had a chance to answer. She was already at the table.

'So?' she said in a stage whisper, leaning forward over Kingston's shoulder, 'Did you manage to get any?'

Charlie blushed. 'Lucy, for God's sake. Shut up and sit down.'

'No need to be rude,' she said indignantly. 'Just tell me.' She dropped down on to a stool so that the air caught in her skirt and made it float about her momentarily before collapsing and coming to rest. The four men stared at her.

She looked from Charlie and Carl to the two strangers. 'I'm Lucy,' she said brightly to Nathan.

Nathan tried not to laugh. 'Hello, Lucy,' he said.

Carl leaned across to her. 'Where's Jules?'

She shrugged. 'Couldn't make it.'

'So you came down here alone?' He sounded appalled.

Kingston pushed his big round face towards him. 'What you worried about?' he said. 'That she'd get eaten down here by one of the scary natives?'

Lucy stretched her arms forward and examined her slender wrists. 'Not much chance of that, is there?' she said to Kingston. 'Wouldn't make a meal for anyone, would I?'

Nathan said, 'We could try.'

She glanced up from her arms. 'Cheeky!' She looked back down again, proudly, and turned them over to study the paler skin underneath. 'Maybe I should take up weight-lifting. What do you think? Put on a bit of muscle?'

Nathan shook his head. 'I wouldn't.'

'You don't need to. Look at you. Perfect proportions.' And then, 'Lovely suit by the way.' She reached across and rubbed the material of his lapels between thumb and forefinger. Charlie and Carl breathed in sharply but Nathan didn't recoil. He was intrigued that she had noticed, because none of his friends had. In the two years since moving into the flat, their business had been good. With the extra money he had been able to replace the second-hand suits with new outfits from a shop on Carnaby Street. The grey material was a finely woven wool, and the jacket was lined in a dark blue mix of nylon, polyester and cotton. He was wearing a white button-down shirt, and a thin leather tie. He wore Chelsea boots that came to a point. He knew he looked good, in a suitably unostentatious manner. He hoped his outfit recalled Paul Weller.

'Not like you two bloody scruffs,' she said, turning to the men. Carl and Charlie were in their own uniform: black biker jackets over sweatshirts and jeans. She ruffled Charlie's hair and he flinched. 'You should take a few lessons from...' She looked across the table again. 'What's you name?'

'Nathan.'

'You should take some lessons from Nathan.' She yawned, and sat back, suddenly bored with her own train of thought. She pushed her bangles back up her arm, and admired the thick coil of silver pressed in against her lightly tanned skin, where it emerged from under the loose cuff of her white, cheesecloth blouse. 'Anyway, did you get some?'

'Yes,' Nathan said. 'They scored.' She looked up, surprised that he was the one to answer. He smiled at her.

'Oh,' she said. And then, with innuendo, 'Oohhh,' and she pressed a hand to her forehead, as she realized who he was. 'You're the—'

'Yes, I am.' He nodded towards Kingston, who grinned. 'We are.'

'Right. Sorry. I didn't think they'd be having a drink with the – I thought you were – You must think me a terrible buffoon.'

He laughed. 'Do people really use words like buffoon?'

She looked up shyly at him from under her fringe. 'Only buffoons like me.' Nathan decided he liked her.

He bought her a rum and Coke. She told him that she lived in Hampstead and Nathan said he had never been there. She said it was nice, but a bit 'stiff' and that too many writers lived there. 'Even the corpses in the cemetery belong to writers.'

'Must be a very unhealthy profession,' he said.

When 'I don't like Mondays' by the Boomtown Rats came on, she raised her hands to silence the conversation, closed her eyes, and mimed the opening piano break with mock pomposity, pumping at the air with splayed fingers for the big chords. And when she leaned into the table to sing along with the first line, Nathan joined her. They laughed and sipped their drinks and kept eye contact.

Kingston said, 'That song's shit.'

Nathan didn't look at him. 'It's not that bad really.'

After another rum and Coke, Lucy stood up to leave. She asked Nathan where he bought his suits and he told her. She asked him whether he had ever been to Camden market. He said he had.

'Meet me there on Sunday, then, by the tube.'

'All right.'

'One o'clock?'

'Done.'

When they had gone, Kingston looked at the door, which was still swinging from their exit.

'I hear posh girls are the filthiest.'

Nathan said, 'I wouldn't know,' and he hoped he sounded like he wasn't interested.

She was waiting for him by the entrance to the tube station, and smiled broadly when she saw him, which made her seem less knowing. They walked up to the canal where the market stalls were, and when they passed the record shop where he and Kingston usually browsed for rarities, Nathan picked out a shop on the other side of the road to comment upon. Ignoring the record shop made him feel like a man of broad interests. In the market they walked among the stalls, and Nathan let his hand hang slack at his side, so it brushed against hers. At one stall Lucy pulled out a T-shirt, marked with The Who's red, white and blue target logo and showed it to Nathan, but he said he didn't want to look like a fan and she told him he was very wise. He appreciated her approval. At another stall, she tried on long silk scarves in primary colours, by wrapping each one around her head to form a turban. When the scarf was in place she raised her arms, fingertips waving as if she had just performed a great feat of gymnastics which deserved applause. Nathan obliged. At another stall, selling joss sticks, and carved Indian boxes, she chose a tiny dope pipe in pewter and rosewood, with a picture of a marijuana leaf on the bell, and when she had paid for it, and it had been wrapped in pink tissue paper, she gave it to Nathan.

'What's this for?'

'Smoking grass, I assume.'

'I mean, why did you give it to me?'

'Because I like you,' she said, and she looked baffled that he should even ask. She moved on to the next stall, which was selling hats, and insisted he try on a black trilby. She placed it on his head and positioned it for him, pulling it down to an angle at the front. They stood looking at themselves in the long mirror.

'I think it's you,' she said.

'I think I look like a ponce.'

'What does that make me?'

Afterwards they walked up towards Chalk Farm tube. They passed a restaurant called Marine Ices, set back from the pavement. A queue had gathered outside.

'Best place in north London when you've got the munchies,' Lucy said.

'Shame we're not stoned then,' Nathan said.

Lucy reached into the neck of her white blouse, and from the light curve of her cleavage, withdrew a joint.

'In emergencies, just rip material,' she said.

She walked him a short distance to a bench under a tree at the foot of the road that led up the hill to Belsize Park. She sat down and lit the joint. Nathan watched. To him smoking dope was about subterfuge.

Sometimes he wondered whether it was that part of the dope-smoker's life which was the most attractive: the keeping of secrets, the maintenance of a life separated from that of others. He had smoked outside, but only in closed-off spaces, like by the gardener's huts in Brockwell Park, or while walking through dense woods on Streatham Common. This was different, and he was excited by how brazen it was. He admired Lucy her ease and carelessness.

She handed him the joint and he hesitated. 'Don't worry,' she said. 'No one will hassle us.' A black guy walked past them towards Camden, hands buried in the pockets of his bomber jacket. He sniffed and glanced around as he walked, and Lucy held the joint out towards him, roach forwards.

'Do you want a toke?'

He walked back. 'Don't mind if I do,' he said, and he pulled lightly so the tip burnt red. When he was finished he handed back the joint, looked at Nathan and, nodding towards Lucy, said 'Lucky bloke', and Nathan decided that he was. The joint was doing its job now. He could feel the light autumn breeze against the warmth of his cheeks. Above him coppered leaves brushed against each other, so that the air was filled with the sound of rush and pull, and cars hummed as they passed. Nathan felt he could sit and watch the cars all afternoon. Today he found cars soothing.

Lucy took a last draw, crushed the roach under foot and stood up. She hitched her skirt back up into position and looked back down the road towards Camden.

'Come on,' she said. 'Ice cream. My tongue's hot.' Eagerly, Nathan stood up to follow her. As he walked he looped his hand through Lucy's arm. He didn't want to let her go.

35

Shortly after nine on the morning of Saturday, 11 June, the Special Branch officer operating the listening post in Mason's Yard, heard what he described to his commanding officer as 'a commotion' in the kitchen. There were raised voices. 'Two of them, sir,' he said. 'Perhaps three.' But the walls were thick, and the low ceilings compressed the sound so he could not make out what was being said. He picked out the words 'enough' and 'car'. He heard what he thought sounded like metal cracking against metal. Just before the incident began he believed he had heard groaning.

The information was relayed to the mobile command unit on Jermyn Street, where Peterson was briefing the quartet of senior officers who would be running the operation that day. Willy Cosgrave and Denis Thompson were also present. Peterson listened to the news on his radio and asked his colleagues for their assessment. One suggested that the hostages were trying to overwhelm their captors. If that were the case, he continued, might it not be necessary to storm the building in support of the hostages?

'But we don't know,' Peterson said.

'No, sir. We don't.'

Another wondered whether the gunmen were fighting among themselves.

'Why would they do that?'

'A difference of opinion?'

'We're guessing.'

Willy said, 'Let me phone Freddie.'

'When I want your opinion, Sergeant, I'll ask for it.'

Denis Thompson intervened. A ringing telephone could have its uses, he said. If the hostages were attempting to overwhelm their captors it might distract them and offer an opportunity to get the upper hand. If the gunmen were arguing among themselves, the ringing of the phone also might interrupt the confrontation and defuse tension. Peterson's face registered nothing. He turned to Willy and nodded. The sergeant picked up the phone, dialled the number and listened for the ringing tone. He faced into the room, where he was watched by the six other men.

The phone had rung four times when one of the officers pointed out the window. 'Look!'

Willy pressed the receiver under his chin and turned to the window, and its unobstructed view of Jermyn Street and the Oyster House.

Nathan and Bobby had retreated back to the kitchen to leave Grey Thomas to sleep off the effects of the wine, chased away by the sour smell of urine and spilt liquor. Eventually, not long after dawn, Nathan fell asleep. He awoke just before eight and found Bobby sifting flour into a bowl.

'Take a cheese sandwich,' she said, nodding towards a plateful. 'We're going to make rum babas.'

Trevor was on the floor by the door, his pistol in his lap. He was holding a half-eaten sandwich. He turned to Nathan and chewed. His face was expressionless. The judge was leaning over a cookbook from the kitchen's collection. Connaston, Sheffield and Stevie were eating sandwiches and slowly dealing out cards for another game of three-bean poker. The mood was sullen and resigned. After nearly thirty-six hours in the kitchen the chefs' whites were grubby and creased. The men had thick stubble. There were dark rings under everybody's eyes from lack of sleep, and Bobby's hair looked imprisoned rather than contained beneath the scarf she wore about her head. Her shoulders were slumped, but she was focused on the task she had set herself.

Nathan said, 'What's a rum baba?'

She looked at him. 'My favourite waste of time.'

There were dishes anybody could make, she said. All it required was the ability to follow instructions. Making the light, bready savarin for a rum baba took something else. It required instinct, a natural sense of when textures felt right. It was the first real dish she had ever made, in her mother's kitchen after her father left. Bobby liked it because it took time. Nothing else mattered when she was mixing the early batter by hand and, at that point in her life, there were lots of things she didn't want to think about. Even when she was waiting for it to rise, she was considering the next stages: how it had to be beaten down to rise again, and then put into moulds and baked and later, while still warm, turned in the thick rum syrup. When she was making rum babas Bobby felt like she was in charge of her world.

'Go wash your hands. I'm going to show you what to do.'

He did as he was told. She explained the importance of warming the bowl, so the yeast would rise, and how the warmth from his hands would aid the process. She pressed the back of her hand against his so he could feel the temperature of her skin. She showed him the yeast, water and milk mixture and the beaten eggs and the unsalted French butter, and how to blend the ingredients to form a batter. When they started to come together, she lifted her hands out and told him to take over. He felt it form a smooth paste beneath his palms. She gave him words of encouragement, and Nathan began to feel the rum baba's power to distract. He liked sharing an experience with Bobby.

There was a sharp intake of breath from the floor.

Nathan looked down. Trevor was looking back at him. His jaw was clenched and the veins in his neck were engorged.

Nathan said, 'What?'

'You keep cooking.' The words were staccato.

'What do you want me to do?'

'We need a car.'

'It's coming.'

'Talk to them again.'

'It's coming.'

Nathan looked away from Trevor to the batter, which he moved with harsher movements so that it began to form a dough. Bobby laid her hand gently on his wrist. She said, 'That's enough.' She placed a tea towel over the bowl, and left it to rise. Nathan stood a short distance away, arms folded, staring at the bowl, deliberately not looking at Trevor, not wanting to engage with him, but the other man demanded his attention.

Trevor had taken from his pocket a box of matches, and now began igniting them in pairs or threes, their heads held together so that they fused. With each ignition there was a small crack and a flash, and a puff of smoke that, with repetition, made Nathan jump. When he looked down, Trevor smiled and sparked up more matches, pursing his lips in concentration. Nathan noticed a shake to the man's hands and a grey pallor to his skin and wondered how much more amphetamine sulphate he had taken overnight and how much more he had on him. Tiny wraps of folded paper ripped from glossy magazines seemed to appear from his pockets at regular intervals and each time the contents of one disappeared up his nose he sensed the other man's grasp on the situation slipping away.

It was when Trevor was lighting his sixth set of matches that Nathan snapped.

'Leave it with those bloody things, Trevor!'

Trevor watched the pink-white flare and then sniffed the puff of smoke, with his eyes closed. 'No.'

'You're driving me nuts.'

'It smells good,' he said. He shook the box to release the last of the red-tipped sticks from their box. He lit two together, sniffed the smoke, blew out the flame and, his eyes wide open, placed the black burnt end on his outstretched tongue where it fizzed in his saliva. He closed his mouth and tasted the residue. 'Just passing the time,' he said. 'Same as you.'

Nathan was relieved when Bobby finally removed the towel from the bowl. It gave him a reason to turn away. The dough had risen to twice its size. Bobby told him to punch it down and beat it again. She admired the regular way in which he worked the savarin mix, even though she understood that much of how he was behaving was a release of tension. Beginners were sometimes too tentative. They fondled the dough, rather than got their hands into it. Nathan was regular and forceful. He enjoyed the sensation of the material and the chance to do something useful with his fists.

She gave him further words of encouragement, but fell silent when Trevor appeared at his side. Slowly she backed off.

'Stop cooking.'

Nathan didn't look up. He worked the dough and said, 'The car's coming.'

'How do you know?'

'I'm negotiating.'

Trevor pushed his face close to Nathan's ear, and shouted, 'No, you're not. You're cooking. You're doing what she's telling you to do.' He pointed across the work surface at Bobby. When Nathan didn't react, he said, 'They're screwing with you.' Nathan worked harder. 'She's screwing with you.' Bobby flinched.

From the basement on the other side of the open doorway, they heard groaning. Everybody turned to look. Grey Thomas stumbled to the entrance and stood, holding himself up with both hands flat against the doorposts. His hair was wild and a white crust ran from the corner of his mouth to the bottom of his chin where a stream of saliva had dried overnight. His eyes were bloodshot and sunken. His skin was grey. His lips were pink and broken. He looked at the faces staring back at him. He opened his mouth as if to speak, then lifted his shoulders, turned his face downwards and vomited violently on to the red tiled floor. It hit the hard surface with such force that it splashed upwards against his trousers and on to the front of the stainless steel cabinets, where it ran downwards in thick red drips of regurgitated claret. Thomas looked down at what he'd done and groaned again. His knees began to give way, and Sheffield and Bobby moved to steady him. The room filled instantly with the stench of bile.

Trevor bashed his pistol down against the metal work surface. He shouted, 'That's enough.' He brought the gun down again. 'I've had enough.' And a third time. 'I want a car.'

Nathan held Trevor by the shoulders and told him to calm down, but the other man ignored him. He had his finger on the trigger and was pointing the pistol at the ceiling. 'I want a car.'

Now Trevor shook Nathan off. He looked wildly about the room until his gaze came to rest on the tableau of Sheffield and Bobby holding up Thomas. The gunman reached into his trouser pocket, tugged out his black mask and pulled it over his head. He walked over to Bobby and, in one fluid movement, like it was something he had rehearsed, something he'd wanted to do for a long time, placed her in a neck-hold, the pistol pressed against the side of her head.

Bobby screamed. 'Get him off me. Get him off me now!'

Nathan took a startled breath and said, 'Don't do anything you can't undo.'

'I'm getting us a car.'

Kingston moved to intercept them, but Nathan held him back. 'I'll deal with it,' he said quickly.

Bobby shouted, 'Let me go, you fucking psycho. Please! Let me—' Her mouth was open and she was throwing her head from side to side, so that her hair escaped from under the scarf. But Trevor just pushed the muzzle of his gun harder against the side of her head and backed off towards the swing doors, his teeth bared.

Nathan walked towards him slowly, his hands up, like he was trying to corner a wild animal 'Trevor, listen to me. You mustn't do the wrong thing.'

'I'm getting the car.' Bobby stared back at Nathan over Trevor's rigid, sinuous arm. Her hands were around Trevor's forearm, but she didn't have the strength to pull it off, and its tightness around her neck was colouring her cheeks. She could smell sulphur on his breath from the matches and nicotine on his fingers and days of unwashed male sweat. She kicked out with her feet, her heel finding the wall of cans that Trevor had built, and knocking them down so that they clattered against the hard tiled floor and rolled away against the kitchen cabinets. She mouthed the word 'please' at Nathan. It was the last thing she said before Trevor shouldered his way through the swing doors and away up the stairs.

There was a brief silence in the kitchen, and then the phone started ringing.

Willy dropped the receiver back on to the handset, and leaned towards the window. The two figures outside in their matching white jackets looked to him as if they might be dancing. The masked man's arm was wrapped high across the shoulder of his companion, whose head was tipped back, laughing perhaps at a shared joke. They rotated as they came through the door of the Oyster House and on to the pavement, their feet tripping about each other daintily, until the kerb broke the fluidity of their movement and they stumbled together on to the road. Only then could they see the gun in the masked man's hand, the barrel pressed to the side of the other person's head. The masked man looked up and down the street. He opened his mouth and shouted.

The policemen stood together at the windows of the mobile control unit, watching. Willy and the officer from SO19 were in front of the window facing down the street. They had the clearest view. The others were arranged behind them trying to take in as much detail as possible.

The firearms officer spoke urgently into his radio. He said, 'Hold fire, repeat, do not fire.' As he issued the order he looked around to Peterson who nodded his agreement.

Willy said, 'It's a woman.'

The other men strained forward. Outside the gunman was bawling. 'I want a car. Bring me a car now.'

'It's the chef,' Thompson said.

A police radio burst with conversation. The firearms officer turned to Peterson. 'I've got two men with a clear line of sight on the target's head.'

Peterson looked at the police negotiator. 'Risk to other hostages inside?'

Thompson said, 'Unknowable, therefore we must always presume it to be high.'

Peterson nodded. 'And those bloody chefs' jackets make a clean shot risky. Maintain the order.' The man from SO19 again told his officers not to shoot. Outside in the deserted street, the masked man was still turning from one side to the other, shouting at the dead-eyed windows of the deserted buildings. They could see Bobby's feet scrambling against the ground, and hear her screams, and could see the way her hands were clawing at the man's arm.

Willy pressed his hands against the glass. 'We have to do something.'

Peterson said, 'We need to get someone out there to talk to him.' Willy swung about, terrified that he would find the commander looking back at him. Instead, Peterson was being helped into a black, bullet-proof tunic. It was while the commander was fastening the last of the clips that they heard the bang.

36

Connaston turned on the television and quickly found a live broadcast of the scene outside the Oyster House. Nathan forced himself to the front of the huddle in front of the set and reached up with one hand to the bottom of the screen as if trying to climb inside. The picture was grainy and unsteady, but even with a black and white picture they could make out the thin figure of Trevor in his whites, topped by the cannon ball of his black-masked head. They saw him swivel and turn, and Bobby's legs emerging from out of the fuzzy shape of his body and back in again. Over the picture they could hear a reporter's voice '... we're coming to you live from central London, where an armed gunman is threatening...'

Connaston shook his head. 'The PM is not going to like this one bit.'

Nathan turned and shouted at him. 'You think I care what she thinks?'

'You should do,' the Treasurer said in a voice as soft as Nathan's was loud.

Nathan turned back to the television, enraged. Looking now at the gun in Trevor's hands, he saw not only Bobby's life in danger but his own. In an instant the whole scenario spread out before him, like it was a set of frames from one of the comic books he might have read as a kid; images so sharp and graphic no one could misunderstand the story.

Bang! Bobby's dead, and there's the blood rolling into the gutter from the gaping hole in her chest.

Bang, bang, bang! Now it's Trevor's turn, his body bucking and twitching under a rush of police bullets.

And now here they come into the kitchen, the men with their guns, ready to end it as fast as possible, each of them with a bullet just for Nathan.

Sheffield was standing to his right. The cook swung about so that his mouth was hard by Nathan's ear, and yelled with such force that Nathan felt his words in his jaw and down his neck and in the centre of his chest. 'If she dies, if he kills her, if he fucking touches her I'll clean this kitchen with your guts.'

Nathan pulled out his own gun and pointed it at him. The cook backed off.

'Calm down!' he shouted back, glancing up at the screen and back again, aware immediately of the tension in his own voice but unable to do anything about it. His hands were so sweaty the weapon felt slippery beneath his palms and the gun was shaking. Blood pumped hard in his temples like the papery skin up there might perforate at any moment and the sudden rush of adrenalin made his legs feel weak and unreliable. 'Nobody do anything.'

Somewhere up above them they heard a muffled thud. He turned to the screen in time to hear its echo a split second later from the television.

Peterson pushed Willy out of his place by the window. 'Who's shooting? I didn't give an order to shoot.'

Outside, the two figures had dropped to the ground, belly to the tarmac. After a few seconds, the masked man rolled on to his back. He lifted the pistol and waved it from side to side.

The firearms officer shouted into his radio, his face turned towards the lapel of his jacket, where the mouthpiece was clipped. The radio came back with a clutter of voices, shouting at each other. 'It wasn't us,' he said, looking up from the radio. 'We didn't fire.'

'Was it him then?' Peterson was pointing out the window. Bobby had her head up now, though they could see that the gunman was still holding on to her arm, the white of his sleeve forming a bridge between them across the slate grey of the road.

Willy said, 'They dropped to the ground after the shot was fired. I saw an impact behind them.'

'I told your men not to fire,' Peterson said.

'My men did not fire.' The air was filled with the noise of men shouting at each other, of police radio and high-volume electronic static.

Willy said, 'I should get on the phone and tell Freddie that.'

There was peace for a second, then Peterson said: 'Do it.'

As she lay on the ground, Bobby tried to work out whether she had pulled Trevor down or Trevor had pulled her down. She knew there was almost no time between the shot being fired and the two of them dropping to the road. She had also known it was gunfire the moment she heard the shot, even though she could not see the police marksmen. She had been around enough hunting rifles as a kid to know exactly what that sound was. She lifted her head and saw immediately that Trevor was uninjured. He was still holding on to her with one tensile hand clasped around her upper arm, the blunt rivets of his knuckles hard beneath the stretch of pallid skin. She tried to pull against his hand-hold and saw his fingers begin to slip away, but the more she moved, the tighter he pinched her until she dropped her cheek to the road and, exhausted from the struggle, from the intensity of the moment, from the days of sleep deprivation and fear and desperation, screamed against the pain. It felt good to scream. It felt necessary. It felt right.

With his free hand Trevor was waving the pistol at the buildings directly opposite. Bobby closed her eyes and took a series of deep breaths, and knew that she had reached the end, here on this dusty London street so far from home, victim of a robbery gone wrong and a sexual predator strung out on amphetamines and his own lust for terror. She pressed her cheek hard down against the road surface and waited for the gunfire that she knew had to be coming.

But all she heard was Trevor's voice, raging incoherently at the air around him. Now, as the seconds passed, she became aware of an ache in her left knee. Then she heard another voice, one in her head which was saying, I'm not dead yet. She revelled in the sudden defiance of the phrase as she repeated it to herself, over and over. I am not dead yet. I am not dead yet. I am so not dead yet. She tried, successfully, to move the damaged leg. Although she couldn't look down to her knee, she believed the pain was caused by the impact when she hit the ground. She was certain she hadn't been wounded by gunfire. Invigorated by the discovery, she also suspected that she could now free herself from Trevor's hold if she jerked her arm away from him hard enough. His hand would have been weakened by the attempts she had already made. That meant she could escape. The problem was she didn't know which way to go.

If she tried to run down the street towards the police cars and the mobile control unit parked in front of the church, Trevor could shoot her before she made it. Even if she tried to shelter in a doorway Trevor might still come after her. Bobby could hope that the police marksmen might get Trevor before he was able to fire, but they had already missed once. And then, of course, there was the chance the police might mistake her for a hostage-taker. What's more she didn't know what her escape would mean for the other hostages. She did not want Stevie and Sheffield to suffer for her foolishness. At least if she made it back to the restaurant, she was returning to a situation she understood. She looked around. She was lying a short distance from the kerb. The entrance was six feet further on, and a few feet after that were the stairs down to the kitchen. It was, she thought to herself, the safest option, if also the stupidest.

She muttered 'Give me strength' under her breath, yanked her arm from Trevor's grip and rolled back towards the pavement as fast as she could.

*

'They're shooting at her.' Sheffield shouted, pointing at the screen, like nobody had noticed.

Connaston shook his head. 'I think you will find they are trying to free her.'

'They're trying to get her killed.' The television camera was panning wildly from side to side, as if there might be more to see out there, but already it was clear that both Bobby and Trevor were moving and unharmed. Kingston was standing behind Sheffield. He leaned forward and spoke gently to him. 'It's all right, mate. She's not hurt. Look! Her head's up.' Sheffield turned to him with a mixture of disgust and outrage on his face, but said nothing.

The phone began ringing. Nathan answered it. 'Why are you shooting?' He leaned over the work surface, supporting his head on one hand.

Willy said slowly. 'It's not us.'

Nathan waved furiously in the direction of the television, like Willy could see the gesture. 'I saw the bullet hit the road.'

'I saw it too, but it's not us.'

'I've got hostages down here.'

'I know that, Freddie. We're trying to work out what happened, but we specifically told our men not to shoot.'

'Somebody fired.'

'We're looking into it right now –'

Sheffield shouted, 'She's coming back in,' and he turned and ran towards the swing doors. He reached them just as Bobby came through, shoulder first as she tumbled down the stairs. The chef rolled to a stop on her side, knees up to her chest, gasping for air and coughing. Sheffield leaned down, put a hand on her shoulder and said 'You OK?'

Bobby took a series of deep breaths, looked up and nodded vigorously, like a runner who had just finished a sprint and had nothing left to give.

Over by the television it was Connaston's turn to shout. 'Your pal's on his way back in too.'

Nathan dropped the phone and made it to the door in two steps. By the time Trevor came through the door, Nathan had his gun drawn. It was pointed at the other man's head.

37

Trevor drew his own gun and pointed it back at Nathan. They stood facing each other, arms at full stretch.

With his free hand Trevor took off his mask. His face was red and creased and sweat ran down the valleys of his scar. He was smiling and Nathan knew he was enjoying himself. In Brixton he had earned his reputation for violence by displaying endless enthusiasm for the mechanics of it. Once, outside a pub, Nathan had seen him kick a man in the head until the victim was reduced to a bloody pulp on the pavement and there had been a rhythm to the stamps and wild boot-swings which made it look like an overcooked dance. When he was finished, he stood beside the man, panting and grinning. He seemed spent.

The tip of Trevor's tongue now appeared over his lip. The two men stared down the barrels of each other's weapons.

Connaston said, 'Well, that's one way to finish this thing.' Trevor shifted his aim to the Tory Party Treasurer and then back to Nathan. His smile didn't waver. He was a man with too many options. At their feet they could hear Bobby, breathing hard.

Nathan said, 'He's got a point,' and slowly lowered his pistol. He waited for the other man to reciprocate. Instead, Trevor shifted his aim to the chef. Bobby pushed herself backwards across the floor, like a crab trying to escape the tide and cowered, white with fear, against the kitchen cabinets.

'If the police hear a gunshot they'll have to respond,' Nathan said. Trevor kept his aim. He looked relaxed. He said nothing.

'Now is not the time for this.' Nathan wanted to sound like he had a strategy. Trevor glanced at the place by the door where he had assembled his collection of knives and chose one with a long, heavy handle. He shoved the gun back in his waistband and squatted down to dig the tip of the blade into Bobby's neck, one knee on her chest. She reached up automatically and grabbed the lapels of her jacket, pulling them together to cover herself. Trevor stared up at Nathan with an expression which said 'Now what are you going to do?' Behind him Kingston was slowly backing off and silently urging the other hostages to come with him.

'You've never done time,' Trevor said. Nathan nodded. He had avoided prison. Bobby lay stiff between them, watching. Only her eyes moved.

'I don't intend to go there either,' Nathan said.

'The first time's all right,' Trevor said. 'After that it shrinks your head.'

'I understand.'

'No, you don't. It makes your brains feel hot.' He smashed the side of his skull with his free hand, curled into a tight fist. 'I won't go there again.'

'It won't happen.'

'I'm dead if I go in again. So—' He jabbed the tip of his knife harder against Bobby's throat and she flinched.

From further back in the kitchen Grey Thomas called out, 'Leave her alone, you bastard.' His voice was high and thin and he sounded hysterical. Trevor got up and turned to face him. He grabbed the restaurant critic and forced him to the floor where he straddled him so that Nathan could no longer see what was happening. He heard Thomas scream and, stepping over Bobby, pulled his gun again. Trevor turned around, smiling gleefully. In his hand was a thick clump of the other man's hair. The restaurant critic curled up on the floor into a foetal position, a hand pressed flat against his cheek. Blood oozed out between his tightly closed fingers and dribbled down his arm on to the white of his chef's jacket. On one side his hair was now cropped close to the skull. On the other it was heavy and shoulder-length. He was sobbing.

Trevor grinned proudly. Behind him, Kingston grabbed the restaurant critic by the collar of his jacket and dragged him bodily across the room and out through the doorway to the other half of the basement into which the rest of the hostages had retreated. Bobby followed, crawling on all fours around the side of the central stove.

Trevor and Nathan faced each other.

Nathan still had his gun pointed at his accomplice, but he knew the other man didn't care. He could see the amusement in his eyes. He knew that Nathan would not shoot him and, in that moment, Nathan understood that everything had changed. He was no longer negotiating only with the police. He would now have to agree terms with Trevor as well, and they would be far less predictable.

'A dead hostage won't make the situation any easier,' he said. He explained this quickly, as if the news had a use-by date. He said he had developed a relationship with the police, that they wanted to see the safe release of their hostages more than they wanted to arrest the two of them. He explained that the cooking talk was just a way to find common ground.

After a few moments he realized that Trevor was listening to him, or at least that he was distracted; the mound of hair was still in his hand, but his fist was no longer raised. Nathan told Trevor quietly that it had been smart of him to take a politician and a judge prisoner, but he had to work his tongue hard to form the words because his mouth was so dry. The other man nodded suspiciously. Nathan leaned in towards him and, in a whisper, congratulated him on having shown the police that the two of them were serious. He said that if Trevor hadn't done it, he would have suggested they do something similar to get their attention. 'It was a smart move, actually.'

Warily, Trevor said, 'Yeah, it was.'

'When we need to do it again, I'll tell you.'

He offered to get some more cigarettes sent in, and Trevor asked for John Player Specials. Slowly Nathan backed off towards the doorway to the room where the hostages were waiting. 'I'm just going to check on them,' he said. Trevor did not move.

When Bobby reached the wine racks she slumped back down on to the floor, her back against a pillar, and took a deep breath, desperate to hold back the tears she felt she deserved. She turned to look away from the others, most of whom were huddled beneath the glass bricks of the skylight set into the pavement, so they wouldn't witness her distress. They were trying to catch a glimpse of the sun they had not seen for two days, and the fragile wash of light against their upturned faces illuminated their pallor. It was all right for them, she thought to herself. They had a shared fear. They were united by their experience. She was alone with hers, the only woman, not just hostage but prey too. She took a deep breath and closed her eyes and thought about other times when life had seemed bleak. She thought about how she had got through those times – when her parents divorced or when she lived in misery in Paris – by actively living in the moment. She had always made sure to find a distraction. As long as she made sure that there was something in each day which brought a little light into the darkness she could get by. That was what she had to do now, she decided. She had to think only about the present and keep finding things to occupy it.

Bobby looked across at Grey Thomas, who was also sitting on the floor, a hand pressed against his cheek. The flow of blood was easing but there had been enough to stain his arm. Bobby picked up the first aid kit which was still there from the night before and moved across to tend to him.

She said, 'Thank you for distracting him.'

'You people never understand, do you. What I wrote wasn't personal, you know. It was business.'

She took a swab from the box. 'It felt bloody personal.'

'Perhaps you need a thicker skin.'

She looked down at him, the wad of cotton wool clasped in her fingertips. 'Before you start talking about skin, perhaps we ought to get you in front of a mirror.'

It was only as Nathan arrived by the wine racks that the notion of his responsibility to the others dawned on him. The emotional anarchy he had lived through as a child, when parental governance was abolished, piece by piece, had also freed him from the need to be concerned about anyone else. The only duty of care he had back then was to himself. He had considered it a luxury – the only luxury – of abandonment, and when he had forced his way into the kitchen two nights previously that was the duty he was committed to fulfilling. Now, though, his own security had become intrinsically bound up with the safety of the hostages. If Trevor had put a bullet through Bobby's head, live on television, it would all have been over. He was sure of that. The police would not have stayed outside. Nathan now knew that his ability to escape was dependent on his ability to protect the rest of them from Trevor. He had placed them in this situation.

Bobby was leaning down over Grey Thomas, mopping at his cheek with the cotton wool, which was already stained a deep red from the wound. Nathan admired the way she was starting to reassert her authority back here. He appreciated her determination.

She glanced up at him over her shoulder. 'Looks worse than it is,' she said, sounding irritated by the work she was having to do. 'The blade didn't go deep.'

'It still hurts,' Thomas said.

'Don't speak,' Bobby said. 'It stretches your skin and opens the cut.' Slowly she applied a dressing to the wound and fixed it in place with surgical tape.

Sheffield was sitting on the floor, looking up. 'Any chance we'll get out of this alive?' he said sarcastically to Nathan.

Bobby stood up and began wiping the critic's blood off her hands with tissues. 'Leave it, Sheffield,' she said, 'We should be thanking him.'

The other hostages looked at her with a mixture of bafflement and anger. Bobby shrugged. 'He protected me,' she said. 'He protected you as well.' She too understood that a change had taken place, that Nathan was no longer the source of danger in this kitchen; that the real threat lay elsewhere, beyond the doorway.

Sheffield was unimpressed. 'Can you keep on protecting us?' he said sourly.

'Yeah,' said Stevie. 'We've enjoyed what you've done for us so far. It's been a gas.'

'Though if you could keep us alive for, say, an hour or two more that would be grand too,' added Sheffield.

'I'm doing my best,' Nathan said.

There was a commitment in Nathan's voice, and a sadness, which surprised the cooks and though their mouths were open to reply they stayed silent.

Bobby said, 'Where is he?'

'Back there, over the other side of the stove.'

She turned to look through the doorway, fifteen feet away. As she did so, her nose twitched. She sniffed the air. Now they could all smell it: something dense and acrid, a stench so powerful and human they could taste it, and in turn they gagged, and covered their mouths and noses with a flattened palm to keep whatever it was at bay, if only for a few seconds.

Slowly Nathan went back to the doorway and looked into the kitchen. Trevor was standing over the stove, watching a plume of smoke rise up from the solid top. He closed his eyes and his nostril twitched as he sniffed. He lifted his hand up and now Nathan could see the large clump of the restaurant critic's hair that he was holding. He dropped lumps of the hair on to the solid top where it fizzed and released another plume of foul-smelling smoke.

'What are you doing, Trevor?'

The other man didn't look up. 'I'm cooking,' he said. 'Just like you.' His voice was cold and unmodulated. He threw some more strands of hair on to the hot metal, and stared at the effect. Nathan watched him for a moment before returning to the others to tell them what was going on.

Bobby looked appalled. 'We can't just stay out here, hiding from him,' she said.

'I think he's settling down,' Nathan said, embarrassed by his responsibility for the situation.

Bobby looked around the basement, at the battered wooden cupboards where the linen was stored and at the metal staff lockers. She turned to Guthrie and said, 'I don't suppose we can take him?' The judge squinted as though mentally reviewing the notion for viability. 'There have been enough heroics for today,' he said. Connaston opened his mouth to speak but Guthrie silenced him with a deliberate shake of the head.

Bobby shoved the bloodied cotton wool into one of the black rubbish bags that were stacked by the lockers. 'Then we might as well put the rum babas in the oven,' she said. She looked down at the restaurant critic. 'And you need to clean up the mess you made on the floor.' She walked back towards her kitchen.

38

A few minutes after Trevor had retreated into the Oyster House, Commander Peterson ordered the withdrawal from duty of the firearms officers on the Jermyn Street side of the building. When the six men arrived back in the church, they were asked to hand over their weapons and ammunition so it could be checked against the inventory they had signed for earlier that morning. The Weapons Issuing Officer had soothing words for his men, who took exception to Peterson's refusal to believe that one of them hadn't fired the shot. To one side of the church, ballistics experts, wearing loose knotted ties over unbuttoned collars, sat in front of a television monitor watching poor quality video footage of the moment it had been fired. The recording had been obtained from the BBC in return for the promise of interviews with senior officers, but the deal was wasted. The experts could confirm only what was already known: that the shot could not have been fired by the gunman because his weapon was pointing in a different direction at the moment the impact hit the road and that, from the direction the dust had flown, it had to have come from somewhere on the northern side of Jermyn Street.

This only intensified speculation that one of the SO19 officers had been responsible, and when the Weapons Issuing Officer reported that all rounds of ammunition had been accounted for, Peterson told Willy Cosgrave to have the four men searched.

'With all due respect, sir, that won't be popular.'

'I'm not here to be bloody popular.'

Willy noted his commanding officer's enthusiasm for investigating his own men, which was greater than the interest he had so far displayed in the complex detail of running the police operation. The men were strip-searched behind canvas screens set up in the corners of the church while their colleagues sat in the pews, watching in sullen silence for the men to be exonerated. They were found to be carrying no other weapons, nor to have any other rounds of ammunition that were unaccounted for.

Towards the end of the morning ballistics suggested a search of the street. Other officers argued that, on the strength of that morning's events, they would be placing men in great danger by asking them to examine the pavement outside the restaurant on their hands and knees, but Peterson overruled them. Two armed officers took up positions on either side of the entrance to the Oyster House, assault rifles raised to their shoulders, while three more, in black jumpsuits and bullet-proof vests, conducted a fingertip search of the road and the pavement. It was twenty minutes before one of the men sat up and raised his hand into the air, holding something that, from the safety of the control unit, appeared to shine in the early summer sunshine.

The thumbs-length of copper-coloured missile was delivered to Peterson in a small, self-sealing plastic bag. He held the bag up so that it dangled between his fingertips and asked his ballistics expert to identify it.

'It's a 303, sir. Kind of thing you'd use for country sports. A classic deer hunter's round, sir.'

Peterson dropped the bag on to his desk, and turned to another of his men. 'Where's the restaurant's owner?'

'I sent two of my boys down to fetch him from his home address this morning for help with intelligence.'

'And?'

'He wasn't there, sir.'

'Do we know where he is now?'

'No, sir.'

Peterson looked out over Jermyn Street. 'Well, I think we've got a bloody good idea where he's been, haven't we.'

39

Marcus Caster-Johns was eight years old when he killed for the first time, and the thrill of seeing the defeated cock pheasant fold in on itself and drop to the scrub never left him. The bird was deposited at his feet by one of his father's dogs. It was the casual manner in which the animal sauntered off, tail aloft, as if it were entirely normal for small boys to bring down game like this, which made him feel most keenly that he had joined an unacknowledged club. If the dog accepted it, then it had to be so.

The only disappointment was that when the pheasant lay on the ground with its long iridescent neck bent shyly over itself it was so dead that Marcus found it hard to imagine it had ever been alive. To understand his new-found power he wanted to witness that moment of death, and to know it was his shot which had been responsible. Sometimes, when he was out shooting with his father, he tried to take the birds when they were directly overhead. He hoped that, by being closer to his target, he would see more clearly the instant he was searching for. But he found the shots harder to make and because the control of his weapon was less assured when he lifted it so high he was scolded by his father for being reckless.

His grandmother, who wore her grey hair long and kept her 'retired' jewels in a box of sweet-smelling cedar, once owned a villa on the island of Capri. Eventually she became too frail to live there by herself and moved instead to the cold and damp of the house below the moor in Northumbria, where she complained about the pains in her joints. Often, when they were alone, she told Marcus stories about Capri, and just talking of the island seemed to warm her from the inside. Her villa was by the sea on the western side of the island, and played audience to sunsets which every evening doggedly repainted the sky. The locals told her that this part of the shore was the only place on Capri where it was possible to witness the green flash, as the falling edge of the sun sunk below the horizon and was dissipated through the water's surface.

'Many evenings I stood on the beach trying to see the green flash,' she said to Marcus, 'but it never presented itself to me. I still believe in it, of course. One does not have to see to know.' Marcus wanted to say: I understand because I too have a green flash, and I too know it must be there to be seen, because an animal cannot go from life to death without the occasion having a place in time to itself. Like so many of these big houses, there were animal heads on the walls: glassy eyed antelope, mouths slack with surprise at their view of the antiques; a ragged and crumbling lion, with yellow teeth and a grey, inflated tongue. Marcus liked to stare at them and imagine the moment when the hunter's bullet extinguished the fire inside.

With time he was allowed to hunt different species and approached the opportunity to take down a deer with great anticipation, because it meant using a telescopic sight which magnified everything. With practice he claimed a number of large animals from the estate but he found the experience more frustrating than shooting pheasant or grouse. The lens did offer magnification, but it also created a separation between himself and his prey. And then, when the shot was fired, the rifle would buck in his hands and, however hard he tried to hold on, he would lose control of the instant. Once, he volunteered to go with the estate manager to the slaughterhouse, where three of the family's pigs were to be dispatched, but he was appalled by the smell and the industrialization of the process. It was clear to him, from the way the pigs turned their heads down, and moaned from deep inside their throats, that they became anxious when incarcerated in the crates used to hold them while the fatal bolt was applied to the head. Marcus suspected they knew that death was imminent and he found something unappealing about the notion. A good death, he decided, should be unexpected.

At first, when he was at university in Leeds, he tried to discard his interest in hunting, but it came to him again early in his second year when he was out walking on the high Yorkshire moors. He saw rabbits shooting up from their burrows and back again, and wished there was more in his hands than just a map and a compass, so he could be an active part of the landscape rather than merely an observer of it. He studied philosophy and became absorbed by the writings of Thomas Hobbes, though he was drawn less to Hobbes' solutions to a brutal world than the idea of the brutal world itself. He decided this was because, by learning how to shoot at an early age, he had been closer to that brutal world than many of the city-dwelling students around him. It made much more sense to him than the silly social games people played with each other in the student bars and from which so often he felt excluded. He found it hard to tell the sort of jokes the girls liked to laugh at. The other men regarded him as a curiosity, and mocked his anachronistic interests in the world of field and game shooting. He was rarely invited to parties and would drink on his own in the city's pubs.

Instead, he liked to imagine himself as powerful within his own world. Once, he managed to take to his bed a girl from his course who was as shy as he was ridiculed, the two of them equally marginalized from the rest of the student herd, and he let his hand slip to cover her mouth and her nose as she lay beneath him. He became further aroused by the sudden thought that he might now be able to match the moment of climax to the moment of her extinction, and to be inside her when it happened. He pressed down harder with his hand until she squealed and bit him and drew blood. She pushed him off and ran from the room and the house. That night, alone in his bed and still unsatisfied, he fantasized about the moment, and imagined the bed lit up by its own flash as deep and as green as the sea at sunset, until his crowded mind alighted at last upon silence. It became in time his chosen fantasy, the one he struggled to reach when sleep proved elusive.

The inheritance of the restaurant gave to Marcus a new kind of power. He felt at last that he had a place in the world that was his own, and not one defined by his relationship to others. And so, when the Oyster House was taken from him by the gunmen, the incident ignited within him an ancient fury. He felt as if his whole purpose had been stolen from him, and that he would only again find peace if he took back what was his. He understood within minutes of hearing the news what this might require of him, and he felt both calm about it and excited by the idea. He was certain his actions would carry within them a clear logic and justification, of the sort that Thomas Hobbes would have understood, and regarded the possibility that he might at last be able to witness the moment of death which he had pursued all his life as a happy by-product.

Standing with his back to the wall, so he could not be seen from the street, he looked down from the open window at the police searching the area outside the restaurant. He was disappointed in himself at having missed the man in the mask, but he had been exhilarated by the process and he was certain there would be another opportunity. Behind him the floor was covered with empty tins of stew and fruit salad in syrup which he had forked cold straight from the can, and deflated plastic bags which had once been filled with white bread that he had either eaten or shared with the pigeons. His supplies of food were dwindling fast, but he was sure he could survive up here for a few days more. Two of the bottles of whisky were gone, but there was at least three quarters left in the third. He poured himself a double thumbs' depth, which he drank in one go. Then he picked up his rifle and with his mind replaying the moment when he had fired the shot, set to oiling it.

40

In the early afternoon Peterson called a meeting of senior officers in the front corner of the church, close to the pulpit. At first they discussed the search for Caster-Johns, and Willy Cosgrave drifted away into mourning for the lunch just gone. Willy hated wasting meals and, as he thought about the slices of waxy cheese caught between two margarine-smeared pieces of furniture-foam white bread it occurred to him that too many of the meals he ate as a policeman were missed opportunities. If he had been at home, it would have been the best, crumbly cheddar with a high acidic end, sliced thick and layered on nutty granary bread with some of his home-made chutney, better still dressed with Dijon mustard and toasted under the grill. He might have made himself scrambled eggs, with single cream and a couple of extra yolks separated from their whites to add richness, and cooked off in foaming salted butter from Brittany. These things did not take effort, he thought to himself. No more effort than making those cheese sandwiches which had been an insult to him at lunchtime. They just needed care, and a dedication to good ingredients. And then he imagined himself out shopping, at Lidgate's, the quality butchers in Holland Park that he liked to visit when he had a bit of spare cash, or even in the cheese shop just behind him on Jermyn Street.

He tuned back into the conversation when he heard his name mentioned but only then because the commander was praising him.

'Cosgrave has done a great job, I think we can all agree.' Willy turned to look at Denis Thompson, who was sitting a few feet away from him on the same pew, but the negotiator was refusing to meet his gaze, and doing so with such intense concentration that Willy knew immediately he was being stood down from the job. He felt not angry, but empty.

The conversation had already moved on. When the siege began the decision was taken to leave the electricity supply connected, partly because the gunmen and their hostages were caught in a basement with little access to natural light, and partly because it gave them the opportunity to watch television. Thompson had argued that it would be better for everybody involved to be able to see the scale of the police operation being mounted around them: reassuring for the hostages and intimidating for the gunmen. That situation had continued unchanged for two days. Now, in light of the events that morning, a more hardline approach was necessary, Peterson said. The power would go off. Conditions would become unpleasant. Thompson would resume negotiating duties.

As the meeting came to an end, Peterson was handed a sheaf of papers. He studied the memos in his hand and, without looking up, said, 'You are relieved, sergeant.' Around him officers returned to their duties, until Willy was sitting alone in the pews staring at the ornately carved reredos by Grinling Gibbons behind the altar. He wondered whether he might look like he was praying for deliverance, and hated the thought that he would appear defeated, though he knew he was. He put on his coat and left the church by the north lobby. For a minute he stood in the flagstoned courtyard that led on to Piccadilly and considered his options. He could go home now to his wife and his kids, and begin his penance, but he didn't want to do that yet. Instead he thought he could make amends for the appalling lunch just gone, by eating lunch all over again in one of the restaurants in Soho. He didn't want anything grand. He wanted comfort food, a meal that would make him feel the day wasn't entirely wasted. He walked along to the electric billboard clutter of Piccadilly Circus, past the enormous burger joint on its northern flank, and turned up Shaftesbury Avenue. To one side was Chinatown and he considered getting dim sum but dismissed the idea because standards were so patchy on Gerrard Street. Instead he made for Jimmy's, the Greek place in Soho, which always did a decent kleftiko, but when he reached the doorway that led down to the basement he decided it wasn't what he fancied after all. He carried on up Dean Street. He thought about stopping off for a Margherita at Pizza Express, but changed his mind and realized he didn't want a bowl of pasta at the trattoria on Old Compton Street either. He walked in long, striding steps around the narrow streets of Soho, ignoring the neon-gilded sex shops and the hostess clubs, and the undressed women lurking in their doorways, trying to drum up trade from the parade of desperation passing before them.

Willy had other appetites. He moved from the location of one restaurant to another, rejecting each one as he came close to it, and choosing to push on to the next, being sure that it would be exactly the place for the sort of thing he needed today. At times he walked in circles.

Eventually he found himself in the fenced garden in the middle of Soho Square, sitting on one of the benches that looked inwards at the small mock-Tudor hut that stands at its centre. The problem, he concluded, was not the choice of food, but the company he would be sharing it with: his own. He did not want to be eating by himself, not while the hostages were going hungry. Not when Freddie was going hungry too. He didn't think it would be good for a man like Freddie, who understood the imperatives of good food, to be left without enough to eat. When the siege began he hadn't wanted the responsibility for negotiating its conclusion. But now the mere thought that he might be eating while those in the Oyster House remained unfed filled him with what he recognized as a father's guilt. He didn't need to send them in the ingredients for a daube or a cassoulet, or anything else grand and complicated. He wanted them to be eating the sort of comfort food that he wanted for himself right now.

Then it occurred to him that he might have stumbled upon the way to edge the siege towards a conclusion. Perhaps he had been sending them the ingredients for the wrong sort of dishes, ones which were too complex and diverting. Denis Thompson had been correct that food was the man's comfort zone. But those dishes might actually have made Freddie too comfortable. He imagined the man could stay down there for weeks if he was kept supplied with the ingredients for intriguing enough cookery. While he was making coq au vin he could bide his time; it was those on the outside who would get frustrated.

So yes, Peterson was right, a new approach was necessary, but still one involving food. For what better way would there be to remind the gunmen of the depth of their predicament than the sort of comfort food they might associate with home? And once they were eating that food, they would instantly dream of their bed. They would dream about being anywhere other than where they were because, as far as Willy Cosgrave was concerned, there was no greater encouragement to sentimentality than flavour. Every great memory he had, every feeling of childhood security, or fondness for his parents and his siblings and his wife and his children, was associated with a particular taste: the cream of tomato soup that his mother had made from scratch, the toffee apples that he had eaten with his brothers and sister at the fair in Frinton when they were kids, the spaghetti bolognese he had cooked for Marion the first time she came to his flat for dinner, the cheese on toast he made for the children on Sunday nights: these were the signposts of memory. He needed to provide Freddie with something which would have the same effect.

With renewed purpose he walked back down to Old Compton Street and stood looking in the window of I Camisa, the great Italian deli on the corner, at the handmade wild boar ravioli, and the strands of egg yellow pasta, and the chunks of fresh parmesan, their cut sides as crumbly as a sandstone cliff. He wasn't convinced it was the right place for his purpose, though. If Italian food was too good it stopped being comfort food because it was unfamiliar. He looked in the window of the butchers on Berwick Street and wondered about sausages and mash, but he was concerned about the choice of sausage. Once a certain quality threshold had been passed – the use of real minced pork rather than mechanically recovered slush – what defined a great sausage was, he knew, a matter of taste. Some people liked a whack of garlic. Others liked handfuls of herbs. Some thought anything but minced belly and loin of pork was an aberration. He abandoned that idea and wandered instead among the fish stalls on Brewer Street market, and looked at the fruit and vegetable stands, with their fine displays of courgettes and red onions, but found nothing there which inspired him.

He became despondent and decided that his great idea was perhaps not so great after all, and traced his steps back towards the church of St James's. He would collect his belongings and head home to Marion and her hurt and disappointment, and try to win her round with a soufflé of some sort. He was not sure she particularly liked soufflés but he knew she understood the effort they required.

He was outside the gates to the church courtyard when he noticed the classical frontage of Fortnum's. He rarely visited the shop because it sat uneasily, in his mind, in that uncomfortable place between tourist trap and ludicrous aristocratic extravagance. Only the very wealthy or the out-of-towner went there to buy their groceries. Still, it was the nearest thing to a supermarket that he was going to find here in the centre of town. He allowed himself to be wafted into the shop through the swing doors, past the assistants in their tail-coats, and walked with soundless tread across the red, wool-thick carpets to the shelves. He ignored the stacks of novelty, Fortnum's-branded teas, in their familiar livery of turquoise and italicized black and made to the back shelves where the more everyday ingredients were stocked, the marmalades and Marmites, digestive biscuits and Oxo stock cubes that even those with titles could not do without. Many things looked eatable. He had never met a chocolate-covered digestive he did not like, for example, and he was very fond of custard creams. But none of it would help make the point he was after. Until he came around into the aisle of canned foods, and realized that he had found exactly the thing for which he had been searching all afternoon.

41

Willy knew that, shortly after 4 p.m., the shifts would change. As the SO19 marksmen came back into the church, Peterson, Thomson and the other senior officers would also leave the mobile control unit for a short debrief. During that period the command unit parked on Jermyn Street would be minded by a young PC, who would only be required to raise the alarm if the phone rang. The senior officers were likely to be away for just ten minutes but Willy was sure that was all the time he needed. He no longer questioned the propriety of what he was about to do. In his own mind he had been stripped of responsibility to his commanding officer. And yet, with great neglect, Peterson had left him with an emotional responsibility to those in the Oyster House. He knew instinctively the risk he was taking, but he surprised himself by how little he cared any more. Years of humiliation by Peterson had led him to this point: those days spent running his errands, those late afternoon lectures on the essence of good police work, the jokes at his expense in front of others. He thanked the commander for this. Willy Cosgrave felt he now understood what was important to him better than he had in years.

He waited in the wood-panelled gloom of the central antechamber outside the church doors and, when he saw Peterson approaching, picked up the cardboard box and headed towards him and the doorway out through the south lobby to Jermyn Street.

Peterson frowned at him as he passed. 'Haven't you gone home yet, sergeant?'

Willy nodded at the box in his arms. 'Got a couple of other things to collect from the command unit, sir.'

'Get on with it then.' The commander moved on through to the church, his officers trailing behind him, like so many eager ducklings behind their mother.

Willy moved quickly. Sitting alone at a desk in the mobile command unit, staring at staff rotas, was a young PC he knew slightly. The officer looked up in surprise. 'Thought you'd gone.'

'Change of plan. Here, take this box. Go put it in the dumb waiter over the road.'

The policeman turned and looked out of the window at the Oyster House. Willy could see where the hair at the nape of his neck had been razored to a light fur that stood up.

'In there?'

'Commander's orders. Take it.'

The policeman took the box, and grunted with surprise at its weight. When he had gone, Willy picked up the phone and listened to the ringing tone. He muttered, 'Come on, come on,' and watched the box's journey into the Oyster House. After three rings there was a clatter from the other end of the line, which sounded like the handset being fumbled.

'Freddie?'

'You've turned off the bloody electrics.'

'Not me,' he said quickly. 'There have been a few changes over here since the fun and games this morning.'

'We're having to do everything by candlelight.'

'I'm sending in a box of stuff, something that might make you feel a bit better. The cigarettes you wanted are in there too.' The PC had just come out of the restaurant and was running back across the street, as though fearing he was a target. Willy watched him sprint past the mobile unit and back into the church.

'You don't sound yourself, Willy.'

'The box is in there now. You don't need power to bring it down, do you?'

'No, we don't. What's going on?'

'I'm off the case.'

'You can't be off the case. You're the one I'm negotiating with.'

'They have other plans now, and there's not much I can do about it. Look, I've got to go. Enjoy what's in the box. I think it's the kind of thing you need right now.'

'You can't do this to me.'

'I'm not doing anything to you, Freddie. I'm just—'

Behind him, Willy heard a click as the door opened. He closed his eyes. 'I've got to go now, Freddie,' he said slowly. Very deliberately, and without waiting for Nathan to answer, he replaced the receiver, and turned to face Commander Peterson, who was standing in the doorway.

42

Bobby cupped the guttering candle flame to protect it from a down-draught of air pushed into the kitchen by the descent of the dumb waiter, while Sheffield took the box out and placed it in front of her. She opened the lid and carefully lifted the candle inside so that a butter-yellow glow illuminated her chin. It lit her smile and then, when she threw back her head and laughed, the long smooth stretch of her pale neck. She picked up a tin and held the candle next to it, so that everybody could make out the familiar blue label.

'My friends,' she said, in a cod French accent. 'For your dinner tonight may I propose to you baked beans –' She dropped the can back into the box and picked up a plastic bag of white sliced bread. '– on toast.'

'Heinz?' Guthrie said.

'Mais bien sur, mon ami,' she replied with an exaggerated Gallic shrug, that indicated anything else would be against nature.

The mood in the darkened, powerless kitchen lifted after that. They found the gas was still connected and lit the burners with scraps of kitchen paper ignited on the candles. The paper burned quickly and soon had to be stamped out to ash on the floor but, as they couldn't see the floor any more nobody cared. Stevie grated up cheese for those who wanted it, from a block of aged Gruyère he found warming in the dead fridge, and Nathan made toast under the eye-level grill. The smell reminded him of Dalberg Road, where white toast with jam was the default choice for breakfast when nothing else was available.

Soon everybody was standing around the stove, eating over strategically placed candles that dropped miniature campfires of light. Beside them mugs of Kingston's latest brew steamed gently against the glow of the candles. Only Trevor stayed on the floor by the door, his presence in the darkness picked out by a berry of burning red at the end of the cigarettes he was now chain-smoking. For the moment Bobby appreciated his chain-smoking habit. It meant she knew where he was.

Connaston attacked his plateful with enthusiasm. 'Now this,' he said, 'is my kind of food.' He pointed with his fork at his sauce-drenched toast.

'Thought you'd be more the smoked salmon and caviar type,' Nathan said.

Connaston smiled at his plate. 'Caviar is something you eat to make a point. Beans on toast is what you eat when you're hungry.'

'It's what *I* eat when I'm hungry,' Nathan said.

'It's interesting what we have in common, isn't it?'

'I don't think you and me have much in common.'

'No?' Connaston scooped up some more of his beans. 'Whatever you say.'

'Go on then, tell me: what makes you and me the same?'

Connaston looked away over Nathan's head, searching the darkness for the right word. 'Not the same exactly,' he said. 'It's more about a shared world-view.' He looked back at him. 'Aspiration,' he said, victoriously. 'That's what links us. I'm all for it, and you're pursuing it.'

Nathan was unsteadied by the other man's certainty. 'You think I'm so simple that one word will do the job?'

'Why did you try to rob the jewellery shop?'

Nathan hesitated. A series of unspoken answers jostled each other.

'You did the jewellery shop job because you wanted money, and presumably you wanted money to make a better life for yourself.' Connaston punctuated his words with mouthfuls of beans and toast.

'You aspire to something better than you already have, and you decided that, rather than expect others to get it for you, you would do whatever it took to get it for yourself. It's pure Thatcherism, my friend – only without the interest in law and order.'

'I'm no fan of Thatcher.'

'I'll take your word for it. You're the chap with the gun after all.' He drew patterns with the tines of his fork in the slick of sauce left on his plate. 'You know, Heinz baked beans really are the bloody best, aren't they? Nothing else like them. Is there any more?' He held his plate towards Bobby, who scooped out a few spoonfuls, before handing out seconds to Kingston and her cooks. The four of them discussed the vital importance of certain brands over others: that it had to be Coke over Pepsi or Hellmann's mayonnaise over some supermarket's sloppy own brand and, watching Kingston banter so easily with the cooks, Nathan suddenly felt excluded from the conversation by his friend.

'It wasn't just for the money,' Nathan said, interrupting. His dining companions looked at him. Kingston stared unhappily at the floor. 'I mean, there was more to it than that. I was trying to teach someone a lesson.' He bowed his head to his plate, as though he wished he hadn't spoken, because the explanation he was prepared to give would never be sufficient. 'It's complicated,' he said to the stove top.

Guthrie said, 'In my experience crime often is.'

Nathan placed his fork on his plate and walked away into the darkness.

Bobby found him a few minutes later sitting down by the wine racks, the hard geometry of his jaw and his buzz-cut hair caught by the smudged light from above. She sat down next to him, and looked back towards the doorway through which she had just come. Somewhere in there, shielded by the darkness, Trevor was sitting on the floor, the red-hot tip of his cigarette floating in the black air, an insect waiting to strike. The air smelt now of his tobacco, and of sweat, and each time she inhaled she thought of the man and his scar, and of the violence that had caused it. She thought of Trevor now as the embodiment of menace, of threat, but increasingly Nathan had become the man who could protect her from it. She pictured Nathan again with his gun drawn and his arm outstretched, only now the trigger was pulled and Trevor was gone and it was all over.

She breathed in again and the image faded; alongside the stench of cigarettes and unwashed people was another, that of decay from the rubbish that hadn't been removed for nearly three days. The bags were being stored next to the toilet and occasionally the smell wafted towards them. They both sniffed the air.

'It's only going to get worse,' Bobby said. 'There's still quite a lot of stuff in the fridges.' Nathan said nothing.

Bobby stretched her legs out in front of her and flexed her feet. 'Have you thought about giving up?' She said it quietly, as though she were counselling a girlfriend to leave an abusive partner.

'It has occurred to me, yes.'

'If you gave yourself up, I'm sure they would be lenient.'

'Life has never been lenient with me before. I can't see why it should start now.'

'Ah, the authentic sound of self-pity.'

'Believe me, I know more than most people about grounds for self-pity. This isn't self-pity. It's realism.'

'You could pick up a skill on the inside.'

He looked at her. 'What sort of skill?'

'Prisons have kitchens.'

'They don't make Wiener Holstein, though, do they?'

'Probably not.'

Nathan ran his hand over his head. 'Thing is, I don't think what happens next is up to me any more.' He understood the importance of what he was saying, but the darkness of the kitchen lent it the air of a confessional. There was relief in admitting his newfound impotence.

'Trevor?' She said it quietly, as if afraid her voice might rouse him.

'He's got the commitment, hasn't he? At times like this it's commitment that counts.'

'If we all got together— '

'Corner him and he'll do what he needs to do. Remember what he did to your waiter.'

They fell silent at the memory of Mr Andrews fighting for breath, a fork stuck in his sagging gullet.

'We need to get the electrics back on,' Nathan said, and he hoped his statement of the obvious made him sound as if he cared about her welfare.

'It would be a start.'

'Some electricity to run the lights, something good to cook on the stove.'

'You need to get their attention.' She hesitated. 'And you need Trevor to be your friend again.'

'So now you're an expert on hostage situations?'

Bobby leaned towards him and whispered, 'I'm a head chef. My job is to make people do what I want them to do by fucking with the inside of their heads.'

He studied her smile for a moment, and tried to return it, but he was distracted by the idea that had just come to him. He knew exactly what he had to do. He knew it was a terrible betrayal, and he regretted that. In another life, he thought to himself, she was the kind of woman he would have wanted as a friend.

43

When Lucy told Nathan she liked to smoke dope in graveyards, she delivered the news in an urgent whisper, her breath hot against his cheek. A few weeks after they had met she took him to a small cemetery on the upper slopes of Hampstead Hill, which was reached by an alleyway, though it was nothing like the piss-stained and fractured passages familiar to Nathan. It was cobbled, and lined with small, perfectly maintained cottages whose walls hung with well-mannered ivy, and the lamp-posts were short and black and made to look as if they might still be powered with gas. The graveyard – a narrow rectangle, fenced in by Victorian railings that matched the lamp-posts – had the same, carefully arranged clutter.

Lucy took Nathan by the hand, and led him on a well-trodden mud and gravel path through the graves, on a route she clearly knew well, to a wide low tomb with a headstone carved with a Celtic cross, which could act as a headboard to this double bed of old, cratered Portland stone. They sat side by side on the tomb. She rolled a joint and told him that she and her friends used to smoke here in their lunch breaks, when she was at school just a little further down the hill. Now she was on a year off before university but she still liked to come. 'I would miss all my friends here, otherwise,' she said, and pointed out the graves of poets and Pre-Raphaelite artists and recited the epitaphs that she said she found 'so terribly touching'. 'Plus,' she said, blowing on the tip of the joint, 'no one hassles me here.'

Nathan told her he didn't spend that much time in graveyards because too many of the people he knew were lying in them, and he said it without particular emotion, as if explaining why he preferred tea to coffee, though he knew the impact the information would have. She moved closer to him so he could feel the softness of her hip against him, and asked who these dead people were. As he explained, she stroked the nape of his neck. He could hear her bangles shifting against each other behind him. He talked about it simply, ascribing to each death a cause and a date but little more, and recognizing for the first time that, with the right person, it might make sense to share this story.

'You really are a fascinating man, Nathan James,' Lucy said, and she kissed him ferociously, aroused by this exciting outbreak of tragedy.

Nathan came to Hampstead often that summer, but took the bus up the hill from Camden because he found arriving off the tube straight into the village with its chocolate-box streets too jarring after the urban clutter of Brixton. Lucy always knew of a party that 'might be worth going to' and if it wasn't much fun there was likely to be another one they could try. They were held by people called Rollo or Sophie or Kate, and took place in big, red-brick houses in leafy streets, where women wearing silky dresses with spaghetti-string straps drank Thunderbird from long-stemmed glasses. They never looked tired like so many of the girls he knew in Brixton. Once, Lucy insisted he come with her to a party that started at 5 p.m., and just the timing made it sound exotic. The party was held in a grand stucco house overlooking Regent's Park, where black waiters in beige blazers carried around flutes of champagne on silver trays. Nathan was intrigued to see these black boys and tried to strike up a conversation with one of them, as if he too might be a tourist here, but the waiter looked bemused and answered in stuttering, heavily French-accented English.

'African,' Lucy whispered. 'Everybody's using African waiters this year.' She told him the party was a 'coming out' event for her friend

Alexa, who was 'very glamorous and a complete dopehead, not that you'd think it to look at her'. She sipped her champagne. 'Of course, it's a bit silly really because nobody actually "comes out" any more, do they, as in go to see the Queen and stuff. It's just her eighteenth birthday cocktail party. There's some bigger piss-up next week. We'll have to go.'

At these parties, people already seemed to know a lot about Nathan, and when they talked to him he could feel Lucy standing next to him proudly, as though she was being vindicated by his presence. The attention made him feel exposed. They told him about the gigs they had been to in Brixton, or the old ska collections they owned, and with each conversation Nathan became more and more puzzled by the desperation of these people to be accepted by him. Often they asked him if he could get them a little dope and he would always oblige, mostly because he didn't want to embarrass Lucy. He found their knowledge of him unnerving, but police action seemed so much less likely when the girls were so pretty and the shoes so expensive.

They had been seeing each other for a few months when Lucy told Nathan he should come for lunch one Sunday with her parents. 'They will adore you,' she said, and he took her word for it that this would be a good thing. He arrived at the door of her house with a box of Black Magic chocolates, which her mother Angela held at arms length and purred over with too much enthusiasm. The house was big and old and each lounge had room for two or three sofas. There were saggy, velvet-covered cushions and shelves infested with books and, standing by itself in a bay window, a small grand piano, the colour of conker. There was quiche for lunch, which Nathan had never tried before and which he quickly decided he would never try again because the flan's filling was watery and loose and studded with pale pink pieces of slippery bacon. There was rough, nutty bread and bean salad, and Nathan felt it was all too much hard work. He wondered why the wealthy would bother to eat unpleasant food when they had enough money to afford something so much nicer.

Lucy's father Andrew was tall and wore baggy corduroy trousers and a loose linen shirt, which made him look like he would need to be tethered in a strong wind, for fear of taking flight. Nathan quickly decided the man dressed like this because he wanted to be thought of as open and easy-going, but he understood that beneath the folds of ill-arranged cloth was a permafrost of hard and long-held opinions. He offered Nathan beer and asked him questions about the 'conditions' in Brixton, and nodded gravely at the stories of police action and poor housing which his guest tried to make sound ordinary and unexceptional. Andrew wanted to know about 'the blacks' and whether they were 'still having a tough time of it'. Nathan shrugged and said, 'Isn't everyone having a tough time of it?' and tried to swallow more quiche.

'That's the reality of Thatcher's Britain,' Andrew said, pointing across the table with the tip of his knife, as he chewed back a thick, damp swab of pastry. Nathan agreed, though he wasn't sure it was anything to do with Margaret Thatcher, however much he hated her, because Brixton had always been like this.

Andrew Cranbourne turned to his wife and said, 'Come the revolution –'

'You'll be the first one up against the wall, dear,' she replied. 'Now pass me the plates.' She stood up and began clearing away crockery and repositioning cutlery, of which there seemed to be a lot.

'They'll still need TV producers after the revolution.' Her husband sawed away at a piece of bread. 'Workers of the world unite and all that.'

Nathan slugged back some beer. 'Actually, it's working men of all countries.'

'Sorry?' Lucy's father sounded mildly affronted at Nathan's intervention.

'It's always being misquoted. The proletarians have nothing to lose but their chains. They have a world to win. Working men of all countries unite.' The Cranbornes looked at him, bemused, so he added, 'My granddad was a member of the Communist Party and he made me learn a lot of that stuff off by heart.'

Lucy leaned into the table. 'Nathan's parents were killed in a car crash when he was little,' she said quickly, 'and he was brought up by his grandparents, but they're dead too now.' She sat back in her chair, satisfied that, with this revelation, she had inherited some of Nathan's tragedy and would therefore suddenly have matured in her parents' eyes. Angela Cranbourne rested the large wooden salad bowl that she was holding against her hip. 'How terrible,' she said and, 'Please do have some more quiche.'

Later, in her room at the top of the house, watched by posters of David Bowie and Lou Reed, Nathan asked Lucy not to talk about the death of his parents with others. 'People think they know all about you when they hear stuff like that. It's one of those facts that gets in the way of all the others.'

She had been sitting next to him on the bed and shifted over now to a window seat, draped with a quilt made from hexagons of randomly chosen material. She opened the sash window, lit a joint and sat with her knees pulled up to her chest. She exhaled out of the window and said, 'I've already sussed that there's lots about you nobody will ever know. You won't let them, will you, Nathan James?'

They had sex after that, because Nathan wanted to prove she could know as much about him as she liked, and when they were finished and were lying lazily across each other, Lucy handed him a large manila envelope that had been propped up on her bedside table. He opened it and inside found a series of forms that needed filling out.

'What's this?' He sat up.

'Application to Lambeth College. It arrived in the post yesterday. I sent off for it for you. It's because you're so clever and smart. I thought maybe you would want to do some A levels like me and—'

He dropped the papers on to the bed and stared at her. Her hand went to her mouth. 'Oh God! You think I'm patronizing you.'

On the other side of the room was a bookshelf and on its top shelf, a large dictionary. He went over and stood there naked, thumbing through the book until he found what he was looking for. He closed the book. 'And you aren't?'

'Well, I didn't mean it like that.'

A month later, on the same bench near Marine Ices where they had smoked their first joint together, she asked him if he thought they should stop seeing each other, and he understood from the way she posed the question, that she already had an answer she preferred.

He said, 'Actually I was going to tell you that I'm going to be away a bit over the next few months.'

She smiled and said, 'I'm pleased for you,' as if they had separated long ago and he had now found a new lover. She looked up and down the road, a traveller in search of a bus that might take her away to anywhere but here. That afternoon, heading south across London on the tube, Nathan realized that he had not taken a single decision during his time with Lucy, and felt with regret another kind of London at his back, the door to which was being closed.

44

It was while Peterson was interrogating him that Willy first began wondering about the best way in which to cook his commanding officer. He knew that the literature on human flesh as a food source was scant because of the obvious taboos, but it had occurred to him long ago that it was a meat like any other. He was sure a half-decent cook could quickly reach some sensible conclusions on the best way to prepare it, if they knew enough about how the animal had been reared. Peterson had forced Willy down on to a chair for questioning – 'What was in the box?' and 'Which type of baked beans?' and, more generally, 'What the bloody hell has got into you, man?' – and the sergeant could see, as the commander bent over him, that, while he was lean, he also lacked muscle tone. He offered up as bald a set of answers as possible – 'Baked beans and white bread, sir, for toast; Heinz; I really couldn't say' – and reminded himself that older animals were usually tougher but more flavourful than younger ones.

Unfortunately, there was no guarantee that the commander would have any flavour at all because that was encouraged by exercise and Willy knew Peterson to be a lazy man. His lack of paunch was down to a disdain for food – 'I'd happily eat a pill for lunch if they invented one,' he would say – which was only one of Willy's reasons for hating him.

Eventually, Peterson became exasperated with his staff sergeant and told him to stay seated on the chair by the door while he and Thompson managed the situation. Now granted the status of a non-person, he could study the way the commander's buttock spread like a soft, white loaf when he perched on the corner of a desk to talk to the chief negotiator, which suggested the rump might well boast a reasonable marbling. Although Willy could see the argument for slow roasting, and enjoyed the mental image of Peterson naked and trussed to a spit for seven hours, the lack of solid fat elsewhere made that an unreliable option. (By contrast, he decided, if he were preparing himself for the table, he would favour slow roasting every time, and he let his hands rest on the comforting envelopes of fat around his thighs.) Clearly the best way to go with Peterson, therefore, would be to braise to a tender fibrousness: seal the meat over a high heat, remove from the pan, cook off a few chopped vegetables in the running fat and add a little bacon. Deglaze with wine, then return meat to the pan and add enough stock to reach halfway up the cut, and cook for three to four hours. He wasn't sure which wine to use with someone like Commander Peterson, and remembered Elizabeth David's rule that wine used in cooking should always be geographically appropriate. If it was a good burgundy with a coq au vin, then perhaps wine would not be right with an officer of the Metropolitan Police Service after all, and he wondered how effective a frothy London ale would prove in such a preparation. He knew the commander was partial to London Pride and imagined pouring gallons of it over his seared body, in readiness for the long slow braise. These thoughts distracted him from brooding on the predicament in which he had placed himself, and lent to Peterson the portion of absurdity that Willy believed he had long ago earned.

The phone rang three times while he was sitting there, but Thompson insisted the calls should go unanswered 'to prove we're not at his beck and call any more'. Everybody in the room stood watching the handset until it fell silent again. Through the window Willy could see officers in the distance holding the cordon at either end of Jermyn Street, standing still, arms crossed, feet planted square, lines of tape fluttering behind them. Closer to, he could see the marksmen in their black jumpsuits, so many statues in doorways. And, here in this room, there was an equal form of stillness and silence. It was mid afternoon on a Saturday in June, and at this point in the siege a virtue had been made of inactivity.

Ten minutes later the phone rang again and this time Thompson answered. The rest of the room listened in.

'We want the power back on.'

'It's good to talk to you too, Freddie.'

'And we want to negotiate with Willy.'

'That's the problem. We haven't been negotiating, have we.'

'I've asked for a car.'

'And a quality bit of chicken and the ingredients for a nice pudding. But you haven't given us anything back.'

'What I haven't done is hurt any of the hostages.' The voice was suddenly harsh and sharp. 'That's what you've got out of it.'

'Now then, Freddie, that sort of talk isn't going to get us anywhere, is it?'

'You're not listening to me, are you? I want the power turned on and I want Willy back on the phone.'

'Can't help you there.'

'Or I will start hurting people.'

'You're not that kind of man.'

'Really?' There was a rustling at the end of the line and then, some distance from the mouthpiece, they could hear Freddie's voice saying, 'Bring her over here, that's right, stand her there,' and then a female voice with an American accent replying, 'No! Please no. Don't do it.' Peterson mouthed the words 'the chef' to Thompson and the negotiator nodded and dropped down at a desk, supporting his head with his free hand as he leaned over the Formica. He called out the other man's name. 'Freddie! Freddie! Are you there.'

There was the sound of the phone being fumbled again. 'We want the power back on, we want Willy on the phone and we want a car with blacked-out windows or – bring her over here – or more people will get hurt.'

They heard the woman's voice again: 'I'll do anything, I promise you. Anything.' There was a scream, and then a single gunshot. After a second's silence, made deeper by the noise that had preceded it, they heard moaning and then the woman saying feebly, 'What have you done?'

Freddie came back on. He said, 'You made me do that.' The line went dead.

45

Arranging to have Bobby shot had been the easy part, Nathan decided: get Trevor to point the gun, let him pull the trigger, listen for the authentic sound of fear. Any fool could do that. It was waiting for the men outside to respond which was difficult. That took nerve. The last of the candles flickered and died and a darkness descended on the Oyster House kitchen which was so complete it seemed to him that the confined space might now be limited only by his imagination. Without sight of the walls there was no geography, no restrictions, only a soundscape of the unseen. He heard Guthrie coughing over on the other side of the stove, a harsh hacking noise that came from deep inside the old man's lungs and later, as the darkness continued, there came a sigh which, by its peevishness, Nathan attributed to Grey Thomas. Somewhere next to him he could hear Bobby sobbing quietly.

Though it felt longer it was only a few minutes before the power was switched back on. Its return was signalled by a click from out by the walk-ins, followed, quickly, by the noise of the motors on the fridges working up to speed. The lights came next, stuttering at first, as if deciding whether to accept the surge of electricity being offered to them. When finally they stayed on they revealed Bobby Heller slumped back against a cabinet, her face streaked with tears. She stared at him open-mouthed and pointed across the room at Trevor, who still had the gun in his hand.

'You let him shoot at me.' There was disbelief in her voice, and the tremble of an anger that was only just under control.

Nathan turned to her and, kneeling up, his hands rested lightly on her shoulder, said quickly, 'I'm sorry. I'm really sorry.' His voice was low, almost a whisper. 'But I needed you to sound genuinely afraid.' He scanned her face, looking for a sign that she understood. 'I needed them to *hear* you sound afraid.' He glanced back over his shoulder at Trevor, who was standing a few feet away. Nathan put his mouth to Bobby's ear. 'I was not going to let him hurt you. I will not let him hurt you. Do you understand?' He sat back a little way, so he could look at her again. 'Do you?'

She stared at him, her mouth open as if trying to frame the words.

He said it again, but this time more forcefully, making it sound like an order. 'Do you? Do you understand that I will not let him hurt you?' She bit her lip and gave the very slightest nod of her head.

'OK then,' Nathan said. 'And it worked, didn't it.' He smiled, encouragingly, looked up at the lights. 'It actually worked.'

She nodded again.

He turned now to consider the damage to the green laundry sack at his feet. Trevor moved closer, shifting his weight excitedly from foot to foot, the gun still in his hand. There was a hole the size of a coin in the bag and the material around it was frayed and burnt. Nathan stuck his index finger through the hole to the first joint and showed it to the other man, who was pleased with the damage he had been allowed to cause.

'Did it come out the other side?' Bobby was standing a few feet away now, still not wanting to come anywhere near Trevor.

Nathan turned the bag over and had a look. 'Why? Do you want a memento?' He could tell she was starting to regain her composure.

'I want to check you haven't damaged my kitchen floor.' She smiled weakly.

Nathan shook his head. 'All in one piece. The bullet must still be in there somewhere.'

Trevor said, 'We could do it again.'

'It's all right, mate. No need for that.'

Nathan felt a larger presence looming over him, and looking up saw Connaston leaning back against the stove, his arms crossed tightly over his chest. Nathan pulled himself up to face him. Trevor moved off into a corner of the kitchen and mimed shooting at the floor, shouting 'Bang!' with each imaginary round and then blowing, Wild-West style, on the tip of the barrel. He turned and pointed the weapon at Bobby, squinting down the sight. She froze. He shouted 'Bang!' again and she jumped. He blew on the tip of the barrel again with an exaggerated pout, and laughed.

Nathan spun around. 'Trevor!'

The other man tipped his head on one side, producing a look of wounded innocence. 'What?'

'Just sit down.' He turned to Bobby to check she was all right and then to the judge, who was looking in Trevor's direction, shaking his head.

'A short-term gain,' Connaston said.

'We've got the power back on,' Nathan replied.

'But at what cost? The police think you've shot someone.'

'It wasn't only about power,' Nathan said quickly. 'It was about neutralizing a threat.' He nodded at Trevor. He was peering inside a packet of cigarettes and shaking it lightly to free the contents from their sticking place. He picked one out, shoved it between his lips and struck a match, cupping the flame unnecessarily, so that it illuminated the rigid boniness of his hand.

Connaston turned back, and dropped his voice to a stage-whisper. 'The authorities will have to act.' He said this gravely to emphasize that the authorities were close friends of his who would not be denied.

Nathan indicated Trevor again. 'It's safer if we can all see each other.'

'None of us will be safer if the police are moved to storm the building,' Connaston said.

'Willy won't let that happen.'

Connaston clapped his hands together and laughed at the ceiling.

'Willy won't let it happen! Fantastic. Well, that's all right then. Willy's on our side.'

'It wouldn't have to happen if you just bloody well let us go.' They turned at the sound of Grey Thomas's shrill voice. He was standing on the other side of the stove. He looked like a badly assembled collection of parts: one hand was bandaged, there was a plaster across his face and his hair was wild and misshapen from where Trevor had hacked away at him. Faced with an audience he took a step backwards. 'I mean, really. We could all of us be safer – couldn't we?'

There was a shout from the door. 'Oi! Pisshead! Sit!' Trevor pointed across the room at Thomas with the lit cigarette that was buried deep in his fist. Thomas opened his mouth to say something, thought better of it and crumpled to the floor, like an inflatable from which the air had suddenly escaped. The knife that Trevor had used earlier was once more back in his hand, and again he straddled the restaurant critic. Thomas shouted, 'Please! Don't cut me again!'

Trevor stood up and turned around. The cigarette was stuck between his lips. The knife was in one hand. In the other he held the rest of Thomas's hair. He grinned, said, 'Hungry anyone?' and threw the clump on to the solid top where it burned to smoke. Trevor seemed pleased with his work. He turned back to the restaurant critic. Thomas was shivering, and a tear ran down his uninjured cheek. 'You stay silent.' Thomas nodded vigorously. He would do as he was told.

Trevor took a drag and exhaled from the side of his mouth without removing it. He winked at Nathan and walked back to the door where he sat down. He held the knife in one hand and idly ran a fingertip across the blade to check it had not been blunted on the restaurant critic.

Connaston turned back to Nathan and whispered, 'You certainly have got the measure of him, haven't you?' The Conservative Party Treasurer did not wait for an answer. He walked back to his position on the other side of the kitchen and sat down next to Guthrie, the victorious orator returning to his seat after the delivery of a great speech.

46

Bobby rested a hand on Nathan's shoulder.

'Come with me,' she said quietly. 'I've got something for you.'

She led him to the preparation table at the end of the stove where, standing on a metal tray, were a dozen golden-brown sponge cakes, each a few inches high and the shape of a tall chef's hat, but tapered slightly towards the bottom. They looked glazed and sticky and around them were puddles of a clear syrup. She plated one and then licked her digits clean, slipping her whole index finger between her lips and withdrawing it with a long suck. 'Rum baba,' she said triumphantly, and handed him a fork. 'There should be cream on the side, of course, but in the circumstances...'

Studying these cakes, Nathan understood what Bobby meant when she described rum babas as her favourite waste of time. Good food was beauty and promise in one tight package, which removed from his mind any other concerns. He attacked the sponge with the edge of his fork. It fell apart into large pieces of glossy, broadly textured cake and suddenly he was no longer thinking about the threat posed by Trevor. Nothing was more important to him now than flavour. Sheffield and Stevie were standing next to Bobby, watching. Nathan slipped the forkful between his lips. He registered a mouth-filling sweetness from the syrup with a high lemony end. It was followed by the surprising denseness of the sponge. After that came the alcoholic lift of rum. He kept his mouth closed, ran his tongue around his teeth and, looking at the others, began laughing.

'That's fantastic,' he said, when he had swallowed, and the cooks nodded as if he had just been introduced to a great truth. They handed the rest of the rum babas out around the kitchen and soon the room was filled with the satisfied clink of silver fork against good crockery.

Bobby watched him eat. 'I thought you needed something to cheer you up,' she said.

Nathan stopped eating. 'Didn't I help make these?'

She agreed that he had. 'And I helped you get the power back,' she said.

'Team work,' Nathan said, glumly.

The return of power had also given them back the television, which was now showing the early evening news bulletin. Nathan noted with disappointment that they were still the first item; he had hoped fame had tired of their situation. A reporter was standing at the Regent's Street end of Jermyn Street, against a background of tired policemen and striped tape waving in the breeze. They showed the grainy footage of Bobby and Trevor from earlier in the day, and reported that more gunfire had been heard from within the kitchen late in the afternoon. The cheerful pose the reporters had assumed the day before was gone now. This reporter did refer to the 'hungry gunmen' but this time sarcastically, pointing out that 'according to police sources' the last food sent in was the makings for beans on toast, as if they had fallen on hard times. There was a discussion between newsreader and reporter about the mood of the police, who were saying only that 'negotiations were ongoing', before the reporter said that, while the police were being circumspect, 'sources' within the government were becoming restless.

'This new government was elected two days ago on a strong law and order manifesto,' the reporter said, 'and yet, less than a mile from Downing Street, armed gunmen are holding senior figures in the establishment hostage. Officials and ministers we have been talking to today have referred to a growing sense of disquiet within Whitehall at the way the police operation is proceeding.'

The item came to an end and they moved on to the latest round of ministerial appointments following the election. Nathan reached up and switched off the set.

His rum baba was half-eaten. He laid down his fork and pushed the plate away.

'Had enough?' Bobby said. She sounded disappointed.

Nathan shook his head. 'It's too good. If I finish it now, the next time I eat one of these all I'll think about is –' He looked around the kitchen. '– this.'

'You're right,' Bobby said. 'A good rum baba should never trigger bad memories.'

He laughed bitterly. 'And out there they still think we're on the beans and toast.'

'Out there they also happen to think I'm bleeding from a gunshot wound to the belly.'

'We need to put them right on a lot of things.' Nathan said. He looked down at Trevor and then back again, casually, as if he were checking out someone in a pub but didn't want them to notice. 'We need them to know exactly what's going on down here.'

'Hang on,' Bobby said. She fetched the copy of *Larousse Gastronomique* from the shelf of cookbooks and opened it to the recipe for mock turtle soup.

Nathan read the ingredients list. 'Is it good?'

Bobby grinned and shook her head. 'It's rank, the kind of thing that should go from cooking pot to trash can without ever troubling the table. But if Willy is the sort of guy I think he is it should tell him everything he needs to know.'

47

Willy sounded baffled.

'Where did you get a calf's head from?'

Nathan put his hand over the mouthpiece and turned to Bobby. 'He's asking where we got the calf's head from.'

Bobby rubbed her eyes. 'Tell him... tell him that you didn't hurt any turtles.'

He turned back to the phone. 'What I'm saying is, Willy, we didn't hurt any turtles.'

'Well, you wouldn't, would you? That's why it's called mock turtle soup. Because there's no turtle in it. That's why it's made with a calf's head.'

'Exactly.' Nathan turned and offered a forced smile to Trevor, who was listening into the conversation and scowling at what sounded to him like another diversion into cookery.

'How does the soup taste?'

'For God's sake, Willy, listen to me. No turtles were hurt.'

There was silence at the other end. 'No turtles were hurt?'

'Right.'

Another pause for breath. 'Freddie, are you trying to tell me something?'

'Yes.'

'Are you trying to tell me –' he sounded unsure of himself, 'that you didn't shoot the chef?'

'Yes.'

There was a moment's silence, as the information was considered.

'Am I right in thinking that you're not entirely able to speak freely?'

'You are correct about that.'

'Freddie, can I ask you this, and please don't take offence. Are you in control down there?'

Nathan held the phone tightly against his chin. 'No, Willy. I'm not sure I am.'

'I'll call you back.'

Jermyn Street had fallen under long, early evening shadows, and in the control unit the strip lights had been switched on to fill the room with a stark and unforgiving glare that exposed the consequences of broken sleep on so many middle-aged men. There were dark stains on the brown, tightly weaved carpet where cups of coffee had been spilt, and a crust of biscuit crumbs and the smell of the under-washed. A few hours earlier police carpenters had completed a three-dimensional model of the kitchen, using information supplied by the cooks who hadn't been working when the siege started, and Peterson now stood over it, considering the narrow alleyways between work areas and stove, fashioned from balsa. He was hoping to identify access points other than the doors at the bottom of the stairs but no matter how hard he looked, there was no other way in. He requested updates on the fruitless search for Caster-Johns, which had now moved to Northumbria, and asked to be told the moment the head waiter was fit enough to be interviewed. In the absence of the restaurant's owner, Mr Andrews was regarded as a vital source of intelligence.

Peterson accepted the suggestion, made earlier in the day, that the hostage-takers were now fighting amongst themselves, and solicited thoughts on how they might best use that situation. There was general agreement that Freddie needed supporting, and that the power had to remain on. Thompson argued that it would suit their purposes if, for the moment at least, they gave Freddie something to take back to whoever he was competing with.

'We should tell him the car will be there in the morning,' Thompson said, 'which gives us the night to consider our options.'

'And in the mean time?' Peterson said.

'Willy builds on his relationship with Freddie. It's worked well so far. Freddie needs to feel we're on his side. He's clearly vulnerable at the moment and that has to be to our advantage.'

Shortly after 8 p.m. Willy called Nathan again and told him that they understood his situation. He said the police wanted to work with him and that arrangements were being made to have a car brought to the front of the restaurant for the morning, as had been requested. He repeated the expectation that, in return for the car, hostages would be released but suggested that he should not mention this requirement to his 'colleague'.

'We need to take this one stage at a time.'

Nathan pressed his hand over the mouthpiece and passed the news on to Trevor, who received it by exhaling a long plume of cigarette smoke.

'OK, Willy,' Nathan said. 'Shall we talk again in the morning, then?'

'We can do, or we could talk for a bit longer now, unless you've got something else that needs doing.'

Nathan laughed. 'Well, I did want to brush up on my German, and the garden needs tending, but it can wait.'

'I was just wondering how the rum babas were.'

Nathan sighed with pleasure and recalled a taste memory of sweet and soft, of the light savarin crumbling away over his tongue and then the boozy hit from the rum. 'That's something special,' he said.

'It takes a greedy man to come up with something like that, doesn't it?'

'Exactly,' Nathan said. 'Only someone who really liked their food would think of soaking sponge in rum.'

'I can't believe you've never tried one before.'

'There are lots of things I've never tasted.'

'Your family not big eaters then?'

'I'm not big on family, Willy,' and Nathan regretted how broken that made him sound.

'I didn't mean to pry.'

'It's fine.' Nathan tucked the handset under his chin and reached up to get a copy of Robert Carrier's *Great Dishes of the World* from the top shelf. He flicked it open randomly to a picture of a roast rib of beef, the quilt of crisp amber fat shining through its crust of coarsely ground salt and pepper.

'Have you always cooked, Willy?'

'Since I was a kid. I come from a large family and sometimes it was better to learn how to cook for yourself than hope to get enough of what someone else was making.'

'You don't sound like a man who would ever let himself go hungry.'

'I used to joke that I hadn't been hungry since 1963.'

'But you don't make the joke any more?'

'I can't. It's sitting up here talking to you. There's never enough time to eat. I was starving yesterday.'

'Sorry about that. It wasn't part of the plan.'

Nathan leaned back against the work surface so that he was facing out into the kitchen. Despite Kingston's best efforts, there was no disguising the chaos: the green sacks with weary people wearing grubby whites slumped across them, the pools of wax dribbling off the side of the stove where the candles had burned themselves out, the vegetable peelings and splashes of sauce that had become smeared across the tiled floors. The hostages looked now like so much human debris – hair tangled, skin grey beneath the lengthening fields of stubble, eyes sunken. Even so Nathan still found his view of the kitchen thrilling. Standing there, scanning the method for roasting beef – 'spread meat with dripping... sprinkle with flour and mustard mixture... tie a flattened layer of beef suet over the top' – he imagined himself working at the stove, and in that moment saw a different life to the one he had led so far. He remembered the cushion of veal beneath his hand and the way the knife had slipped so easily through it. He recalled turning the escalopes in the egg and the breadcrumbs and watching the meat contract as it hit the hot fat. He pictured his hands in the savarin mix, gently kneading the dough and had again a sense of being lost in the moment. Here in the kitchen he had felt in charge of the ingredients, and absorbed in the process, and he wondered if he had stumbled upon the one job that would have given him satisfaction.

'I could have been a good cook,' Nathan said, almost to himself.

'You sound to me like you already are.'

He looked down at Bobby, who was back in her place on the floor. 'The chef here taught me a lot.'

'But there's always more to learn.'

'Lots more to learn.' He paused and turned the book over so that he could read the cover. 'Do you know a book called *Great Dishes of the World*?'

'Of course. Robert Carrier. It's a classic.'

'They've got a copy down here. Nice pictures.'

'Good dishes too.'

Nathan flicked through the book to another recipe. 'What's this? Boo-le-base?'

'The fish dish?'

Nathan read the text. 'Yeah.'

'It's pronounced Boo-ya-bess.'

'Boo-ya-bess? It looks great. Do you think you could sort us out the ingredients for one of these, Willy?' He turned over the page and scanned the list, most of which he had never heard of. What was a rascasse? What were patacles? What were sarans and perches? What was this world that had its own vocabulary and grammar? On the other side of the kitchen Sheffield and Stevie groaned. 'Too difficult for you boys, is it?' Nathan said, shouting across the stove. He was grinning at them. 'Not up to it?'

Willy said, 'I suspect they're objecting to the fact that a bouillabaisse takes a good two days, if you do it properly, and they're probably hoping to be out of there sooner than that.'

'OK, not one of those then.' Nathan looked across to Trevor. He liked to keep a constant watch on the man, to know where he was in relation to both himself and, more importantly, to Bobby. He was by the door, a foot up on the frame, picking at dirt under his fingernails with the end of a match. He looked absorbed but Nathan knew he was listening.

Willy said, 'I'll sort you out the ingredients for a really good breakfast instead.'

'Thanks, Willy.'

'Do you like black pudding?'

'Never had it.'

'Better get you some of that then.'

'Excellent.'

There was a dirty silence on the line, with only the hiss and whirr of the city distilled into a rush of background noise.

'And Freddie?'

'Yes?'

'Look after yourself tonight, will you?'

'I'll try to, Willy.'

Nathan hung up the phone. Next to the recipe for bouillabaisse was a photograph of raw fish, crammed together, belly to fin, in a glazed pottery bowl. Nathan studied it. 'When I get out of here,' he said to himself. He closed the book, and looked over at the man who was blocking the way.

48

At 8.45 p.m. a chauffeur-driven Jaguar drew up smoothly outside the church of St James's, as if it owned the kerb. Commander Peterson, who had been warned of the visitor's arrival, was waiting by the gates on Piccadilly and, as the car came to a halt, he crossed the pavement in two easy strides and climbed in. At the same time, the driver got out, closed the door, and stood on the pavement, leaning back against the car.

'Came from the Opera House,' the car's passenger said from his corner of the leather backseat, and he brushed away imagined specks of dust from the satin lapels of his dinner jacket. '*Rigoletto*,' he added. He shaped the word extravagantly to emphasize the richness of the night he had left behind.

Peter Dryden pressed a button on the inside of his door and the tinted window slid down a few inches, so he could look up at the darkening sky over London. Peterson knew Dryden slightly from meetings at the Cabinet Office, and recognized him as one of those senior civil servants who regarded high-ranking police officers as functionaries who had got above themselves. He had a spare, angular look and kept his grey hair neatly clipped. His suit was uncreased, even though he had been wearing it for hours and his black leather slip-ons had a substantial heel. He smelt lightly of cologne.

'I was in the middle of a briefing,' Peterson said, irritably.

'Of course, commander,' Dryden said. 'You must be terribly busy.'

Peterson stared into the generous space between himself and the driver's seat in front, and thought how poorly it compared with the Rover he was required to use.

Peterson crossed his legs and said, 'What can I do for you?'

Dryden yawned and made no effort to cover the gape of his mouth. 'Bit of a mess, this isn't it?'

'Sieges are never tidy.'

'Of course not, commander.'

'We're doing everything we can to bring it to a swift and peaceful conclusion.'

'Of that I have no doubt.' Dryden sighed. 'But it is rather more of a mess than is strictly necessary, don't you think?'

He turned and looked the police officer up and down, before meeting his gaze. Peterson became aware of the lazy curl of his unwashed shirt collar and the grubbiness of his jacket.

'Not everything has gone as we might have wished.'

Dryden laughed. 'Glad to hear it, friend. If this was what you were after we'd all be in trouble, wouldn't we?' He leaned towards the window, as if suddenly intrigued by something going on in the road outside that only he could see. 'All this hungry gunman malarkey. Coq au vin and baked beans. It's made us look like we're running a bloody hotel.'

'We've been taking expert advice from our highly trained negotiators.'

Dryden winced, theatrically, for the other man's benefit. 'First kill all the experts,' he muttered. 'Bane of everybody's life, don't you think? Because of them we have the nation looking to a bunch of thugs for cookery tips. Then the next moment, one of them is out in the street threatening to shoot dead a hostage.'

'It was unfortunate, but nobody was hurt.'

'I understand another shot was fired this afternoon.' His voice was colder this time, less familiar. Peterson had the sense of a man working his way down an agenda, and only he knew what the next item would be.

'A misunderstanding, we think.'

'I'm not sure we can afford very many more of these misunder-standings.' He made the last word sound as if it were isolated between quotes marks.

'Again, nobody was hurt.'

'Mr Peterson –' The police officer blinked at the failure to acknow-ledge his rank. It was an irritating ploy among Whitehall mandarins who liked to remind senior officers that they were used to briefing people of much greater office. '– this situation does not exist in isolation. There are other realities which must be considered.' The pleasantries were over.

'Such as?'

'Proximity. Location.'

'I am aware of London's geography.'

'Then I'm sure you can see how embarrassing this all is.'

The commander had seen the evening news and understood Dryden's point. He said, 'I cannot allow political considerations to influence my running of this operation.'

Dryden sank back into his seat, as if it were moulded to his form. 'Spare me the homilies, Mr Peterson. The police observe political considerations every hour of every day.'

'We are doing everything we can to bring this to a safe and peaceful conclusion.'

Dryden tapped his fingertips against his lips for a moment in thought. 'I am certain you are working to the very furthest extent of your capabilities,' he said. His voice was moderated and restrained again.

Within a few days, he said, parliament would reassemble after the General Election, to choose a new speaker. At that point the newspapers should be responding to selective leaks of the forthcoming Queen's speech, talking up the new law and order agenda, and the government's commitment to use its vastly increased majority to push through tough, crime-busting legislation. The populace had expressed a taste for blood which the politicians were committed to satisfying.

'In those circumstances,' Dryden said, 'It would be rather embarrassing, would it not, if, less than a mile from parliament, the Metropolitan police were still shovelling the finest ingredients available in London down the gullets of a couple of armed thugs?'

'That's a gross exaggeration of the situation.' Peterson felt the discussion slipping away from him.

'The feeling in the PM's office is that we need to make an example of these men.' He paused. 'There is no particular need nor, dare I say, appetite for a trial.'

Peterson let this information sink in. 'This is the Prime Minister's view?'

Dryden laughed patronizingly and waved him away. 'The PM is far too busy to concern herself with details like this. I am simply communicating to you the view of those in her office, who know her mind.'

Peterson saw it all: the men gathered around the polished rosewood table in a corner of Whitehall, shaking their heads over tea and biscuits at the turn of events; the muttered agreement of 'something must be done'; more than any of this, the Commissioner of the Metropolitan Police, making the tactical decision that he should no longer defend his commander from the politicians. Let them make operational decisions on this incident, if they felt it held so much political significance. Sacrifice the second-rater, so as to keep control of the rest of his policing agenda. Best, though, to keep his hands clean. So it is agreed that Dryden should be the one to bring the news. Swap chain of command and dress uniform for dinner jacket and the light smell of cologne. So much more civilized that way.

Peterson stared out of his window at the officers manning the gateway through to the churchyard. 'What do you suggest? That we go in, all guns blazing?'

'Deployment orders went out to Hereford this morning,' Dryden said. He proffered a sheet of paper and as he did so, turned away to consider the traffic rattling past, as if the document were no longer anything to do with him. It was marked 'Top Secret' and carried the royal seal.

Peterson read it. 'You're sending in the SAS?'

'It was felt the moment had been reached.'

'And you didn't think it was worth consulting me?'

Dryden pulled back his sleeve and consulted his watch. 'That's what I'm doing now, commander. I'm consulting you.' He looked out of the window, as if preoccupied by the thought of something he had forgotten to do. 'And now I ought to let you get on with your work. You will be contacted about the agreed course of action and you are to offer the Hereford boys all necessary assistance.' He pointed out of the window. 'When you get out, could you tell my driver I'm ready for him?'

Peterson was back on the pavement watching the tail lights of the Jaguar merge into the star field of the late evening traffic when an officer brought him the news: Mr Andrews was awake and talking.

'Apparently, sir, there may be a staircase hidden somewhere in the building.' Commander Peterson considered the officer, and thought about the leverage the information might have given him if it had been available half an hour earlier.

49

Late one evening in the spring of 1843, the body of James, 6th Duke of Roxborough, was found at the bottom of the narrow stairs which ran from the back entrance of the Jermyn Street Oyster House in Mason's Yard to the attic. One leg was twisted underneath him, and a shiny wax seal of blood lay from his left nostril to his top lip. His eyes were open. The *London Gazetteer* later reported that the Duke had 'enjoyed a fine supper' and was assumed to have fallen 'most unfortunately, suffering the effects of his consumption, while in search of relief'. In the gentlemen's clubs that surrounded the Oyster House, the coverage was read hungrily and none of it was believed. The Duke had not dined there that evening, though it was known that his young wife Emma regularly entertained her lover, the Earl of Strathmore, in the private dining room on the second floor, where there was a day bed of blue velvet and the walls were decorated with sprays of peacock feathers. According to the gossip at both the Carlton Club and the Reform, Roxborough, learning that his wife and Strathmore were feasting on venison, cabinet pudding and each other, had gone drunk to the Oyster House to confront them. At some point he had lost his footing and fallen to his death, and it was said with authority that the younger, fitter Strathmore had helped the Duke on his way.

The inquest into his death accepted the explanation given in the *Gazetteer* and the back staircase quickly acquired a reputation as a dangerous place for scorned and cuckolded men. Though the only other death recorded there during the nineteenth century was genuinely caused by too much claret, men who came to confront love rivals fell regularly, broke bones and lost their pride. The danger of these narrow flights became a feature of the restaurant and in the kitchen head chefs liked to threaten their young cooks with 'a swift exit down the back stairs' if they failed to meet the expected standard. In the 1870s, when the Prince of Wales began his affair with Lillie Langtry, the use of the back stairs at the Jermyn Street Oyster House added to the lustre of risk that was associated with the relationship in the years before her position as mistress was tacitly acknowledged by the court. As a result, the destruction of the building by the Zeppelin's bomb in 1915 was regarded not only as having taken away a much-loved restaurant but also as having destroyed a significant piece of London's social history.

Colin Bellamy explained all of this as he leaned over a set of architectural drawings liberated that evening from the archives at the Museum of London, where he was the chief curator. He had been dozing on the sofa when the call came, and his grey, wiry hair was wild from where it had sunk into the cushion. His moleskin waistcoat was unbuttoned, though he wore at his throat a brown bow-tie which lent him a hint of formality.

'Whether any sign of the staircase should prove extant within the building as it stands today is an intriguing question,' he said, and he pushed his glasses down off his forehead so that he could read a note in a fine italic at the bottom of a sheet. It was just after 10.30 p.m. and a small group of officers was gathered around the trestle table, hastily erected in front of the altar for the purpose.

Peterson gazed at the curling, yellowed sheet. 'Is the staircase story widely known?'

Bellamy looked over his half-lenses as if at a promising student who was destined only to disappoint. 'By those with an interest in such things, of course.' He looked back to the table. 'Though only as a piece of history, which is to say, that which once was.' He pulled up a set of plans dated April 1916, which showed at its centre an overhead view of the building's footprint and, at the bottom, a front elevation which closely matched the Oyster House as it now was. Bellamy's finger hovered over a corner of the building, where it backed on to Mason's Yard.

'See here. It was designed to be rebuilt on a set of ninety-degree angles.'

'As you would expect,' Peterson said, hoping to sound like he was keeping up with the explanation.

'On a green field site, perhaps,' Bellamy said, allowing the final sibilant in 'perhaps' to continue for a second longer than was necessary. 'But this is not a green field site.' He pulled out another sheet from underneath, and it attempted to roll itself back up into a tube. He called over two officers, gave them kidskin gloves and told them to hold the edges down. 'And please do be gentle.'

This sheet was much older. The parchment was almost brown and in places the ink was beginning to fade. Nevertheless it was still possible to make out the overhead view of plans for an entire street, laid out with pavements, entrances and windows and, to one side, the church in which they were now standing. In the top left-hand corner it was dated 1664. Beneath that was a coat of arms and the name Henry, Earl of St Albans.

The historian pointed at it. 'Full name, Henry Jermyn. He it was who bought from the Crown the plot upon which all that we see now stands. And look here too.' His fingertip was just above the line that marked out the shape of the street, as he traced its position along the page. 'The proposed building works are somewhat wider to the south in what is now Ormond Yard than they are to the north in Jermyn Street.' He stood back from the table and scanned them from left to right. 'Further, we can see in the lines of division between the separate properties, both acute and obtuse angles.' He pulled off his glasses and massaged the bridge of his nose. 'You must understand that many of these properties would have been built to order and a great deal of negotiation should have taken place to ascertain the exact shape and form of each one, engendering competition between the aristocratic gentlemen who were patronizing the project.'

'It's getting late, Mr Bellamy.'

'Am I boring you? Because I have a willing sofa to which I can happily return.'

'I need to know if there is a staircase hidden in this building. People's lives are in danger.'

'As I cannot tell you whether such a thing exists, you need to know instead *why* there might be a staircase hidden in this building.'

Peterson took a deep breath. It had not been a good evening. 'Anything you can help us with, Mr Bellamy.'

'I understand,' he said tartly. 'We clearly have a mismatch between the intentions expressed here in the seventeenth century and those expressed on the plans to rebuild the property after its destruction in the Great War.' He called over another officer and gave him the 1916 sheet, which the constable struggled to hold in front of him. He peered over the top, like a child trying to see what was going on in next door's garden. 'Presumably, if we were to visit the land registry we should find that the legal space occupied by the property at 87 Jermyn Street matches that on the original plans. And yet, having been built only on right angles, as was the fashion at the beginning of this century, it cannot entirely fill the plot allotted to it.'

'So there could still be a staircase running from the attic to the basement of that building,' Peterson said, as if talking to himself. He was staring at the plans too, willing them to give up their secrets.

'Absolutely no idea,' Bellamy said. 'But it seems likely to me that there's a bloody great void between number 87 and at least one of the buildings on either side –' he indicated its position on the older of the two maps. '– Which would be of some width on the southern side, tapering as it travelled north, possibly to a point on the Jermyn Street side. Perhaps one contains a staircase. Perhaps neither of them do.'

In the next hour, Peterson dispatched two teams of officers to enter the top floors of the buildings at either side of number 87 from the roof, with orders to investigate the walls. He asked Colin Bellamy to remain on site to provide advice to his men by radio and, grudgingly, the curator agreed to do so. He took off his jacket, folded it carefully and placed it on a pew as a pillow which he lay upon, his hands across his chest as if in prayer. At the back of the Oyster House, in Mason's Yard, officers from Special Branch, listening into the microphones placed around the outside of the building, reported that they could not detect any sound of the hammering from above and Peterson gave the go-ahead for his men, who had already cracked off large slabs of crumbling plaster, to begin work on the bricks behind.

'We may just have got our first real advantage,' Peterson said to Denis Thompson, shortly after midnight.

Thompson yawned. 'As long as they don't know the staircase story too,' he said, 'which is unlikely.' He sipped his lukewarm coffee.

50

Yesterday

The men from Special Branch were correct. The work taking place on the top floor of the neighbouring buildings could not be heard in the basement kitchen – but it could be felt by anybody who happened to touch the wall at the right moment or who, like Sheffield Tony, was leaning back against it in the one place where there was a gap in the otherwise continuous line of work units.

He felt the vibrations in his shoulders and looked immediately to the ducted ceiling, as if expecting to see the cause there. He turned and looked at the wall itself. He felt a thud, and then another.

Stevie was sitting opposite him, his back against the stove. He had his eyes closed but Sheffield knew he was awake. He whispered, 'Did you feel that?'

'Feel what?' Stevie didn't open his eyes.

Sheffield felt a third thud. 'That.' He stood up and placed his hands flat against the white-tiled wall. 'They're trying to bang their way in.'

Stevie opened his eyes. 'Sit down,' he hissed from his place on the floor. He looked over at Trevor, who was now watching Sheffield lean into the wall. 'Tony! Sit!' Reluctantly Sheffield dropped to the floor next to the other cook, his back to the stove, so that he could consider this suddenly fascinating stretch of white tiling.

'I know what they're doing,' he said, still in a whisper, but sounding victorious.

'It's probably a tube train heading into Piccadilly Circus,' Stevie said. He closed his eyes again.

'They're looking for the staircase.'

'Jesus, Sheffield. Not that old wives' tale.'

'They're up there, looking for the staircase. That's what they're doing.' He stood up again, unable to stop himself, and pushed his hands against the tiling and imagined them becoming soft to the touch so that his palms slipped through it into some undiscovered void behind. But the thuds and vibrations had ceased.

'Still, no harm in looking,' he said, under his breath. He rapped lightly on the wall with his knuckles and listened for a hollowness. He knew the staircase story was probably just that – a story – because all old restaurants had their myths and legends. In a Yorkshire hotel where he had once worked it had been the tale of the commis chef who got caught in the freezer overnight and whose ghost was said still to haunt the kitchens. In another it was the story of the cook who severed an artery during service and who, before dying, bled into the meat juices to accompany the beef. In the chaos following the accident the thickened gravy was still served, and met with such acclaim that many diners asked for seconds. It was said that, every year on the anniversary of the death, the cooks stood around the gravy pot, cut themselves and bled into it, as a mark of respect. The practice had died out only a few years before Sheffield arrived, the other cooks told him mischievously, but there was talk of reviving it, and he found himself staring at his older colleagues' arms for unusual scars.

All these narratives would have been based on some element of truth, Sheffield thought to himself, just as there really had once been a staircase that ran from this kitchen to the attic. What if it was still there? What if he were the one to find it? And what if he were the one to lead them all to freedom and be the hero? He imagined his family, watching on television in Yorkshire, as the escaped hostages appeared at a top-floor window, led by Sheffield, waving to the crowd below. He saw his father pulling the cigarette away from his lip and leaning forward in his armchair and acknowledging at last that his son was a man he could be proud of. Sheffield liked that image very much, and he held on to it as he pushed his hands harder against the wall, willing it to give, lost in a child's fantasy. He was hungry to perform an act of heroism. But his hands did not sink through the tiles and he could not tell whether the space behind was hollow.

'There is no staircase,' Stevie whispered. 'Now sit back down.'

Reluctantly Sheffield dropped back again on to the floor next to Stevie. He attempted to straighten his chef's jacket so it didn't look such a mess, but to little effect.

'Do you think your mum and dad know you're in here?' Sheffield said, as he tried to flatten his lapels.

'They don't know where I am,' Stevie said. 'Haven't spoken to them in years. I wasn't exactly what they were hoping for.'

'Know what you mean. My dad decided I was a poof because I wanted to be a chef.'

'My dad decided I was a poof because he found me in bed with the bloke from the post office.'

They both laughed. Sheffield said, 'Ever cook for them?' Stevie shook his head. 'You?'

'Once,' he said. 'Not exactly a triumph.'

It was a year after he had left home, he said. He and his father weren't talking and his mother suggested he come back for a night and 'rustle up a bit of tea for him. You know your dad. Thinks with his stomach, he does.'

Sheffield consulted cook books for days after that until alighting on a recipe for pigs' trotters bourguignon, the boned feet stuffed with foie gras, minced pork, bacon, button onions and mushrooms and glazed with a rich red wine sauce. It looked complicated but he concluded there was no point doing something simple if he was trying to prove to his father that he did a man's job. He could see that the Frenchness of the dish might put him off but that was balanced by the use of pigs' trotters. His dad loved trotters. It was the kind of cut a Yorkshireman understood. So he singed the trotters himself to remove any hairs and boned them out and braised them for hours in red wine and shallots.

He spent two days making his own stock and *jus* for the sauce, and followed meticulously the seventeen stages to make the stuffing and the garnish, and worked carefully to fill the pigs' feet, and to reform them and wrap them in foil ready to be steamed.

His father was not there when he arrived at the family house so his mother left him to work in the kitchen, and by 7.30 p.m. he had the table laid and the candles lit and all the food ready to serve. His father did not return from the pub until 9 p.m. He smelt of ale and was unsteady on his feet. Ignoring the candles, he turned on the lights. Sheffield refused to be downhearted by this slight to the atmosphere he had created and placed the dish in front of him. His father lit a cigarette and sat back from the table, smoking.

'What's this?'

Sheffield told him.

'Pigs' feet? Didn't think it was worth spending that cash of yours to get me a nice steak?'

'There's foie gras in there.'

'What's that when it's at home?'

'Goose liver.'

'Liver? I hate liver.' He stubbed out his cigarette in the puddle of sauce next to the trotter. 'I'll get me a pie for supper down the pub.' He left the house again.

Sheffield watched the last thin wisp of cigarette smoke snake upwards from the plate.

'I'm sorry, love,' his mother said. 'It's being on the unemployment that does it. He's a good man really. He just needs a job.'

'Haven't spoken to him since,' Sheffield said. 'Speak to my mum sometimes, but I don't think she knows where I work.'

Stevie pulled his legs in under him so that he was sitting cross-legged. He dropped his head down and yawned. 'It's beginning to feel like the outside world doesn't exist any more,' he said. 'All that's left is this. It's us, here, and these walls and these people.' The air stank now of rotting food and sweat.

'That's why I'm trying to find the staircase,' Sheffield said.

'There is no staircase.'

'You don't know that.'

'Nothing is ever that simple.' He nodded across the room at Bobby and Nathan. 'Go ask chef. She'll tell you. She's been here the longest.'

They watched Nathan and Bobby, who were sitting on the floor side by side with their knees up, hands out in front of them, as though they were comparing nails.

Stevie whispered, 'Do you think she's going a bit Patty Hearst?'

'Patty what?'

'Hearst. Stockholm syndrome. Where the hostage falls in love with the gunman. Joins the cause. Like that rich American girl?'

Sheffield shook his head. 'No. It's the other way around. He's the one falling in love with her.' He pushed himself up from the floor. 'I'm going to talk to them about the staircase.'

'There is no bloody staircase,' Stevie hissed again, but to no effect. Sheffield was already on the other side of the kitchen, and Trevor was on his way over there too.

After talking to Willy, Nathan sat down on the floor next to Bobby with the Robert Carrier book. He flicked through the recipes, stopping every now and then to ask for descriptions of dishes. He wanted to know what gazpacho tasted like and what moules mariniere was and, as she answered his questions, he made it clear that a list of ingredients wasn't enough. He had never eaten mussels before, nor drunk much white wine, so it didn't help if she told him that moules mariniere was one cooked in the other. He needed more than that. He needed her to tell him about the texture of a mussel and its soft, mediated taste of the sea. He had to know how the wine changed its nature when heated with onions and herbs and butter, and how it became sweet from the juices released by the shellfish during cooking. At each recipe he asked if the dish was difficult, and she understood from the question that he wanted to know whether it was something *he* would find difficult, so she told him almost everything was easy 'as long as you control the recipe and it doesn't control you'. She filled his glass from a bottle of a 1964 Cheval Blanc that she had found at the bottom of the wine racks, its label stained and torn around the edges, and tried to tell him about the wine's great reputation and its even greater value and the balance of fruit to acidity which was now at its best, but he was absorbed by the pictures in the book.

Nathan rested his finger on a photograph and asked her to identify the dish. She leaned over the book. 'Quiche', she said, 'aux fines herbes.' He stared at the page. She said, 'It's a kind of egg and cheese flan with herbs.'

Nathan said, 'That's not right. I've eaten quiche and it didn't look anything like that.'

'You've eaten quiche?'

'Shock horror. Man eats food not from can.'

'Sorry, but quiche is just not one of those dishes you associate with armed gunmen.'

He ignored the jibe and, without looking up from the page, said, 'Anyway it didn't look like that. It was wet and soggy and part of a very bad day.'

'Bad quiche is a terrible thing,' Bobby said, trying to sound sombre. 'It can make the very best of days awful. I'll have to make a good one for you sometime.' Soothed by the wine, she was quietly amused by the bizarre assumption in her last sentence that there might be a future, like theirs was a holiday friendship which would survive the return home.

The picture showed the quiche surrounded by fresh green herbs on a green plate, which, in turn, was lying in a meadow. It was a stupid place to put a quiche, Bobby thought to herself, though she understood the point it was making, about the link between the grass which the cows ate to make the milk, that went to produce the hard Swiss cheese that gave the quiche its flavour, because she had learnt all about that early on. When she was growing up in Ohio, her father used to hunt partridge which he brought home, their gnarled-twig feet tied together on pieces of muddy twine. The first thing her mother did after plucking them was cut off their heads. Then she inserted two fingers into the neck cavity to pull out the crop so she could see what the birds had been eating before they took the bullet. If the crop was filled with maize, as it usually was, she made small cornbreads to go with the roasted birds. If it was barley, she braised the grain with bacon and served it as a side dish.

'Let your ingredients lead the way,' her mother said. 'They always know more about your dinner than you do.'

Bobby recognized that Nathan had none of this knowledge. He had no terms of reference for any of these dishes, nor for the ingredients or the way they related to the place that produced them, just an instinctive understanding of food and a great curiosity. She supposed he could learn the rest later.

'Do you know all these recipes off by heart?' Nathan said.

'Some of them, if I've cooked them often enough. Others I have to look up. Mostly I have to remember what mistakes not to make, but I've always got my scars to help me with that.' She waved her hands at him.

'Show me.'

She held her left hand up, and ran her finger over the white lines carved into the skin of her palm. 'These ones remind me to keep control of the blade when I'm opening oysters.' She showed him the side of her hand where there was a series of a pale pink burn marks, lined up from the ball to the knuckle of the thumb. 'Those remind me that things which have been in the oven are seriously hot. As you can see, I have a tough time remembering that one.' She lifted her right hand, and showed him a much larger burn scar covering the back of her hand. 'That one tells me that anything with too much water in it will cause hot fat to boil over.'

'What was it?'

She blushed and said it was a thick sirloin steak, cooked at the restaurant where she had worked before the Oyster House. 'We were rushed during the dinner service and I had to get one out quickly, so I chucked it into the deep-fat fryer just to crisp it up.'

'Did it do the job?'

'Yeah, and it crisped me up nicely too.' She shrugged apologetically. 'I still make mistakes cooking. And when I get my own place I'm still going to be making mistakes.'

'You got plans?'

'Oh sure,' she said, 'So it would be kinda good if I got out of here alive.'

'What are you planning?' he said, consciously ignoring her sarcasm.

She looked shyly at her feet. 'I don't know. Simple, light food. A few Mediterranean flavours. None of those starchy tablecloths. Kind of place you could go to three nights a week and not be bored.'

'It sounds good.'

'It will be.'

'What will you call it?'

She shook her head. 'I'm not going to jinx it.'

She looked at her hands again then dropped them into her lap. 'What about you?'

'How do you mean?'

'Scars?'

He examined his hands. 'There's this one.' He showed her the deep white crater in the knuckle of his right hand. 'I got that from punching out Margaret Thatcher.'

'You're kidding me?'

He told her the story, and she had to put her hand over her mouth to smother her giggles, for fear of waking anybody who was already asleep. Then he showed her the tattoo, with its snaky, amateurish trails, and explained why it was done and how Kingston had one to match, and the medicine they had to take, and she looked over to where her kitchen porter was standing, by the sinks.

'He's a good man, you know,' Nathan said quietly. Bobby said nothing. 'And he really didn't know anything about this. He was trying for a fresh start. Everything that's happened here is my fault, not his.'

She was silent for a moment, as if lost in thought. 'It's a weird name, Kingston,' she said.

'His real name's Jeremy.'

She turned to Nathan, one eyebrow raised.

'You can see why he wanted to get rid of it, can't you,' Nathan said. 'It wouldn't have been easy growing up in Brixton being called Jeremy.' He acquired the nickname when he was still at primary school, he explained, because, one year, he had gone to Jamaica for three months to visit his father who lived in Kingston. When he came back the other children thought there was something thrilling about where he'd been and changed his name to match the journey he had made.

'Still, Jeremy,' she said again, as if trying it on for size. 'It's a nice name.' She sipped her wine.

'He's a nice bloke.'

Bobby put down her glass and returned her attention to her hands. She was not yet willing to accept that her kitchen porter was as much a victim in all this as she was. She splayed her fingers, as if drying her nails. 'No job for a girl, this,' she said.

Nathan held his out too. 'Hands don't tell you anything,' he said. 'Some of the most violent men I've known have had soft girls' hands.' Casually, she reached over to take hold of his right hand in hers, as if inspecting him. Her fingers were underneath his. Her thumb was on top, and he could feel the warmth of her palm and the pressure of her thumb on his index finger, and he became aware of the film of sweat on his skin. She leaned over to study the scar made when the nail had punctured him on election night.

'You mix in interesting company.'

'Too interesting,' Nathan said.

Before she could reply, Sheffield arrived beside them, and she let go of him.

'Chef, I've been thinking—' He got only halfway through his pre-pared speech before she stopped him.

'It's a myth.'

'But what if it's not?'

'What are you thinking? That we take down the walls using three knife steels and a ladle?'

'There's lots of heavy stuff in a kitchen. And anyway, it's not like we've got anything else to do. If the staircase is there –'

Sheffield looked up. Trevor was standing over them. His arms were crossed, but the knife was still held in one hand so that the blade was next to his face. His scar was reflected in the polished metal, but made uglier by distortions on the surface of the metal from the attentions of wire-cleaning brushes.

'Staircase?'

Quickly, Bobby said, 'It's a story. It's a waste of time. There isn't one.' She was trembling involuntarily.

Trevor stared at Bobby with undisguised hatred. He was tired of the way she tempted him, just by being here, and of the games she played, pretending she was unavailable to him. Pretending she was too good for him. She was like all women, Trevor decided. 'Tell me.' He pointed at Bobby with the knife and instinctively Nathan raised his hand to protect her. Trevor smiled as he rested the tip of the blade against the palm of Nathan's hand. He was at ease, with a blade in one hand, and people at his feet. He jabbed his arm sharply, which made Nathan wince. A drop of blood fell from the ball of his hand and splashed on to the tiled floor. Nathan looked at the damage. There was a small puncture in the centre of his palm which he squeezed with his other hand. Beneath the pad of his thumb, where the blood seeped sticky and hot, he felt another piece of history being written on his palm.

'There's a story about a staircase,' he said, trying to sound as if he took the insult to his skin as nothing more than horseplay. 'Hidden behind the walls. Sheffield thinks the police might be looking for it.'

'But that's all it is,' Bobby said. 'A story. This place was rebuilt at the beginning of the century.'

'Better if we found it first, though,' Trevor said. 'Just need to get busy, don't we?' He dropped down opposite them, the confrontation with Nathan apparently forgotten by a mind with a talent for living in moments so much shorter than any clock could mark. He pulled from his pocket more of the home-made envelopes fashioned from pages torn from glossy magazines and unfolded one to reveal a crush of grey-white powder.

Nathan said, 'No more,' like he was some lousy gambler, whose luck had stayed bad.

Trevor grinned at him. 'Been saving these ones.'

The first wrap of speed went up his nose, in a long noisy snort. He tipped the next one down his throat, swallowed hard and swallowed again, as if he was trying to move an obstruction. He rolled the paper into a ball, flicked it away, blinked three times, and then slowly opened his eyes wide.

'Go easy,' Nathan said.

'Better be sure,' Trevor said in a monotone, and he swallowed a third. He ran his tongue around his teeth and held a wrap out towards Nathan. 'Kill the sleep demons.'

Nathan shook his head. 'Grass and hash, me. Nothing else.'

'Suit yourself,' he said and he twitched, trying to move the wiry legs of the phantom insect that had landed on his cheek. Nathan watched this dangerous man, his brain now fizzing with speed, and another image came to mind: of a window hung with blankets, and a man with unwashed hair and a room that smelt of damp, sweaty dog.

52

It was when his suppliers stopped being pleased to see him that Nathan knew things had to change.

'You got giant's trousers,' Brandon said. When Nathan looked blank the tall Rastafarian patted him on the thigh with one big, leathery hand.

'You pocket's too big,' the Rasta said, and he dragged deeply on a thumb-thick joint of grass. Brandon stood in the middle of the room staring straight ahead after that, bouncing lightly on his heels to a Burning Spear bass line, played low on the hi-fi in the corner of the living room. On the wall was a picture of Bob Marley, head thrown back, hair flying. There were bongs and chillums scattered about a low, ceramic-topped coffee table and leaning up against one of them, a block of black cannabis resin the size of a paperback book.

'When you come, the gear all go,' Brandon said.

'That right,' said an older man with greying dreds like frayed rope, who was fixed to the centre of the sofa, hands palm down on the brown velour. 'Gear all gone.'

'Nu'tin for others.'

'Bad for busy-ness.'

'After you, Nathan, we ain't got no more busy-ness. You buy every 'ting.'

He had outgrown them, Brandon said. It was time he went

elsewhere and they gave him the address of a house in the suburbs to the west.

'Go see Swallow,' Brandon said. 'Swallow see you right.'

Andy Swallow worked from the front room of a dilapidated 1930s semi-detached house, in a street full of them close to Heathrow airport, where the constant thrum of landing jets lowered the sky. There were blankets hung behind the front door to stop any light escaping through the window above it, so the house looked empty. There were heavier blankets over the bay window in the living room and more over the doorway from living room to hall, so that walking through the house was a matter of pulling back drapes of thick, dusty material that clung to the shoulders as you passed. Inside, electric heaters filled the padded space with dull noise and soporific warmth. There were old mattresses on the floor around the edge of the room, draped with Indian-patterned prints, and in one corner there was a pile of cushions, the bed for Rizla, the mongrel dog who made the room smell damp and feverish. When Nathan was there the dog was always asleep unless Swallow roused it to accept a blow-back, slipping the burning end of a joint into his mouth and then exhaling to send a plume of smoke through the roach towards the animal. Swallow thought this was very funny.

Swallow held court here every night until dawn, surrounded by the unchoreographed assortment of bikers, hippies and punks who made up his clientele. He did business, toked on passing joints and kept up a constant chatter about the drug habits of the famous, which he claimed to know about because he had supplied the gear or been the supplier to the supplier.

Nathan hated going to see Swallow. The car journey through London's low-rise suburbs depressed him. The streets here were so uniform and spread out, compared to the eccentric clutter of his London, and the sight of the man's pinched features peering from behind the blanket when he knocked on the window to gain access, made him feel weary. He hated the way Swallow said, 'You're like me, Nathan,' because he didn't want to be like Swallow at all, and he worried that sitting on the mattresses would leave a stain on his suit. He hated the way the man tried to get him to diversify his business by offering up bags of speed or cocaine at knock-down prices so he could 'feel up the market. Buy Charlie from me, Nathan, and you could clear four figures a day in no time.'

'You know me, Andy. Strictly grass and hash.'

'Go on, try a bit of whiz. Just to get you home. Give him a wrap of sulph, someone.' And he was offered a torn page from a porn mag containing a crush of grey powder which looked like ground gravel, rustling in the cleavage of some wet-lipped model. Nathan declined. He'd tried amphetamine once, watching Prince Buster at the Kilburn National Ballroom. It made his throat hurt and the music sound tinny and insubstantial. Anything which interfered with Prince Buster had to be a bad idea. As for cocaine, he didn't like what it did to people. Grass and hash made people quiet. If you smoked too much of that the worst that would happen is you would fall asleep. Snort too much coke and it was broken bottles and broken heads. It was fury and anger and paranoia. Anyway coke was class A and Nathan didn't think it was worth the risk.

But he put up with all of this because Swallow had a constant supply of good quality resin and grass straight off the flights into Heathrow, and he never complained, however much Nathan and Kingston wanted to buy.

'You're like me, Nathan,' Swallow said one day, as he weighed up three pounds of Lebanese red. 'You take care of your customers.'

'I do my best.'

'You do better than best,' he said. He looked up and, in a voice ringing with profundity, said, 'You do bestest.' He nodded slowly at the importance of his observation. Swallow was very stoned. Andy Swallow was always very stoned.

'He's an arsehole,' Kingston said one night, on the drive back. 'And that dog smells like one.'

'I know, but if Brandon and the boys can't deal to us any more what are we supposed to do?'

Kingston didn't take his eyes off the road. 'Bring it in ourselves.'

Nathan appreciated the notion and made enquiries around Brixton about how he could move up the supply chain, but his contacts claimed either not to know what went on at the level above them, or said they were not in a position to talk about it.

'It's a Jamaican 'ting,' Brandon said.

'My best mate's Jamaican,' Nathan said. He knew he sounded desperate.

'You a rude boy, Nathan,' Brandon said, 'but you still a white rude boy. No place for you in a Jamaican 'ting.'

Eventually he was reduced to asking Swallow. The dealer furrowed his brow. 'I get it, Nathan. You're just like me. You got ambitions. I never sit still.' The dog snored. The lizard didn't move.

'So you can help me?'

'I got some contacts, yeah.'

For all his meaningless chatter, Swallow was telling the truth, and in the spring of 1981 Nathan and Kingston made their first trip to Amsterdam. They borrowed a Mark II Ford Cortina from Kingston's brother Raymond, which they fitted with a compartment hidden under the passenger seat, and took the car ferry from Harwich to the Hook of Holland. It was their first trip to anywhere else in Europe and they felt light and free. They drank glasses of pale, frothy beer at the outside cafés in the Leidseplein and strolled the cobbled, canalside lanes looking for the famous coffee shops where they could smoke dope without fear of arrest. They wandered through the red light district, gawping at the ageing, melon-thighed hookers in their lit shop windows, and ate thin chips with spicy peanut sauce from the self-service cafés near Dam Square.

'How can a whole city be so chilled?' Nathan said one night, as they were sitting in the Bulldog Café on the Leidseplein, skinning up some Nepalese Temple Ball.

'Helps if you stop trying to bang people up for smoking a bit of spliff,' Kingston said.

'This city must be stoned all the time.'

'I would be if I lived here.'

'Funny, but if I could smoke any time I liked,' Nathan said, 'I wouldn't want to,' and he twisted the tip of the joint to a tight finish.

They were in the Bulldog the night before they were due to pick up their consignment, watching the glossy music videos that were being shown on the giant projector screen over the bar, when a news bulletin came on. The two men watched in silence.

Nathan said, 'Has dope ever made you hallucinate?'

'That's the high street,' Kingston said.

'And that's Atlantic Road.'

They didn't understand a word of the Dutch commentary but the pictures told them everything they needed to know: there were upturned police cars, blazing, outside the shops on Atlantic and Railton Roads. There were buildings on fire and policemen hiding behind riot shields and shots of crowds lobbing bricks in great arching parabolas down the cluttered Brixton Streets.

'It's all gone off,' Kingston said.

'And we weren't there,' Nathan said.

'It's a firestorm.'

'We should have been there.'

'I need to phone my mum.'

Kingston went back to the hotel but Nathan stayed where he was, hoping to see another report. Instead there were only videos by Teardrop Explodes and Stevie Wonder, and a churning sensation in his stomach which he identified as guilt for having missed the Brixton uprising that had been talked of for so long. In a stoned haze he imagined describing the pictures to his grandfather and Terry laughing at the stories of flying rocks and police injuries. 'This is how it starts, Nathan,' he could hear the old man saying. 'This is where the revolution begins.' And Nathan wondered whether it really was the beginning of something or just the very end.

Later, when they were back home, they agreed it was the news of the missed riot which had made their smuggling operation a success. They were so distracted by the television pictures and what they had heard on the phone from Kingston's family that they didn't have space in their heads to be nervous about the ten pounds of North African product hidden under the back seat.

'Do you think we could arrange for a riot to kick off every time we go?' Nathan said, and Kingston laughed.

But within a few days of returning to Brixton, Nathan began to imagine himself back wandering the leafy canals of Amsterdam where life seemed so straightforward and the girls were pretty. Too many shop windows were boarded up in Brixton and too many buildings burnt out. Rubble still lay in the streets off Coldharbour Lane and Nathan couldn't escape the feeling that it had been his neighbourhood which had been the real loser, not the police. He tried to talk about this to Kingston, but for days after their return he was in a continuous, febrile rage which Nathan attributed to his frustration at having missed an opportunity. Kingston served up every new outrageous rumour about the riot – the stories of police brutality, of injuries that went untended and innocent bystanders beaten – as though they were verifiable facts and spat them out in short, sharp, bloody sentences.

'My family needed defending,' Kingston said, when Nathan mentioned his cold silences and hot retorts. 'The fascist pigs needed to be taught a lesson, and I wasn't here.' And his voice trembled with the sort of authenticity he had not heard since Terry had been in his prime. That was when Nathan began to think about a life elsewhere. He understood Kingston's fury. The man's family lived in Brixton and family was roots. But Nathan had no family and recognized his attachment to the area as a matter of convenience.

So he organized more trips to Amsterdam, and worked with Andy Swallow to distribute the dope across wider areas of London. Soon Nathan built up a thick roll of banknotes that he kept under a loose floorboard in his room and its increasing weight represented to him the promise of a new kind of freedom. He still didn't like Swallow and regarded it as a mark of his professionalism that he could work with the man; as long as Swallow continued to find distributors for the dope that he and Kingston couldn't move he was content to carry on doing business with him.

Over the next eighteen months, though, Andy Swallow changed.

'He's always got a cold,' Kingston said.

Nathan laughed. 'It's not exactly a healthy lifestyle, is it? Not the sort to get into the jogging craze, is our Mr Swallow. '

He lost more weight from his already skinny frame, so that his cheekbones became sharper. His bloodshot eyes retreated into his face and he developed a nervous shake and twitch. He hung extra layers of blankets over the windows. Soon the reason became clear: fewer and fewer joints were being passed around the room out near the airport. Now the album covers that lay about the room were being used for crisp lines of cocaine which Swallow snorted hungrily from one side of the sleeve to the other across the diagonal, as if the drug might be trying to escape him. Whenever Nathan visited there was always at least one plastic bag of white powder lying on the floor, its contents spilling into the dirty weave of the carpet, and the clients who came no longer sprawled on the mattresses but sat with their knees pulled up to their chests, rocking back and forth against the wall. He began to wonder how much of the profit from their trips to Amsterdam was disappearing up Swallow's over-tended nose.

Nathan was just about to tell him that their relationship was at an end when Swallow announced he had been given information about a new 'business opportunity'. He said it could be very lucrative.

'Too rich for me, though,' he said. 'I'm not like you, Nathan, you see. I don't want to get into anything too big. I just want to stay here –' He reached out, picked up a discarded bag of coke from the floor and weighed it in the palm of his hand. He stared at it lovingly, as if he had forgotten Nathan was there. 'I just want to do the thing I need to do.' He handed Nathan a business card. It was thick. The corners were bent down and one side was crusted with traces of cocaine where it had been used repeatedly to cut lines. But Nathan could still see it had been expensive to produce. The type was in gold italic, which he could feel under the pad of his thumb.

'Go see Mr Phillips,' Swallow said, nodding towards the card and sniffing. 'He's not like me. He's like you. He wears suits.'

Nathan studied the address. It was in an expensive part of London he didn't know but wanted to, which made the proposition all the more attractive. And he liked the idea of doing business with a man who wore suits. He felt it was more appropriate than this stagnant room with its wheezing dog.

Late one wet afternoon in April 1983, he put on a white shirt with a buttoned-down collar and a new, grey all-wool suit with narrow lapels which he had just bought on the King's Road, and took the Victoria line to Green Park tube station. From there it was a short walk to the address on the card: the premises of a jewellers called Richmond Phillips and Co. whose back-lit, velvet-padded window was studded with bands of silver and gold and slivers of fine cut diamond and emerald. Nathan had never seen anything like it and he found the display thrilling. Part of the appeal was its location: Richmond Phillips and Co. occupied a prime spot in the middle of a narrow covered arcade of equally expensive shops which ran all the way through a Georgian building from Piccadilly to Jermyn Street. It was, Nathan decided, exactly the sort of place where he should be doing business.

53

Trevor had been trying to knock down the east wall of the kitchen to find the lost staircase for over two hours when the judge's asthma attack began.

At first, when he started his assault on the place where the work units met the tiled wall, there was an air of resignation among the hostages. Why shouldn't this be happening at three o'clock in the morning on the fourth day of an armed siege? What right did they have to expect normality or anything resembling it? This – the sharp, repeated, head-jarring crack of knife steel against wall – was how it was meant to be. Most of them curled up against their own knees to keep at bay the noise of the impact and the sight of the dangerous man with the heavy-bottomed saucepans in his hands. They tried not to imagine what damage he could do if he turned his attention away from the wall to his hostages, but after all this time the anxiety had become a part of them. Many found it impossible not to let it overwhelm them.

Trevor succeeded in prying the work unit next to the dumb waiter away from its sticking place and Sheffield, who had abandoned any hope of sleep, took a deep breath and decided to help. He was tired of being afraid. He was tired of cowering in the corner. He needed to do something. Now the atmosphere changed. The two men took to hitting the wall with the heavy-bottomed pans, one after the other, so they filled in each other's off-beat and crowded the air with guttural shouts of effort which soon dissolved into laughter. Nathan asked if he could have a go, then Stevie and Bobby joined in, and even Connaston asked for a turn. He swung the pan wildly and with little coordination, spinning a full 360 degrees before making contact. Bobby put on a tape of the B-52s and they took revenge on the walls that had held them for so long to the bouncing, joyful chorus of 'Rock Lobster'. Suddenly it wasn't Trevor or Nathan or a jewel heist gone wrong which was responsible for the situation they were in, but the Oyster House itself. They were determined to do it harm and egged each other on to ever greater assaults on the fabric of their prison. They applauded each new piece of masonry or tiling that fell to the floor and every time Bobby swung the pan she high-fived her cooks and ran in a small circle with her hands in the air, the prize fighter on a lap of honour. Expensive French wines were opened and swigged straight from the bottle. Cigarettes were smoked. Congratulations were offered. Outside in Mason's Yard Special Branch officers, who earlier in the evening had turned up the volume as far as it would go in a futile attempt to hear what was being discussed, had to pull off their headphones because the noise was so harsh. Peterson was roused from a few hours sleep up in the gallery to be told that it sounded like the inhabitants of the Oyster House kitchen were having a party.

'Has Cosgrave tried calling them?' the commander said, dragging his hand across his hair to smooth it back into place.

'Yes, but nobody picked up. I don't think they could hear it over the music.'

It was when Trevor snorted more speed off the stove-top, head down, one finger pressed hard against a nostril to close it down, that they were reminded of the reality of their situation. Trevor's unruly laughter gave way to shouts of aggression directed against the wall, then against those he thought were standing too close to him or laughing at him or, finally, challenging him. The hostages recoiled and drifted back to the corners of the kitchen. The music went off. Now it was just Trevor and the wall, and he attacked it with an even greater violence.

On the other side of the kitchen, Nathan stood next to Bobby, watching. He said, 'Maybe it's better he's got something to do,' but he didn't sound convinced.

Render crumbled. Ancient red London brick shattered and great plumes of dust rose up. Clouds of it billowed across the kitchen, surging down the narrow alleyways between the stove and the work units, causing everybody else to bend double and cough and choke and to shout out, 'Trevor, for God's sake' and 'You have to stop, we can't breathe'. But Trevor did not stop. He no longer looked like a man who knew how to stop. This, now, was what he was about.

It was ten minutes before anybody noticed that Guthrie was in distress. He was on the floor by the doorway through to the walk-ins, head tilted back, gasping for breath. All colour had drained from his face and his hands clawed at the floor as though he were trying to escape its hold upon him. Bobby dropped down next to him and pulled open the top buttons of his chef's jacket.

She said urgently, 'Mr Guthrie? Can you hear me?'

His eyes flickered open and he hissed the single word 'Asthma'. Clouds of dust were breaking over the stove and dropping down around them and Trevor's hammering against the wall echoed off every hard surface so that, in her rising panic, she felt surrounded. Bobby looked up at Nathan. She didn't need to say anything. In a few strides he was next to Trevor, a hand on his shoulder, shouting, 'Stop! The judge! You have to stop!'

Trevor shook him off, and lifted the pan to swing it again, but he hesitated. He turned to Nathan, his improvised weapon still raised over his head.

'What about the judge?'

'He's in trouble.'

'Let me see.' He sounded excited.

Guthrie's bloodshot eyes were wide open now, his features held in a cold place between surprise and fear. He tried to speak but there was just the wet suck of his tongue coming unstuck from the roof of his mouth as he fought for air. Bobby held on to his hand and caressed his head.

She said, 'He needs help.'

Nathan said, 'We've got to get him out of here.'

Trevor leaned back against the edge of the stove, pulled the gun from his waistband and pointed it at Nathan. 'No,' he said. 'The judge stays where he is.'

54

'The man is going to die.'

'I said, he stays here.'

Nathan took a step towards him. Trevor jabbed the barrel of the gun into his chest, forcing Nathan to raise his hands. The veins in Trevor's neck were up and proud, and another pulsed violently in his temple. He reached under the hem of his jacket and withdrew a knife, so that both hands were occupied.

'Please, Trevor.'

Trevor pursed his lips and, with a simple controlled movement, slashed at Nathan's chest. Nathan looked down at the fine cut in his jacket, more with surprise than pain and registered the blood soaking into the material. From her place on the floor Bobby gasped. Nathan pressed one hand against his chest. 'It's OK,' he said. And to Trevor, 'What's happening here?'

Trevor looked down at the judge. 'Southwark. March 1978.'

Guthrie nodded vigorously and blinked, as he tried again to take a breath.

'Oh yeah,' Trevor said slowly. 'Now you remember.'

Nathan pointed at Guthrie. 'He was the judge at your trial?'

'It was when they said his name on the telly.'

'Jesus, Trevor. This is not the time for it.'

'Didn't recognize him without the wig.'

Nathan looked from Trevor to the judge and back again. 'If he dies and we didn't do anything to stop it, things will be very, very bad.'

'He sent me down for five years.'

Nathan looked back at the old man now writhing on the floor. His eyelids flickered. The loose elderly skin of his brow was creased in great ploughed furrows. He could see from the whiteness of Bobby's fingertips, just how tightly Guthrie was holding on to her hand as though, if he let go, he would be swept away.

'And if you let him die they'll throw away the key.'

'I'm not going to prison.' There was no desperation or tone of agitation in the man's voice this time. He was stating a fact.

'It was the jury that sent you down, Trevor, not him. He's just the judge.'

'He gave me five years. It should have been two.'

Guthrie's eyes were closed. No sound was coming from his mouth now, but he was arching his back, and his fat, drying tongue was pushed up against his swollen lips. Bobby cupped the back of his head with her free hand to stop it slumping back against the wall. She leaned down and, in an unsteady voice, whispered, 'Take a breath, just one more deep breath and you'll be fine. Please. Do it for me.' She scanned his face for any sign that he had heard her.

Nathan looked back to the other man. 'Let him go, Trevor.'

'He stays. I want to see him hurting.'

'He needs help.'

'Nobody ever helped me.'

Bobby looked up, desperately. She said, 'Please, Trevor, you have to—' She stopped mid-sentence, and looked back at where the judge's hand was held in her own. His fingers had been clawed, pressed tight against the back of her hand. Now they had released their grip, though no colour had returned to their tips. For a moment she did nothing, desperate not to acknowledge the change. If she did not recognize that something had happened, then it hadn't. The judge was still all right. The judge was still with them. And then, slowly she opened her fingers. His hand slipped off hers and fell away limply to the floor where it landed with a feeble slap of skin on cold tile. She leaned down so that her ear was over his mouth. She moved across and leant against the left side of his chest. She prodded at his wrist and at his neck with two inexpert fingers.

Finally she sat up and said only, 'He's dead.'

There was silence. Trevor licked his bottom lip, and twitched, so that his head flicked a few inches to one side and back again. He pointed his gun at Sheffield and Stevie. 'Put him somewhere.'

Sheffield said, 'Outside?'

Trevor shook his head. 'Fridge.'

Next to them the phone began ringing. Trevor put down the gun and, with his free hand, ripped the phone from the wall. The receiver dropped off and dangled towards the floor on its stretched coil. They heard a man's voice, small and reduced from this distance, calling, 'Hello. Are you there, Freddie? Freddie?' Trevor used the knife to slice the wires that attached the phone to the wall. The receiver fell silent. He threw the entire handset across the room. It crashed into the wall and dropped to the floor.

The hostages stood staring at their captor. He stared back at them, the knife lifted. There was a smudge of Nathan's blood on the blade's leading edge. He said, 'I'm in control'. Nobody argued with him.

55

Richmond Phillips smoked Cuban cigars from Davidoff's on St James's Street and extinguished them in a jade and silver ashtray from Ospreys. He liked to lob the butts across his office to the lacquered Chinese rubbish bin in the corner, a gift to himself from Harrods and, though he regarded himself as a good shot, he made an effort to miss so they landed in a puff of ash on the carpet.

He pressed a button on the intercom box on his desk and asked his secretary to come in. Nathan turned to look at the young woman in the tight black skirt with the flash of red lipstick. Phillips nodded towards the wreckage of his cigar. She slowly bent over, legs straight, to pick it up, so that the skirt rose up just high enough to reveal the dark top of a stocking. For a moment all her seams straightened. She stood up, dropped the butt in the bin, indulged her employer with a smile and left the room.

'It's the small things that make my life worth living,' Phillips said, as if to himself.

He looked at Nathan. 'Nice suit.'

'Thank you.'

'Where's it from?'

Nathan looked inside his jacket, to indicate it was just one of many. 'Alfred Dunhill.'

Phillips gave a nod of approval. He was wearing a salmon pink shirt with a double cuff by Lewin's of Jermyn Street, and a wide-shouldered, navy-blue double-breasted suit from Gieves and Hawkes of Savile Row. His brogues were from Church's and his tie, which lay for now in a tidy spiral on the green leather-topped reproduction desk, came from Liberty. He was a big man in his early forties. His hands were thick and square, so that the narrow band of gold on the fourth finger of his right hand looked under-engineered, and he had a light tan. He spoke with the kind of smooth, rounded vowels that someone with this desk and this secretary should have.

He said, 'You don't look like one of Swallow's cohort.'

'I'll take that as a compliment.'

'What's he up to?'

Nathan rolled his eyes. 'About four grams a day.'

Phillips smiled, to indicate that he understood the joke to be both good and a little too obvious. 'You know what this is about?'

'I assume you're not looking for someone to invest in a golf course.'

'Not right now, no.' He swivelled around in his chair so that he was facing the window that looked out over the rooftops above Piccadilly. 'Tell me about yourself.'

'How do you mean?'

Phillips did not look at him. 'What do you do? How much do you turn over a week? What's your –' He paused. 'Racket?' The word sounded like acquired vocabulary.

Nathan told him everything: about cannabis, both resin and leaf, imported from Amsterdam via flights into Heathrow; about a retail distribution network covering Brixton, Peckham and Camberwell and a wholesale business across the rest of London and beyond; about price maintenance, and the need to know your clients, and an almost clean conviction record. He used the language of business that he had read in the newspapers, and cast himself in the role of strategic thinker.

Phillips interrupted him. 'How much money have you got on you now?'

'I didn't bring the cash to invest with me.'

'Not what I asked. How much? Right now? In your wallet?'

'I don't know. Fifteen pounds maybe? And a bit of change.'

'Bloody amateurs.' Phillips jumped up and reached inside his jacket. He pulled out a thick wad of £20 notes, held together by a gold money clip. 'That's £400,' he said, shaking it at Nathan. 'Do you know why I'm carrying £400?'

Nathan shrugged.

Phillips leaned over him. 'Because I fucking well can.' He slipped the money back inside his jacket. 'If you take off that suit, you're just another one of Swallows' oiks, aren't you?' He dropped back on to his seat heavily, so that it creaked beneath him. 'You probably ought to sod off now.'

Nathan didn't move. He placed both hands flat on the arms of his chair, to avoid crunching them into the fists that he was eager to make. Phillips was a big man, Nathan thought to himself, but heavy. One well-placed punch is all it would take to topple him backwards. That would take the smirk off his over-fed face. Instead, he said, 'I've got money. And Swallow works for me now, not the other way around.' His words were clipped and controlled.

Phillips opened a drawer and took out a new cigar. Silently, he clipped the end with a silver cutter, allowing the discarded part to fall to the floor. She could pick it up later. He lit it noisily, using a beige onyx cigarette-lighter in the shape of a crouching lion, and puffed across the desk.

'£30,000,' Phillips said. 'That's a 10 per cent share of the consignment. Return will be in the order of 1000 per cent. Think three hundred grand. We supply the distribution. And we're not talking a few weight under the back seat of a Hillman Imp. This is containers, in through the docks at Tilbury.'

'What's the product?'

Phillips sucked on his cigar. 'Cannabis sativa, types many and various.'

'Not coke?'

'Later, maybe. For now we'll take control of the hash market, won't we?'

Nathan thought gloomily of the rolls of cash hidden under the floor of the flat on Acre Lane. Up to that point the £6,000 he had managed to accumulate had seemed a monumental achievement. Now it looked meagre, starved down there of light and warmth, unable to grow, and even with whatever Kingston had put aside they were a long way from the required sum. He knew this was not the moment to ask whether he could buy in for a smaller share. It would only further weaken his position.

Outside police cars rushed by on the rain-slicked streets, sirens calling. Phillips went to the window. He looked out over London.

'Do you know that most of the gentlemen's clubs around here merely suspend membership if you are required to go to prison. They'll even give you a refund.'

'I'm not planning to spend time in either.'

Phillips smiled and for the first time it looked like he meant it. 'A chap like you could do a lot of damage with 300k, I imagine,' he said, and he let the hand holding the cigar hang slack at his side for the moment, so that smoke climbed up beside him. 'Bit of property down by the water. That's what they all want these days, apparently. A view of the river. Smell of the Thames.' He pointed at him with the burning tip of the fat Cuban. 'You should get into wharf apartments. Do them up, sell them on, turn over the cash, invest in a few shares. Service industries. Get yourself a Porsche with the proceeds, and a nice girly with big knockers. Tell that smelly tosser Swallow to sod off. Get yourself out of Brixton.' He blew smoke into the room. 'Join the human race.' He yawned and made no effort to cover his mouth. 'Except you haven't got the thirty grand, have you.'

Nathan did not react even though he could hear the angry pump of his heart in his ears, and feel a cold sweat accumulating around his shirt collar. 'What guarantee do I have that I'll see my money again?'

Phillips pressed one finger to his lips and frowned, like a child trying to work out a maths question in his head. 'I imagine that if I try to run away with the dosh, you'll send one of your wog friends up here to bump me off.' He needed the money by the end of June, he said casually, as he looked at his watch. Their meeting was over.

Phillips's secretary led Nathan back through the network of corridors and stairwells that honeycombed the building above Princes Arcade and out through the jewellery shop. For a while he stood looking in the window, trying to calm down. He tensed and uncurled his fist and tensed it again and imagined smashing the glass; he took pleasure in the thought that he might bloody himself doing it. Blood should be spilt over this sort of humiliation, he thought to himself. It demanded a serious gesture, something unforgettable to all involved.

It was coming up to seven o'clock and the two shop assistants were lifting the black velvet cushions from the display and placing their contents in a large wood-fronted cupboard at the back. One of the women smiled at him through the window. He smiled back and imagined he looked like some lovesick groom-to-be, hunting in the wrong place for an affordable ring. As the cushions were lifted up he noticed the four-figure prices, written in black ink on tiny white labels, and calculated quickly that there was more than enough there to pull together the money he needed, even allowing for the cut the fences would take. He imagined the big fat cigar dropping from Phillips's shocked hand as he discovered the robbery: the shattered glass, the splintered cupboard, the empty cushions. He liked very much the idea that he could challenge all of Phillips's assumptions by ripping him off, and he felt his heart beat slow from its adrenalin-powered hurry, and his breathing fall shallow. The fury was passing, to be replaced by the kind of clearness of mind that he knew was vital to the achievement of his goals. He wanted to hurt Phillips, and he would do so but in his own way and in his own time.

Around him, office workers emerged from the doors between the shop units on either side of the arcade and headed towards the Piccadilly and Jermyn Street exits, and the promise of a little evening daylight. The shutters at the northern end were brought down first, with a sharp clatter of metal on metal. As the caretaker passed Nathan on his way to perform the same task at the Jermyn Street end, he announced it was closing time. Nathan followed him down with the remaining shop staff. He was the last to leave and about to walk out, when a thought occurred to him.

'What happens if you get caught in here after closing?'

The caretaker nodded towards the wall. 'Emergency lever. Pull that and it releases from the inside.'

'Right,' Nathan said. He stared at the big, red metal handle.

'Sir?'

'Yes?'

'I wouldn't mind getting home for my tea.'

'Of course, sorry.' Nathan stepped through the archway on to Jermyn Street, and turned around to watch the heavy, articulated shutter roll down to the ground, locking away for the night both the premises of Richmond Phillips and Co. and its polished inventory.

56

A few days later Nathan returned to Princes Arcade, wearing overalls and a yellow hard hat borrowed from a friend who was working on one of the building projects that had sprung up around Brixton since the riots of 1981. Under his arm he carried a roll of plans for a development of low-rise flats that was being constructed along Railton Road and he stood now in the middle of the arcade staring at them, apparently absorbed by the architect's drawings. To either side of him were the doors that led into the building. He deliberately did not look at the premises of Richmond Phillips and Co. a few feet away, partly so as not to draw attention to himself, and partly because he wished to keep his mood in check, and just the sight of the window reminded him too sharply of the man whose name was above the door. He wanted to save that anger for a time when it might be needed.

Instead he waited until a middle-aged woman went through the door to his right and followed her before it closed.

A staircase went straight down from behind the door and at the bottom of that there was a T-junction where it met a short corridor. There were doors at both ends. The woman went through the door to the left. He tried the door on the right first. It was locked and when he knocked there was no answer. He knocked on the other door, pulled the hard hat down over his eyes and stared down at his plans. He glanced up briefly to see it opened by the woman he had followed.

'Fire safety check,' he said briskly, before she could say anything. 'This is–?' He pointed through the doorway.

The woman said, 'The office.'

'Sorry, love. I've lost my bearings. Which office, exactly?'

'Xenon. The nightclub. The owner's not here at the moment, though. Perhaps you could call and make an appointment?'

'Only take a second. Don't need to trouble him, do we?' He pressed a finger on the middle of the plans and walked in. 'So *this* is the office. Excellent.' As though he had been searching for it all morning. There were two desks with phones, typewriters and piles of paper. To one side was an old leather sofa and on the walls were vintage film posters. He pointed at the door through which he had just come. 'And that's the fire exit from here?'

She nodded.

'Where does that door lead?' He pointed at the other side of the room.

'Into the club.'

He turned the plans around in his hands. 'Of course it does. I had the damn thing upside down. Always doing that.'

'I could call Carlo,' she said, 'And check when he could see you?'

'Really, two more minutes. That's all. I'll just have a look out there and then I can leave you in peace.' He went through the door and closed it behind him. He was standing in the corner of a large nightclub which, in the bald glare of the daytime lights, looked cold and unwelcoming. To one side of him was the DJs' booth. On the other side, running perpendicular to the booth, was a long stage, at waist height. At the other end of the room he could see the bar, where in the distance a waiter was stacking bottles, with a clink and rattle that broke the room's silence. There was booth seating along one side, upholstered in turquoise and green, some carpeting in the same colour as the seats, and a blond wood dance floor. The ceiling was hung with a complicated lighting rig and the walls were crusted with swirls of unlit neon.

Nathan turned to the door he had just come through and noticed that the bolt on the Yale lock was stuck back in its housing. He tapped the round, brass keyhole where it was sunk into the door and it snapped back into place, locking the door. Responding to the knock the secretary opened it.

'That one's always sticking,' she said sheepishly.

'Nothing to worry about,' Nathan said, throwing her a friendly wink. 'This kind of lock is often doing it. The key, please? I'll check that and then I'm gone.'

She retreated back behind the door and returned with a small, chrome Yale key. He smiled and closed the door on her, and gave the keyhole a knock once more so it was locked again. With his back to the bar he took from his pocket a small tin containing a block of dull yellow wax. He gently laid the key on top of the wax and pushed down hard to get a clean imprint. He turned the box over and tapped it on the bottom so the key dropped out, and repeated the process so that he had an impression of the Yale's other side. Finally, he closed the tin, put it in his pocket, wiped the key clean on his overalls, and used it to unlock the door.

'That's me all done,' he said, returning the key. 'Everything as it should be.' He took a pen from his pocket and quickly scribbled some notes in the margins of the plans.

'Can I tell Carlo who was here?'

'Tell him it was a random fire inspection,' Nathan said. 'He'll understand.'

The following week Nathan told Kingston he had found a great club in town. 'We should try it. We don't do enough of that, these days.' When Kingston looked unconvinced Nathan gave him three £20s and told him to get himself an outfit from the Bonmarché on the High Street. 'Something smart,' he said. 'Something a bit trendy instead of those baggy-arsed jeans you always wear.'

Kingston bought a zoot suit in black satin that shimmered under the lights, with loose pleated trousers that fastened high on the waist and came to a cuff at the ankle. He wore black slip-on dealer boots and, underneath the jacket, a white collarless shirt, fastened at the throat.

Nathan nodded approvingly as he gave him the once-over. 'You look like the high priest of pop.'

'This is a good thing?'

'Where we're going this is a very good thing.'

They took the tube from Brixton to Green Park and walked east along Piccadilly, past the shuttered entrance to Princes Arcade, to where a queue of clubbers was spilling out of the doors on to the street. Kingston studied the punters: the girls in their black leggings and T-shirt dresses beneath men's black jackets, or rah-rah skirts with fishnet tights, their candy-floss peroxide hair captured by black felt fedoras tipped back far on the head; the boys in their box-shouldered jackets of primary colours, sleeves rolled up, and their jeans, artfully torn at the knee, wearing Kickers and Rayban Wayfarers. He looked up at the word 'Xenon' picked out in a scribble of green neon and turned to Nathan.

'What's this about?'

Nathan tried to look innocent. 'What do you mean?'

'Why have you brought me here? This isn't us.'

Nathan placed both hands on his friend's shoulders and leaned in to whisper in his ear. 'Through there,' he said, pointing at the door, 'is our future.'

57

At 6 a.m., an hour after telephone contact with the Oyster House had been lost, Commander Peterson took a call from the duty desk at the Cabinet Office and placed another via the switchboard at Kensington Barracks. After hanging up he wrote a short message on a piece of the church's headed notepaper, the only stationery he could find. He signed and dated it, and handed it to a junior officer with instructions that it was to be delivered immediately to an address two streets away. Then he made himself a cup of coffee and took it with him to a bench out in the gardens on the west side of the church that looked towards Jermyn Street. Willy found him there ten minutes later.

He sat down next to Peterson and sipped from his own cup of instant coffee. A ragged arrow's head of geese from St James's Park flew overhead, honking at the morning air, and they both looked up to watch. Willy felt calm and relaxed for the first time in days. He knew exactly what he was going to do and he knew it was the right thing. Over the years he had put up with a suffocating weight of humiliation and abuse. He had turned a blind eye to the commander's behaviour because, as long as he took no part in it – and he made sure not to – he wasn't compromised. After the first time a guest of the commander's had put money in his top pocket it was clear Peterson had said something to his visitors because it never happened again. Willy declined any free theatre tickets that were offered to him and in time those situations stopped arising as well. He had long ago accepted that his promotion prospects were severely limited. But for years he had concluded there was a way in which to do the job, and then take satisfaction from his life away from the force.

All that had changed over the past four days. Having experienced real responsibility, having led the negotiations for so many days, he could not imagine going back to that office at New Scotland Yard. He was no longer prepared to be patronized. He found it impossible to imagine looking at Peterson on the other side of his desk without wanting to punch him.

Willy looked down to his coffee cup and said, 'I thought I ought to tell you that I'll be resigning from the force when this is over.'

'I won't try to dissuade you.'

'I wasn't expecting you to.'

They fell silent again. There was an uncommon quiet in Central London this early on a Sunday morning. The only sound was the breeze in the old plane trees of the churchyard, and the call of songbirds. Willy watched fronds of steam rise from his cup. 'I know you've never thought much of me as a copper –'

'I don't have an opinion either way.'

'– and I know we've never seen eye to eye. But I just wanted to say that everything I've done over the past few days has been with the best of intentions.'

The commander yawned. 'It's too early for a sermon, Cosgrave, even for a Sunday.'

Willy leaned forward and rested his elbows on his knees. He felt his shirt tug itself loose from the taut waistband of his trousers. 'I just think it's still possible to end this thing peacefully.'

'That's your considered opinion, is it?'

'Freddie wants to bring it to an end.'

'But he's not in control down there, is he? Do you think Freddie was the one who cut the phone line?'

'No, I don't.'

'So it makes no difference any more what Freddie wants, does it?'

Willy took a deep breath, to subdue the frustration. 'Please...'

'Yes?'

'Don't do anything hasty. We've got through it so far without loss of life. That has to be the most important thing, doesn't it?'

Peterson drained his coffee cup and stood up. He crushed the poly-styrene in his hand, and looked to where the last caramel-coloured dregs had dripped into his palm. 'Do you know the problem with you, Sergeant?'

Willy stood to face him. Quietly he said, 'I've already told you I'm leaving the force.'

'The problem with you—'

'So I don't have to take another one of your bloody lectures, do I?' The sudden intensity in his voice surprised and pleased him. He felt comfortable standing in the empty churchyard, toe to toe with the commander, with only an audience of sparrows.

'The problem with you is you never see the bigger picture.'

Willy laughed. 'What? The bribes stuffed in your top pocket by those contacts of yours? The cosy drinks with the porn mag publishers and the dodgy nightclub owners?'

The commander glared at him. 'You are so far out of order, Cosgrave.'

'The free boxes at the Royal Albert Hall? The case files buried as a favour to your pals? I've seen all of it.'

Peterson's chest swelled with rage. Willy saw him raise his hand and make a fist. He laughed again and shouted back, 'Go on, hit me. I'll enjoy it much more than you will.'

For a moment he stood, chin up, awaiting the blow, willing it to come now, aware of the impact an assault by his superior officer might have on any severance package he could negotiate. Peterson raised his arm higher, so that Willy could see the hard, pink geography of his fist. Slowly he lowered it again.

'Get back to the kitchen, Cosgrave,' the commander said, 'where you belong.' He turned and walked back towards the church.

Willy called after him: 'Killing a few people just might get you that promotion you've always wanted.'

Peterson did not look back.

For an hour Trevor stood by the door, looking through the small window, bouncing on his heels, as if expecting someone to come. He took no more speed but Nathan could tell from the sweats and the uncontrolled twitching that the drug was still in charge.

Sheffield and Stevie placed Guthrie's body as far back as they could in the walk-in fridge, behind the sacks of Maris Piper potatoes, while Bobby insisted on treating the cut to Nathan's chest.

'It's not deep at all,' she said quietly, as she dabbed at it with a cotton-wool swab, moistened with antiseptic.

Nathan winced. 'That's why you should leave it.'

'Not down here,' she said. 'Too great a chance of infection.' When the wound was clean she laid another piece of cotton wool over the top and taped it into place.

'He's getting more aggressive,' Bobby said, as she tore the last piece of tape from the roll. She felt Nathan take a deep breath, his warm chest rising and falling beneath her hands.

'You don't know what he's capable of,' Nathan said, and he thought about the man lying on the pavement outside that south London pub, his cheek torn from the corner of his mouth and halfway to his ear, his hair matted, blood pouring from one nostril and out on to the pavement slabs.

Bobby shook her head. 'He's capable of anything,' she said, but she did not look up from the dressing on his chest, in case he saw how afraid she was. She swallowed. 'He's capable of everything.' Nathan buttoned up his blood-stained chef's jacket.

She rubbed her face with her open hands. She couldn't remember when last she had slept, and her eyes felt now as if they were crusted with sand. Every muscle ached and her head spun with fatigue. 'What are you going to do?'

'The only thing I can do. The only thing I've got left. I'm going to talk to him.'

Trevor didn't look away from the window when Nathan spoke. He blinked and swallowed and stared ahead.

'You need to get some rest,' Nathan said. He was leaning back against the wall, next to the door, looking into the kitchen. The others were looking back at him. Kingston mimed grabbing Trevor around the neck, furiously. He was making no attempt now to hide his contempt and fury. Nathan shook his head. He might well need Kingston's help, but not yet.

Quietly he said, 'You can't deal with this thing if you're strung out.' Trevor said nothing. 'I don't want to end up inside either. You know that. Neither does Kingston.' He looked back across the kitchen. Kingston stared back at him and squeezed the knuckles of one hand in the other, which made them crack. Nathan looked away. 'So you can trust me. I'll keep an eye on everyone while you get your head down for an hour. Then, when you wake up, you can do the same for me.'

Now Trevor turned to look at him. His eyes were bloodshot. Sweat ran down his scar and dampened his collar. He said, 'We need to sort the hostages.' He turned and walked towards where Bobby was standing with Stevie, by the far end of the stove.

'I told you,' Nathan said urgently, following him, not willing to let him get away. 'I can watch out for them.' He glanced to one side and, gratefully, saw that Kingston was moving quickly around the other side of the stove so they could intercept him at the same time. Now Nathan nodded his agreement. He needed his friend's help.

But Trevor had sensed the two men closing on him and grabbed Bobby's wrist so violently and with such speed that she lost her balance and began tumbling towards the floor. She screamed as Trevor yanked her upwards again. 'I need to sort you first,' he said, his jaw tensed.

It was the moment Nathan had come both to expect and fear. Without checking to see where Kingston was, he ran up behind the other man and flung both arms around his neck to pull him off. Trevor let go of Bobby and spun around, with Nathan still holding on.

Kingston lunged too, but again Trevor was too fast, throwing the tip of one shoe hard into the other man's crotch like he was trying to launch a football deep into the back of a net. Kingston dropped to the floor, turned in on himself, his hands buried in his damaged groin. Now Trevor reached up, grabbed Nathan's hands and pulled down on them sharply as he bent over. By the time Nathan realized he was being thrown over Trevor's head and on to the floor, gravity had taken hold and there was nothing he could do about it. He tried to break his fall with one arm, but heard the crack of bone as he landed on the hard tile floor, and knew his forearm had snapped. The pain shot up his arm to his shoulder and back again. He had barely grasped which way was up when Trevor reached down, grabbed him by the collar and pulled him into the sitting position.

Nathan saw the flash of blade, held tightly between Trevor's knuckles, a split second before it made contact with his left eye, which was wide open in shock. There was no time to blink or turn his head away. The searing pain coincided with a burst of white light that died immediately to nothing. He felt the next punch between the eyes and deep inside the place where the soft cartilage of his nose met his skull. After that he felt them only as heavy, jarring impacts that muffled the sound in his ears and made him feel sick in his stomach, until, at last, he felt nothing at all.

58

Nathan ordered them each a Xenon house cocktail – a Suffering Bastard, made with 151 per cent proof rum, because it sounded serious and male – and they stood by the bar, watching the clubbers on the dance floor. Kingston nodded his head lightly to the beat and, as each track mixed into the next, Nathan glanced at him to gauge his reaction. In most things Nathan led the way, but in the serious matter of what music was worthy of their attention, Kingston remained the senior partner, just as he had been the first time they spoke to each other fifteen years before, at the school gates. Nathan may still have been delighted when he chanced upon rare platters of vinyl by the Paragons or the Skatalites, during their occasional expeditions to the record shops of Notting Hill and Camden, but nothing would win a place in the front section of his music collection unless Kingston had first indicated his approval with a slow nod of the head and the single word 'Sweet!'

Xenon was not the place for the off-beat shuffle they were used to. Here it was 'Temptation' by Heaven 17. It was David Bowie's 'Let's Dance' and the driving, jangly guitars of 'Oblivious' by Aztec Camera. There was a briskness to this music which Nathan decided was the sound of optimism. Most of the bands to which they had graduated only understood how to lament or rage. There was no place in their songs for happiness, and the contrast between this and what they were used to made Nathan forget for a moment the real reason for coming. He wondered instead whether bringing Kingston here had been a mistake.

He leaned across to his friend and, nodding towards the forest of animated bodies on the dance floor, said, 'Wankers.'

'I don't know,' Kingston shouted back over the music. 'Looks like they're having fun to me.' Nathan felt wrong-footed by his friend's enthusiasm, and irritated with himself, because he too thought they looked like they were having a good time out there. He had only been trying to maintain his credibility. A cloud of dry ice belched across the dance floor and was quickly sliced in two by a sweep of green laser light, scanning the club's darkness from top to bottom. The dancers raised their hands in the air so that, as the triangular sheet of light lifted over them, they looked like swimmers sinking beneath the swirling surface of the sea.

The track changed: there were loud hand claps, short and sharp as a snare drum, which echoed over a male falsetto, announcing the beginning of 'Wham Rap'. The crowd cheered and threw their hands in the air again, and clapped along to the beat. Kingston swigged the last of his cocktail, put his glass down on the bar and shouted at Nathan, 'Come on, we're going to dance.'

Before he could protest Kingston was gone, manoeuvring into the swaying crowd with a delicacy Nathan had never seen before. He followed on behind, tripping over the feet of the clubbers around him at first, until he reached the middle of the dance floor, where Kingston had carved out a space for himself; where there was room for his huge shoulders and the light could reflect easily off the fine polish of his new black suit. Now they were both inside the crowd, moving with it, all elbows and hips, and turning to each other to mouth the lyrics they were surprised to discover they had heard often enough on the radio to know by heart. They reached the middle of the rap and were struck by the thrilling conceit that this song was about them. They shouted the words, pointing at each other like their fingers were loaded revolvers:

If you're a pub man,
or a club man,
maybe a jet black guy with a hip hi-fi,
a white cool cat with a trilby hat...

They laughed at the epileptic stutter of the lighting-rig above them and Nathan dragged his friend into a tight embrace so that he could shout in his ear. 'I don't wear a trilby!' Kingston pulled away and threw his arms wide, as if this omission was unnatural. 'Why not? You're a white cool cat...' They danced in their own spotlight amid the slender girls with their happy upturned faces, and the boys with their retro sunglasses, shining in the darkness, and the baselines which they felt in their feet and their stomachs. The girls turned on the spot and smiled at Nathan until they turned away to another part of the crowd to share the joy.

But one girl kept smiling at him, her face lost in the crowd and then found again, like a boat in a heavy sea, as she attempted to move closer through the thickening crush of bodies. He danced on the spot, scanning the silhouettes for the face which, though glimpsed fleetingly, was familiar. Until finally a cluster of shoulders parted in front of him and she came through, grinning, eyes wide and threw her arms around his neck without ever losing hold of the beat.

'Nathan!'

'Lucy?' The soft ripeness had gone from her body to be replaced by something more rigid, but the enthusiasm of her smile was there, and they turned, their arms looped around each other.

'Buy me a drink,' she shouted in his ear, and they barrelled off through the crowd to the bar, leaving Kingston mirroring dance moves opposite a white girl with peroxide dreads.

He ordered Lucy a rum and coke, and she told him she drank white wine these days. She thanked him anyway, rubbing the ball of her hand carelessly across her nose before emptying the glass in one go.

'It's so good to see you,' she said, leaning into his ear, so he could feel the heat of her breath. 'You look exactly the same.' She tugged at the lapel of his suit, to indicate, affectionately, that he would obviously never change.

He told her she looked different. He said that she had done something with her hair, that she looked older, more mature. 'I am more grown-up,' she said, giving the phrase a girlish lilt, and turning from him to scan the room.

'How are your parents?'

She looked suddenly bored. 'Fine, I suppose.' She turned back to him, eyes ablaze again. 'Come with me!' She grabbed his hand and pulled him through the crowd towards the main doors.

'Lucy!' But she only grinned, and dragged him more urgently into the women's toilets just beyond them.

'I can't come in here!'

'Nobody cares,' she said, as she ran along the line of cubicles, past the girls attending to their make-up in the mirror opposite, or hand-sculpting their hair back into place. She took him into the last cubicle, locked the door and, still grinning, reached into the front of her white shirt. Nathan stood with his back to the door and waited for her to withdraw the inevitable bag of coke from the cup of the bra whose contents had once so intrigued him. She brushed at her nose with her hand again and dangled the bag between thumb and forefinger. She giggled, and turned to the cistern where she carefully cut a line, the restlessness replaced now by stillness. She was absorbed by the complex task of keeping the drug in place.

She offered Nathan a five-pound note, already rolled into a tight tube. 'Think of it as a little gift,' she said brightly, in a half whisper, aware of the chattering women outside the door. 'For old times' sake.'

'Too much of the old booze already tonight, actually,' he said. 'The two don't mix for me. You go ahead.'

'Suit yourself,' she said irritably, turning away to the toilet and putting one knee on the closed seat, so that she could steady herself over the line that she had cut on top of the cistern. 'You always were a bit of a stiff.' She went to work with the five-pound note.

'I'll see you back out there,' Nathan said to the curve of her back, and she nodded but did not reply. Nathan looked for a moment at her taut, slender frame, jack-knifed over the toilet, before letting himself out.

Bacak in the club, Nathan found Kingston on the dance floor. 'Was that Lucy?' When Nathan nodded, he mouthed, 'She's lost weight.' Nathan tapped the side of his nose with his index finger and mimed a quick snort.

'Lot of it about,' Kingston said, nodding in time to the music.

'Follow me,' Nathan said. 'Something I need to show you.'

He took him beyond the stage, where a dance troupe had just begun a jerky, robotic routine to something by the Eurythmics, to a door. He took out a key, unlocked it and pushed them inside the empty office. The music withdrew to a dull, muffled thump. Nathan flicked on the lights. He turned and tapped the lock housing so the bolt sprang back into place then slipped the latch so it couldn't be opened from the outside. He opened the door on the other side and put that on the latch too so they could get back through it. He led them up the staircase.

At the top he said, 'Give me one of your shoes.'

'What for?'

'Just for a minute.'

Kingston pulled off a boot and Nathan used it to wedge open the door out to the arcade. Kingston limped out behind Nathan into the deserted corridor of closed and shuttered shops, and felt the cold stone of the tiled floor beneath his one unshod foot. Princes Arcade was lit after dark by four overhead lamps with low wattage bulbs, so it was cast either in shadow or a deep bronze glow that made it look like it was receiving the last of a setting sun. Nathan led his friend to the premises of Richmond Phillips and Co. and looked admiringly at the black painted frontage, as though he were planning to buy it.

'This place is going to make us our fortune,' he said. He explained about Phillips and the deal he had offered; about the impossible amount of money they needed, and the way the man had patronized him, and the solution to the problem that he had hit upon.

'It's perfect,' Nathan said. 'We make the man suffer by ripping off his stock. At the same time we come up with the cash.' He said he was planning to do the job on 9 June. 'It's the General Election,' he said, and when Kingston looked blank, added, 'Police will be too busy to pay any attention to what we're doing down here.'

Kingston looked at the empty shop window. 'We don't do burglary,' he said.

'We haven't done it before. That doesn't mean we shouldn't. We can pull off anything if we plan it well enough.' He pointed back to the fire exit they had come through. 'Once we're up here we've got the place to ourselves. We can take all night if we like.'

'But the risk—'

'Shall I tell you the real risk? The real risk is in not doing this. The way we make our living is going out of fashion, Kingston. Dope's yesterday's thing. Coke is the drug of choice now. When even Lucy Cranbourne is snorting lines off the toilet you have to face facts. And I don't want to start dealing coke.'

'Neither do I.'

'So we need an exit strategy,' Nathan said, enjoying the phrase. He turned back to the unlit shop. 'And this is ours.'

59

'He's coming round.'

Nathan tried to open his eyes and felt immediately a deep ache, centred on the left of his face. The wound there felt deep and, even without touching it, he knew it was catastrophic. He attempted to move his hands to his head to check for damage, but the evidence of his broken arm took his breath away. There was a tightness around his chest from the ropes which were restraining him, and around his wrists, where his hands were tied together behind his back. He took deep breaths, trying to fight off the intense waves of pain.

He heard Bobby say, 'Don't struggle,' and he managed, with great effort, to open his right eye. The lids stung as they broke away from where they had become gummed to each other by congealed blood. Bobby was sitting on the floor opposite him, her legs crossed. She was tied up with the cord from one of the linen sacks, so that her arms were pinned to her side. Her hands were also behind her back. He could see Kingston's head, looming over Bobby's. They had been tied together, facing in opposite directions. Now he could feel another body against his.

He said, 'Who am I tied to?' Bobby leaned towards him apologetically. 'I'm sorry. I didn't quite –'

Nathan ran his tongue around his bruised and swollen lips. He took a deep breath. 'I said...' And he tried again.

'Me,' Sheffield said. Nathan turned his head a little and, recognizing the voice, said, 'Thank you,' though it came out as a noisy mumble.

'Stevie and Thomas are next down the line,' Sheffield said, 'and our noble Lord has a corner all to himself.' They were seated in a row on the west side of the kitchen, so that Kingston was looking north through the doorway towards the wine racks. Nathan managed the single word, 'How?'

Bobby looked embarrassed. 'He locked us in the fridge at gunpoint, then took us out in pairs.' Nathan was about to ask where Trevor was when she pre-empted him. 'He's asleep.' She nodded towards the other side of the kitchen. 'He crashed out by the dumb waiter about ten minutes ago.' Nathan looked down at his chest. With his right eye he could see that a spray of deep red, now turning rust-brown around the edges where it was drying, lay across his jacket; proof, as if it were needed, that his nose had also been broken.

Bobby swallowed, preparing herself to break difficult news. He could see her staring at the left side of his face. 'You have been wounded,' she said, enunciating every word, as though his hearing might also be impaired. Nathan tried to muster a smile; something that said this was hardly news. She shook her head. 'No, I mean –' She looked to where his left eye should be, and away again. 'You are badly injured.' Nathan nodded and said quietly, 'I understand.'

Bobby swallowed again. 'Kingston was about to tell us how you ended up down here.' She leaned her head back against her kitchen porter. 'Weren't you, Kingston?'

'I thought they should know,' Kingston said, gloomily.

Nathan took another deep breath, and heard the air squeeze its way in through his swollen nostrils and over his thickened, uncooperative lips. When his chest rose, every part of him ached at once, so that he felt like a single bruise.

'Go on,' Bobby said.

So Kingston told them: about the trip to Xenon, and the jeweller's shop, and Nathan's scheme to rob Richmond Phillips.

'I told him it was a bad idea,' Kingston said.

'But he didn't listen,' Bobby said, keeping eye contact with Nathan.

'He had it all worked out,' Kingston said, and he made such planning sound like a great misfortune.

'Then what happened?'

Kingston turned his head as far as he could, to talk over her shoulder. 'The next day,' he said, 'he insisted we went back.'

It was just before lunch, and shoppers wandered Princes Arcade, browsing in the windows of the shirt-makers and the art dealers with the casual confidence of people who knew they could buy but didn't want to.

'Look at it,' Nathan said, leaning towards the shop window. Clusters of gold and silver and sharp cut jewels glittered against their black velvet background. 'It's all there.'

'And at night, they lock it in that cupboard?'

'No alarm. No special safe.'

Kingston leaned towards Nathan and, through pursed lips, whispered, 'Maybe the reason they don't do nothing special is because they don't think anybody would be stupid enough to try ripping this bloke off.'

'That's because they didn't bank on a couple of smart boys like us.' Nathan looked up and down the arcade. 'Come on. We shouldn't hang around here too long. Let's get something to eat.' They left via the Jermyn Street exit, and Nathan led them across the road to the restaurant immediately opposite. It was hushed inside the Oyster House, and the room smelt richly of food and furniture polish. Kingston looked at the thick red carpets, and the mahogany bar with its brass rails, and took a step backwards.

'Let's find somewhere else,' he said.

'This will do fine,' Nathan said. 'People like us can eat anywhere.' Before a waiter could approach them he sat down at a table located at the top of a set of stairs that went down to a basement. Reluctantly, Kingston sat down side-on to his friend, so they both had a view out through the window.

'Anybody can do anything they want to,' Nathan said. 'The world is changing. Didn't you feel it last night?'

''Spose so,' Kingston said, uneasily.

'Life feels like a grind most of the time in Brixton, doesn't it? And then you end up in a place like Xenon and you realize it doesn't have to be like that.' He looked around the room for a waiter.

'I don't know,' Kingston said. And he added, as if it were part of the same thought, 'Natalie wants me to move in with her.' He said this quickly.

Nathan looked at him with surprise. He had met Kingston's girl-friend a few times. She was a small round woman with a wild burst of Afro hair and a big laugh and a five-year-old son called Joshua, who liked to use Kingston as a climbing frame. She had been to the flat on Acre Lane, and had cooked them a meal, while Kingston and Josh rolled on the floor roaring at each other like cartoon lions. Nathan knew she made Kingston happy and he was pleased for him, but he hadn't realized the relationship had reached such a point.

'That's a big step,' Nathan said.

'What can I tell you? I love her.'

'Bloody hell.'

'And the kid's great too.'

'Instant family.'

'It's what I want.' Kingston laid his big black hands flat on the white of the tablecloth. He wanted to hold on to the soft material. 'Anyway, she wants me to move in with her and Josh. And –' He hesitated. '– she wants me to pack in our thing.'

'She wants you to leave the business?'

Kingston turned his shoulders further away. 'Stop trying to make it sound like we're a couple of plumbers.'

Nathan thought quickly. He said, 'Excellent!'

'You mean that?'

'Of course.' Nathan leaned in towards his friend. 'We do this one last thing together and then we both give it up. We'll have enough cash to do whatever we like. We can get out of Brixton.'

'I don't want to leave Brixton.'

'Course you do.'

'No, I don't. It's my home.'

'But last night, in the club. Couldn't you feel it? The energy that's out there? Anything's possible now. We should have a piece of that.'

'Anything's possible for you, Nathan. I'm still a black boy from Brixton.' He indicated the various waiters who were crossing the restaurant, ignoring them. 'They don't even want me here.'

Nathan turned to look, and agreed. 'It does feel like we're invisible,' he said.

'That's what I'm saying.'

'Excuse me!' Nathan shouted across the room. 'I said, excuse me!'

A large moon-faced man with a soft fat neck overflowing his collar looked up from the other side of the room, where he was self-consciously rearranging cutlery at a table.

Nathan said, 'Can we get something to eat? You know. Food?' Sarcastically he mimed using a knife and fork. The man gave a tight, unhappy nod and walked up the stairs to the bar area.

'You're right,' Kingston said. 'We're invisible here.'

'But when we've got money we won't be invisible any more,' Nathan said, turning back to him. 'That's how it works.'

'I'm not doing the job,' Kingston said, addressing the tablecloth. 'I'm not interested.' And then, 'I'm out.'

'If it's what you want.'

'It's what I want.'

They fell in to a cold silence. They were used to being silent together. It was one of the pleasures of a long friendship, the understanding that being together did not always mean talking to each other. But this silence was different. It was filled with the other things they should have been saying. Nathan turned to the window. Suddenly he sat up in his seat. 'Bloody hell!'

'What?'

'Richmond Phillips. Coming our way.' Outside Phillips had reached the kerb just beyond the entrance to the arcade and was looking for oncoming traffic before crossing over towards the Oyster House. 'He mustn't see me here.' Nathan turned and looked at the staircase behind him. 'I'll go first. You wait a minute and follow me down.'

As he stood up, Nathan bashed into the head waiter who was about to present menus. They bounced apart. 'Watch where you're going,' Nathan barked.

'Well really!' Mr Andrews said, hugging the two menus to the curve of his chest for protection.

Kingston looked up apologetically, as Nathan rushed away down the stairs. 'He gets like that when he's hungry.'

Mr Andrews fixed Kingston with a glare of pure disgust, then shouted after Nathan. 'Sir, the toilet is at the other end of the dining room.' But he had already disappeared into the kitchen. At that moment the restaurant's front door opened. The head waiter turned to look and immediately replaced his scowl with a broad smile that deepened his jowls and made his eyes crease away into his face.

'Ah, Mr Phillips, how lovely to see you. Always a pleasure.'

As Mr Andrews moved to greet the new arrival, Kingston stood up and went down the stairs and through the swing doors. He was brought to a halt by the heat in the kitchen, and the clatter of pans and the sheets of flame chasing each other to the ceiling. Nathan was nowhere to be seen, but in front of him, across the other side, there was an open door which led out into a backyard. Before he could move towards it he was stopped by a woman with peroxide hair held back by a blue and orange scarf, who came around the end of the stove, drying her hands on a tea towel tucked into the apron tied at her waist.

She tipped her head back to look up at him and said, 'You the one they sent for the job?' She had an American accent and when she looked at him, she closed one eye as if sizing him up.

'Job?'

'Kitchen porter. You're not from the agency?'

He glanced behind him at the swing doors, expecting to see the head waiter coming down to apprehend him and then back over her head at the exit. He pointed at the open door. 'Actually I was looking for my friend.'

'Your friend? He's a cook?' She looked around the kitchen.

'No, he's... He was just leaving, through the back.' He waved at the door again.

'Didn't see anybody. I was just out back.' She pointed towards an open doorway. She laughed and said, 'Sure you're not here for the job?'

'Really, I'm just following my friend.'

'That's a pity,' she said, and she looked him up and down. 'A big man like you would make a great KP.'

He pushed past her and backed away towards the open door, trying to keep her at a distance with a smile. 'I'm sorry. Hope you find someone soon.'

'Me too, sweetheart. Me too.' She turned from him, no longer interested in what he had to say. 'Sheffield, how long on those steaks?'

Kingston was already out the door and into Mason's Yard before the cook had a chance to reply.

'It just made me think,' Kingston said. 'I needed to get away and there was a job going.'

Bobby said, 'You came back a couple of days later, right?'

'I almost came back the next day but I didn't want to seem too desperate. It was like Nathan said. I would be invisible here. It was the best place to get away from everything. Or at least, that's what I thought.'

Nathan's right eye was weeping, but he could at least now keep it open. He and Bobby looked at each other. 'So,' she said, 'when did he tell you about his smart idea to get Trevor on board?'

60

It was a Thursday night and they were in the Prince of Wales pub at their usual table. Nathan had just returned from the bar with two pints and was putting them down, when he announced casually that he had found someone to help him with 'the thing' they had been talking about.

Kingston had been reaching for his pint but, when he heard the name, his hand dropped on to the table. 'Trevor's mad.'

'I can handle him.' Nathan sipped his pint and scanned the bar for likely customers.

Kingston leaned forward and hissed. 'He hurts people.'

'Most of that stuff's just rumour. He probably made the stories up himself.'

'You even saw him do it once.'

Nathan bristled and refused to meet his eye. 'I can control him.'

'He'll want to go armed.'

'Might not be such a bad idea.'

Kingston's mouth dropped open. 'You wouldn't know what to do with a gun. You barely know what to do with a knife and fork.'

'Anyway, it's not your problem any more, is it?'

'We're still mates.'

Nathan pushed his unfinished drink away from him and stood up. 'Give my regards to Natalie,' he said, and he left the pub.

For days after that Kingston walked fearfully about the streets of Brixton, concerned that he and Nathan would meet by chance, as they often did, and that the conversation would start again. Once, on Coldharbour Lane, he ducked into the market to escape him. On another occasion he disappeared into the depths of Woolworth's on the High Street where he examined the shelves of objects he didn't want to buy until Nathan had finished paying for his newspaper. The subterfuge was foolish but he couldn't stop himself. Each day, when he descended into the underground station at Brixton, he felt only relief because he knew now that they could not meet. But then, arriving for work, he would forget about the plan and instead of cutting down Duke Street to the Oyster House would walk through Princes Arcade, which took him past the premises of Richmond Phillips and Co. He tried to speed up each time he came upon it, pretending to himself that if he didn't have a chance to look in the window he wouldn't have to think about what Nathan was planning to do there and the risks he would be taking – but it never worked.

One morning, four days before the General Election, while on the way to the tube, he saw Trevor from a distance. He was wearing a short sleeved T-shirt which made the rigid architecture of his arms all too obvious. His cheeks were gaunt and his gaze was fixed on a place nobody else could see. Kingston understood what Trevor was capable of. He knew how much enthusiasm he would invest in the robbery of a jewellery shop, and how important to him it would be that he was organized for maximum violence. That evening he returned to the flat that he had only recently moved out of, knocked on the door, closed his eyes and waited.

'You can't say I didn't warn you,' Kingston said.

Nathan swallowed hard against the pain in his arm and his face. 'You warned everyone in the building.'

Kingston leaned back towards Bobby. 'I shouted a bit,' he said, sheepishly.

Bobby had been sitting with her head turned as if she were looking at the back wall, the better to hear what Kingston was saying. 'A bit?'

'OK. I shouted a lot. The neighbours were banging on the walls.'

Now she turned back to Nathan and shook her head. 'You were right about him,' she said.

'How do you mean?' Nathan's words flowed into each other.

'You told me he was a good man.'

Nathan took a deep breath, the air vibrating in the clogged-up channels of his blood-clotted nose. 'And a good friend,' he said, and he dropped his head.

She leaned back into Kingston again. 'What exactly did he say?'

'In between telling me to mind my own business, he said that if he couldn't do the job with someone who knew him really well he needed to do it with someone he could rely on in other ways. He told me he wanted Trevor's criminal experience.'

Bobby looked sadly down at her lap and then up again. 'So you chose a psychopath,' she said quietly.

A silence fell on the kitchen now, as Nathan and Bobby stared at each other. Nathan wanted to say something. He wanted to explain how the plan was meant to have worked. He wanted her to understand that none of this had been intended, but he knew now that nothing he could say, nothing he could do, would make up for what had happened. She continued looking at him for a moment, and then turned away to face the wall, as if distracted by the view.

That was when they heard the noise: a low groan from the other side of the stove, which quickly coalesced into words. Trevor was awake.

He said, 'This place stinks,' and he stood up. He shook his head, and a shiver swept over his narrow frame. He looked around, sharply, as if he thought he was being watched from the corners of the room.

'It's the rubbish sacks,' Bobby said, and then regretted opening her mouth.

Trevor pulled his gun. It was a reflex now. His hand felt undressed without a weapon in it. 'I didn't say speak.'

Trevor looked towards where they were stored beyond the doorway and then back to Bobby. 'Where do they go?'

'Out front,' she said in a small voice. 'Since they bricked up the back door.'

Lord Connaston was tied, by himself, to a set of drawers in the back corner by the sinks. Trevor pointed his weapon at him. 'You. Take out the rubbish.'

Connaston said, 'I'm tied up.'

Trevor put away the gun, withdrew a knife and used it to cut him free. Connaston stood up, rubbing his hands, and shook out his legs. His greying stubble was so thick now it was close to forming a full beard, and his hair hung down loosely over his ears.

'What do you want me to do?' He was compliant.

'The rubbish,' Trevor said. 'Take it upstairs. Put it outside.'

'And then?'

'Come back. You run, someone else dies.'

Connaston nodded.

Trevor pushed the tip of his blade against the Treasurer's bearded cheek. 'Understand?'

He said, 'I run. Somebody dies.'

With his free hand Trevor reached up and turned on the television. 'I'll be watching,' he said, though the picture on the screen was of a Sunday morning church service.

'We've become rather boring news, apparently,' Grey Thomas said from his place on the floor, where he was bound to Stevie. He was sitting with his knees up to his chest and his feet together. 'They're not interested in us any more.'

Trevor looked at him. He didn't have to issue a command. Grey turned away, fearfully.

Connaston lifted the black plastic rubbish sacks out of their place by the fridge, one by one, and carried them over his shoulder through the kitchen to the stairs, amplifying the smell of decomposing vegetables and rotting meat which was already infecting the kitchen. The other hostages turned away and swallowed hard in an attempt to avoid the smell which was now so strong they could taste it. Trevor flicked across the channels and back again until he found a morning news programme which had interrupted a discussion on the intense politics of the week to cut across live to the siege. In the distance now, they could see Connaston emerging from the Oyster House, and throwing each rubbish sack on to the pavement before going down to fetch the next one. Over the images, a reporter was explaining, excitedly, that there was clearly a development in the four-day-old siege, but that nobody was entirely sure what it meant. And still Connaston worked, lifting the sacks up the stairs before returning for the next.

He had just dropped the fifth black plastic sack on to the pavement and was about to come back for the last, when they saw him fall to the ground.

61

Marcus Caster-Johns awoke to the sound of the wine bottles that lay at the bottom of the rubbish sacks clanking against the pavement. He had fallen asleep in the early hours of the morning over his rifle, having drunk the last of the whisky, and now had to peel his cheek off the smooth varnished walnut of the butt. He looked around the room. On the first day, when his possessions were arranged tidily, he had congratulated himself on the detail with which he had planned the operation, but the moment the need to piss arose, he realized that he hadn't quite accounted for everything. The empty whisky bottles were quickly refilled with urine so that at first they were warm to the touch and now stood in a row against one wall, looking as if their seals were once again to be broken. His faeces were harder to dispose of, and though they were tied away inside empty plastic carrier bags, the room still stank of human excreta.

The room looked as it smelt. The floor was scattered with half-finished cans of food, whose contents had spilt out on to the carpet and lay in dark, sticky pools of fruit syrup and unheated stew. In one corner was the camp bed with its tangle of stained bedding; in another, a pile of rubbish. In undertaking to reclaim ownership of his family's Oyster House, Caster-Johns had hoped to strike a pose that his late father would have recognized as heroic. He wanted to be viewed as an adventurer, and in his drunkest hours here had imagined the old man sitting in the corner of the room, perched on a hunting stick, thick tweed jacket buttoned high, admiring the effort his son had made.

But squalor had a way of encroaching upon the life of Marcus Caster-Johns, and had shown no willingness to spare him here. The feeling of disappointment, the sense that he had not proved equal to the challenge that his parents had placed before him, was only more dispiriting for being so familiar. Still, at least here there was a route to redemption, a chance for him to prove his worth in a way which nobody could argue with. He looked over the top of his rifle at the bearded, grey-haired figure in chef's whites who had just dropped the rubbish sack on to the pavement. The man looked briefly up and down the street, then turned and walked back into the restaurant.

Caster-Johns thumped the table with frustration. He had missed another opportunity. Then Connaston appeared at the door with a second bag of rubbish. He hesitated for a second before placing it down on the pavement next to the first and Caster-Johns understood that this was a clear-out. He knew there were more bags to come and that he might have a little time. He did not recognize the man at all. He was certainly not a member of staff. He knew what they looked like, and this man was not one of them. Nor could he be a customer. No customer of the Jermyn Street Oyster House would look like a tramp. Mr Andrews would never have allowed it. Following this train of thought it became obvious to Caster-Johns that he was therefore looking at one of those who had taken the Oyster House by force. He closed his left eye and focused with his right on the sight. He watched carefully as the man dropped the fifth bag onto the pavement and he realized that this was his chance and that there would be no other.

The first shot missed, though the target dropped to the ground and lay motionless on the pavement. Calmly, Caster-Johns slipped the bolt and reloaded. He took aim and fired again and he knew, as he squeezed the trigger, that this time he had got it right. The way the top of the man's head burst open reminded him of the ripe watermelons he had practised on as a teenager in Northumbria, before the deer shoots, and there was a density to the sound of the impact; a deep, ripe tone that spoke pleasingly of something very hard meeting that which is soft at the core. As he looked down from the window, he saw the final twitch of the man's left foot, and he felt that he had come as close as it was possible to witnessing that moment between life and death which he had pursued for so very long.

He was transfixed and exhilarated by this image and it was a few seconds before he realized that he was leaning out of the window, the rifle still in his hand. He heard a shout to his left and looked across to see a small group of policemen some distance away, outside the church, pointing up at him. Calmly he retreated back into the room. He stood holding the rifle, butt down to the floor, surveying the mess and thought that it didn't matter any more. Nothing mattered. He had done what he had set out to do. He had killed one of those who had tried to take from him what was his and whatever happened now that fact could not be argued with. He was not a disappointment. He was not a failure. He was a Caster-Johns. He was someone of whom his father could be proud.

Somewhere down below he heard a door slam and then another and a third. Soon he heard the rhythm of footsteps, beating up the staircases and along the corridors. Behind him the sun came out and he felt against the back of his neck the sudden blush of warm sunshine, and he thought of his grandmother on the beach at sunset, her long, fine hair hanging loosely over her shoulders, and the thought of her warmed him further. He went to the door, unlocked it, and returned to stand with his back to the window, his arms outstretched, his eyes closed. In the final seconds before the men arrived outside the door, he decided that this position might be misunderstood as one of surrender and he congratulated himself on the clarity of his thoughts under circumstances which he knew would have crushed lesser men.

A voice outside shouted, 'Police! Open the door!'

'It's open,' Caster-Johns said gently, as if ushering in room service, though he was not at all surprised when they kicked it in. His rifle was pushed hard now into his armpit and his cheek was against the warm walnut of the butt. His right eye was at the sight, through which he saw briefly the two armed policemen from SO19, though his finger stayed away from the trigger. He had just enough time to wonder once more what the moment of death would feel like before the officers opened fire.

The three bullets hit him in the chest with such force that they lifted him high off the ground. When he impacted upon the sill of the open window, he tumbled backwards out of it, arms flailing over his head, mouth open, as if gasping with pleasure at the surprise arrival of a long-lost friend.

Marcus Caster-Johns was dead before he hit the ground.

62

Trevor arrived at the flat on Acre Lane shortly after 7 p.m. on the night of the General Election, wearing the black Levi 501s and the light crewneck jumper that Nathan had given him the money to buy. Trevor showed him the three Browning P35 pistols lodged in his waistband. Thousands of them had come back with the British troops returning from the Falklands War, he said, taken as souvenirs from the Argentinians, and many of them had ended up being sold off cheap in the pubs of South London. He had another two at home, he said proudly.

'Three seems a bit much for tonight, though,' Nathan said, and he tried not to hear Kingston's voice in his head.

'One each and one just in case.' Trevor offered one to Nathan but he declined.

'You carry them.'

Nathan gave him a black leather zip-up jacket, like the one he was already wearing. It tapered slightly to the waist and had tabs that fastened on round chrome studs. In the lining there was a nylon zipper bag folded flat. There was a black balaclava in one of the pockets. Trevor took it out and tried it on. He looked at himself in the mirror and posed with one of the guns, enjoying what he saw.

'Take the mask off. I've got to put some make-up on you.'

'You what?'

'They won't let you in with that tattoo. I'll also try to do something about the –' He searched for the right word. '– mark under your eye.' Trevor's hand went to the scar, as if discovering it for the first time, and it occurred to Nathan that it was so much a part of him now, he no longer even thought about it.

Nathan applied the foundation quickly, hating the intimate feel of Trevor's skin beneath his fingertips. He dusted it with powder to take away some of the sickly sheen, and gave him a beret, which he said he should wear pushed far back on his head. Nathan was not generally interested in pop, but he had seen pictures in *Melody Maker* and the *NME* and knew the image he was trying to achieve. A bit of eyeliner would have completed the makeover, he thought to himself, but he wasn't about to suggest it.

'I feel like a nonce.'

'You look right, though. And it's only till we get inside.'

Nathan's instincts were correct. The elegant middle-aged man in the lounge suit who manned the door at Xenon did check Trevor out, but clearly placed him in the category headed 'eccentric' rather than 'threat'. Downstairs, Trevor was allowed to abandon the beret, though they kept their jackets on, and stood by the bar sipping the one cocktail Nathan had allowed them. After a few minutes Trevor nudged Nathan and indicated something lying shyly in his palm. Nathan looked down at the folded piece of glossy paper.

Trevor said, 'Whiz? Get you in the mood?'

Nathan considered the offer without meeting Trevor's eye. He wanted to tell him to leave it, that there would be time for the stimulants later, but he knew Trevor wasn't that kind of man. In any case Nathan had brought him along precisely because he had done burglaries before. If he couldn't have Kingston with him, he wanted the confidence that would come with the other man's experience and if Trevor had rituals before a job, and those rituals involved a snort of amphetamine sulphate, he couldn't interfere. He didn't want to knock the man off balance.

He shook his head. 'Maybe later.'

Trevor said, 'Fair enough,' and retreated to the toilets. He returned a few minutes later blinking against the flash and crack of the lights. He looked invigorated and centred, Nathan thought hopefully. Quickly the club filled up. The music began to thump and Nathan felt Trevor next to him slipping into the aggressive pumped-up dance, all punching fists and elbows, that was popular in the clubs of Brixton when the hardcore New Wave and post-punk stuff started playing. It was out of place here, though, amid the shiny sound of pop and the girls with their lipgloss and big hair. He laid a hand on Trevor's shoulder and when he looked up, shook his head. Trevor stopped dancing but continued to shuffle restlessly on the spot.

'Bloody relax,' Nathan said, sharply.

'I am relaxed,' Trevor said, and a muscle beneath his eye twitched. Nathan imagined he was here with Kingston instead, and enjoyed the image of his friend out on the dance floor, turning on the spot, tips of his shoes together, heels up, knees bent, a big grin on his face, enjoying the moves he was pulling.

By 9.45 p.m. the club was full. Artificial smoke rolled across the dance floor and lasers scanned the room. The crowd heaved and rolled to the music, and at the bar drinkers piled up three or four deep, straining to get their orders taken. It was just as a fire-juggling act came on to the stage that Nathan spotted her, coming through the main doors, her arms raised, fingers marking the beat. Lucy looked about the space, eyes bright with excitement, and craned to shout something into the ear of a friend, as they moved towards the centre of the floor.

Nathan turned around so his back was to her, grabbed Trevor by the shoulder and told him it was time. They pushed their way through the herd of clubbers to the edge of the room, Nathan choosing a route which would take them as far away as possible from Lucy and down to the door in the corner. As the jugglers chucked their burning Indian clubs to each other, so that great ribbons of flame arched across the stage, Nathan unlocked the office door. They pulled on their masks and Trevor offered Nathan a gun. He hesitated for a moment but this time took it, getting instruction from Trevor on the safety catch. When he was sure the catch was in place, he stuck it in the waistband of his trousers. This time they let the door out to the stairs pull shut.

Just as they were about to head up the stairs Nathan hesitated. He turned around.

'Did you hear the door from the club lock shut?'

Trevor shrugged. 'It's a door. It's got a lock on it.'

Nathan stared past him. He tried to recall checking that the bolt was free from its sticking place. He lifted his hand in a fist, as if replaying the moment when he would have rapped the housing with his knuckles. He was certain now that he hadn't. He had been too absorbed by the business with the masks and the guns and the safety catches.

Trevor said, 'What?'

Nathan hesitated and stared past him. 'Nothing,' he said, turning away from the door. It was too late to stop now. They were here and ready to go. He told himself nobody would notice and if they did, by then the job would be done and they would be out of there. He nodded at the stairs. 'Come on.' At the top they let the fire exit out to the Arcade close behind them.

It was as silent and empty out there as it had been the first time he had visited with Kingston. Nathan looked from one side to the other.

'Follow me,' he said, 'keep close.'

They darted the short distance across to the other side, and then moved briskly from the shelter of one doorway to the next, until they reached the jewellery shop. Nathan was certain nobody would bother looking through the tiny holes in the shutters at either end and he was equally sure, if they did, that they wouldn't be spotted. Being dressed entirely in black, they would merge into the shadows. Still he did not want to take chances.

In the doorway of Richmond Phillips and Co., Nathan pulled from his pocket a small glass-cutter. He had practised with it at home and was confident he could cut a useful hole in the glass of the door. But when he pressed the blade against the pane, at the place where Richmond Phillips' name was etched out in gold lettering, there was a sharp crack and a black line spread from one side to the other.

'Bugger,' Nathan said. He ran his finger along the crack, wondering whether, with enough pressure, the glass might just fall in, but there was no give. Trevor was hunkered down beside him, scanning the arcade, from left to right. Nathan reached into the inside pocket of his jacket for the small length of lead pipe that he knew was there. He weighed it in his hand, than tapped Trevor on the shoulder and told him to stand up and back off a little way.

He was about to swing the metal at the glass when he was distracted by the sound of giggling off to his left, followed by the high sound of female voices.

'I told you. I saw someone coming out here.'

'Who was it then?'

'Well, I don't know, do I?'

'We should go back.'

'Stop being such a wimp.'

He turned around in time to see Lucy and her friend peering out from the alcove by the fire exit. Nathan gasped the single word, 'Fuck!'

Trevor turned to look. In one swift movement he pulled out his gun and pointed it at the two women, who froze where they were, their mouths open.

'Trevor! No!'

Nathan heard the other man shout 'Back off!', followed instantaneously by the sound-burst of gunfire. The women threw themselves back towards the safety of the fire exit.

Nathan dropped the lead pipe, so that it clattered against the hard tiled floor and grabbed hold of Trevor. 'Follow me,' he said. 'I know a way out.'

They ran for the Jermyn Street exit, Trevor stumbling backwards, the gun in his hand. Glancing over his shoulder Nathan could see the women peering around the corner. So Lucy was unhurt, he thought to himself. That was something. Nobody was meant to get hurt on this job.

He stared at the shutter and then at the control panel to its right.

Nathan pulled down on the heavy lever and heard a deep clunk from somewhere inside the shutter's frame.

'I said, back off!'

Trevor was squatting down in front of the shutter, pointing back at where Lucy and her friend had come from. He looked up at Nathan.

'They're just girls.'

'They saw us.'

'Restaurant across the road,' Nathan said quickly, turning to look through the mesh of holes at the fractured image of the brightly lit window on the other side of Jermyn Street. 'Back door in the basement.' He reached down and pulled on the shutter so that it lifted a couple of feet and, as he did so, dropped down and rolled out through the gap. He felt Trevor behind him and assumed he was following. He looked back just long enough to see him wedged underneath on his knees still aiming into the arcade.

Nathan shouted, 'Trevor! Now!' and he heard his own voice echo back at him down the narrow street.

He ran across the road, pushed his way into the Oyster House and stood panting in the doorway. Even through the mask he could smell the wine and the roast meats, overlaid by the scent of cigarette smoke. The room was filled with voices and the clink of metal on plate which didn't stop immediately as he came through the door. Within seconds the fat waiter he remembered from the day he was there with Kingston was standing in front of him.

Mr Andrews bowed a few degrees from the waist and said: 'Good evening, sir. May I help you?'

If it had not been for the balaclava, the waiter would have seen a blink of surprise.

Mr Andrews smiled thinly and moved closer to Nathan, in the hope that he might back him out the door. He believed that the width of his barrel-chest and his shoulders, correctly positioned, could be used to bar entry to anybody, should he so choose. When there was no response he moved closer still, and repeated the question. 'I said, sir, may I help you?'

Before Nathan could answer, there was a crack of gunfire from outside.

He swung about at the noise, only to be pushed backwards into the restaurant by Trevor, who was shoving a pistol into the waistband of his trousers as he ran. Together, the three of them stumbled backwards across the dining room. Mr Andrews managed to say only, 'Really!' as they fell into the table at the top of the kitchen stairs. None of them knew it yet, but the siege or the Jermyn Street Oyster House had just begun.

63

In the kitchen they flinched when they heard the shot, and stared up at the screen, rigid with shock. They saw Connaston's body jerk on the ground, and turned away from the grainy picture. Only Trevor didn't move. He stared unblinking at the television, trying to work out the shape of the insult that had been committed against him. And when they looked back and saw him, his jaw tensed, the veins in his neck engorged, they knew that he would hurt one of them very badly because of what had happened.

'Try to keep calm, Trevor,' Nathan said quickly, though his nose was so blocked by congealed blood and his lips so swollen and cracked, that the words were barely intelligible. Trevor walked over and, with a loud grunt of effort, hit Nathan around the right side of his face with the butt of his pistol. The impact opened a new cut across his cheek and sent up a spray of fresh blood, which splattered against Bobby's whites. Nathan groaned and his head lolled forward.

For the first time in four days Bobby began to sob uncontrollably, dropping her head down so heavily, that Kingston had to lean in the opposite direction to keep them upright.

'Stop,' Trevor said.

Bobby looked up and blinked against the tears and the advancing panic. 'I can't,' she said, apologetically. A rush of images came to her: of her misery in Paris, of her grandfather's funeral, of her parents at opposite ends of the family kitchen table announcing their plans to divorce. Each one had felt, in its time, like the end of her world. Now she felt only a curious nostalgia for them, as if they were moments of innocence, when she had not been able to comprehend just how bad life could be.

Trevor walked across to Grey Thomas and untied him from Stevie, before retying the cook to the place where Connaston had been. The restaurant critic whimpered as he was pulled upright and a dark, wet patch grew on his inner leg that filled the room with the smell of hot fresh urine.

'I need to show them,' Trevor said. 'They have to know they can't do things to me.'

He pulled Thomas around the room, one arm about his neck, flicking switches. He turned on the food processor. He turned on the deep-fat fryer and the tape-machine, nudging the volume up to maximum. The B-52s started again, the high, trembling organ and cymbal-clash ringing out over the grinding sound of the kitchen machinery. Trevor took Thomas to Kingston's cleaning station and examined the knives until he found the one he wanted.

'You the restaurant critic?' Trevor said.

Thomas nodded.

'They pay you to eat?'

He nodded again.

'We should give you something to eat.' Trevor's voice was flat and emotionless, drained of colour.

Now he pulled Thomas back around the stove and out through the doorway towards the changing lockers. He laid him on the ground so that all Kingston could see from his position facing into that part of the basement was the man's short legs. Trevor straddled him and leaned forward so that he too could not be seen fully.

But they could hear what was going on. Trevor said, 'I'll give you something to eat. Something special.'

Thomas shouted, 'No! Please!' and then screamed, his screams becoming sharper and wetter until it sounded like he was being smothered. And all the time the girls of the B-52s continued singing. And the guitars kept playing and the drums kept beating and the food processor kept grinding.

When Trevor came back into the kitchen his jacket was smeared with blood and there were splatters on his cheeks and neck. But it was his hands which had taken the full force of the haemorrhage. They were smothered, as if he had cleansed them in blood, and held between them with unusual delicacy was a thick cone of flesh a few inches long. Trevor took it to the deep-fat fryer and dropped it in, where the moisture caused the hot oil to fizz and boil angrily.

Strapped behind Kingston, Bobby could not see what was going on. She tried to look, but she was too low down behind the stove.

'What's he doing?' she said, her voice now thin and tentative. She could hear Thomas moaning softly somewhere beyond the doorway.

'You don't want to know,' Kingston said.

'Tell me.'

'I can't.' Kingston said.

Trevor stood over the deep-fat fryer, jabbing at the bubbling oil with a slotted spoon. 'This is how to cook,' he said, 'come here, fishy fishy,' as he chased the piece of flesh about the vat. He laughed and pressed it against the side of the fryer so that it released more moisture and the oil bubbled with renewed intensity. He lifted it out of the boiling oil after a couple of minutes and subjected his trophy to a close examination. Now deep fried, its nature was obvious; the restaurant critic's tongue was the last thing to be cooked in the kitchen of the Jermyn Street Oyster House.

He carried it back through the doorway on the spoon, like a child in a school sports day race, to where his victim lay. Again he straddled him.

'Eat this!' he shouted.

'Eat it now!'

And a final time.

'Eat it.' They heard Thomas groan, and Kingston could see his feet beating against the ground, a wild, unfocused scramble of heel against tile. He saw Trevor sit up. His arm went to something at his waist, and then there was the hard sound of a single gunshot. The B-52s track came to an end and now all they could hear was the repetitive whirr of the food processor.

Quietly Bobby said, 'Oh God.'

The thumping base and the harsh guitars of the next B-52s track kicked in, filling the silence.

Trevor lifted up the restaurant critic's body and carried it over his shoulder to the swing doors. He pushed it through them and stared at it while he wiped his hands on his jacket, watching the doors fall still.

Now he went back to the remaining hostages. He looked at them, weighing up alternatives. Nathan said, 'It didn't need to be like this,' in a slurring mess of vowels and missed consonants.

Trevor ignored him and concentrated his attention on Bobby. She tried to speak. She wanted to plead with him, to shape a convincing argument as to why he should stop and go away and leave her alone. She wanted to protect her cooks. She wanted to protect herself. She wanted everything to end. But when she opened her mouth nothing came out, and she seemed to Trevor to be looking up at him in awe as he reached down to cut the rope that was securing her to Kingston. She felt his hard, bony hand against her ribs and around the small of her back and then on the side of her breast, and nausea rose up inside her. He pulled away at the ropes hungrily, hand over hand, at the treat whose time had finally come. Behind her she felt the reassuring bulk of Kingston's body floating from her, as if she was being drawn away by a fierce current from the safety of the shore, and she turned to grab on to him so that Trevor could not separate them, but she felt Kingston shrug her off. She wanted to shout out at him, 'Why are you doing this, Kingston? Why won't you look after me?'

It was as she turned to him that she understood why he had let her go so easily. He was up on one knee, his face fixed in a rigid mask of focused hate. As he stood up, he turned and launched his full weight at Trevor, arms outstretched, fingers splayed.

And that was when the lights went out.

64

At 6 a.m. on the last day of the Oyster House Siege, Commander Roy Peterson received a telephone call from Peter Dryden at the Cabinet Office in Whitehall, informing him that the decision had been taken to bring the incident to an end by force. Unless there was a reason to do so earlier, the SAS would move in shortly after 5 p.m. that afternoon. Peterson was told to telephone the switchboard at Kensington Barracks and to ask to speak to a Colonel Newson. A few minutes later, when he did so, his call was rerouted back across London to a boarded-up shop unit on Arlington Street, just a few hundred yards from the church of St James's. The men from A Squadron of the 22nd SAS Regiment had set up a forward base there twenty-four hours earlier and were training now on a plywood mock-up of the kitchen.

Peterson and Newson discussed the need to move the media positions back up Regent Street and St James's Street so the television camera could no longer get a clear shot of the restaurant. It was agreed this would be done at midday. Newson then asked Peterson to sign over his command as was required under the government's Military Aid to Civil Power arrangements and, once they had finished speaking, the policeman scribbled off a note on a piece of the church's headed paper, the only stationery he could find. He gave it to a junior officer for immediate delivery. After drinking coffee in the churchyard he gathered together his senior officers by the pulpit and explained what was going to happen later in the day. He issued an order than none of this should be revealed to his staff sergeant who, he said, 'has become emotionally involved in the case and is no longer reliable'. Although Denis Thompson had been irritated by Peterson's attitude towards Willy Cosgrave, he accepted what the commander now said, and blamed himself for what he regarded as the mistakes made in placing him at the forefront of negotiations. Cosgrave was told only that he had been stood down again, and sat in the church pews gloomily reading the Sunday newspapers and their accounts of the formation of a new government. It was what he had expected after their conversation outside the church.

The sound of gunfire shortly after 9.00 a.m. made Willy drop his paper, and he moved quickly towards the south lobby and the doorway out to the mobile command unit, but the route was blocked.

'Commander's orders,' the officer said. Willy opened his mouth to speak but before he could say anything they heard three more shots and the solid thump made by Caster-Johns' body landing on the street.

'You have to let me through,' Willy said, staring past him in the direction of the restaurant, as if he could make the walls invisible.

'I suggest, sir, you return to the pews and await the commander.' The words were polite but the tone was not. Willy did as he was told but stood at the back of the church under the clock, listening, his eyes closed, in the hope that his ears alone would tell him what was going on. He was there when he heard another gunshot, this time muffled, which he was sure had come from within the restaurant; when he tried again to get on to Jermyn Street the officer charged with keeping him inside stared at him as if he were an idiot. Willy retreated back into the church and sat in the pews, his head in his hands.

The television cameras were quickly moved away after that, and a team of four men from the SAS came around to the front of the Oyster House. In the early hours of the morning the police teams investigating the walls of the buildings on either side of the restaurant had found a void, but only in the wall to the west, rather than to the east where Trevor had been looking. Peering down through the hole by torchlight they reported that the space was four feet wide at its southern end, tapering to a point at the northern end and, when he heard the news, Colin Bellamy gave a gentle bow in recognition of the congratulations that nobody had offered him. Of more interest to Bellamy (though of none to the police) was the news that there were clear signs on the walls – bricks jutting out a few inches to support long-lost treads, a dark, jagged outline – that there had once been a staircase here. 'It is pleasing to see that some good has come of this affair,' Bellamy said, 'at least in historical terms.' Again he was ignored.

The news of the void, which had been communicated to the men on Arlington Street via the Cabinet Office, was considered carefully. It was agreed that it offered desirable opportunities for surprise. Later, however, the explosives experts of the SAS concluded that the presence of kitchen cabinets and metal work surfaces against that wall made it almost inevitable that hostages would be badly injured by daggers of flying steel, even if they used the smallest of directional charges. There was no benefit to surprise if the outcome was the wounding of the very people they were trying to free.

Instead, the soldiers reverted to their first plan: a simultaneous assault through the recently bricked-up backdoor at one end of the kitchen, and the skylight over the wine racks at the other. Explosives were confident that their directional charges could take out both lumps of brickwork in one piece, while sending the majority of the blast waves outwards and away from the kitchen rather than into the space itself. Apart from a little temporary tinnitus caused by the noise the worst assessments only came into play if somebody was leaning against the backdoor itself and that, they decided, was a risk they had to take, given the obvious deterioration in the situation.

At 9.50 a.m. the power to the Oyster House kitchen was switched off. A few seconds later the explosives were detonated simultaneously and a team of six men from the SAS, dressed in black, their faces hidden behind the sort of balaclava masks Nathan and Trevor had worn when they arrived, came into the kitchen, preceded by stun and smoke grenades.

In the darkness Bobby felt the air suck away from her, followed by a bang so loud it was less a noise recorded by her ears than a sensation that affected her entire body. At the same time, Trevor let go of her wrists and, as he had been pulling her upwards, her balance was gone. She fell forward on to her front, where she lay, her hands pulled down tightly over her head. Next to her she heard Kingston's guttural shout followed by new voices calling for weapons to be dropped and everybody to stay where they were. There were more shouts. She took a deep breath and something dark and acrid hit the back of her throat and made her cough with such force that she thought she was going to be sick. She curled in on herself on the ground. There were further voices and then she heard the high-velocity whine of four bullets very close by. She knitted her fingers together and pulled down hard as though she might be able to force herself beneath the cold hard tiled floor.

And then came the call of 'Clear!' And again, 'Clear,' 'Clear,' 'Clear,' as if it were a chant being picked up on the football terraces. She heard the whirr of the motors on the fridges kick back into life and, even with her eyes closed tight, could now sense a lightening in the room. The music of the B-52s came back on and, just as quickly, was turned off again. She felt a hand on her shoulder and slowly allowed her hands to slip away from each other. Bobby rolled over and looked up through the whorls of smoke at a man with close cropped sandy hair and black coal smudges around his eyes. A rifle hung slack on its strap around his neck and in his hand was his mask.

'You're all right, Miss,' he said, though very quietly as if he were talking to her from behind a thick door. He smiled, 'It's over.' And when she squinted at him, trying to understand exactly what he was saying, he said, 'Can you hear me?'

She rubbed her hand against her left ear. 'It's a bit deadened,' she said, and heard her own voice as soft and distant as his had been.

He smiled again. 'Don't worry,' he said, loudly. 'Just the noise of the blast. Won't last long,' and this time his words were a little crisper. 'Here, let me help you up.' He wrapped one large hand around her upper arm and she felt herself being propelled upwards.

Smoke lay over the kitchen but even through it she could see, lying in front of her, two bullet-punctured bodies. She turned around. 'Stevie? Sheffield?'

'Yes, chef,' they said in unison and coughed loudly against the smoke. Two soldiers were cutting through their ropes with large hunting knives and the cooks were soon standing, rubbing their wrists and their arms.

'You both OK?' she said, and they told her they were. She looked down at her feet. Nathan looked up at her. His ropes were already off, and another soldier was examining his wounds, and gently laying his broken arm in his lap. He leaned into his radio and said, 'We need medics down here.' And then, as if the thought had just occurred to him, 'one possible fracture, plus eye trauma.' He looked back to Nathan and smiled reassuringly. 'You'll be all right, mate.' Nathan said nothing.

Bobby turned from him to the dead bodies on the floor. She looked back at Nathan, and saw him open his mouth in preparation to say something. She shook her head to silence him.

'There were two gunmen, you see,' she said to the soldier, and she coughed.

'It's all right miss. You take your time.'

'I'm just saying, there were two of them.' She pointed at the two corpses. 'And you've got them both.'

She turned to Stevie and Sheffield for support. Sheffield kept eye contact. Immediately he understood. 'Yes,' he said, still looking at Bobby. 'Two of them.' And then to the soldiers in the kitchen. 'And you got them both. Well done.'

'Yeah,' said Stevie. 'Good job.'

She looked down at Nathan and again he opened his mouth. 'Don't try to talk,' Bobby said gently. 'Let them sort you out first.'

The soldier who was tending to his wounds threw Nathan a chummy wink. 'You listen to her, mate. Do what she says. There'll be more than enough time for talking later.'

When the smoke from the army's stun grenades began to clear, two of their bullets were found to have penetrated the stomach and chest of a man who had fallen to the floor close to the doors. He was wearing chef's whites, and was lying on his back. His eyes were open, and his lips parted to present an oval of surprise. Once an SAS officer had pressed two fingers against his carotid artery, just below his jaw, and satisfied himself that the man was dead, Bobby came and knelt by the body, as if in supplication. The chef drew a finger through the crimson puddle spreading across the victim's chest, checking the liquid for consistency, then leaned down and whispered into Kingston's face, 'You weren't supposed to die.'

65

She was helped up the stairs and out into the sweet morning air, where the harsh blue lights of the police cars and ambulances that jammed the street flickered impotently in the daylight. To her left, thick ribbons of smoke escaped through the gaping hole where the skylight over the wine racks had once been, and around her police officers and medics thronged the narrow pavement trying to bring order to the chaos of the aftermath. A body on a stretcher, its identity obscured by the spread of a red blanket, was being wheeled away towards an ambulance. She assumed it was Connaston. On the other side of Jermyn Street, she saw a second body being strapped under its own blanket. She had no idea who it belonged to, but accepted that she would find out in time. She felt there was a lot she didn't yet know. Stevie and Sheffield came up behind her, each of them with an army escort at their elbow. Nathan followed on, his good arm slung over the shoulders of a soldier who deposited him on to a stretcher and into the care of a nurse. A blood-stained swab was already taped in place over the left side of his face.

Bobby looked down at him. He mouthed the words, 'Thank you,' and then winced with the effort.

She said, 'A lot of people died,' and she scanned his face for a reaction. 'Kingston's gone.'

He gestured for her to lean down to his mouth. He whispered, 'I'm sorry.'

She stood up and nodded sadly. 'Hope they sort you out,' she said, nodding towards the left side of his face. She felt it was the most she could say to acknowledge what he had done to protect her down there.

He looked down at his broken arm, which the nurse had laid across his chest, in preparation for putting it in a sling. He shrugged, as if to say it was nothing in the circumstances.

He opened his mouth to speak but she shook her head. 'Don't talk.' After a moment's thought she said, 'Don't say anything you don't need to.' She let her hand rest on his. His nurse said, 'It's good advice.'

He nodded his understanding. 'I'll come and see you,' Bobby said. She watched as he was wheeled away to a nearby ambulance. For the first few seconds he craned his head upwards to keep her in view but finally he dropped back on to his pillow and looked up at the clean expanse of London sky.

Now her own nurse was at her elbow, a cleanly scrubbed young woman, with blonde hair pulled back in a ponytail, and white smock top, and a snowfield of a smile. 'Come with me, love. We'll get you checked over by the doctors.' Sheffield and Stevie were already moving towards an ambulance in the care of their own nurses, and Bobby was going to follow on when she noticed a man standing motionless in the middle of the road amid all the activity, staring at her. He was solid and round and he appeared less to be wearing his stained police uniform than to have made an accommodation with it.

The nurse tugged gently at her arm. 'You coming?'

'Just a second, honey.' She shrugged her off and walked over to the man.

He smiled awkwardly. 'You Bobby?'

She nodded. 'You Willy?'

'I am.'

She was aware that whatever she said now was not going to be adequate. 'Thanks for keeping us fed,' she said.

'Just a few bits and pieces.' But they both knew they weren't.

He looked over her shoulder to what remained of the entrance of the restaurant. Inside was a scene of destruction. The floor of the dining room was strewn with shattered glass. Tables and chairs were overturned or completely splintered and layered with shards of crockery and glassware. Bobby knew it was nothing compared to the damage which had been done to the kitchen below.

'Freddie?'

Bobby shook her head. 'He didn't make it, I'm afraid. They—'

'Yes,' Willy said. 'I understand. I was afraid of that.' He added, 'He knew his food.'

'He was hungry in a lot of ways,' she said, 'and he knew how to eat.'

'That's the most important thing.'

'It's what I tell all my cooks. Every time, I tell them that.'

'Do you think you'll cook here again? I never managed to get to the Oyster House.'

She turned to consider the wreckage again. 'I don't think anybody would want to eat here again, after what's happened.'

'No. Probably not. Though I always liked that kind of food.'

'It was all right, in its own way,' she said. She looked up and surprised herself with a sudden surge of emotion. 'It was mine,' she said.

She looked back at Willy, embarrassed, and attempted to rub away the tears. 'Sorry.' She gave an apologetic smile and sniffed. 'It's been a bit of a weekend,' and she laughed at the understatement.

'Of course.' He looked up at the building. 'Probably become one of those menswear shops.'

'Like Jermyn Street needs another one of those.'

They were silent. Bobby looked down at her feet and was suddenly aware of how she must look: of the grubbiness of her whites, smeared with Nathan's blood and the dirt of four days, of the streaks through the dirt on her cheek where rogue tears had run. She ran her tongue around her unbrushed teeth and breathing in now, she smelled herself.

She looked up at him and blinked. 'Anyway, thank you for making it bearable down there.'

'Just doing my job.'

'Now go home,' Bobby said, hoping she sounded motherly and

concerned. 'Raid the fridge. Make yourself something good to eat.'

Willy shook his head. He took a deep breath and looked at his feet. 'Don't think I will. I'm not really hungry.'

Acknowledgements

A variety of cookbooks were at my side during the writing of this novel. Both Robert Carrier's *Great Dishes of the World* and the *Larousse Gastronomique* appear in the text but were also referred to regularly during its writing for recipes and for other more random culinary detail. Other books do not make their way into the narrative, but I am still grateful for the wisdom they offered: *French Provincial Cooking* by Elizabeth David; *Roast Chicken and Other Stories* and *The Prawn Cocktail Years*, both by Simon Hopkinson with Lindsey Bareham; *New British Classics* by Gary Rhodes; *White Heat* by Marco Pierre White; *The Reader's Digest Complete Guide to Cookery* by Anne Willan; *The Heritage of Southern Cooking* by Camille Glenn. I am indebted to the chef Chris Galvin, originally at the Wolseley on Piccadilly, now with his brother Jeff at the eponymous Galvin on Baker Street, who gave me his recipe for Wiener Holstein.

Of course, books and recipes were never going to be enough. Both Alistair Little and Simon Hopkinson shared with me their memories of London's restaurant scene in the early 1980s, when they started out as chefs. Angela Hartnett of the Connaught (and her then head chef Neil Ferguson), was brave enough to let me work in her kitchens. Likewise, Henry Harris of London's Racine invited me into his kitchen for the day. He also agreed to read the book for any culinary inaccuracies.

I would like to say that all errors are his, but I suppose I ought to take responsibility for any that appear.

I am obliged to Julian Barnes for his thoughts on wines and to my mother, Claire Rayner, who shared with me her acute medical knowledge. The staff of the Church of St James's on Piccadilly answered my questions with endless patience. Dennis Hackett, founder of the menswear chain that carries his name, kindly gave me access to the premises of Hackett at 87 Jermyn Street where the fictional Jermyn Street Oyster House is located. The geography of the building is exactly as described. Carlo Spetale, the founder and owner of Xenon on Piccadilly, recalled the heyday of his club, where I and my friends once danced, with great candour. The research department of the *Observer* newspaper came up with superb sources of detail on the politics and culture of the late 1970s and early 1980s, and on the results of the 1983 General Election. Vanessa Engle's documentary for BBC4, *Property is Theft*, on the Villa Road squat in central Brixton, was a pointed reminder of what this corner of Lambeth was like at the time. All writers working now should acknowledge their debt to google.com. And so I do.

I owe thanks, and a few pints, to the Friday night boys: Mike Burles, Jamie Thompson, Frank Nelson, Rob Whitaker and Steve Hartley. All of them arrived in Brixton long before I started living here and had invaluable memories of what it was like back then. They also let me bore them rigid with a running commentary on this book's progress, often over a night's drinking at the Hamilton Arms on Railton Road, now sadly replaced by a corner shop.

My agent Pat Kavanagh was, as ever, both supportive and wise. My wife, Pat Gordon Smith, played cheerleader-in-chief, did not complain when I insisted on using her as a sounding board and turned out to be a marvellous DJ. The selection of CDs from 1983 that she found for me provided the kind of soundtrack that any writer attempting to go back in time needs. I could not do what I do without her.

But it is to my editor, Toby Mundy of Atlantic Books, that I owe my greatest debt of gratitude. He was there when the idea for this novel was born. He stayed resolutely by my side throughout its writing, and proved himself a patient, insightful and gifted editor right to its end. I am very lucky to have him.